THE GREAT MADNESS

Since its first publication in 1929, *The Great Madness* attracted generations of enthusiastic readers. It is a unique combination: an eventful war novel, depicting life in the trenches like the best European examples of World War I literature; a powerful manifestation of solidarity toward fellow Jews and admiration of Jewish heroism during wartime that belied the traditionally meek image of Jews; and a deep personal quest, leading the author from Hungarian patriotism to the revelation of his Zionist identity. None of these qualities have lost their fresh, intriguing taste a century later.

—Professor Avner Holtzman, Department of Hebrew Literature,
Tel-Aviv University

Avigdor Hameiri's documentary novel, based on his own service in the Austro-Hungarian trenches of the First World War, provides a unique insight into the experience of Jewish soldiers on the Eastern Front. As a devoted Zionist and Hungarian patriot, Hameiri marries many personal contradictions while surveying the terrible scenes around him. Dr. Peter Appelbaum, who has retranslated the novel from Hebrew with extensive annotations and the inclusion of previously untranslated poetry, has done a huge service in making it known to a wider readership. He has brilliantly retained the lively, ironic and sometimes directly humorous tone of the original while conveying Hameiri's unsparing views of the battlefield. Appelbaum's annotations are invaluable in explaining Hameiri's frequent references to aspects of Judaism and to literary and political personalities. This translation is a major addition to the canon of First World War literature.

—Glenda Abramson, Professor Emerita of Hebrew and Jewish Studies,
University of Oxford

This hidden gem is one of the most gripping stories about the horrors and folly of war in world literature. Based on his personal experiences as a Jewish officer in the Imperial Army of the Habsburg Empire during World War I, Hameiri takes us into the trenches of the Eastern Front and then into Russian captivity at the twilight of the Czarist regime. One of the most extraordinary aspects of this unusual book is its optimism and the unyielding belief in the human spirit despite the barbarity, the depravity and the devastating apathy that was part of that long and terrible war.

—Yaron Peleg, Kennedy Leigh Reader in Modern Hebrew Studies,
University of Cambridge

The Great Madness is a remarkable literary document of the Great War, using the familiar format of the memoir-novel to tell the lesser-known story of the Jewish soldiers in that war. Hameiri's choice to write in Hebrew suggests that he was writing for an audience who did not experience the war first hand, to the Hebrew reading public in mandatory Palestine, and—indirectly—also to future generations. With wit, irony, and a keen eye for details, Hameiri presents a host of credible characters and with masterly control of literary tropes he describes the impossible, the chaos, the horror, and the total madness of the battlefield. The English translation preserves Hameiri's unique literary style and brings his work to many more readers and back on the shelf of European literature of the Great War where this novel belongs.

—Tamar S. Drukker, Independent Research, Formerly, Lecturer in Hebrew
(Education), SOAS University of London

THE GREAT MADNESS

Avigdor Hameiri

Translated and edited by
Peter C. Appelbaum

With an introduction by Dan Hecht

A joint publication between

BLACK
WIDOW
PRESS

Black Widow Press is an imprint of Commonwealth Books, Inc., Boston, MA. Distributed to the trade by NBN (National Book Network) throughout North America, Canada, and the U.K. All Black Widow Press books are printed on acid-free paper, and glued into bindings. Black Widow Press and its logo are registered trademarks of Commonwealth Books, Inc.

Joseph S. Phillips and Susan J. Wood, Ph.D., Publishers
www.blackwidowpress.com

Stone Tower Press is a Rhode Island corporation. All design, production, and printing is done in the United States.

Publisher: Timothy J. Demy, Ph.D.
www.stonetowerpress.com

Cover Art: František Reichentál painting and sketch. Used with permission of copyright owners Ken Kaliski and Karen Pearse.

Design, Typesetting & Production: Kerrie Kemperman

ISBN-13: 978-1-7338924-6-9

Printed in the United States
10 9 8 7 6 5 4 3 2 1

The publication of this work
was made possible by a generous grant from
the Max and Anna Levinson Foundation
and the assistance of Rachel Blackmon
and Jim Kates and Zephyr Press.

Contents

Introduction

"From Paradox to Madness: The Personal Battlefield Experiences of Avigdor Hameiri in the Great War"

Dan Hecht, Department of Literature, Tel Aviv University

In 1926, ten years after being taken captive by the Russians during the Brusilov Offensive, the writer and poet Avigdor Hameiri began to publish his war diary *Haparadokson Hagadol* (*The Great Paradox*) in the daily newspaper *Ha'aretz*. He had only completed eight chapters when the editor, Moshe Glickson, stopped publication because of lack of interest. However, the overwhelming success of the novel *All Quiet on The Western Front,* and its translation into Hebrew by Ya'akov Horovitz, sparked renewed interest in the experiences of a Jewish officer in the blood-soaked war, and Mitzpeh Publishers quickly published Hameiri's novel, now entitled *Hashigaon Hagadol* (*The Great Madness*). The book became an unprecedented commercial success—in fact the first Hebrew bestseller in the new *yishuv*. Anatoly Steimatzky, younger brother of Yehezkel Steimatzky, founder of the original store of Steimatzky Books, the oldest and largest bookstore chain in Israel,[1] wrote to Hameiri: "These were the days when supplies of your book *The Great Madness* were exhausted at the end of each day." According to the journalist Uri Kesari: "*The Great Madness* could be seen everywhere: on the beach, in gymnasia corridors, in the hands of boys and girls, students, railway workers, in cities, towns, *moshavot,* homes, outdoors—everywhere."[2] The popular success of *The Great Madness* led to its being dramatized and produced in 1936 at the "Sadan" theater.

The Great Madness was also a great artistic success for Hameiri, who had been previously been known as a poet who dabbled in short stories, mainly on themes related to the Great War and Russian Civil War in Odessa, and the founder of the satirical theater *hakumkum* (The Teapot). *The Great Madness,* Hameiri's first published novel, contained many new literary devices. The novel is considered a documentary novel since it is loosely based on Hameiri's autobiography and based on actual events, even though it has its share of the supernatural. Hameiri's personal biography, and his crisis of identity, fluctuate within a broad and sometimes radical spectrum of experiences in Jewish, ethnic, and Christian Hungary. Recognition of these contrasts is essential for proper understanding of this novel. In a certain sense, the war is merely a background and theater set for the national awakening of the novel's protagonist. Avigdor Hameiri departed for war from his Budapest home as a Hungarian Jewish journalist and Hebrew poet who had already one volume of poetry under his belt, but his journey actually ended in the Land of Israel. The protagonist of *The Great Madness* not only fought on the Galician Front in the east, but also embarked on a journey of spiritual apprenticeship rooted in his hybrid identity as both Jew and Hungarian. In the end, he would part, at least from a perceptible point of view, from the latter and devote himself solely to Zionism.

Avigdor Feuerstein

Hameiri was born Menahem Avigdor Feuerstein on 20 Ellul, Tar'an,[3] 5 September 1890, to his father Zvi Meir Hakohen and his mother Hadassah Rushovski, in the village of Ódávidháza (Hungarian: the home of old David), at the time part of the Austro-Hungarian Empire, now Stare Davidkovo in southwestern Ukraine. It was the one of the smallest villages in Bereg District, no more than 1 kilometer long with one lonely road. Of the population of about twenty families, half were Jews, the balance were Hungarians and Ruthenians, who served as "shabbes goys."[4] This area of Carpatho-Ruthenia was very poor and intensely religious. "My cradle is the Carpathian Valley, the most despised, poorest, darkest region in all the countries of cultured, civilized Europe," he wrote.[5] His mother died when he was very young and he went to live with her father, David Rushovski. His grandfather's personality and devotion to Hebrew played a seminal role in development of the young Hameiri's life, and he inspired the awakening of literary awareness in the young boy. Hameiri's grandfather appears repeatedly in different citations and aphorisms—especially in his poetry, stories and articles—as a guide in the ups and downs of his stormy life. He saw his grandfather as the source of his most important ideals and principles—Hebrew and Zionism—which were intertwined and derived meaning from one another. His grandfather was not a Zionist, but his zealousness for the Hebrew language, and inculcation of his young grandson with love of the ancient language, turned Hameiri in the direction of the awakening Hebrew nationalist movement. "He imbued his two grandsons with love of the Hebrew language—my brother and myself. Somehow, I became infected with the rhyming bug—I sought and found a rhyme for everything. I even cried in rhyme."[6]

From a very young age, Hameiri was drawn to the Hebrew language, and got to know the poor but God-fearing Jews of Carpatho-Ruthenia. After a number of years wandering among various Hungarian *yeshivot* and being expelled from the Pressburg Orthodox *Yeshiva* at the age of 15, "in part because of Zionist activities," he continued his studies at the the *gymnázium* of the Budapest Rabbinical Seminary (*Országos Rabbiképző—Zsidó Egyetem*). From then on, he wandered between the two contrasting worlds of Hungarian Jewry—the strict Orthodoxy of the Pressburg[7] *yeshiva,* and Neologic Reform movement of the Budapest Jewish Rabbinical Seminary, "whose entrance, in the eyes of the Orthodox Jews, was tantamount to a gateway into apostasy."[8] This is a key moment in the division of Hameiri's soul between simple, devout, secluded, Orthodox, and modern, urban, Hungarian Jew who became part of society. Two worldviews collided: one aloof and introverted, the other outward looking and integrating with local society. Both shared a common denominator, which Hameiri clearly recognized—antagonism towards Zionism. The rabbinical seminary "...eschewed the fledgling Zionist movement [...] but did allow faculty members to lend a helping hand to various cultural projects associated with the revival of Hebrew, most notably Eliezer Ben Yehudah's great dictionary."[9] These two habitats which influenced the young Hameiri's growth sharpened his attraction towards Zionism, and opposition to the two movements in Hungarian Judaism, and designated him a special, isolated place only for himself.

With his arrival in Budapest, Hameiri became a true urbanite, and remained so for the remainder of his life. He began to work as a journalist in Hungarian newspapers. This job took him to the bustling Budapest coffee-houses, where he became friendly with the Bohemians of the city. In the first chapter of *The Great Madness,* he details the life style of a modern man who works into the wee hours of the morning, and then socializes in coffee houses of a large city. "Hameiri's life is that of a 'Bohemian.' He sees himself as a kind of European representative, whose obligation it is to inspire our lives with the light of his world view."[10] In 1910, Budapest had about 500 coffee houses, "There were more cafes in Budapest than in Vienna… In Vienna you could spend a few hours in a café. In Budapest you could live there."[11] The poet Dezső Kosztolányi (1885–1936), who knew and influenced the Hameiri of those contemporary coffee houses, nicknamed Budapest "the coffee city (a kávéváros)." In an article dated 15 March 1914, in the newspaper *Az Ujság (The Newspaper)*, a paper to which Hameiri also contributed, Kosztolányi asserted that the British say "my home is my fortress," yet the people of Budapest say "my coffee house is my fortress." Hameiri spent many a late hour in coffee houses such as the Café New York which in those days was home to the Hungarian literary elite. Busy city life with ethnic Hungarians, all intertwined in the spirit of literary rejuvenation, bolstered his Hungarian identity which had been, up to that moment, that of an isolated Jew among Jews. The atmosphere in those coffee houses bonded Hameiri with his Hungarian colleagues and he felt welcome and at home. This sentiment differed completely from the one he would experience later in the circle of Hebrew writers. "There, they were members of 'my own' Magyar race. But here,

I am amongst different races: Russians, Poles, Bulgarians, even Magyars!!"[12], he wrote in Israel, where he felt out of place. These words attest to the special breed of Hameiri—a Hebrew poet with a Hungarian beating heart.

In just such a coffee house around 5:00 a.m. on the symbolic date of 1 May, Hameiri met the most important Hungarian poet of his era—a man who influenced his worldview and his poetry more than anyone else. His name was Endre Ady (1877–1919). Ady was, at that time, in the midst of a literary controversy whose echoes penetrated even the hallowed walls of the Jewish Rabbinical Seminary. Hameiri, already a controversial figure in the seminar for his Hebrew writings and attraction to Zionism, took Ady's side, and became known as an "Adyst." During the first meeting between the rebellious, stormy poet and his young, up and coming admirer, the inebriated Ady heard that Hameiri fought for his good name in the seminary, and had even translated one of his poems into Hebrew. Hameiri told him to his face that, had he lived 3,000 years ago, he would have been counted amongst the Prophets of Israel. His namesake the Prophet Ezekiel would have been named Ady had he lived at the present time. When he heard this, the drunken Ady gave him a kiss that was, in Hameiri's words "much deeper than that of a woman…".[13] These words give an idea of Hameiri's admiration of Ady, which manifested in true, personal love, artistic inspiration, and even an attempt to adopt Ady's model—the Hungarian patriot and proletarian warrior, who suffers his people's pain like a prophet and emissary—in the context of Zionist national renewal.

Turn-of-the-century Hungary was in cultural ferment, conveyed in the periodical *Nyugat* (*West*), to which Ady and Kosztolányi contributed regularly. Hameiri too was swept up in this enthusiasm by the excitement of Ady's writings. His attitude to Ady's poetry gives us an insight into how he possibly wanted posterity to write about him: "decadent; immensely powerful; renewer of the language; archaic style; member of the oldest aristocracy; poet of the proletariat; unequaled patriot; burning socialist."[14] These words are key for understanding of Hameiri's world view on a poet's place and task in society. He is an admonisher at the gate, bound heart and soul to his people's ancient past, the chronicler of his people who longs for its renewal. This view was separate and different from the one which he inherited from his grandfather, and acquired by Hameiri himself. Hameiri clung to two simultaneous world views, both of which were realized in his works. Writing Hebrew in a Hungarian context and milieu had a unique and unusual impact on his Hebrew: Zionist poetry, but with Hungarian form and passion.

The Dry Branch of the Jewish Tree

The Jews of Hungary were unique from a point of view of cultural diversity. Jews in the Austro-Hungarian Empire had acquired full citizenship and equal rights from their beloved Kaiser Franz Joseph in 1867. From that moment, the process of integration began its inexorable course. Assimilation tore the social fabric of Hungarian Jewry into two groups: on one hand the inflexibly Orthodox, on the other the Neolog (Liberal) modern group. The Empire's enlightened attitude—allowing its Jewish minority to preserve its identity and way of life, demanding absolute national loyalty in return—made Hungarian Jews enthusiastic patriots. By contrast, espousal of Hungarian national identity meant rejection of, even recoiling from, Zionist national Jewish revival. Hameiri was revolted by Neolog assimilationist Hungarian Judaism, which blessed Hungarian poetry and culture, but spurned Hebrew poetry and nationalism.

Post-World War I Hungary suffered violent upheaval, which had far-reaching consequences. The Treaty of Trianon tore away large tracts of the country including Transylvania, and millions of ethnic Hungarians, about 30 percent of the Hungarian population, found themselves without a homeland. Additional wars with neighboring countries left governmental chaos in their wake, including a Communist revolution and a short lived Hungarian Soviet Republic. Persecution of political refugees and terror followed. Jews were not spared, and terrible pogroms broke out. For assimilated Hungarian Jews, who had so identified with Kaiser Franz Joseph and the supranational Austro-Hungarian Empire, this presented the end of an illusion, and a wake-up call to which few paid attention. Despite pogroms, many Jews chose radical opposition to Zionism as proof of Magyar identity. A few even cooperated with conspiracy theories about the double loyalty of Jews on the battlefield, in the spirit of the German "stab in the back" theory. Hameiri, who fought in the war, rose to the rank of officer, was wounded twice and taken captive for the sake of his homeland, called these Jews "emissaries of the devil" and didn't spare the rod with them. "We young Jews of Hungary have suffered too much in recent years to write about these gentlemen in a romantic tone and handle them with kid gloves," he wrote Nahman Sirkin (1868–1924) in the early 1920s. He added in contemptuous German: "No mother's body has spat out such whores."[15] Hameiri, a unique representative of Hungarian Jewry which was referred to at the time as the dry branch in the tree of Judaism, was planted between those two worlds: On one side, assimilated Neologs, on the other, strict Orthodoxy from the region of his youth. Both divergent poles were strongly opposed to establishment of a Jewish state in the Land of Israel, and clung tenaciously to their Hungarian homeland. Hameiri attacked the Neologs with sharp words: "Official Jewry has done everything in their power to deny all memory of Judaism as Judaism…how these gentlemen have trampled our Jewish souls with their roughshod legs, and by so doing delayed our redemption by several centuries…"[16]

But, with this, Hameiri evinced the same powerful national pride with which assimilated Jews tried with all their strength to prove their Hungarian identity. This pride led him, a few years later, to volunteer for military service for a war based entirely on patriotism and nationalism. As he said, if Hungarian Jewry differed from other countries it was only by virtue of its patriotism for the Austro-Hungarian Empire, which acquired freedom of religion, and ritual and social integration within the fabric of Hungarian life. The writings of Joseph Roth and Stefan Zweig, both products of the Habsburg Empire, reflect a deep yearning for the lost days of the Kaiser and his Empire which had been destroyed by the war.[17] "If there is truth to the claim that Hungarian Jews are a separate entity, then that is due to a unique tendency — wrongly ascribed to 'assimilation' alone. This tendency is *Uberpatriotism* and *tragic* love of Hungarian Jews to their native land unexampled in other countries with Jewish assimilation. This love is much stronger than mere ambition to imitate and assimilate[18] a foreign culture. It derives from a tragic source, a source of human sanctity—a natural love of the land, the homeland, and its soil. This is the love of native land, its atmosphere, and the first images of childhood."[19] Hameiri speaks of a native love for one's homeland, of an atmosphere of distant, childhood memories. Hameiri the Jew is conscious of the fact that Israel was his people's native homeland 2,000 years ago. But by the same token he knows that "for the last 600 years, my blood has been part of a foreign land, my existence is tied to it. This not a literary or mere theoretical consideration, but the blood of my fathers and my fathers' fathers."[20] Hameiri's identification with Hungary is *ethnic* despite the fact that he is Jewish, and forms a bond of blood with the Hungarian language. It gives him an intimate connection with the most important Hungarian poets and authors of his time at a crucial cultural intersection, and sends him out to fight and be wounded in the terrible slaughterhouse of World War I. Yet despite his Hungarian national pride of land, homeland and soil, Hameiri still fluctuates between the rich land and produce of a concrete, beloved homeland, and a suffering spiritual homeland, that demands much pain from him. To the end of his life, he maintained this double national loyalty.

On the other side of the coin, Hameiri was disgusted by and recoiled from the dark and gloomy Orthodox Hungarian Judaism that he knew from his youth in the region of his birth, centered around the city of Munkács.[21] The main reason for this visceral dislike was their burning hate for Zionism and Hebrew. "That fiercest and most sinister hornet's nest at war with any form of light, especially Hebrew culture, which at that time, the early days of the Zionist idea, was tied in their minds to 'that heretic Herzl who guzzles pork and slaughters pigs at the Western Wall in God's name, using the Tetragrammaton.'"[22] Hameiri's opposition to this sect of

Hungarian Judaism began at a young age, with his Bar Mitzvah address which concealed and integrated Zionist ideas, and ended with his being expelled from the Pressburg *yeshiva* and all the other *yeshivot* in Hungary. This was not unusual: many Hebrew authors suffered from the same complex. The difference was, that progressive Jewry did not demand such total assimilation with the state. Therefore, Hameiri deserves his own separate place. As a Hungarian Zionist Jew, he belonged to a religious minority in a country that stood alone and anomalous on the European continent, with a strange language and roots that extend from the Ural Mountains and Upper Volga River, and within this minority, he stood in the middle, between the assimilated and strictly Orthodox, each of whom, for their own separate reasons, rejected Zionism.

Hameiri's Documentary Novels: A Nationalistic Perspective

Reaction to the novel was overwhelmingly positive. Critics praised it for being engrossing and for the depiction of the Jewish experience on the battlefield. Moshe Kleinman (1870–1948). editor of *Haolam*, called it "a high and noble artistic creation."[23] There is no doubt that its unequivocal critical success was related to the great commercial success of *All Quiet on the Western Front*, which appeared at more or less the same time. Hameiri also had the advantage of supporting the *yishuv*'s fight to emphasize Jewish experience and Hebrew writing. The fundamentally different writing style of this novel compared to his prior short stories also contributed to the book's great success. Hameiri's previous short war stories had focused on specific events and individual experiences such as Jewish bravery in the light of antisemitism, contempt for senior military leadership, exposure of cruelty and horror, and the supernatural. By contrast, *The Great Madness* attempts to ground the novel in a pseudo-documentary context. This is done by means of chronological development of the story line, within its center a distinct protagonist who undergoes significant change in values and points of view during the plot's exposition. This inner development accompanies the protagonist from the outbreak of war and national enthusiasm that sweeps the streets of Budapest—through conscription and basic training, into the field of battle, his wounding, convalescence at home, and return to the front, until he is taken captive in June 1916.

The Great Madness is a novel of education which describes the vicissitudes of a Jewish journalist from Budapest, whom World War I changes from carefree Bohemian to enthusiastic Zionist and, at the same time, to exceptional officer revolted by the upper officer class. In this way, Hameiri's two viewpoints—one Jewish, the other universalist—are intertwined and realized in the novel's protagonist. This is his own one-of-a-kind trait that made this one-of-a-kind novel possible.

In the novel's introduction, Hameiri declares that it represents memories and impressions from the front, with nothing added or diminished. Only the facts are reported. This introduction stands out in light of criticism of Hameiri's short stories as "inauthentic" because of the supernatural dimension in many of them. Previous research has indicated that Hameiri not only polished and balanced his memoirs, but also added, molded, even placed contradictory historical facts in the narrative, such as the Balfour Declaration which is supposedly published while Hameiri is at the front. In fact, by the time the declaration was really published (2 November 1917)

Hameiri had already been freed from Russian captivity. There are other examples of stylistic design that make it clear that the protagonist of the novel is not entirely the narrator Avigdor Hameiri.

Several of the protagonist's characteristics underpin the concept of Hameiri's development from carefree youth to Jew with Zionist awareness. However, Hameiri had this awareness from a young age. He was already a Zionist in the Pressburg *yeshiva,* and active at the Budapest Rabbinical Seminary in the Hungarian Zionist student association "Maccabiah." before the war. The novel's protagonist reveals no Hungarian identity, and observes the war patriotism and enthusiasm with astonishment. Hameiri enlisted willingly despite his Zionist awareness: "I stood by the truth of my Jewish nature long before the war, and nevertheless, went to the front even before I was conscripted—I volunteered the year before."[24] In order to reinforce the transformation from lack of national awareness to radical Zionism, no mention is made in the novel of Hameiri's volunteering or war enthusiasm. Quite the contrary, he excludes all religious or national identity. It seems as if he is totally occupied with pleasure and material matters:

> "Hello! Is this City Hall? This is the editorial office of *The People's Voice*.[25] This morning I received a red slip. What is it for?"
>
> "A red slip? It means you have to present yourself for conscription."
>
> "Conscription? What do you mean? I have to be a soldier?"
>
> "So it appears."

"Can't it be managed without me? I really am very busy. Especially in the mornings, when I sleep. Surely you know what newspaper work is like."[26]

Hameiri's enthusiastic conscription stands in stark contrast to his post-war pacifism resulting from Hungarian socialism and even Marxism inspired by Endre Ady. This pacifism comes to expression later in the novel, which rode on a wave of pacifist anti-war sentiments in other novels such as *All Quiet on the Western Front.* Ady's pacifism is described in chapter 10, "The Commander of the Muse" when the instructor in the officer's academy identifies Hameiri as a journalist and friend of Ady:

> "You're a good friend of that lunatic Endre Ady?"[27]
>
> "Beg to report: No, sir."
>
> "What, no? I say you are. Do you deny it?"
>
> "Yes, I deny that he's a lunatic, sir. Endre Ady is the greatest Hungarian poet of all time."
>
> My instructor stares at me, removes his hand from my shoulder and after a moment's pause says:
>
> "We'll soon find out. I believe that he's opposed to the war. We'll see if he recovers his senses now and gives us some rousing war poetry. If he doesn't… If he doesn't…"
>
> His face becomes grim and harsh as a shrunken horse-radish.
>
> "If he doesn't, you'll have to forget him, as if he died a scoundrel's death."[28]

The instructor who rejoices in battle sees Ady as a radical pacifist and lunatic since in those days, much like today, those who oppose war and nationalism are often denounced as traitors and enemies of the people. In poetry and in prose Ady protested the war, and like many other European intellectuals was repaid with vilification.[29] In the novel, as continuation of his astonishment at the shouts of the crowd, the protagonist remains a pacifist in contrast to Hameiri who, as already stated, volunteered for what he saw as the good of his country:

> I walk on, but a few steps later a premonition of danger drives me back. I read it and it warms my heart:
>
> "The Free Journalists publicly declare that the people of Tolstoy, Pushkin, Gorky, Andreiev, Romain Rolland, Shakespeare, Barbusse, Bernard Shaw, Wilde, Wells, Sinclair, Whitman, Anatole France (and many, many others) have never been our enemies, we shall never raise our hands against them, and may the hand of anyone who does so be withered, etc., etc."[30]
>
> Among the writers who had signed the manifesto—myself.
>
> Very good. Bravo. Excellent.
>
> Beside it, another notice. I read it and momentarily become sober:
>
> "... and whoever dares to spread the false spirit of pacifism and dishearten the protagonists of the

> homeland, will find that I shall have the power to break him like a cracked reed, etc., etc..
> Signed: Graf Tisza, Chief Minister."[31]
> So it's one against the other. Me against Tisza, Tisza against me. Fair enough. Bravo, in fact. Very good.[32]

The protagonist of *The Great Madness* is dragged down to hell while still confused by the "madness" of sharpening swords for war. However, he becomes infected with patriotic fervor, apparently as a logical method of converting from patriot to Hungarian Zionist.

> But the strangest thing of all is that when the tall officer slaps me on the shoulder and shakes my hand, saying that I would make a good soldier–I feel a kind of pride. Why should I deny it? Why lie to myself?–It's a fact: I am flattered. What does it mean? Only yesterday I would not have sat at the same table with him.
> What is war?[33]

The confused protagonist has signed a pacifist petition. However, the moment he receives praise from his instructor, he feels a kind of creeping national pride, whose source he doesn't understand. He is disoriented, and sees no connection between himself and the storm of national sentiments in the streets. The novel's protagonist is a reflection of Theodor Herzl, seer of the Jewish state and Hameiri's cultural protagonist. Herzl was also a journalist in a large city in the center of Europe who at first didn't particularly concern himself with the fate of the Jewish people.[34] In the first chapter "Opium," the young journalist finishes his work late at night, continuing on to a coffee house in the company of friends, young women and strong drink. They overimbibe and ridicule the possibility that war could break out, while pale, delicate Dr. Garai prattles drunkenly about the need for war:

> The ancient hate of the vicious beast in the primeval forest, which grinds its teeth in our blood, cries out for release. It is choking there, side by side with man.[35]

This early, hedonistic exposition contains hints of the hell awaiting the jovial throng, indifferent to what is to come. In the following chapter, "Madness," the direct opposite of the first, the pale, delicate Dr. Garai becomes aroused by the national call to arms in the streets and infected by the mad drumbeats of war. When the protagonist mocks him and his fake patriotic bravery, he hurls a word at him that instantly complicates the novel by introducing a Jewish bias, and sets the protagonist's Zionist education in motion:

> *"Jew!"*
>
> I am thunderstruck.
>
> It's ages since this word has been uttered in such a manner among us. I cannot restrain myself from answering him, but my throat is parched and my tongue paralyzed.
>
> "Garai!" I final call out, almost in tears.

> It must have reached him. Dr. Garai hears. He turns back, comes up to me and exclaims with a stinging, sarcastic hiss:
>
> "How can you know what a homeland means?"[36]

Garai undergoes a dramatic change within one chapter, from hedonistic, light-hearted Bohemian to ardent nationalist swept up by the madness of war. His attack sends the novel's protagonist on a journey that lasts throughout the novel. The same type of defined moment in time that Herzl experienced when the French public called "Death to the Jews!"[37] Similarly, in *The Great Madness,* this is the moment that introduces the indifferent protagonist to the context of his maturing and complex relationship to war, when he first encounters what he calls the "madness" of war, in the streets of Hungary. He is confused. "Homeland? What does that word mean?" During this tempest, someone whom he thought of as a coffee house friend destroys his personal and nationalistic world. From that moment, the stunned protagonist's journey towards national and Zionist awakening begins.

From a literary and developmental point of view, the book's loose documentary content forms the mold of a stirring *fabula* which serves as a successful dramatic national and pacifist "argument" for the Jewish perspective of the battlefield.[38] In many places, despite the aforementioned introduction to the novel, Hameiri testifies to the impossibility of depicting the reality of his experiences, and that he refrains from doing so due to principle. "The well-known desire to depict absolute reality in writing is a distorted requirement that can only end in failure. It's like serving the goose with the bones and the beak. Any author worthy of the name doesn't, even in a biography, present a literary personality exactly as he was in life. Even a literary dish is not presented without preparation, spices and salt, in other words without imagination."[39]

In *The Great Madness,* there is autobiographical overlap with historical facts, but Hameiri arranges, explains, and massages them into a single literary unit. "The central design of *The Great Madness* is the combination of radical contradictions, with linguistic and thematic dimensions, from single sentences to the entire book."[40] Hameiri remains faithful to the same contradicting word combinations prevalent in his poetry, legacy of his spiritual father Endre Ady. We can see this in a single sentence, when he hears on the front that there is both a British and German program to give Palestine to the Jews: "What joy!—How terrible—Palestine!—Treason…!"[41] The protagonist is torn between two identities: loyalty to the army of his homeland, and his longing as a diaspora Jew for the Land of Israel. This complex of thoughts in the protagonist's mind of the while lying on his bunk serves as a metonymy for the general narrative, in which he passes from one loyalty to another:

> After all, I think, isn't there an element of treachery in it? Even to think for a moment about another country? All right, I'm a Zionist.
>
> But not during the war! Good God! To be thinking of another country. another homeland, right here at the front, in the midst of the war?! Never![42]

Jewish Pacifism

> I had learned about the world and society, and understood the secret of militarism and capitalism and all the rest...[43]

As already stated, *The Great Madness* belongs to the wave of post-war pacifist literature. It objects to war, mocks the upper military echelon, and sides with the company of simple soldiers. This viewpoint is a kind of Marxist connection between the soldier suffering in the front line trenches and the unskilled worker exploited by the ruling classes. Pacifism, a universal concept based on brotherhood between nations and erasure of national borders, contradicts the feeling for homeland which, during the course of the novel, gradually weakens in the protagonist's heart in favor of Zionism. The pacifist overtone, that sees the simple soldier as a victim of the nobility and upper echelon who use patriotic sentiments to feed an entire generation into the meat grinder, was very popular in the poetry and literature of the Great War. On the Western Front, for example, the Christmas Truce that occurred 5 months after the start of the war saw football games between the British and Germans in no man's land. The French socialist Louis Barthas (1879–1952) describes how heavy rain forced the French and Germans to leave their dugouts so as not to drown, allowing them to spend a few moments together in the face of the forces of nature:

> Frenchmen and Germans looked at each other and saw that they were all men, no different from one another. They smiled, exchanged comments, hands

> reached out and grasped; we shared tobacco, a canteen of jus [coffee] or pinard.
>
> If only we spoke the same language!
>
> One day a huge devil of a German stood up on a mound and gave a speech which only the Germans could understand word for word, but everyone knew what it meant, because he smashed his rifle on a tree stump, breaking it into two in a gesture of anger.
>
> Applause broke out on both sides, and the "Internationale" was sung.[44]

Another compelling example of such pacifism is the apology of the protagonist of *All Quiet on the Western Front* to the French soldier whom he has killed, calling him (purposely) *Kamerad*. Hameiri details a similar sentiment shared by soldiers on the Eastern Front for their Russian counterparts, down to the very same tobacco:

> They, too, are daydreaming, Together with us. We are merged together, separated only by the mighty longing to be with them physically, too, here, under the sun.
>
> How we love them, those men over there, who are suffering with us, dreaming of the sun, of love, of women, of God!
>
> Suddenly fat Rosenberger says:
>
> "I'd give five years of my life to be the first to run across to them and give them a warm, fraternal greeting!"

> "To do that and then die," says the lanky Tyrolean, as if continuing Rosenberger's thoughts without a break.
>
> "I'm keeping a box of Memphis cigarettes that my Ada sent me for the first one of them that I meet," continues Barchi the professional hoodlum.[45]

The uniqueness of *The Great Madness* compared to other novels in this genre lies in its distinctly Jewish pacifism, the sanctity of the Sixth Commandment "Thou shalt not kill." The concept of pacifism that erases national boundaries, supports socialism, and the ideals of international brotherhood was a complex one for Jews who saw in the war an opportunity to prove their bravery and loyalty to the homeland. Approximately 300,000 Jews fought on various fronts in the Austro-Hungarian Army for their beloved Kaiser Franz Joseph. The Jewish soldier's dilemma was further complicated by Zionist feelings. Hameiri, who developed Marxist sympathies after the war, came to see "homeland" as a chauvinistic demand for war. In the 1930s, during the spread of fascism, Hameiri said: "This abomination annihilates every drop of faith in what is called 'homeland' and 'homeland's distress,' which forces defense of 'people' and 'homeland.' Before your body is riddled with shrapnel, before you breathe your last young breath, something else dies—patriotism. The homeland, bravery—all the beautiful things with which you deceive yourself and which make you feel that it's worthwhile to die for someone or something in a war such as this!"[46]

Another expression of post-war pacifism is hate for military officers of high rank. From a Marxist point of view, this is a war between classes—officers are the hegemony that enslaves simple soldiers, sends them to their death, and shoots them for cowardice. In this regard *The Great Madness* resembles *All Quiet on the Western Front*. Lieutenant Stubniak and Colonel Figer resemble the hated Corporal Himmelstoss, ultimate villains who show cowardice at the moment of truth. In contrast to war-frenzied officers, prostitutes remain uninfected by the madness of approaching war, and mourn the cities being emptied of young men. They accompany their departing menfolk with a strange parade, another non-realistic component of the novel that doesn't pretend to be literary. They symbolize realization of the lofty, realistic pacifist ideal compared to the madness taking over everything else, and personify the desire for life and eroticism compared to blood lust and death:

> The whores won't let him finish. The word "homeland" drives them mad:
>
> "I spit on your homeland, you louse!" one of them screams, and the others follow suit, weeping and raging, blending into a terrifying, upsetting chorus of synchronized lamentation.[47]

In the novel, whores are explicitly preferable to officers: "Who sits beside an officer? A whore: worse still, another officer."[48]

Officers are depicted with mockery, images that correspond to the madness of war, desire for death, cruelty, and abuse of subordinates:

> The army officer, if I thought of him at all, had always appeared to me to be a useless and superfluous creature in God's great world. A sleek

> creature, strutting about like a clockwork doll, its bones, from head to foot, dry as sticks. It seemed to have a sort of coagulated wine jelly instead of brains inside its skull.[49]

The speaker is so nauseated by the officer's image, that he won't even sit at table with him. The protagonist is himself an officer, reporting from the source how awful it is to live amongst officers, how disconnected they are from the people. The real war is between the ruling class, hierarchy, and military officials, not between nations.[50]

> How much love there is among us, the common soldiers. How much hate there is "up above" among the officers. After the last attack we expect to have a long rest.[51]

From Hameiri's socialist viewpoint, senior military officers identify themselves as people of means who preserve the status quo at the expense of the junior soldiers, amongst whom worker's brotherhood reigns. The officer is the personification of all the sick manifestations, pomp and mute stupidity of the military in man. But this is not a specific legacy of the Jewish officer. Hameiri describes Captain Schlesinger as someone imbued with all the military and personal characteristics that make him a successful commander in the field. Jewish bravery is as convincing here as it is in Hameiri's short stories:

> By now there is no doubt whatsoever that the Jews excel in sheer bravery, even more than the purest Calvinist Magyars. Events keep confirming this fact, however unpalatable it may be.[52]

By this, he confirms that negative characteristics of the upper echelon are not a Jewish legacy. He cites the economist and sociologist Werner Sombart:

> Jews are incapable of being officers. Quite true. Being an officer requires a certain empty-headedness, and Jews have different qualities.[53]

In the novel, socialist-pacifist values and stereotypical Jewish characteristics seem to correspond and are part and parcel of the same narrative. It is no coincidence that many Jews, amongst them Albert Einstein, Stefan Zweig, Arnold Zweig, Karl Kraus,[54] spoke out against the hopelessness of war and national consolidation. Jews who spoke for cessation of all violence and hostilities, and counseled Jewish identification with universalism and pacifism, were often viewed as traitors to the nation and in favor of the rising bolshevism. One of the novel's strengths is the fusion between national Jewish recognition and a pacifist theme, with resultant bravery. "The uniqueness of *The Great Madness* amongst other European war literature lies in its Jewish point of view, manifested by its universalist and pacifist themes, changing it into a personal testimony on the impossibility of the Jewish situation during World War I."[55] The glowing nationalist patriot, pale, delicate Dr. Garai, is swept up by blind war frenzy, but at the end of the day, does not volunteer and obtains an exemption. By contrast, the novel's protagonist volunteers, serves, and becomes an excellent officer.[56]

War Poetry

This new edition of *The Great Madness* makes me (and everyone who appreciates the works of Avigdor Hameiri) very happy. It is due to the diligent work of Peter Appelbaum, who has already published the first English translations of Hameiri's novel of captivity *Hell on Earth,* the fascinating novel *Voyage to Savage Europe* and short stories about the 1918–1920 Odessa pogroms, *Of Human Carnage*.[57] In the current edition, the English-speaking readership has the first opportunity to read all the poetry which is embedded like precious stones in the body of the original text. Without these poems, it is impossible to plumb the depths of war madness reflected in the novel and sense the nuance of the specific Jewish, pacifist sentiment. If we examine Hameiri's war poetry through the prism of his parallel growth as a Jew and Hungarian in comparison to his Zionist-humanistic perspective, we find the image of a new and stormy world, which sheds additional light on Hameiri's previous poetry. The powerful impressions of his difficult war experiences blend together with his tempestuous creations and powerful imagery. "Hameiri's war poetry is, in many respects, a continuation of the first chapter of his creative life."[58] However, they represent a completely different world and higher stylistic level that did not exist in his earlier poetry. For example, the contrast between increasing feeling of the absurd and disharmonious in presence of powerful, colorful battlefield images.

The combination of contradictory words, especially those of a powerfully visual nature, are expressionistic tools much used by Hameiri in his war poetry. "As in other expressionist creations, contrasts are created by combination of material which grates powerfully on the reader's sensitivities."[59] These oxymorons are achieved by use of colorful, contradictory and graphic words. The poem "Pinkish Stain," for examples, contrasts the virgin white snow with the stark, battlefield red blood: "It's only a blood stain, red on white."[60] This poetry is the ultimate manifestation of pacifism, universal human brotherhood and total rejection of war and senseless killing. In these poems, war resembles a condition of madness, the battlefield is a lunatic asylum and soldiers are its inmates.

> Tens of thousands around me go insane
> But my mind – it still remembers.
> In a moment my time will come
> And no one can foresee when.[61]

This verse presents the concept of fighting soldiers as "madmen," and war as a non-normative, unjustifiable condition. The feeling of annihilation is ever present, as is the immanence of approaching death. The writer reacts to it in different ways—indifference, madness, relief, sorrow. These components intensify this feeling of impending doom while life continues as usual:

> In another moment or two – a molten spark will
> explode
> My dreaming brain into ten thousand pieces.

And you – you, my canine comrade
Sit and wait a few moments
Sighing for my inarticulate life.[62]

In this poem, the poet's only companion is a dog, the "best friend," of man, who himself has deteriorated to the level of animal. During war man descends to his most primitive level, that of a dog. The dog will continue living after the soldier dies. It's not a question of if, but when he dies.

The Wounds of War

During the 1930s, Hameiri was an active participant in the Antifascist Marxist League. As a World War I veteran, he was an important asset to the pacifist movement in Israel which arose as a reaction to the *yishuv*'s increasing militarism. Hameiri's published poetry twenty years earlier had rejected war, emphasizing the Jewish pacifist point of view manifested by "Thou shalt not kill." This complemented universalist Marxist rhetoric which depicted exploitation of simple soldiers by the Kaiser, state, and army. His inspiration for these ideas came, amongst others, from the cultural leaders of Hungary. As a World War I veteran, Hameiri was a central speaker at "Antifa" meetings, sometimes dressed in his old officer's uniform, declaring war against war—real war, not a flowery phrase for revolutionary war. His burning hatred for "art for the sake of art," which he saw as writing without moral underpinning, blended with a specific Marxist, political viewpoint.

The Left welcomed Hameiri warmly. As a World War I veteran, he constituted a committee spokesman of the first importance. At his literary half jubilee, the Jerusalem Worker's

Union wrote to him: "In your role as an author-fighter, you have fought for and against us, but the wounds of love are dear to us. Your vigorous expression of the suffering of the workers and working youth atones for the war which is our heritage and flows from the great pain of a poet who aches and strives for universal peace and brotherhood."[63] "Antifa" also heaped praise on Hameiri: "You have rebelled against the usual lies of the counterfeit fascists and raised the flag of pure nationalism in support of human brotherhood in the spirit of working humanity. You have voiced a warning on behalf of the people to the *yishuv*: Fascism will not save us! Our destiny is forever linked to the war for worker's independence! The antifascist movement sees in you one of its oldest comrades, an example of the combination between a man of creative activity and war, who serves our shared goal heart and soul."[64]

Hameiri's Marxist leanings preferred the *fabula* and plot to psychological groping and theoretical views reflecting intellectual thought processes. For him, art was a tool of social improvement, like the Prophets of old. Beauty and aesthetics were Greco-Roman concepts, while the Prophets reached the summit of human morality, neglecting art which sanctifies form to achieve its aims. He believed that the approach of "art in service of art" was destined to blur, conceal, and confuse anyone who would die for the homeland in the future. "*L'art pour l'art* reflects lovely poems about the beauty of nature and life but conceals the ugliness of suffering and miserable subjugation!...*L'art pour l'art* stuffs your children with aesthetics, and, when they grow up, leads them like lambs to the slaughter on the altars of international arms manufacturers!"[65]

Therefore, *The Great Madness* is a novel of realism crammed with incidents and images, and relevant historical contexts (albeit sometimes inconsistent and inaccurate).

The novel also contains some surrealist and mysterious moments. During the years preceding publication of this novel, Hameiri published a series of short war stories whose signal element is fantasy. These stories present mysterious, unnatural events, to intensify the feeling of horror and dread on the battlefield. *The Great Madness* differs greatly from these war stories, but there are moments of fantasy, such as the procession of whores, the furniture in the protagonist's apartment that weeps when he departs for war as if they were members of his family, and the clock that ticks to him that he will not return. Another section that deviates from the novel's realism is the evening when the protagonist arrives at his destination in formal attire. When he takes off his dirty jacket, it weeps because it has become soiled with mud. By contrast, his uniform laughs:

> Who was it said that objects could cry? Some Roman. Didn't he know they could laugh, too? The Rav Hatanya knew it.
>
> The congealed blood weighs on my heart. And the uniform laughs at me: "ha ha ha! That's the reward for all your trouble. You hopped from star to star, from one constellation to another."[66]

Echoes of the great madness of empires, dynasties, kaisers, dukes, and tsars now seem very far away, and there are other causes for war and human fear. The "shell shock" of World

War I, and world-wide loss of more than 8 million soldiers and 5 million civilians, did not prevent future war. A second world war followed two decades later, even more destructive than the first and fraught with a terrible destiny for the Jewish people. The newly arisen Jewish State has already known many wars and a great deal of bravery. However, in the years before the Second World War, Hameiri still had the privilege of sitting back and analyzing, from a socialist point of view, the entire concept of war as a contradiction:

> The war is a great paradox, sir. Kant's question of the "*Ding an sich* (thing in itself)"[67] ought to be resolved empirically, not logically. Only one solitary reality within us is "a thing in itself," and that is the divine part of us, which we observe as a wild beast, or a uncouth animal, guzzling flesh with gold teeth, holding its fork in its left hand. We used to believe that man was the crown of creation, and that is was bread that turned him vile. Now the war has come to show us that man does not live by bread alone,[68] but chiefly by the blood of the homeland's enemies, whom it is a divine duty to destroy, root and branch. And that means that we have no idea of the true meaning of the sublime creation which is the sergeant, or His Excellency the Colonel.[69]

With the passage of time, it seems as though there never was a war in which this Jewish conflict was so dominant, to the point of severe conflict between Zionism and the Diaspora, and exposure of the inherent contradictions of this hybrid paradox. Hameiri, who began to serialize his novel with the title *The Great Paradox,* eventually decided that war, more than being an inner contradiction in man's animal nature, is really an illogical external spiritual condition, one of madness. The true paradox in the war from a personal point of view, was the fact that, as a Zionist, he fought for one physical homeland while his heart was given to a second spiritual homeland, which he would eventually choose. The paradox is found in the depths of his divided soul, split between Shem and Japheth. Only a human paradox like Avigdor Hameiri, totally rooted in two cultures, faithful to two homelands, split between assimilated Judaism and strict Orthodoxy and fraternal to ethnic Hungarians, was capable of creating such a novel replete with contradictions. It contains the comedic and the fantastic, the shocking and the amusing. A unique novel that comprehends the dilemma of the individual human condition and embraces the entire world, both Jewish and pacifistic. Hameiri's soul is the real battlefield, both Jewish and Hungarian. The sparks created by this friction are the wonderful madness that rise from it into the reader's heart.

Editor's Preface

The first English translation of Avigdor Hameiri's first great World War I novel *Hashigaon Hagadol* (*The Great Madness*)[1] by Jacob Freedman appeared in 1952,[2] followed by Yael Lotan's translation in 1984.[3] Both translations have long been out of print. My previous translations of *Bagehinom Shel Mata* (*Hell on Earth*),[4] *Ben Shinei Ha'adam* (*Of Human Carnage*),[5] and *Masa Le'Eropa Haperait* (*Voyage into Savage Europe*)[6] have led me to believe that an edited, updated English translation of *The Great Madness* is overdue.

The first eight chapters of *Hashigaon Hagadol* were published 1925 and 1926 in serial form in the newspaper *Ha'aretz*. The book itself was published in 1930, around the same time as *All Quiet on the Western Front.* Not only was it similar to *All Quiet,* but it overshadowed it for Hebrew readers. However, much to Hameiri's chagrin, it never received the world-wide acclaim of *All Quiet.*[7] Hameiri's iconoclastic personality as well as language problems in the original Hebrew (with no contemporary translation) contributed to the lack of outside readership.

The Great Madness is in many respects a greater novel than *All Quiet.* Hameiri served on the front for a longer time (2 years as opposed to 6 months) than Paul Bäumer, and the palette of characters is vastly greater, comprising representatives of the entire polyglot Habsburg Army. Instead of the poor farmer Stanislaus Katczinsky, Hameiri's companions are Pály, a young Magyar, Margolis, a *yeshiva* student, and Uncle Osterreicher, a middle aged Orthodox Jew. Hameiri never forgets for a minute that he is both a Jew and a Hungarian. The novel provides a uniquely Jewish glimpse into the role of Jewish soldiers in the World War I Austro-Hungarian Army, and also the Magyar experience. The novel is replete with assimilated and converted Hungarian Jews who try in vain to hide their Jewish origins. Like Paul Bäumer, Hameiri is greatly disillusioned with life at home on leave. He has the added experience that whores have become nurses, and wives have become faithless whores. His experiences of the follies of war turned Hameiri into an avowed pacifist, which did not endear him to a nascent Jewish state preoccupied with development of a Jewish defense force.

Hameiri's books require endnotes if they are to be properly understood. Holtzman has published an annotated version of *Hashigaon Hagadol* in Hebrew, but as of now there is no annotated English version available. I have sought to remedy this deficiency by translating and expanding on these notes.[8] Hameiri was well educated in Torah and Talmud and had a wide secular interest, so the scope of these endnotes is wide. Because this is essentially an action novel, however, the number of endnotes is, except for chapter 28, fewer than for my other Hameiri translations.

The original version contains several pieces of poetry, most not included in the Lotan translation, and some in the Freedman translation. Strangely, the later only contains 27 instead of the full 33 chapters of the original. It does not include chapter 17 (a poem, "Hanina Beni," not included in the Lotan translation either), but also chapters 20, 21, 22, 27, and 30. For the sake of completeness, and because I believe that one significant line of poetry is as good as if not better than several pages of prose, I have included all in this revised edition.

The spectrum of poetry is wide. Hameiri talks of his loneliness, having no one to leave behind and grieve for him if he dies. In the symbolist poem "Hanina Beni," Hameiri compares the life of Hanina Ben Dosa during Mishnaic times after destruction of the Second Temple, with the chaos and destruction he sees around him. Other poems depict the Angel of Death visiting him while he is keeping watch, and mass death and burials at the front, without anyone to mourn or weep over the graves. In "Blood and the Rose," he compares the blood-red rose to a woman having intercourse with him one last time over his grave, and cynically depicts God as laughing at his creation. In "The Nest," Pály is his *Doppelgänger*. Hameiri was well aware of the poem by that name: indeed, he published a volume of Hebrew translation of Heine's poetry (almost impossible to do because of the deep equivocations and multiple meanings hidden underneath seemingly simple words).[9] Finally in his longest poem, "The Dog," Hameiri describes the relation of his own bitter feelings to that of a barking dog. He rails against the cruel war like a dog howls at the moon, and they warm each other on his grave. Perhaps only a dog can give vent to the cruelty of this war by barking and howling. The last verse of this poem reminded me of the last verse of Bialik's "Ba'ir Haharega" ("In the City of Slaughter"), when the poet rails and raises his fist to God at the injustice of the Kishinev pogroms (1903 and 1905).

As in all his works, Hameiri has a biting and acerbic wit. He sees the human condition, with all its vicissitudes, with great clarity. The text of *The Great Madness* is full of laugh-out-loud comedy alternating with the cruelty of war and immediacy of his front line battle service. His writing is infused with a sense of compassion for the helpless victims of war, caught up in a process over which they have no control. He is wounded twice in 2 years, the second time very seriously. Unlike *Hell on Earth,* where hallucinatory episodes are common, most of *The Great Madness* is direct and down to earth. The exception is the Grand Guignol chapter on the Russian Christmas with Cossacks drinking blood mixed with wine, a severed head under the table, and nailing a soldier to the wall. This chapter may have been influenced by Hameiri's contact with the German writer of the macabre Hanns Heinz Ewers.[10] The book ends with Hameiri, together with his whole unit being taken captive by the Russians at the start of the Brusilov Offensive (1916).

Even when described briefly, Hameiri uses the finest of brushes to describe his characters. One of the unique aspects of this book is the description of representatives of the polyglot Habsburg Empire: German speaking Austrians, Hungarians, Czechs, Slovaks, Serbs, Croats, and Italians. He reserves his finest brush for the priggish, cruel Colonel Figer and his three comrades Pály the faithful, handsome young Magyar, Margolis the adaptable *yeshiva* student always ready with a quip, or to help repair telephone communications, and Uncle Osterreicher the pious Orthodox Jew who prays regularly but fights just as bravely as other soldiers. The fates of all three, especially Pály and Margolis, are followed in his second war novel, *Hell on Earth.*

Throughout this book, I have drawn on Yael Lotan's translation as my outline, complemented and expanded by the earlier translation by Jacob Freedman and my own interpretations, translating and expanding the notes by Holtzman in his 1989 Hebrew re-edition. The Shapira brothers kindly granted copyright approval to reedit an English translation of their grandfather's novel. I thank Jonathan Orr Stav and Ilana Hairston for permission to modify and expand on their mother Yael Lotan's translation. I thank Tim Demy for his support and encouragement in this new edition of an old masterpiece and Dan Hecht for his introduction and assistance in poetry translation. Thank you to Gina Palmer who was exceptionally helpful and meticulous in transcribing material from numerous Hameiri files. I thank Ken Kaliski and Karen Pearse for copyright approval to use their grandfather František Reichentál's painting for the book cover as well as his sketch of Hameiri. Bialik once said that reading translation is like reading the original through a veil. This is ten-fold true for poetry, which requires an expert eye and touch. As always, my wife Addie and daughter Madeleine provided their own kind of support. If this new edition makes this World War I masterpiece more widely read and appreciated, I am content. Any mistakes in translation and editing are mine alone.

Peter C. Appelbaum
Land O Lakes, FL
August 2020

Author's Preface

THREE years I spent in that colossal madhouse which spread over half the globe, wherein a billion frantic people rioted in a variety of frantic postures—enthusiastically, tearfully, exultingly, cunningly, naïvely, sadly, lovingly, defiantly.

I witnessed the madness break out and rubbed my eyes with amazement. In my bewilderment, I was swept into its midst by a certain character dressed in a glittering uniform and sporting a long pointed moustache. He called himself by the strange name of *General Feldwebel* ("General Sergeant-Major").[1]

Then I, too, found myself falling victim, prey to the violent waves of smashing confusion. I steeled myself to prevent my brain from becoming benumbed, so that I could soberly observe the poor wretches around me as well as my own unfortunate, well-liked self.

Did my eyes see aright? Was my mind clear? It is not I who should answer this question, not I, the madman observing himself.

Vaguely I remember disputing with Maeterlinck his reason for not obeying his physician, Doctor Einstein.[2]

Then the dispute too faded in my mind.

For three years I lived in the Great War, in the Austro-Hungarian-German front line facing the Russians, and there I wrote down what I saw as a sentient human being. I began to make notes two days after meeting the sergeant and finished the last chapter in Chortkov,[3] the first station of my captivity in Russia, thirteen years ago.

I have neither embellished nor coarsened my notes, nor did I add to or subtract from them. I made my notes and waited for the finale, for the return to sanity.

But in the meantime I had also observed the Jew, who in the midst of the madhouse remained a Jew—enthusiastic idiot, holy clown, ancient child, and despised lover of man.

I had not set out to observe the Jew in myself and in my comrades-in-death, but that is how it turned out.

Looking back, I'm glad it did.

Avigdor Hameiri

I dedicate these notes to Albert Einstein, one of the only sane men in a world of insanity, who didn't follow my sergeant's orders.

Chapter 1 | Opium

ALL QUIET in the editorial office. A tense, sweaty silence. The silence of feverish labor. Each colleague is buried in his own work, in hasty ant-like activity which consumes the nerves. Nerves – electrical wires, positive and negative; the brain – that ethereal machine – excretes and secretes its moving images upon the white paper. A ceaseless, continuous stream of activity.

Should you raise your head for a moment, between one subject and another, you'll hear the scraping of pens and the mysterious beating of hearts. From time to time – blowing of cigarette smoke, combining with ticking of clocks on the many desks.

Prolonged rustling silence.

Suddenly: telephone!

"Hello! Stockholm, yes."

It's my turn to take it. I pick up the receiver on my desk: "Hello." I write down:

"(a) Professor Brunner proposes to establish an international university in The Hague, taught in Esperanto.[1] The proposal is scheduled for acceptance tomorrow; (b) A lecture by Professor Einstein on the theory of relativity, in Leipzig, brought tears to the eyes of the small audience.[2] There is a proposal in Germany to build an observatory which will bear his name; (c) Edison is about to complete his electrical screen, which will be able to stop any kind of war in the world;[3] (d) Speaking at a court dinner yesterday, Kaiser Wilhelm[4] said that as long as he is alive, there will be no war in Europe; (e) At an interview with the Brahmin Lamondi, the Hindu priest expressed his opinion regarding opium smoking. "For us true Hindus," he said, "opium is superfluous. Only uncivilized European barbarians need it. The sublime smoke would show them in a dream, at least, the real purpose of man in life: to extirpate the 'I' and the 'Thou' within us and to recognize both as divine;"[5] (f) The Austrian Colonel Redel, who, as it was conclusively proved, has sold all the plans of the fortress of Przemysl to the Russians, shot himself this morning with a revolver left on his desk by two fellow officers. – End."[6]

I dish up these boring items into as tasty a dish as I can, call it a day, and ring the bell.

The door opens and the girl from the press comes in.

"Here are the last cables."

Similar offers are made from all the other desks: "Here take these too."

Everybody has finished.

A great sigh of relief. Now we can hear the noise of the machines downstairs.

We all stretch, looking at our watches: 3.30 a.m. I get ready to leave. A couple of minutes later the messenger brings us the newspaper.

Nobody looks at it.

We go out to "lunch." Coming out into the street we are hit by the concealed hum of the city's night life. The trams are at rest. Street lights have been extinguished, spacious mansions slumber the sleep of the just, only the more intimate cafes are full.

We go to the "Royal Orpheum"[7] and enter its crowded cellar. Seated at our table, my friends ask me for the latest news. I tell them: an international university. Einstein. Edison. Kaiser Wilhelm. The Brahmin and the opium. The traitor colonel. Laughter. Kaiser Wilhelm is caught in the act. "So long as he lives there will be no war." Ha ha. That means, he really is thinking about war. What an idiot – a war in the twentieth century! Ridiculous! Edison and Einstein are funny as well, as are Brunner's university and Esperanto. Mister Edison can build himself a house with his electrical barrier screen.

Only the Brahmin interests us. Especially our friend, pallid and delicate university lecturer Dr. Garai.[8]

"Perhaps the Brahmin would pay us a visit as well," says the doctor, and his grayish face grows grayer. He lights a cigarette before the meal, and draws the bitter-sweet smoke deep into his lungs. He sips the sour soup, at intervals chewing the cigarette tobacco and tasting his cherry brandy. After a few sips, he tells the waiter to take the soup away and bring him a sausage fried in lemon juice.

The music blares around us and the cabaret girls join our table. Someone offers them Tokay laced with a little absinthe. They all drink.

They are five young girls. One from France, one from Canada, one from Dusseldorf, one from Melbourne, and one from Worms. But they all understand the international language of the Orpheum. It's a language of the night, the language of wine, women, and song.

"Here's to Professor Brunner's university!" says one of my friends and turns to the girls:

"Well, and what will you do if war breaks out?"

They all burst into delightful laughter. Each of them has a remedy for this ridiculous war.

"I'll dance to the sound of firing at the front."

"I'll crawl into the muzzle of a cannon and have them shoot me home."

"I'll get the whole front drunk with Bordeaux wine, until the enemies start to dance arm in arm and leg to leg in a frenzied can-can."

"I'll sit between the enemy soldiers and make eyes at them," says the French girl, sweetly coquettish. "First at one, then the other. I'd like to see if they can recover enough to fight!"

"God help us all then," says one of my friends. "They'll eat each other alive because of you."

"And what about you?" Somebody asks the tiny pale girl from Melbourne. "You're such a holy marble Virgin Mary, what will you do?" The statue-like child raises her tragic eyes and says in an almost sing-song voice: "I'll be a nurse and kiss the blood off the foreheads of the silly wounded men. Who knows how many bridegrooms I will have there?" – she adds, her voice gently serious. "Who knows how many of the kisses that I imprint on my lovers' foreheads will dissolve with their last sigh?" She begins to weep quietly.

We all burst out laughing She really does believe in the possibility of war!

Our friend, the anemic and delicate Dr. Garai, rises from his seat, goes over to her, takes her on his lap, kisses her and says:

"You're a fool, my little sick bride. The Brahmin is wrong, after all. You don't know what the Brahmin said. He said that Europe needs opium in order to love, to forget herself, to reach the level of the Higher Man, physically sense Spinoza's logos in the blood.[9] Well, darling, he doesn't know us, doesn't know Europe. It's they, the Hindus, who need opium in order to hear the music of Bach[10] in a dream, and dream the secret of the great fusion of the 'I' and the 'Thou.' We have already reached it, without the need of smoke. Do you know, my pale beloved, what is our 'categorical imperative'"?[11]

His "pale beloved" stares at him as if he were drunk. What sort of words are those? What is he talking about?

And he goes on:

"Our categorical imperative, my darling, is 'love thyself as thy neighbor!' – You and your neighbor, but the neighbor comes first.[12] Darling child, we're already approaching Mars and Alpha Centauri[13] – by machine. And we are also drawing near to ourselves – and God – by the dynamics of our brain, and so…"

The girl interrupts:

"And you, old man, do you love me?"

"Yes, my child, I love you beyond measure, more than myself. They say that you have an infectious disease and that you want to kiss me. If it gives you pleasure – here I am, kiss me."[14]

"And would you kill someone, say, one of your friends, out of jealousy for me?"

"Jealousy? – What is jealousy? Is there a pleasure in the world greater than that of giving a friend the woman we both love more than life itself?"

The girl jumps off his lap as if stung by a viper:

"In that case, get the hell out of here to the desert! You monster!" But he continues quietly, as in a dream:

"All the same, nobody really knows what lurks in his own heart. The great love known to the children of the primordial planets, which bears the culture of life, has already come to us; and yet – that devil still exists, that Satan Cain, who has to be released, has to be given an outlet and set loose."

"By perforating the brain," someone suggests mockingly.

"Of course," Dr. Garai proceeds, "war is necessary. War! The ancient hate of the vicious beast in the primeval forest, which grinds its teeth in our blood, cries out for release. It is choking there, side by side with man.[15] The great war will come, the blessed catharsis, the searing spiritual surgery. We'll emerge from under the scalpel like a patient recuperating from an appendectomy, having got rid of the suppurating infection together with the diseased member, inheritance of our revered savage forefathers.[16] How can Martians visit us as we are now? Who will they visit among us? The *Australopithecus*?[17] Or you, my darling Melbourne Lilly? Yes – to free ourselves from the force of gravity means to conquer the universe! To create a neutral field between rebellious man and the crawling beast within us, means – to be united with God!" –

"Waiter! Josti! Again there is no more wine and no more absinthe! Do you really love me!"

The waiter arrives, for at least the tenth time. The drinks, the music and the dancing rock us gently on the waves of our singing blood, and we sit on and sleep with eyes open.

A woman's voice whispers dully into my ear:

"Where I come from, in Worms, it's forbidden to stay up till dawn."

"Oh, Worms? – ah, Worms, Worms… That was Varmiza, Varmisha. Do you know, sweetheart, who lived in your town of Varmisha? – Rashi, Rashi, Rabbi Shlomo Itzhaki, that wonderful good old man, whose commentaries I learned by heart…"[18]

One of us suddenly sobers up and says:

"Let's go. They want to sweep the hall."

The hall is empty, quiet and cold.

"Josti, the check!" We each hand our open purses to the waiter. He takes what is due him and says, bowing:

"Good morning, brothers. *Au revoir.* Go home, or it will be dawn. It's already –"

But he doesn't know the exact time either.

When we come out, there is a regular procession of nocturnal revellers singing obstreperously and tripping the light fantastic along the entire length of the street. Passing a policeman who stands in the middle of the road, they drag him along, dancing and kissing.

The air is quite cool and very pleasant. Street lamps have already been extinguished and one of the city clocks strikes the morning hour.

In my dream I discuss Dr. Garai's "categorical imperative" with Flammarion, in pure modern Hebrew.[19] When I rise in the evening twilight I find a red slip – a conscription order – on my table.

2 | Madness

FOR ABOUT four years I have not seen the morning sun. Newspaper offices usually close around 3:00 a.m., and who can go to sleep straight after work? After work one socializes, and social life lasts till dawn. Social life means music, art, philosophy, women, dancing, science. In the morning one goes to sleep before sunrise, so as not to bump into people. People are strange creations. They are creatures of financial concerns, preoccupied, dried up, foolish. Very good citizens but sickening and boring to talk to. "How are you?" "Fine, thank you. And you?" "Thanks. All right, still alive. A thousand sovereigns would save me." That's humor. "What's the news?" "The news?" You tell him the news. "What's the news? None, but that the world has grown honest." The theory of relativity. At the end of the day he, the citizen, dear reader, really despises you in his heart of hearts. After all, it's for him that you sweat and scrawl And then, what are you? – a lazybones, who spends his nights with cabaret girls.

Fear of the citizen surmounts all other fears. You rush home at dawn, turn on the light and read a book until about eight o'clock, then fall asleep.

You get up around 4:00 p.m. Once again to the coffee house to work for a couple of hours or more. Poems, stories, articles. Then, a visit to the editorial office. Then you go and cover the theater, or a concert, until about 10:00 p.m. or later. After all this, hard work creating a newspaper, until 3:00 a.m.

Then the same thing, all over again.

Four years of this. The life of a night owl.

The red slip hardly sobers me up. Should I go to the City Hall? Very good. But when? – 10.00 a.m. is not good. One is sure to run into people there. Perhaps it can be done by telephone. I go to the editorial office and ask for the City Hall on the telephone.

"The City Hall, please, Miss."

"City Hall!"

"Hello! Is this City Hall? This is the editorial office of *The People's Voice*.[1] This morning I received a red slip. What is it for?"

"A red slip? It means you have to present yourself for conscription."

"Conscription? What do you mean? I have to be a soldier?"

"So it appears."

"Can't it be managed without me? I really am very busy. Especially in the mornings, when I sleep. Surely you know what newspaper work is like."

Laughter on the telephone. Then:

"We're very sorry. But it appears that one cannot die heroically by telephone. Impossible." And that's that.

They laugh. So it has to be a serious matter.

A few colleagues enter.

Now I am laughing:

"One can't die heroically by telephone. One must join the human race."

"Have you been in town? The city's gone crazy."

My lodgings are two minutes away from the office. Just around the corner. No, I haven't been into town.

"Let's go downtown. I tell you – people have all gone mad. Really!" We go downtown, and find it all agog. There's a parade down the street. A soldier carries a flag, followed by a mob of urchins shouting deafeningly.

"Long live the war! Long live the homeland! Long live Emperor Franz Josef the First![2] Long live Kaiser Wilhelm, our noble friend! Long live King Victor Emmanuel of glorious Italy!"[3] – And the hymn:

> "To your homeland firm be,
> As a rock in your loyalty, O Magyar !"

Peculiar. It's a long time since we last heard this pious refrain. Where did it hide, before suddenly bursting out from the mouths of this rag-tag rabble?

"Homeland" – what is the meaning of that word?

"The song of our primate ancestor, the *Australopithecus*,[4] that's what this song is," somebody says behind me.

I look back: there is the pale and delicate Dr. Garai.

"Well, what do you think?" I ask him.

"You know what I think."

"Do drop your paradoxes, my friend.[5] Oh yes, have you received a red slip?"

"Yes. I arranged it by messenger."

There is one among us who is not greatly amused by Dr. Garai's "arrangement," and that is me. I see something in that jubilant crowd which the others miss. I can't believe my eyes. I look again and rub them.

"What's this? Can't you see? Look!"

Beside the flag-bearer, to his left, bursting with national pride, marches our dear friend, the famous Italian anarchist Signor Grappulini.

"But he's been in prison for the past six months, hasn't he?"

"What do you mean, in prison? — Haven't we been raising hell for months, leaving no stone unturned to improve his prison conditions? Haven't we enlisted the influence of all our prominent friends to get him released?"

"They must have forced him to go free," somebody says. But it's clear that he himself doesn't believe it.

We all stare at the speaker; what nonsense! Force someone to fight against all his own ideals? Why, even in Tsarist Russia they don't do such things!

The mob reaches the "Meteor" coffee house and stops. Signor Grappulini is still in front.

"This is madness. Grappulini and war?"

But facts are facts. Signor Grappulini enters the coffee house and sternly orders all the customers – "Out!" This is an order that brooks no disobedience. He is accompanied by several policemen and a young officer who pulls out his sword and waves it around – "Out! Out!"

The customers come out and Signor Grappulini gathers the mob around him, places the flag bearer on a table in the terrace, then stands on table and begins to make a speech.

He harangues enthusiastically, with face flushed crimson, blood streaming through his heart and lungs. "In the name of the great ally Italy, in the name of the nation of Michelangelo, of Machiavelli, of the sainted Garibaldi…"[6]

We push our way in. This is a delightful business. Grappulini orating in the name of our ally Italy,[7] enthusiastically calling for war. In the name of Garibaldi. He's quite a fellow, that one. He's making fun of the whole business. After all, we know him. He's a humorous sort of lad. Soon everybody will be laughing. He's making a huge joke of everything. Some naïve person in the crowd, an artless fellow who can't take a joke, calls to the frothing speaker:

"Well, what's stopping you from dying a heroic death? — Go, and good luck to you!"

We've hardly turned around to see who it is when a cry, a yell of pain, is heard, and we see the tactless heckler's face bloodied. He is arrested at once and taken away. The crowd rages and the entire street seethes and foams:

"Long live the war! Long live our ally Italy! Long live the gracious and all-powerful Kaiser Wilhelm!"

Somebody laughs. And after the laughter, an outcry. His face drips blood as well.

"Let's get out of here. It's dangerous."

"Why? We can stand by and listen in silence."

Dr. Garai bends and whispers in my ear: "I want to see if there isn't a single man or woman in this entire crowd who is opposed to the war."

"But you see there are, and they get beaten up."

The speaker grows ecstatic. The homeland is in danger. We must break the teeth of the Serbian dog, tear out the French serpent's tongue, cut off the British lion's head, shatter the skull of the Russian bear!

"Bravo! Bravo!"

We look at the crowd: the faces are all exultant, they are all in agreement!

Finally, the anthem:

> "To your homeland firm be,
> As a rock in your loyalty, O Magyar !"

By now there's not a mouth in the whole street that isn't open in song.

"What's the meaning of all this enthusiasm?"

"These are all mercenaries. Can't you see? It's a mob."

Dr. Garai studies the frenzied crowd, listens to the speaker and then turns to me with slitted eyes and declares very emphatically:

"We are all mistaken, my dear man. We're all much too clever by half. Did you hear what he said? – the Serbs have crossed the Danube. They are coming closer and closer."

"But that's a lie."

"What if it's true?"

"Then we would all know it."

"You know everything, my dear fellow. But did you know this – that the masses are ready to march to their death with a song on their lips?"

"I don't see that yet. I do see them shouting."

Dr. Garai becomes provoked:

"Don't be a wise guy! They're all willing to go, all of them!" I fall silent, and he continues solemnly:

"Do you know what it means to march towards death?"

"No I don't."

"To march towards death means searching for a new meaning in life."

"Opium. Divine madness. We're rotting away..."

He says that and leaves us quickly. Simply vanishes.

We laugh.

The fevered enthusiasm of the crowd kills the laughter on our lips.

"The People. The Heaven-blessed People."

The hymn comes to an end, followed by a dramatic declaration:

"Whoever wants to volunteer to join the sacred war for the defense of the homeland – step forward!"

The mob begins to push and shove against the table until it becomes positively dangerous. Everybody volunteers.

"Put me down too."

I can't believe my eyes: our fragile, sallow Dr. Garai.

I blink and laugh: what a wonderful joke.

Dr. Garai fastens his weary eyes on me indignantly:

"What are you laughing about?!"

I break into a guffaw, take his hand and clasp it: "You're a splendid fellow, a true war hero. Well then, go. The homeland is in danger." Dr. Garai throws me one last parting look, withdraws his hand from mine and rushes to the table. I follow him, still convinced that he's only joking.

But no – he has really registered.

"What's all this?"

"We'll see how it'll turn out." Dr. Garai, looking like someone who has faithfully done his duty, returns from the table, his face beaming, his fragile frame erect.

I go up to him: "Congratulations!" I go to shake his hand, but he avoids me. He stares at me piercingly, his expression full of suppressed hatred and anger mixed with scorn. He turns to go. I grin and he walks away, then turns back and spits out one word at me:

"*Jew!*"

I am thunderstruck.

It's ages since this word has been uttered in such a manner among us. I cannot restrain myself from answering him, but my throat is parched and my tongue paralyzed.

"Garai!" I final call out, almost in tears.

It must have reached him. Dr. Garai hears. He turns back, comes up to me and exclaims with a stinging, sarcastic hiss:

"How can you know what a homeland means?"

My head begins to spin. I close my eyes and lean against a lamppost.

Somebody pushes me. I rouse myself and go to the editorial office.

The office is deserted. I sit down and wipe my sweating face.

The emptiness is frightful.

On my desk lie last night's cables: the Einstein Observatory, the international university. Esperanto.[8]

And in the streets – an uproar.

I can't go on sitting here. I must go out.

An artillery regiment passes by. On both sides of the street a multitude of women give the marching soldiers money and cigarettes.

Some of the women throw themselves on the soldiers' necks and kiss them.

"To your homeland firm be…"

3 | Able-Bodied

THAT RED slip. Strange. I have to appear before the authorities by their order. This is the first time in my life that the authorities have ordered me to do anything. Before that, they have always addressed me with requests, whenever it had the need to do so. Now it's an order.

Below, in the lower margin of the slip, is a footnote: "This slip is not a conscription order in itself, only an order to appear at headquarters."

I haven't the vaguest idea what this footnote means. But it's late and I have to go to the editorial office.

The editorial office is all agog.

"Dear Mr. Stupid," they greet me. "Sit down and get it into that superior head of yours that there's a war on. On one hand the homeland is in danger, and, on the other, it's embarked on world conquest."

"I don't understand."

"Tomorrow the Hussars enter Belgrade, capital of the great Serbian people, in order to change the king's name from Karageorgevic to the simple and beautiful name Karolyi.[1] Why have such a peculiar name as Kara-geor-ge-vic?! Pfui! On the other hand – my colleague, the current theater critic, continues – the great Cossacks want to cross the Carpathians."[2]

"So let them cross. Why not?"

My colleague is perplexed. He hasn't even thought of that. But really, why not? Whom would they disturb?

"It really would be a shame if they didn't cross," comes a voice from the sports desk. Cossack dances are beautiful! Just the same, I hope that they won't cross."

"Why shouldn't they cross?"

"Why?! Didn't you learn at school that the Carpathians are 'God's barrier,' the fortress of the Magyar gods? Who would never allow an enemy to pass over them?"

"Oh, the Cossacks can't even read and write!" interjects our lady colleague who edits the women's section. "They didn't learn it at school, so they'll have no difficulty crossing them," she concludes, rather happily.

The girl from the press room comes in to ask for copy.

We are all thrown into consternation There isn't any copy yet.

Work begins with customary feverishness.

I'm still preoccupied with the footnote on the red slip. My colleagues explain it to me: "When were you born? In the nineties? If so, you aren't yet subject to conscription. Unless, that is, the homeland being in danger in the Carpathian sector, they might want to know if you have some connection with that part of the country, in which case they'll ask you to volunteer."

"I see."

So we work until 3:00 a.m. Since it's hardly worthwhile to go to bed until 7:00 a.m., we don't lie down.

Only when we finish working do I realize that my colleague Dr. Garai isn't there. Where is he? – No one knows. He hasn't come in at all that night. I tell my friends about Dr. Garai's behavior in the street. Nobody can understand it. He's a bit cracked! Good!

But his parting words the previous day give me no rest. There are many forms of insanity but this one – such an attitude, to remind a person of his *Jewishness*...? It's obvious that something is behind all this.

In the morning we go to headquarters.

There we find Dr. Garai. None of us pay any attention to him. He notices it and becomes irritable. He is also somewhat drunk.

My turn comes. The recruiting officer explains the red slip and the footnote.

"If you, sir, have any connection with the Carpathian provinces, then you can volunteer to go there. The homeland must be defended. Those wild Cossacks may break in. Well?"

"Of course I'll go."

The recruiting rises, shakes my hand, enrolls me, and adds:

"Please undress. Over there, in the corner."

"Naked?"

"Yes, yes. Naked."

"Can't it be done without this?"

"No. Someone may be sickly. We must examine everyone."

"But I'm not sickly."

Suddenly a tall soldier comes up to me and yells:

"Undress! Understand?"

"Please don't speak to me in that tone."

The tall officer comes up to me, almost touches his nose to mine, glares. and says through gritted teeth:

"What did you say? How dare you adopt such a tone?! Do you think this is a newspaper office? Here we use another tone altogether, my friend. You enlisted. Well, then, now you're a soldier and must undress. At once! Understand?"

A dark curtain seems to fall from my brain and my heart is filled with regret. Why did I enlist? So that a clown dressed like an idiot could abuse me? While taking off my clothes I think: to die for one's country is understandable. But to endure such boorishness?

If that's how it is from the very outset, what's going to happen in a week or two? – It's really revolting.

The doctor examines me.

Meantime, a few of my colleagues join me and we stand in line. Naked. But Dr. Garai is missing. Where is he?

The doctor asks me a few questions, then says in a confident voice:

"Able-bodied, fit for duty. Next!"

Some are rejected. One of them protests loudly at the disgrace. He's healthy and able-bodied!

We get dressed and return to the recruiting official. He hands me a new slip, saying:

"From now on you're in the army and may not take a step without orders. Go into that room and wait."

"I have to inform the editorial office."

Once again the tall officer comes up to me:

"No informing, no editorial office!!"

"I have to say goodbye to my sister and my family."

"Where does your sister live?"

"On her own homestead, in Bereg province.[3]

"In Bereg province? Why, that's in the Carpathians! You'll be sent there tomorrow! You're going to protect your sister from the Cossacks. Idiot!"

Suddenly he offers me his hand to me and says:

"You're going to be a marvellous soldier, my friend. You'll chase the Cossacks right back to Moscow! And when you return you'll get a first class decoration! Before it's all over, we'll make a man of you and you won't go on messing about with ink and all the rest of that nonsense!"

When my colleagues and I meet in the other room we find out that Dr. Garai has not enlisted. He has obtained an exemption.

"We too can still get exempted, as newspapermen," says one of my colleagues.

I am completely stunned by all that has happened to me. My head feels heavy as I haven't slept. Only the word "able-bodied" keeps reverberating in my insides, from heart to brain and back. I able-bodied? Me? I am fit to wear a uniform like that officer? – What a travesty!

A few minutes later another officer-type enters and orders us to come along with him. I eye him from helmeted top to toe. A boorish fellow, with waxed moustache whose points are twirled up towards his small eyes. A stumpy, powerfully built man, he keeps spitting with gusto, in constant punctuation of his rapid words, talking at top speed.

"Who are you?" I ask.

"Me?" he replies with scornful arrogance. "I am the *Feldwebel* (sergeant), that's who I am!"

"I see," I say, and extend my hand to him as I politely introduce myself.

He doesn't take my hand. "Never mind, never mind!" he flashes back at me. "We'll have time enough to get acquainted. You'll become fed up with me yet, gentlemen!"

Outside in the courtyard he announces: "Is there anyone who wants to go to his apartment to fetch something?"

Of course we all do.

"I knew it!" the sergeant says scornfully. "Very well!"

"Everyone can go home, take whatever he wants, and in two hours' time – it's now 8:15 a.m. – at exactly 10:15 a.m., you'll all be in this courtyard ready to travel. Not a minute later, understand?"

Out in the street we all heave sighs of relief.

I walk to my apartment in a daze When I enter my room the furniture begins to cry.[4] I reprimand my things: "you fools, am I going away for a long time?" I can't understand the whole business yet. The seething streets. The anarchist Grappulini turning orator, haranguing the crowd, and shouting: "Long live the King." The pale, sickly Dr. Garai insulting me: *Jew*. I am able-bodied. The officer fuming at me and ordering me, in the familiar person,[5] to undress. The churlish *Feldwebel,* too, refusing to shake my hand, speaking to me contemptuously. But the strangest thing of all is that when the tall officer slaps me on the shoulder and shakes my hand, saying that I would make a good soldier – I feel a kind of pride.

Why should I deny it? Why lie to myself? – It's a fact: I am flattered. What does it mean? Only yesterday I would not have sat at the same table with him.

What is war?

I begin to pack my things in a suitcase. The concierge comes in.

"Where to? Where to? What's happened?"

"I'm able-bodied, granny."

"What d'you mean, able-bodied?"

"I'm able-bodied, don't you understand? I'm able bodied!"

The old woman understands at once. She begins to quietly blow her nose, then wipes her eyes and bursts into tears.

"Why are you crying, foolish dear? If I'm able-bodied, does that mean you have to cry?"

The old woman weeps bitterly, and her tears get under my skin. "Woe is me, able-bodied," she mumbles, "Oh, my only son was able-bodied, too! He died in the barracks a year ago, of tuberculosis. He caught a cold and died there. Oh my, oh my... And now you, sir..."

"I won't catch cold. I won't die of tuberculosis."

But her bitter wailing shakes me. I reassure her:

"You remain here, my dear granny, and take care of my library and everything, and I will write you love letters, dear lady, just like your son. You know, he was really smart, to die of tuberculosis without a war. Then I will return to you, a hero on the battlefield, on my homeland's altar!"

But the old lady is inconsolable. She weeps and weeps, meantime pushing more things into my suitcase – another shirt, another apple, another sausage, one more handkerchief.

Memories of my dead mother rise up before me. For years now I have not been conscious of feeling motherless.

"Oh my, oh my," the old woman moans, "what shall I say to the dear lady? What shall I tell Mamselle Mansie, who loves you so much, sir? Woe is me!"

"Tell her that I'm able-bodied, dear lady. That for the first time in my life somebody said to me that I am able-bodied.

Do you know what that uniformed general said? – He told me that I will be a great soldier, and will chase the Cossacks all the way back to Moscow!"

At that moment I again feel a sort of pride.

The old woman suddenly remembers something of great importance. She looks at me, eyes beaming with precious hope, and says:

"My dear boy, but you have important, influential friends, who could get you out of this trouble! Don't you have a close friend who's a prominent general?"

So I do. I remembered that the senior ranking general, General Schweitzer, an invalid and a fine Jew, knows and likes me. He's practically a Zionist.[6]

The old woman seizes this straw of hope and will not let go:

"Please, sir, go to him. I beg you, go to him! He won't let you…he won't let you … oh my…Please go! I'll go to him for you."

"Don't you go, my dear. He won't see you."

"He won't see me? – Me, who gave an only son to the Kaiser?!" she exclaims, holding her head proudly.

She is all set to get dressed and go to him, but I prevent her.

"All right, all right, granny. I'll go to him myself. In any case, I should say goodbye to him."

"Promise you'll go, sir!"

I promise.

If I'm to call on the general I must dress correctly. So I put my jacket on correctly and leave the house and my maternal concierge to wail and moan.

General Schweitzer, a Jew of humble parentage, who was a *yeshiva* scholar some seventy years before, is deeply moved to see me.

Only two weeks previously he revealed to me and to my fellow Zionists his warm Jewish heart, and great regret that due to his advanced age he could not take part in our great and ancient hope. And now, without warning, I appear before him as a candidate for a heroic death. He begins to cough and his eyes well with tears.

"The homeland is cruel, my dear child," says the old general. "She is cruel, very cruel, because she knows we love her."

Suddenly he asks:

"How old are you, my boy?"

"Twenty-four, Excellency."

The tall patriarch begins to trembling visibly. He rises from his chair and I stand up as well. He comes up to me, takes both my hands and asks, as if he already knows the answer:

"So you've volunteered?"

"In a certain sense, yes, Excellency."

He takes my head between his hands, kisses my forehead and says, deeply moved:

"May the Lord God of Israel preserve you, as He has preserved His people from generation to generation."

He grips my hand firmly, continuing:

"Go in peace and blessing, my dear son, and should God grant you the privilege of fighting to protect the walls of Jerusalem, don't forget me there, at the Temple W..."

His words break, his voice cracks. He turns around and goes out of the room. I see his neck twitching convulsively. Is he weeping?

I leave his room and go out.

There in the corridor stands my old concierge in her Sunday best, waiting for me with bated breath.

"Well?" she asks, heart pounding. "What did he say?" She looks like a quivering human question mark.

"What did he say, my dear? He asked me to pray for him at the Temple of Jerusalem."

The old woman stares at me as if I had gone mad.

I turn and leave her; she stands there, glued to the spot, and doesn't even follow me.

But as for the general's request, I am no wiser than she.

What do the Carpathians have to do with the walls of Jerusalem?

4 | A Lonely Soul

I sit down and write the following:

The Pinkish Stain

This is the path that I have prepared,
To set out on my journey with glorious grief;
How good that finally my legs are so inclined,
How good that finally there is no other way,

How good that nothing binds or holds me here
No healthy future, no trembling heart;
No home, no wife, no vineyard,
Nothing to regret, nothing to repent,

I will start my journey with hidden steps
In the fullness of cheering, madness-provoking,
And no woman's cheek to dry my tears,
My mother's body is the wide, wide earth,

My withered sinews have hardened to steel,
Death's brightness in my eyes and in my heart, through war's alarms,
A flaming sunset lights my way –
The world-bright name of the bleakest ancient
Hebrew hero on my lips.[1] –
And if I fall on a snowy plain in the potency of my youth –
No matter; it's only a blood stain, red on white.[2]

Why deny it? A sort of festive spirit seems to be singing inside me during this final leave-taking. Myriads of feelings jostle within me, clash, quarrel, and finally compromise, fuse, and weld into one mighty, pleasant emotion which manifests itself in the form of an all-embracing happy sigh of relief:

At last!

At last to go away. Perchance to die.

Every day of my brief life passes through me in a flash, beginning with the hazy memory of my mother, invoking the warm sweet taste of her milk on my palate, and ending with Dr. Garai's terrible, scornful look when he spat out the word: "Jew!"

My beautiful, romantic orphaned childhood, my upright and stately grandfather, ordeals at the *Beit Midrash*,[3] my happy-pathetic fellow students at the Talmud academy, my wanderings, my first love for the white nun who peered at me through the high latticed window, all the deaths – in our family and others – the beautiful, voluptuous, ugly women, Vienna, Berlin, Paris, Amsterdam, our homestead, my sister, my Latin grammar declensions and conjugations, dear bald Rabbi Akiva, all the blows I received and meted out, the scrawled manuscript of the inebriated Endre Ady, whose first translator I had the good fortune to be,[4] Professor Judah Blau,[5] who hated me for not attending his lessons diligently, my brilliant Bar Mitzvah address, and again my dead mother, my daughter, who was born when I was nineteen and whose whereabouts are unknown to me, and Mansie, my latest mistress, the young and drunken singer-dancer, whose foulness of speech reaches tragic-sacred dimensions…

A film of stirring events, flashed upon the screen by some divine hand before an invisible, laughing and suffering audience.

And at the end of the film appears the word:

Jew!

How does he know that I am a Jew? Who told him? Not I. We have all been working together for years in this editorial office, and not one of them ever knew who was a Jew and who wasn't. Who could be bothered with such things?

Then suddenly: Jew.

And with such disdain!

At last, I will go. The big city and the whole heavy world have been weighing on me to the point of suffocation. Now I'll leave them, go away to my dead mother who is waiting for me. That would be very pleasant. At long last.

I'll go. Alone. Proudly. Heroically, with a smile on my lips.

I'll make one last mighty gesture of defiance, at heaven and earth, and be on my way.

Now all my friends and acquaintances will realize my true worth.

Up to now they have all taken me and my friendship for granted. Now, when I take leave of them forever, they will feel the chill of death.

Not through me, but through them.

So I go to say farewell. In sequence.

Strange. It turns out quite different from my expectations. They all smile proudly and earnestly, wish me an heroic death. With genuine love and warm handshakes, they all say, one after the other:

"That is the beautiful fate of the poet. Now all your poems will be garlanded with the blazing glory of a hero's death."

"You won't have to wait before the petty-minded critics place you in the pantheon – a hero's death!"

"I will always be happy, to have had a friend who died heroically." That is the constant refrain of all the farewells: a Hero's Death.

They're all very happy.

I am silent and thoughtful. I suddenly become aware that in all this heroic outpouring there is also the word "death."

None of them seems to notice. Only I do.

Death. And what a death! A shattered human carcass lying in a field, before being tossed into a lime pit by a medical orderly. And that's that…Pantheon! – Oh my God…

I want to utter a mighty cry:

"You whores! You whores! I'm going to die in a lime pit, and you'll stay and go to the theater, the cabaret, to drink, to laugh, to live! You whores!"

A terrible thing. Friends.

Is there really not one single soul among all my comrades and friends with whom I have drunk wine and suffered – one solitary person who would say, or at least feel: "Poor wretch! A living man going to die?"

The streets are a seething cauldron.

On my way to City Hall I pass some acquaintances. They are all flushed with joy, and all tease me:

"Where are you going to in evening clothes?"

Indeed, I am dressed formally: a black evening jacket, a starched shirt.

"Where to? I'm going to a *dance macabre*," I reply.

Meantime, curious rumors, and all sorts of secrets, are flying, Secrets upon secrets.

"Have you heard? They've caught and arrested four spies. Among them Vera, the Russian dancer. Vera Radowskaya."

"What? Vera Radowskaya? What nonsense!"

"I myself saw her being led away in chains."

"In Szeged they have brought down a French airplane with four Serbian officers in it."[6]

"Our soldiers have entered Belgrade and they are advancing further."

"Hindenburg, the German commander in chief, has given an order to capture Moscow in a month."[7]

"Yesterday an enemy airplane was seen flying above the post office."

"This morning a Hussar caught the Serbian heir to the throne."

"He's being held here, in the barracks."

And more of the same.

I arrive at the City Hall confused and excited. The sergeant receives me very cordially. Smiling broadly, he asks:

"Well, young man, did they shed many tears over you?"

I am stunned by this crude fellow's condescending joke.

He adds: "They're all whores, my friend, all whores. Now you've only one friend in the world – your rifle. And even it will desert you when you die."

We prepare to go to the railway station. Everything is done at top speed – the Cossacks are in the Carpathians![8]

"We have to chase them out at once." The sergeant almost apologizes: "We're all in a hurry and that's why everything's in disorder. No uniforms, no marching, no instruction. We'll chase out the enemy and return, then we'll start everything properly, practice, get ready, become first-rate soldiers. Don't be afraid. Not everybody gets killed. Just don't shit your pants, boys! And no need to regret life. It isn't worth it.

"They're all whores, all of them! There is not a friend in the world. They are all drinking friends, not dying friends. Whores! Pfui!"

He orders us too to spit in a chorus. The whole gang spits as one man:

Pfui!

Suddenly there is an outcry outside the gate. A woman's voice, then immediately after the sounds of many women shouting, crying, rushing about arguing, jostling. Before we can make it out they rush in, eighteen women in all, rush in and fall upon us, weeping, wailing and lamentation, each of them hugging one of the men, and before I know it there, around my neck, is my own Mansie, wailing like a wounded animal, choking with bitter tears:

"You won't go. Oh my, you'll stay! Ay ay ay! Where are you going? I'll go with you! Oh my heart! I shan't leave you! I shan't leave you! I shall not leeeave youuu…!"

The wailing seems to rend the heavens. The barracks square is crowded with them. The whole place overflows with desperate hysteria.

The sergeant stands there, confounded, speechless.

The commissioned officers come out of the barracks to look.

"The hell with it! one of them yells. Get them out of here!"

But the sergeant doesn't move. He looks on, watching the women clinging to their sweethearts, in mute silence now, sobbing softly, spasmodically caressing, clinging to their necks like fruit from a tree.

Another officer says:

"Leave them alone. Let them say goodbye!" Silence falls in the barracks square. Only here and there a soft moan from the depths of the heart rises from the ranks.

The officers walk down the stairs, approach us slowly and looked at us. One of them observes the women closely, saying

"Look, look – they are all whores."

"True," says the other.

All the weeping women are amateur or professional whores.

My Mansie is a cabaret girl.

The officers remain mute, touched to the heart.

Then one of them addresses the women – politely, courteously, with sympathy and respect:

"Dear ladies, do calm down. You have a great and sacred duty to the homeland, so –"

The whores won't let him finish. The word "homeland" drives them mad:

"I spit on your homeland, you louse!" one of them screams, and the others follow suit, weeping and raging, blending into a terrifying, upsetting chorus of synchronized lamentation.

"Arrest them, dammit! Throw them the hell in jail!" one of the officers shouts, but the others calmed him down:

"There's no need. They're whores after all. Let them cry a little." The whores cry, groan, sob quietly and finally fall silent.

The sergeant gives the order to march. The procession begins and the street women follow it, each one beside her man, walking in silence. When we come out of the courtyard into the streets. more women join – first one, then three more, another two and then six more. Policemen in the street are astounded and stare:

"A parade of whores," they whisper. They know them all well. When I part from Mansie, I say to her:

"Don't cry, little sister. What more do you want? I'm going to die a hero's death. You should be proud of me, sweetheart."

"I spit on you, idiot!" Mansie bursts out furiously, and subsides in a storm of tears, bitter, heart-felt, sacred, and sincere to the point of fainting. She is almost prostrate.

When she recovers she faces me, grasps my shoulders, looks straight into my eyes and says in a dry, fatalistic voice:

"Don't die a hero's death. Don't be a hero, Avigdor. Come back as a private, tattered and torn, but without medals and glory. Alive!"

She looks at me some more, her eyes overflowing again, then makes up her mind:

"Well, then, go. I'll wait for you."

"You'll wait to toast me with a glass or two, Mansie!" I say, kissing her.

Her eyes blaze and she doesn't kiss me back. Then a moment later she speaks in the same dry voice:

"I shall not drink anymore. Not until you come back. This very day I'll leave the cabaret and go to nursing school."

She kisses me and weeps. She doesn't wait for the train to leave.

My only soulmate.

A common whore.

5 | Journey to Bushmanistan[1]

FROM THE City Hall we are taken to the barracks square. There the sergeant hands us over to his assistant, who looks us up and down, his lips parted in a sardonic smile:

"So-o-o-! In evening clothes! – Would your honor like me to find him a beautiful young lady as a dancing partner?"

"No, thank you."

"No? What a pity. I'd have offered him my sainted grandmother. Fall in, gentlemen!"

We stand in line. Sixty very different men, among them several journalists and a few artists. The sergeant examines all of us, joking casually. He talks about the degenerating intelligentsia, who will finally be made into useful people. I take out a cigarette and want to light it, meantime offering the case to the sergeant. He fixes his piggy eyes on me and shrieks:

"Get it out of my sight! I'll knock it out of your hands! Where d'you think you are – in a saloon?! Or in your newsrag office? Stand at attention! Don't you know where you are?!"

"Yes, in Bushmanistan," I answer, groggy for lack of sleep, hoping that he won't understand the word.

The men laugh.

The sergeant is frantic. He turns this way and that in a towering rage, looking for a word but not able to find it. He faces us, violently agitatedly gnashing his teeth, and spits violently: Pfui! Then he enters the building.

Before we can give voice our opinion and our disgust with this all of this, he comes out again:

"By order of His Excellency, the colonel, you will now go home and return in the morning ready for travel. Dismiss!"

We don't dismiss. We simply turn away and leave. Thank God. One more night without a sergeant.

The street is a boiling, seething cauldron. Shouted military orders, a long line of artillery men followed by a brigade of infantry, war material, cavalry, orders, singing, shouting, tears, mothers' wails, the national anthem, homeland, beautiful genteel ladies hugging, kissing, strewing flowers on ordinary privates, embracing and kissing them, snatches of bombastic harangues from coffee house cellars…

I haven't the strength to stand on my feet. It seems the best thing would be to go home and snatch some sleep. Until tomorrow morning.

My concierge is almost out of her mind with joy:

"Have you have been released, sir?"

"Yes. Until tomorrow morning."

She bursts into tears.

"Don't cry, granny. I want to snatch some sleep. In a few minutes I shall be free."

"What?" the old woman asked, her moist eyes shining with renewed hope. "What, sir? In a few minutes you will be – ?"

"Yes, granny. In our dreams we are set free from all that weighs on our psyche. Professor Freud is mistaken – quite mistaken. Dreams give us precisely what we *don't* want in reality, not even subconsciously.[2] The subconscious is a part of God above, my dear, and God is absolutely good, unlike our sentient nature, which is absolutely idiotic. The threshold of the subconscious is not our creation, my dear, for if it were our creation, why then…"

I must have finished that last sentence in my dream. I feel the hands of the concierge tucking me in, so I don't catch cold, and perhaps I hear her sobs, too, deep in my slumbering soul, and her voice saying:

"My poor unfortunate gentleman, in his despair he drinks and babbles. Oh, the unfortunate man, oh my …"

I don't sleep long. Evening comes and I'm compelled by habit to rise. Sunset pulls a man out of bed. I get up, dress, and go to the editorial office. As I enter I recall that I have absolutely no business there. Indeed, the entire editorial staff is new to me. Strange people are sitting there, sweating in our places. My old friend Dr. Garai is among them. He too is a stranger to me. A complete stranger.

"*Servus*!" I say to him as usual, and at once feel that I have no right to greet him in this familiar manner.[3] He looks at me, nods, and whispers, like a distant acquaintance:

"Good evening."

A cold shiver runs through me. I want to cry. I run out of there, run home, that is, to the Orpheum cellar: home.[4] That place too has changed somewhat. The dancers are much the same, but one can hear crying in the corners. Drunkards are smashing more glasses than usual. The strange rumors are confirmed. Vera has in fact been arrested. She is a spy. How very strange. Darling Vera? That sweet Russian, whose kiss is always given from her warm and ardent heart, who loved Budapest better than she loved her own little girl, that Slav angel whose soft veins run with the Orpheum's sparkling wine…? Did she deceive us? Was *she* involved with politics? – Such stupidity can only be invented in the empty heads of policemen and officials.

And more: the waiter Dubos has also been arrested, and important political documents have been found on his person. He has revealed the topographical secrets of Budapest to the French government. This is the summit of fearful suspicions, because Dubos is of Hungarian stock. His wife and children don't speak a word of French. *He* speaks Hungarian, but *they* don't know any French.

And more shocking reports of that kind. Madness is rampaging among us like a drunken specter.

Suddenly two of my journalist colleagues arrive, approach me hurriedly and thrust a manifesto for me to sign:

"Read it and sign!"

"Why should I read it? Here's my signature. Later, if you want to get the money for it, go to the granny at my apartment. She has all my belongings in her possession."

I sign. They take the sheet of paper, approach a few of our writer friends and leave in a hurry.

This madness is beginning to confuse my brain more and more. The strange reports bubbling out of my champagne glass mist over my eyes and nerves, and after a while I begin to feel that the whole business is nothing but a stupendous joke, and that in another hour or two I'll sober up.

Morning dawns.

They start to sweep the cellar, and ask me to go home. It's a crisp, cool morning. I walk home distraught and melancholy. The old granny is still sleeping the sleep of the just. I take my suitcase, which has been ready since the day before, and leave my apartment in despair.

The furniture looks after me with sleepy eyes, and the grandfather clock rings after me:

"Tick-tock, tick-tock, go away and don't come back, tick-tock"...Out in the street I pass a notice-board and see an announcement – a manifesto of the "Association of Free Journalists."[5] At the bottom, among others, my name appears as 11.

Should I read it?

I walk on, but a few steps later a premonition of danger drives me back. I read it and it warms my heart:

> "The Free Journalists publicly declare that the people of Tolstoy, Pushkin, Gorky, Andreiev, Romain Rolland, Shakespeare, Barbusse, Bernard Shaw, Wilde, Wells, Sinclair, Whitman, Anatole France (and many, many others) have never been our enemies, we shall never raise our hands against them, and may the hand of anyone who does so be withered, etc., etc."[6]

Among the writers who had signed the manifesto – myself.

Very good. Bravo. Excellent.

Beside it, another notice. I read it and momentarily become sober:

"... and whoever dares to spread the false spirit of pacifism and dishearten the heroes of the homeland, will find that I shall have the power to break him like a cracked reed, etc., etc..

Signed: Graf Tisza, Chief Minister."[7]

So it's one against the other. Me against Tisza, Tisza against me. Fair enough. Bravo, in fact. Very good. Let's go to the dear sergeant.

Fortunately I don't understand a single word he says. When he laughs, I laugh. But I don't allow his anger to get under my skin. I remember yesterday's affair with the cigarette, and again offer him one. He strikes it from my hand, the case falls, and I'm too lazy to pick it up.

"Follow me!"

We follow him and reach the railway station. Inside the train they thrust us all into a long compartment, jammed with men. With great difficulty – or, perhaps I ought to say, quite easily – I sit on a bench, because I cannot do otherwise. The crowd presses me down.

The compartment rages and storms: sad and obscene songs, cursing and blasphemies, laughter, derision, drunken kisses.

When things quieten down a bit, the confusion really begins. I don't know any of the men around me. They are mostly peasant and artisan types, drunk or half drunk. I take a book out of my valise and begin to read: Mechnikov's *An Optimistic World View,* translated by Dr. Liani Arpad and published in *Science*, Budapest, 1908.[8] I light a cigarette and settle down to read.

Suddenly a black gob of spit, tobacco spit, falls from above and lands right on my book. I wipe the book with my handkerchief and become furious. I look up – a rookie is smoking and spitting. Oh well, he doesn't mean to offend me. But such uncouthness.

I go on reading and smoking.

"Who has a light?" somebody asks.

Somebody snatches the cigarette out of my mouth, lights his own with it and throws mine out of the window. Then he nonchalantly turns back to his business.

What's this?

My wits return and I am amazed. I want to call the conductor. Some of the other passengers notice me, get the drift of the situation, and burst out mockingly;

"Oh Mr. Conductor! Mr. Conductor! Where's the conductor?"

"He died a hero's death!"

"Hush! He's been elevated to the rank of general!"

"His Highness Mr. Conductor!"

Laughter on all sides.

I continue reading. Now I understand the situation. I begin to grasp the meaning of it. Better to suffer in silence and read the book.

Before I've absorbed the next sentence in my book, there is general pushing and shoving around me. Somebody shouts: "Let me out! Let me out! I have to go out!" The crowd surges, laughter and shoves – and again the same voice: "Who has paper? Who has paper!" Suddenly a rough paw snatches my book and tears out a handful of pages.

The man rushes out into the corridor, not before thanking me in all seriousness:

"Thank you very much. Excellent paper."

I close my eyes like one drunk with pain, and my left temple begins to throb painfully.

"*Servus* comrade! Well, how do you like this wonderful Land of Bushmanistan? Glorious, isn't it?"

A friendly pat on the shoulder wakes me up and opens my eyes: my fellow-recruit, Count Cziraky, the young Bohemian, my fellow night-owl, looking filthy all over. I stare at him quizzically, and he laughs:

"Isn't it charming? When did we ever go on such a democratic jaunt?"

6 | Lacrimae Risusque Rerum[1]

ORDERS, BELLS, yells, noises, shouts, kisses, whistles – and the train moves off.

Drunken singing, mingled with lamentations of tortured mothers and other heart-broken women, turns into a pleasant Eldorado[2] of nematode-men deranged with the madness of the blood-stench in the air.

It opens with a minor incident, hardly serious enough to interrupt the commotion. One new recruit, a jolly Budapest wine club rounder, whose bellyful of schnapps flames with the sad hurrah of war frenzy, tries to cut capers. He climbs on top of the train so as to bid farewell to the dear city with a flourish of his hat and a shower of wet kisses for the splendid palaces. The train passes under a bridge – and the wag suddenly finds himself headless. The sharp arch of the bridge severs his drunken head from his shoulders like a sword.

Somebody tries to crown the severed head with a hero's garland.

"The war's first victim!" he gasps, awe-stricken.

"Victim, hell!" someone else says. "A plague on his gizzard! Does anybody who falls under the wheels of a troop train get to be a hero and war victim?!"

They go on raising a rumpus. They won't let the jolly casualty be canonized by the sacrament of war.

"Who'll pay him the last respects?" asks a voice.

"Him? To that contemptible shirker? That cowardly blackguard, who slips out of the hands of the homeland and chooses to die by accident, instead of dying honorably on the field of battle?! Let the dogs devour him!"

"The Holy Father himself will come from Rome to bury him," rumbles a deep voice from one of the overflowing bunks.

"The Pope?"

"Yes, the basso voice continues. "The Pope is the apostle of peace on earth and shows great honor to the carcasses of peace."

"Ah yes, the Pope," says a squeaky voice from under my bunk, and begins to sing the famous popular ballad, *The Gates of the Vatican*:

The gates of the Vatican open very softly
Ho ho ho, very softly!
The Holy Father is awaiting someone there
Ho ho ho, he is awaiting!
The triple crown he takes off very softly
Ho ho ho, the crown
His holy heart is slowly beating
Ho ho ho, it is beating!
The lovely maiden weeps with sorrow
Her handsome cedar-strong lover gone for soldier
Ho ho ho, for soldier!
The Holy Father comforts her: come hither.
Ho ho ho, come hither!
Don' t cry, my darling, I'll bring you peace
Ho ho ho, I'll bring you peace!

We journey to the tune of this sprightly song for almost three entire days. In normal times it would have taken half a day.

Fortunately I have my narcotic: Mechnikov's *Optimism*, and a bottle of Törleyi Cointreau.[3]

On the evening of the third day, we get off at some little town or other, and are at once loaded on to a huge cart pulled by four German horses.

The rain is coming down in torrents.

After about four hours of riding in the rain we hear a thunderous voice:

"Fall out of the cart!"

Fall out. Not get off, of course. The darkness is total. We jump off the cart into the pitch-black night, straight into a flood of deep gutter mud, splashing its clammy dirt up to our faces. I sit down in the mud. The cart is very high, I cannot judge its height in the dark and the jump lands me in the mud up to my waist.

It's easier to sit than to rise. But there's that voice again:

"Scramble out!"

A sergeant's voice. A real sergeant's voice.

We scramble out. We knead the mud like the Children of Israel in Egypt kneaded bricks.[4] The sweat pours off my face. My body feels heavy as lead. My lower half is soaked with mud and my belongings inside the valise are soggy as well.

We scramble out, lit erratically by the sergeant's torch, which concentrates not on the road but on our faces. As if the darkness of the dark isn't enough – we have the darkness of the light, as well.

Finally the order comes:

"Get up!"

They lead us into some sort of ruin, roofed by the sky. We might have enjoyed the beautiful starry sky, if we could have seen the stars through the clouds and raindrops didn't blind our eyes.

The sergeant carefully passes his torch over the grimy walls and gives the order:

"Drop dead!"[5]

We drop down dead tired, right where we stand along the walls, bags under weary heads. Fatigue overwhelms the cold in our bones and we sleep all hunched up, body and soul. The living dead.

Daylight is brutal. Only now I can see my situation clearly. Fearful cold makes my weary limbs quake. I don't have the strength to move from the spot where I have collapsed.

I look around and watch my fellow soldiers. Something is happening: everyone is bestirring himself, cheering up and trying to adapt to the conditions. That is hardly surprising. However, everyone also tries to show that he is a seasoned soldier, familiar with military uses and practices. At the same time they all try to mock and despise the "softies" among us. A few have even managed to pick up some army expressions by hearsay, to show that this is the center of existence, the center of life, sum total of the world and all that's in it, the end of human existence, and quintessential goal of human civilization. Everything else is meaningless, superfluous, pitiful, and laughable.

Oh yes – we've all been living in error until that day and never knew that the be-all and end-all of our lives was this: militarism, the war, the homeland, the sergeant.

One of the men, a lecturer at the Eastern Academy, who has spent his life in its cloistered confines researching the Persian language and its poetry, and is famous for knowing all of Firdusi's *Shahnameh* by heart in the original,[6] suddenly becomes vociferous with vile, blasphemous cursing directed against all those who complain about the intolerable conditions.

"What would you like," he asks angrily, "His Excellency the Colonel to give you his own warm bedroom?!"

I grow curious to know who this colonel is, before whom university professors are so humbled.

"Who is he?" the Persian scholar snaps back. "What difference does it make who His Excellency the colonel is? Yes, my friend, His Excellency the Colonel is not simply the colonel. He is *Herr* Colonel to you! Watch your tongue. You are supposed to be an intelligent man, I believe!"

"Nevertheless," I persevere, "who is the *Herr* Colonel?"

He looks at me with irate eyes and says in a menacing voice:

"The *Herr* Colonel is the man who has three shining gold stars on his collar. I should have thought that an intelligent person would know that much!"

For a second I feel like laughing in his face, but am at once seized by a deep shame that, though an intelligent man, I have not known this much.

My head begins to ache. Only then do I take proper stock of myself. It's a frightful spectacle:

A man in a stiff, broad-brimmed hat, a dinner-jacket and pressed trousers with patent-leather pumps, lying on the ground covered with mud from soles to stiff shirt-front, seized with shame at not knowing what the simplest soldier knows. I observe myself closely and a wave of hilarity sweeps over me: it's fantastic. A great comedy with a very unusual "hero." Staged, it would be an artistic triumph.

But at that moment in my benumbed brain I seem to hear a soft, tragic weeping. I look around me – nobody is weeping. On the contrary: they all seem exuberant, happy, and eager to show that they know the sacred meaning of the word "colonel."

Who is crying, then? – I become completely disoriented and, for a moment think I see granny my old concierge, weeping. But should I actually be able to hear her crying? I must be delirious with exhaustion and a chill. I feel feverish. Then it suddenly became clear to me – I look at my jacket and see that it is weeping.

I recall the Latin idiom, *sunt lacrimae rerum.*[7] Oh yes, inanimate objects can shed tears. This garment, whose black cloth is saturated with a paradise of ideas and ideals, mighty longings, and Flammarion-like dreams[8] – it's crying. My head hurts to the point of distraction. I turn my thoughts away. I close my eyes and envision the Philharmonic Hall with its magnificent orchestra playing the "1812 Overture" – and my jacket cries even louder. The overture, after all, is a military march. The Marseillaise blends in with the bells of the Muscovite Kremlin, in danger of destruction by the red flames rising[9]... And the colonel, a Napoleon with gold stars on his collar.

Again I force my mind to turn away, and see Hamlet with the skull in his hand, wondering aloud how with "Imperious Caesar, dead and turned to clay" it might have "stopped a hole to keep the wind away."[10]

My jacket sobs pitifully: Poor Hamlet, the young prince, who failed to launch great wars in honor of his royal father, killed by a cruel king whose only ambition is to govern his armies by means of innumerable sergeants, and the colonel: Julius Caesar,[11] whose soldiers captured the pyramids, while the gold stars on his collar gleam in the Eastern sun…

Good God, is there nothing in the world but colonels and sergeants and wars? And why didn't I realize this before? So there is no theater, no books, no Rodin, no Isadora Duncan, no Tolstoy, no Endre Ady, and no Rav Hatanya… ?[12]

"No Rav Hatanya?"…

A pleasant warm shudder runs through my body. No, no, not that. The author of the *Tanya* was not a colonel and had no sergeant. There is still a corner in the universe where the soul of my jacket can rest and weave garlands of thought…

A pleasant fever shakes me. I'm drunk. But I can hear my jacket's lamentations quite plainly:

Woe, woe, woe! Woe to that sanctity! The *Tanya* author is gone… The author of the *Tanya* has been banished somewhere and awaits the Messiah… Look at me: I am not your garment, but your *inner self*, all covered with mire and filth. A scholar on whose garment a (fat) stain is found deserves to die.[13] Oh oh oh… Who are you? – don't reject me, don't cast me off, or you shall be lost forever…

A brutal hand grabs me by the scruff of the neck:

"Strip down! Strip down, or I'll strip the hide off you! Undress at once and put this on!"

A soldier, but not an ordinary one. He hands me a uniform. I stand up and take off my jacket – and put it on again.

Ay! This sentimentality is out of place. The jacket is crying? – well, let it cry. If I had got a flogging, I'd have wept as well.

I take it off and fling it on the ground with ruthless determination, while my head spins fearfully.

Somebody starts to sing:

> Farewell, top hat!
> Farewell, Shakespeare!
> Adieu, Max Linder,[14]
> Song, ideal and dance!
> Goodbye, nights with lovely women –
> All that was but emptiness and vanity.
> Long live His Majesty's buttons!
> Long live our sergeant!

I take my new garments and examine them. They are caked with filth. The trousers are soggy. Instead of being dried properly they were left to turn moldy. The tunic has caked with dried blood on it.

Frightful.

I put them on. My intoxication grows worse. Someone inside me laughs. How do I look? Blood. I feel my gorge rising. Quickly I open the valise and take a sip of the Cointreau. Pleasant warmth. A soothing, healing dizziness.

The garments laugh. What is this? – The tunic is laughing and the jacket on the ground cries.

I put my jacket in the suitcase. It goes on crying inside.

I'm very drunk. Why did I drink? It's even worse… Who was it said that objects could cry? Some Roman. Didn't he know they could laugh, too? The Rav Hatanya knew it. The congealed blood weighs on my heart. And the uniform laughs at me: "ha ha ha! That's the reward for all your trouble. You hopped from star to star, from one constellation to another."

Now... suddenly a shriek:

Attention!

That means, stand up straight, respectfully. We all stand up respectfully, motionless. The sergeant enters and the place seems frozen still. He goes from one man to the other, studies each one closely, and is satisfied: Good. Good. Good.

When he comes up to me he bursts out laughing. I recognize it at once – it's the laugh of my blood-soaked tunic.

"You're a fine fellow! Where's your jacket? Surely you also have a top hat. And how do you feel about the war in general?"

I can't understand: why me, of all men? Why is he honoring me with this serious question?

"About the war? War, sir, is a great paradox." I reply cautiously, my head still spinning.

"What? What? What kind of dox?"

"The war is a great paradox, sir. Kant's question of the *Ding an sich* (thing in itself)[15] ought to be resolved empirically, not logically. Only one solitary reality within us is 'a thing in itself,' and that is the divine part of us, which we observe as a wild beast, or a uncouth animal, guzzling flesh with gold teeth, holding its fork in its left hand. We used to believe that man was the crown of creation, and that is was bread that turned him vile. Now the war has come to show us that man does not live by bread alone,[16] but chiefly by the blood of the homeland's enemies, whom it is a divine duty to destroy, root and branch. And that means that we have no idea of the true meaning of the sublime creation which is the sergeant, or His Excellency the Colonel. – So, Kant was mistaken."

The sergeant concurs with a broad laugh:

"Ha ha ha! You're right. Who is that fellow Kant?"

"Some pathetic hunchback, a slacker, who wrote a book about eternal peace. The idiot."[17]

"Ha ha ha! You're a valiant fellow, my friend! the sergeant slaps me on the shoulder. You'll make a first-rate officer. Even though you do talk some incomprehensible nonsense, here you'll soon learn to talk like a human being. Very good."

He looks at me and my clothes and breaks out into a chuckle.

As for me, my heart melts inside me, I don't know why.

Laughing and weeping. The tunic and the jacket holding a mad concert… Oh my head!

Fortunately, just then the door opens. Two soldiers bring in a tremendous bucket reeking of tobacco mixed with black coffee.

"Black coffee!" someone exclaims with satisfaction.

Coffee *before* breakfast? – Now I know that things are really happening in this great world.

The sergeant stiffens and growls:

"Make pigs of yourselves!"

7 | Nightmare

MORE THAN a month has passed since I put on the bloodied uniform, and I still don't know what has actually happened. It's all like some sort of cheap melodramatic movie based on a corrupted Theodor Amadeus Hoffmann tale, entitled "The Nightmare."[1]

It all comes, like a bolt from the blue, with a mad and terrifying announcement:

The sergeant explains to us that there is no time for us to train properly, because in actual fact we're already at the front and must first drive the Russian pigs out of our homeland's vineyards. Meantime the sound of cannons begins to be heard, followed by shrapnel shells, each of which could demolish a good-size house. The sergeant instructs us on "The Gospel of Patriotism," and the customs and usages of a decent man, who prays not to God but to His Majesty the Kaiser. The sergeant spreads the gospel, the shells keep falling, in quick succession then in volleys, enough to drive one mad.

The sergeant is explaining the nature of the good soldier and the meaning of death, when suddenly a shell falls, stopping the word "death" right in his throat. He explodes into a thousand fragments, all that is left of the him are rags of flesh and bone.

The next sergeant, who replaces him, is a soft and cowardly man who prays constantly and urges us to pray as well, each to his own God and in his own tongue. With studied casualness, he asks men of different faiths to teach him one prayer of their own. I teach him the Prayer for Travel:[2] he is very pleased and promises me a battle decoration in the near future.

The Russians are coming closer. We are entering the heart of the front; some of us are killed, two go mad in the midst of the terrible cannonade. Our commanding officer shoots them where they stand. The Russians can be seen plainly. Dead bodies pile up in the space between the two front lines. Medical orderlies fall like flies. We are ordered to fire in the air, out of sight, at the invisible enemy. None of us understands what we are doing. A few are beaten with butts. The rain begins to pour, rifles are clogged with mud and bullets explode in the barrels, killing those who fire them. A man begins to cry and somebody shoots him. The roaring grows louder. Somebody yells: "The Russians are fighting empty-handed! They have no guns, only clubs!"[3] A companion lying beside me in the mud tries to shoot, falls flat on his face and dies, blood oozing from his lips.

Somebody yells: "Mother!" Two soldiers are fighting hand to hand, clawing and biting each other. The sergeant shoots them both dead. I ask for bullets and the sergeant tosses me some, shouting: "Bravo! Bravo! Be merciless! You're an unusually intelligent man! A medal!" Night falls slowly, and rain drenches us to the bone. The firing stops and our hearts expand with hope. Somebody grunts wearily: "We've driven them off! Let their bloody memories be blotted out as far back as their criminal ancestor Esau the Wicked!"[4] I look at him, he understands me and goes on: "Keep shooting, young Maccabee![5] Only shoot at the head and not the legs, or *he* might walk home to Moscow lame, so help us!" I rejoice to meet a Jew, and laugh and shout to him in Hebrew: "Hurrah, hurrah! Come over here, to me!" The Jew crawls over to me on all fours, lies down at my side, and doesn't move anymore. His head droops to the ground. He is dead. Now the firing stops and the order comes to stop shooting and clean the guns.

I search my dead comrade's pockets and find twenty-two crowns which I hand to one of the medical orderlies. I examine the identification tag around his neck. Simon, son of Jacob Berger, infantryman, twenty-three years old, doctor of philosophy, from the village of Hatrag. I dig him a grave with my friends and see him off with a few words: "Go on your way, my friend, and should you reach the True World, please send us a brief telegram – tell me what the truth really is." The kindly sergeant joins the "funeral," asks if the dead man is a Jew and loudly repeats the Prayer for Travel, with mispronounciations of a non-Jew.

We drink some black coffee, and once again the yelling and the firing begins. We gulp down the dregs and resume firing. The sky clears and there, on the side, floats a vaporous moon. Leisurely, as if casting its pallid, amorous white light on young lovers. The battle grows hotter and fiercer. Men are falling, here, there, everywhere. Some are only slightly injured and overjoyed to be carried behind the lines by medical orderlies. The work becomes an act of madness. Sweat pours off us, lungs are raw screaming orders, shells exploding, exhausted men groaning, one of them curses: "You up there, damn you! What are you shining at so peacefully?!" I look at him and see that he's yelling at the moon. "Look at her, how she mocks us, the dear moon! At least it's not singing couplets to us!" He shoots and shoots and meantime sings:

Oh the wonderful moon
The sweet silvery moon!
Piff paff boom!
Night-blossom blooming
Piff paff boom!
The whole world's drunk
My blood has turned to wine
Piff paff boom!
My darling, your cheeks
And your tender lips
Piff paff boom!
Kiss me thus, quiet quiet,
Silence – in a dearest night lullaby
Piff paff boom!

We strain every fiber in our bodies, the roaring overwhelms our minds. Somebody yells: "Hurrah! Once more the sweet silvery moon!" The singer starts again:

Oh the wonderful moon
The sweet silvery moon!
Piff …

He falls silent. Somebody yells: "He's dead! Let someone else sing!"

I yell back, while firing: "Idiot! Pig!" and he answers: "You know the words – sing! Piff, paff, boom!" Another man falls. Another one is wounded and cries out in pain. Shot in the belly. Suddenly an order: "Get up! Attack!" We see men, shadows, moving through the moonlight towards us. We jump up and run towards the shadows, firing at them the whole time. They fall one by one. Terrible shrieks: "Hurrah! Hurrah!" I too yell: "Hurrah!" Meantime I wonder: What if the poet Zalman Schneur[6] is among them? Or my friend, Professor Piotr Vassilyevich? Hurrah! Hurrah! Darkness, rain, we penetrate the enemy line, which surges against us. We stab each other with bayonets. I stab in the air. Shouts: Stab! Stab! Curses, swearing, blaspheming. Strange languages, which I cannot understand. Strange men. Strange animals. Savages. "We have to kill them! Stick 'em! Stick 'em!" I stumble in the mud and fall down. A boot kicks me in the side. I'm not dead yet. I'm alive, and men are running over my body. A sharp stab in the ground near my left ear. I am shocked and choke. I make an effort and rise, hitting and stabbing in the air. Ay! I've bayoneted someone! I hear a voice: "Don't drive it in! It's me!" It's one of us. The bayonet passed through his armpit. I hear a very close shot and feel a frightful blow in my right leg above the knee. Ow! The bullet has gone through the bone. Frightful pain. I shout: "Orderly! Orderly! Stretcher-bearer! I'm wounded!" – Someone supports my upper body, drags me along, another one comes and helps him. They put me on a stretcher and carry me away. One of them asks: "Where were you hit?" I'm so happy to be leaving the "wild party" that I answer: "Where was I hit? – On the field of honor, on the altar of the homeland!" He gets mad at me and wants to throw me off the stretcher: "You're faking! You're not wounded, dammit!" I yell back at him: "May you and your sons suffer from my wound, friend! Ow!" He asks again: "Where were you hit? – In my right leg, on which I don't lay phylacteries!"[7] Ow! – The wound is hurting, hurting badly, it even makes my head hurt… We enter some sort of depot. They are bandaging me and meantime they ask: "Where's the bullet?"

"What d'you need the bullet for? Ow ow ow!"

"I'm asking you – where's the bullet?" the orderly yells.

"Ow, I don't know! What do you need the bullet for? His Imperial Majesty Franz Josef the First has enough bullets! Ow! It hurts!"

"Did the bullet come out?"

"I don't know. How should I know? Ow, bandage it, it hurts terribly!" My eyes water and I am happy. One of them says: "The bullet went through. Tough luck! You won't be home long!"

I'm panic-stricken:

"What? Am I going to die?"

"On the contrary. You'll recover fast and come back pretty soon. Bad luck!"

They finish the bandaging and carry me away. The pain grows worse. I feel tremors running through me. The swinging of the stretcher is very soothing. I close my eyes.

The cannonade grows much louder. Screams of wounded men from afar. I hear one of my medical orderlies saying:

"Such luck! A leg wound!"

I feel that my wound is beginning to numb my brain. I feel better like this and soon fall asleep.

When I wake up I find myself in the hospital train. Click-clack, click-clack. Going home.

What has happened here?

8 | A High-School for the Intelligentsia[1]

FROM THE military hospital I am transferred by high command to the *Unteroffizier*'s juridiction,[2] to learn proper ways of standing, walking, firing, and discipline. To start with, they test us to see if we realize exactly where we are. To be exact, the *Zugsoffizier*[3] explains, we are now attending a "high school for the intelligentsia."

"What you learned in your useless colleges," says our new teacher, "were all sorts of fancy but useless intellectual wisdoms. I too learned to read and write like the rest of you. But that isn't all. Any lawyer or professor can read and write. What you have to learn here is a little army intelligence. Why, you don't even know how to stand straight! Now just imagine that the first lieutenant were to pay us a visit today – would you even know how to greet him? You, for instance" he turns to one of us, "how would you greet the first lieutenant? Well, how?"

"Good morning, *Herr* First Lieutenant!"

"Bite your tongue, boy! I knew it! And you're not even ashamed, either. A soldier who has already had the privilege of being wounded, and still chatters 'good morning' and all that nonsense! You don't greet the first lieutenant like you greet some professor or a scullery maid whom you want to fuck! You don't greet the first lieutenant at all! What do you do? You stand before him like this – like a statue, not moving a limb, head up, holding your breath, eyes straight, straight into his but without seeing anything at all. Not what's around you, not your other comrades, not the whole wide world, nothing! Not even he himself. These limbs are not made for signaling, like a whore! A man's body was created for one single purpose: to stand before the first lieutenant, take in what he says, and see the thoughts inside his head. A soldier has to be nothing but ears and eyes, no other subtle nonsense and cleverness of any kind! Now let's see your lousy talents. We'll pretend that the first lieutenant is approaching us this very minute. I give the order: 'Attention!' and you do as I told you. Well, get ready – one, two, three, ATTENTION!!!"

I stretch my limbs, close my eyes, and stand immobile. The NCO bursts into crazy laughter and then yells:

"You i-di-ots!"

I open my eyes and see that the other men have all closed their eyes like me.

"What a useless bunch!" says our instructor despairingly. "I can tell that you'll never be real men! Why did you close your eyes? Huh? Why? You think we're saying our prayers? When you pray, you have to shut your eyes so you won't see God, God forbid! But the *Herr* First Lieutenant isn't God! God can never give you a medal! And he can't send you into solitary confinement for three days either, where you'll be blinded by the darkness! So once more – here goes!"

Not only once more, but fifty times more. What a crowd lacking in the most basic intelligence! The NCO is exhausted with despair. "They keep shutting their eyes!"

Suddenly, a catastrophe. The first lieutenant actually arrives. The instructor utters a hoarse shriek, like the whistle of a chimney in a horse-meat sausage factory:

"AttenTION!!!"

The first lieutenant approaches, stands before us, and our teacher informs him with steely words:

"First Lieutenant, sir! Beg to report: There's no news!"

Shocking. No news. But why the frightful shriek? The first lieutenant inspects us from helmeted top to toe, closely, seriously and silently, then says calmly:

"At ease. No need to shit your pants. I'm not the devil!"

The weather is splendid. The autumn sun spreads out its dazzling abundance, and the breeze carries intoxicating, overripe scents from some happy faraway place. I remember: Naples, Sorrento, Zara,[4] Monaco, the French Riviera…

The first lieutenant finds that our postures are all wrong.

They make us stand opposite the barracks wall. The wall is pure white and with the sunlight upon it can hardly be looked at. The officer takes out a pencil, goes up to the wall and draws a perpendicular line. Then he says:

"When I stand before you, look at this line. Look straight, don't budge. Understand?"

We understand.

Our instructor gives the command:

"AttenTION!"

We freeze and stare at the blinding wall. The light begins to sting my eyes. I close them and then remember – it isn't God who is standing before me, but the first lieutenant. I open my eyes again. I will look – come what may.

The officer approaches the first in the line, inspects the man's face and makes a contemptuous gesture: "Fall out, dammit!"

The disqualified man stands aside, to the left. After him the second and the third and the fourth. All are disqualified.

I am staring ahead, condemned to blindness, with my remaining strength. My eyes are watering. No, I shall not close my eyes. I can hear the instructor saying to the rejectees: "You wait, you epileptics! Just you wait! I'll tear the lashes from your eyes! I'll teach you manners!"

I hear this and gather my failing powers, staring straight at the blinding wall.

The officer comes up to me and looks at me. My eyes are watering, great teardrops trickle down my cheeks and my eyes can no longer see anything but a great, dancing sun, its radiance hot as red pepper.

The officer goes on looking at me calmly. He takes a cigarette from his pocket, lights it, draws great draughts of smoke, and blows them into my eyes.

But I will not close my eyes. It's all the same to me now. I simply won't.

The officer smokes and smokes. Finally he comes up to me, pats my shoulder amiably, and pushes me to the right:

"Bravo! good fellow! ... Wipe your eyes."

I step to the right and wipe away my tears with a great sigh of relief. I'm filled with an extraordinary sense of pride.

What a triumph! What price all my literary triumphs compared with this one?! I'm a good fellow! Bravo!

I notice that the first lieutenant has a slight limp. Then I remember: That's him. He's the officer about whom they say all sorts of unpleasant things. They say that when he first served in the war he did all he could to avoid the fighting, and when nothing helped, he put his revolver in his pocket and shot his own foot through his trousers.

Since then he's been "home," behind the front, teaching new recruits the ways of war.

"Pfui!" I think to myself, "Such cowardice!"

Having concluded his first inspection he goes to the rejectees and stands before them disdainfully. Wrinkling his forehead contemptuously, he asks :

"You – wish – to become – soldiers?"

"Who wishes? I wish it?" comes a voice from the gang and I wonder who dares be so bold…

A snort of laughter is heard.

The officer draws himself up abruptly, flings away his cigarette and bends his arms like a bear about to pounce. He approaches the impertinent joker and says through his teeth:

"What did you say? What was it you said, you miserable wretch?"

"I said…"

"Shut up! I didn't ask you! – What did you say? What was it you said to me?!"

"I –"

"Shut your trap! Sergeant," he turns to our instructor, "three days in solitary confinement, no food or water, and no daylight! At once! Take him away!"

The unfortunate man is grabbed tightly by the sergeant's hands and meantime he mumbles:

"No daylight! Wonderful! I'll be able to close my eyes."

The first lieutenant overhears him and flushes crimson:

"Stop!"

He goes up to him, so close that their noses almost touch, and asks:

"So you're wisecracking, are you? – Sergeant, tie him to the wall for four hours!"

To be tied to the wall means being tied up so that you stand on your tiptoes with arms held high above your head.

The price of a wisecrack: three days solitary, fasting and darkness.

The next day they tell us that each one of us will have to take a special "intelligence test." A different test for everyone. The sergeant takes out a sheet of paper and reads us the subjects of the tests. One man must explain, in five minutes and with exemplary brevity, the difference between a buck private and His Imperial Majesty Franz Josef the First. Another will have to say what he would do if he receives an order to shoot his own mother. A third must explain in a single sentence who the Russians are. A fourth must display his prowess in cursing and swearing. The fifth (that's me, because I'm a writer) must enumerate the ten virtues of war… and so on.

We are given a few minutes to prepare for the tests. I summon up all the angels of thought and all nine muses, as well as all the evil powers, to help me find the following virtues: 1) War strengthens the muscles; 2) It teaches you to suffer; 3) It accustoms you to death; 4) It teaches to kill without hatred; 5) It teaches us to respect the *Unteroffizier*; 6) It takes us to places we haven't seen before; 7) It provides work for the unemployed; 8) It destroys the poor who have nothing to eat; 9) It carries us to the hereafter; 10) It makes our violent death a heroic one.

I communicate my exalted ideas to the sergeant in the hope that he will be overjoyed. I fail. He looks at what I had written, studies it carefully, and says with classical simplicity:

"Shit!"

"Pity," he adds. "You're a talented fellow, but you lack basic intelligence. The virtues of war are that it breaks, kills, murders, destroys, annihilates, castrates, defeats, demolishes, exterminates and buries!"

"Whom?"

"Whom? What do you think, whom? The bloody enemy, that's whom! Well, wise guy, you've failed. Now I'll give you a chance to take another test, so that you won't be ashamed in front of the first lieutenant. You see that hill over there? It's half a kilometer away. On top of it there's a shelled fortress, with only one wall left. You've got to run and get there in twenty minutes, and without stopping to rest, you've climb that wall, stand there and sing the Hungarian national anthem. Now – one, two, three!..."

I run as fast as I can.

Behind me I glimpse the first lieutenant riding on a horse, behind him the NCO, who overtakes him on foot.

After I climb the wall I sing "Hatikvah.'"[5]

The sergeant motions me to come down. When I'm on the ground he pats my shoulder and says pityingly:

"Bravo, old man. You've got the will but not the ability. You've got no voice and no musical ear. That was no way to sing the Hungarian anthem. It was way off pitch. Pity."

"Well, what's going to happen to me?"

"What's going to happen? We'll see. You've a lot to learn."

After a while the entire platoon arrives. We hold all sorts of maneuvers and then march home. There are a good many puddles on the way and, to avoid soiling my boots, I take a little detour around one of them. Suddenly I hear the order: "Halt!" The whole platoon stops. The officer rides up to me, orders all my comrades to one side, and me to stay behind the puddle.

"Now," says the officer, "up-and-down seven times!"

"Up-and-down" means lying down full length and getting up. In the puddle. Seven times.

I carry out the order and come up looking filthy as a pig.

"There now," says the officer, pleased. "Now answer my question. Have you read the Bible?"

"Yes, sir."

"D'you remember Gideon and the three hundred men who lapped the water?"[6]

"Yes, sir."

"Can you tell me Gideon's reason for choosing the ones who lapped?"

I'm at a loss. Truly, I never tried to understand that capricious act, which even my great teacher, Professor Bacher, didn't explain to me.[7] But then an idea flashes through my mind.

"Yes, sir," I say, "I do know! Gideon got rid of the squeamish men and chose those who were not too finicky. A soldier who recoils from filth will never make a real soldier, Sir!"

The officer raises his hand and then offers it to me. He shakes my hand, saying:

"Bravo, stout lad! You'll rise high! You'll make a man yet. If you don't get a medal in this life, I'll see that you get it on your tombstone!"

My comrades look at me enviously. As for me – I am overjoyed.

What a big deal! A medal on my tombstone!

9 | His Majesty the Button

THROUGHOUT all these confusing events, in the midst of the mental turmoil which has gripped me for the past few weeks, a curious realization has grown in me and become a strange problem for which I can find no answer. It's the inner respect that I increasingly feel for people whom all my life I have completely disregarded as of no more value than a dried up lemon peel – officers.

What did I think of officers before?

The army officer, if I thought of him at all, had always appeared to me to be a useless and superfluous creature in God's great world. A sleek creature, strutting about like a clockwork doll, its bones, from head to foot, dry as sticks. It seemed to have a sort of coagulated wine jelly instead of brains inside its skull.

I rarely met this creature in my social life, and never noticed it, even in passing. A total absence of all regard. I thought to myself that if such a creature were to stand between some object and myself, it would not block my view; it would resemble glass. I would never dream of sitting at a table with an officer. Who sits beside an officer?

A whore; worse still, another officer.

It never even occurred to me to ask, what are these creatures for anyway? Only once did the thought cross my mind accidentally. I was reading a book by Bölsche[1] on the purpose of creation, and it led me to the great "Why?" Then, among other questions and associations, I asked myself what was the actual purpose of creating, say, the grasshopper, the frog, the officer?

Even after I had learned about the world and society, and understood the secret of militarism and capitalism and all the rest, I still could not understand the function of that creature in this stupid, ugly system. Even in a stupid, ridiculous regime I could find no good reason for the existence of this character in a stiff, strangulating collar, with a whip under its arm with which to flog the poor husband who wishes to avenge the honor of his silly wife, who falls for that living flagpole.

I recall that Bismarck had always been surrounded by those strange beings, who used to stand around him like the stone pillars surrounding the great linden tree in the Grunewald Park in Berlin.[2] Whenever linden-tree Bismarck moved, they moved. When he stopped, they stopped. But what did those flagpoles do when Bismarck was thinking? He might have been thinking venomous, bitter, murderous thoughts of killings and attacks – but what did *they* have to do with any thoughts of any kind?

Which reminds me of Werner Sombart's lecture on the Jews[3] – Jews are incapable of being officers. Quite true. Being an officer requires a certain empty-headedness, and Jews have different qualities. That was what Sombart was saying, and we accepted it as self-evident, a statement of the obvious. To be an officer one needed a whip, a waxed moustache, a dog – and the officer himself.

These thoughts come to me unexpectedly during the "school for the intelligentsia." They come suddenly, in a lucid interval, when I catch myself treating my first lieutenant and his ilk with respect, not only in military matters but in other matters as well, such as questions of culture, art and literature!…

What's going on?

The first lieutenant, Herr Print, an Austrian, is a pleasant enough fellow, enjoys conversations on cultural subjects and considers himself a connoisseur of the arts. After "work" he condescends most graciously and talks to us about all sorts of things. At such a time he seems to be a different man. He enjoys joking and argues with us as equals.

In the course of these discussions I come to learn some of his views.

For example: Michelangelo was a great artist, but there is one defect in his work – his women are neither aesthetic nor beautiful.[4]

Or: Karl Marx was a contemptible careerist who failed to reach a high position, so he hit on the idea of flattering the lower classes and confusing them with dangerous ideas.[5]

Or: The greatest of all German composers was Haydn. It was he who composed the Austrian national anthem as well as all the military signals of the Austrian army.

Wagner was also a great artist – there are some military leitmotifs in his music, too – but having failed in the July Revolution he became a revolutionary himself. His artistic punishment was that his revolutionary work, the "Polonia" overture, was a miserable failure.[6]

As for Tolstoy, the secret truth about his ideas is that he was thrown out of the officers' corps because of poor military abilities. So he became a preacher of peace and all that. It's really a pity – he might have been a blessing to the world if he had remained an officer all his life.[7]

As for the Bible – it's a book of war,[8] but the Jews, being helpless and lacking the means to make war, made it a gospel of peace.

"What about Jesus of Nazareth?" we ask.

"Christ? He was a real biblical Jew. The most Christian thing about him was his apothegm. 'I came not to send peace, but a sword.'[9] Peace can be a compromise, not an ideal. Pity Nietzsche came so late – he should have been born before Christ, then the whole world would have accepted his doctrine, the doctrine of 'war for war's sake, for the intoxication of the knife.'"[10]

"But Nietzsche's day will come. It will surely come."

One might have thought that such views would strengthen my old attitude towards the first lieutenant, and yet…

And yet I fall into a strange weakness. I no longer despise him and his colleagues with the shiny buttons. On the contrary, I find that in our conversations, in all my dealings with them, I am trying to win their approval and match their wishes and views.

It all began with that very first examination, when I was declared "able-bodied," and when that superior officer at headquarters gave me his hand and said, "You'll be a marvelous soldier, my friend. You'll drive the Cossacks right back to Moscow, and when you return you'll get a first class decoration!" Ever since then, whenever I get a compliment of this sort, I feel a sort of pride.

When, a few days before, the officer gave me his hand over the horse's neck and said, "Bravo! You'll make a man yet," I felt *flattered* by those words.

I search in vain for an explanation for this strange development. I regard them with respect, why deny it?

Marx, a careerist; Michelangelo's women, ugly; Wagner got his comeuppance; pity about Tolstoy. The Bible – a record of war, Jesus of Nazareth…

I am unable to resolve my predicament, until a seemingly trivial fact brings it home to me. I had written a letter home to Mansie, and when I re-read it, found the following sentence: "Our first lieutenant is a really intelligent man. He'll see that I rise through the ranks!"

I tear that letter into shreds.

At such times I am aware that this feeling has crept into me and is weighing me down. Like a stone thrown into a hollow tree – the tree keeps growing, encrusting the decay around the stone, but the tree itself doesn't disintegrate.

I grow desperate: have I really been condemned to die young with this rock inside the core of my being?

In place of Rabbi Pinchas of Koretz[11] – First Lieutenant Print. In place of two luminous, supremely wise eyes – His Imperial Majesty's polished uniform buttons. When His Majesty the Button stands before me, and I draw myself up straight and tight, hand to trouser-seam, I feel that I am fulfilling my duty faithfully and honestly, and that I have a purpose in life. Moreover, that to be an officer is the highest purpose of all, and whoever wins a posthumous medal is the most fortunate of men and his mother would be blessed among women.

I really feel all this. A week ago, yesterday, this morning. Ye gods of Flammarion, what has happened to me?![12]

I can't even tell this to anyone. It's impossible. And not out of shame, but simply because we all share this feeling, every single one of us.

Consider further that, in the army, and especially in military academy, there is a very strict law which says that a candidate against whom there has been the slightest imputation may never become an officer.

It means that a candidate who has done nothing wrong, but about whom the slightest accusation is spread, is automatically rejected and sent to the front as a private. Thus if anyone who may be mad at me wishes to hurt me, he need only malign me to others, and it's all over. It doesn't matter if there is a shred of truth in the allegation or not – no one will inquire and try to find out, no one will want to hear your defense and wretched self-justification. If anybody says that you have stolen as much as a silver spoon, you're finished. You have already been condemned to disgrace, to be sent back with a guard of dishonor to the replacement camp and thence to the front, to be the beloved sergeant's dog. In the meantime everybody will stare at you with repulsion enough to bury you alive.

At first we are all stunned by the idiocy of this brilliant principle, but then it happened when one of my closest friends, an artist with a brilliant reputation as a painter, fell victim to some slander. Headquarters heard about it and the order came to send him back to the troops, as a reject from the officer's academy.

The wretched fellow didn't dare look any of us in the face. He packed his things and left, accompanied by general scorn.

As he approached the gate, I saw him turning his head back, looking at me. His eyes expressed the silent question: "Et tu?"

I couldn't even run after him and whisper to him that I spat at the entire madhouse with him, and that you don't need an officer's respect and agreement, or the eulogies of a drunken sergeant, to die and rot in the grave.

No, I didn't run up to him and I didn't say it. I stood amongst the people who scorned him and, by saying nothing, scorned him as well.

I, the man of culture, disciple of Rabbi Akiva, the Gaon of Vilna, Professor Ze'ev Bacher, Camille Flammarion and Tolstoy.[13]

I enter the room, take out my small mirror, gaze at my reflection, and spit at it.

"God damn your soul!"

10 | The Commander of the Muse

IT SEEMS that my first examination in the officers' academy went off well. I didn't realize that I was taking part in the charade of disqualification from the academy to which my poor friend was subjected following the slander. Though passive, my part was quite important. That performance, I soon discover, was used as a test to measure our embryonic officer-like intelligence. While our condemned comrade is leaving the courtyard, he is the cynosure of hundreds of contemptuous and pitying eyes. Our great-hearted instructor, First Lieutenant Print, stands by and examines us with a critical eye, to detect which of us might be so weakened as to sympathize with the expelled man.

Anyone who falls into that trap is doomed to disqualification before long. To our hard-boiled instructor's real satisfaction, none of us is trapped. We all, thank God, show appropriate contempt for the man who is leaving. Bravo! Excellent! I soon find out that my own role is rather trickier than the others; our officer-teacher pays greater attention to my humble person than to the others. After the condemned man is gone, the first lieutenant comes up to me, puts his hand on my shoulder and asks:

"D'you write in the newspapers under the name of 'Albert Kova'?"[1]

"Beg to report: Yes, sir."

"You're a Hebrew poet, too, in the language of the Bible?"

"Beg to report: Yes, sir."

"You're a good friend of that lunatic Endre Ady?"[2]

"Beg to report: No, sir."

"What, no? I say you are. Do you deny it?"

"Yes, I deny that he's a lunatic, sir. Endre Ady is the greatest Hungarian poet of all time."

My instructor stares at me, removes his hand from my shoulder and after a moment's pause says:

"We'll soon find out. I believe that he's opposed to the war. We'll see if he recovers his senses now and gives us some rousing war poetry. If he doesn't… If he doesn't…"

His face becomes grim and harsh as a shrunken horse-radish.

"If he doesn't, you'll have to forget him, as if he died a scoundrel's death. I hope you understand me. Try to understand me."

"Just as you say, sir."

The officer lights a cigarette, offers one to me to my great joy, and when I light it he asks me with a half-derisive, half-solemn chuckle:

"What is your opinion about absolute honesty and justice?"

I see at once that this man knows all about my life, my habits and ways, my literary work over the years, and decide not to succumb. But I don't want to provoke his vile arsenal of vulgarity and corruption, so I answer with a similar chuckle:

"Beg to report: There is no absolute honesty and justice in the world, sir."

"And will never be?"

"Beg to report: There will be, sir, but only when there are no more wars in the world."

"You ought to add," he says, "when we will emerge victorious from all the wars in the world!"

"Beg to report: Yes, sir, we will *all* emerge victorious from *all* the wars in the world."

The first lieutenant inhales a lungful of smoke and says in the tone of a man who is momentarily disconcerted and has no ready answer:

"Very well. We'll argue about that another time."

Then he orders a field drill.

He keeps his promise – the argument about absolute honesty and justice comes up between us again and again. It's extremely difficult for me. There are moments when I feel that I'm going to collapse under the strain of these discussions, which grow into a very unequal duel. He holds the revolver of absolute authority and I have nothing but words. A battle between might and mind.

If there would have been any among my comrades who also take some part in these discussions a single one who dared not nod with fawning approval to the vile opinions of this living lexicon of murder, it might have been possible to turn the contention into a triumph for the thinking mind, or at least into banter. But there isn't a single one. The fellows all smile at us, a disdainful officer-like smile, approving the lieutenant's words and pitying mine. And so I gradually become the laughing-stock of the regiment, and all my efforts to win approval end in failure.

"I'm sorry for you," our teacher says to me, with genuine pity and affection. "As a soldier we have a very good opinion of you, but as a man – it seems that your education has ruined you."

The result is that while most of my friends have risen to the rank of corporal, or even platoon leader, by the second month, I have not even made it to lance corporal. I am still a lowly rookie, although I have already been to the front and even been wounded. I feel deeply ashamed.

But then suddenly something happens to change my miserable status.

At the end of every course at the officers' academy there is usually a ball, a cabaret evening, to mark the end of the three months training that precedes departure to the front. All the men who are known to have some talent, literary or artistic, take part in the "cabaret," and as it happens, our class has a good few such talents – writers, painters, actors, dancers, opera singers.

When the order comes to prepare for the ball, I find myself excluded from the plans. First Lieutenant Print, that connoisseur of art and literature, doesn't see his way clear to include me in this artistic endeavor. Success in this matter would help greatly to advance me to the rank of commissioned officer, and he, fearing that I might do well, certainly doesn't want this to happen. A dangerous pacifist like myself should go to the front as an ordinary soldier, and if he should prove himself worthy of it there, bravery itself would bring advancement.

However, arousal of the artistic impulse awakens the conscience in some of my comrades, and they feel uneasy about my exclusion.

Then one of them, who has already risen to the rank of corporal, maybe even *Zugsführer* next month, takes me by the arm for a stroll. He is a handsome young man, with blue eyes and typical officer's good looks, whose well bred Christian appearance has helped his success at the academy. Back in the city he had already acquired an early reputation as a writer and poet, and published a small volume of verse.[3]

"I can't bear to see your suffering, my dear friend," he whispers to me. "You must participate in the ball."

"I'm not suffering at all," I lie.

"That doesn't matter," he replies. "It won't do. We can't do without you."

Suddenly he bends his head closer still and whispers in my ear:

"Unfortunately I can't do anything myself. Because, you see, I myself… I'm a Jew… But someone else…"

So – this noble Christian officer type is a Jew as well. I'm not particularly surprised. In Hungary this isn't uncommon.

My friend continues:

"I couldn't stand it if there were not a single Jewish voice in that entire ball! You must take part."

"Why the Jewish overtone?" I ask.

"Because he is against the Jews and forces us – me – to deny them."

I understand, and promise not to spoil things for him.

It seems he has tried, through other people. He is afraid to recommend me to the first lieutenant. To do that, a genuine Christian is required.

The following day, when we return from afternoon training, the first lieutenant's messenger comes:

"*Herr* volunteer! The first lieutenant orders you to appear before him at once!"

"By your order, sir!"

A few moments later I stand before him. The great gentleman receives me with official coldness. He addresses me not in the familiar second person, as customary when officers speak to cadets, but in the formal third person,[4] indicating a chilly, almost insulting attitude.

"We have decided that you must take part in the ball, as a poet and reader."

"At your command, sir!"

"Would you like to write a poem? he asks, and quickly adds "because even if you don't want to, you have to."

I think for a moment, gazing at the Commander of the Sacred Muse. He goes on:

"You must write a poem and read it at our ball. The subject must be romantic, patriotic, sentimental and clearly military. Do you understand?"

I understand. Romantic, patriotic, sentimental and clearly military.

Yes I understand, but then the ordinary civilian, who cannot hear such an order without smiling, comes to life within me, and I restrain my smile. He concludes:

"The length of the poem – a quarter hour's reading before the public. Understood?"

"Understood, honored sir. But may I ask a question, sir?"

"Ask!"

"How wide must it be?" I ask, and at once regret it.

The first lieutenant opens his prominent eyes wide, steps up to me in true officer's style and shrieks at me through gritted teeth:

"Attention! Miserable ink-licker! About face, march!"

I carry out his order, but when I reach the door he calls me to attention again.

"It's now 3:00 p.m. You're to produce the poem by 7:00 p.m. this evening!"

"At your command! By seven."

This last order gives me the courage to make a request.

"What is it?" he asks suspiciously.

"Sir, would you permit me to go to the coffee house and write there?"

He thinks for a moment and says, mockingly but without ill-will:

"You coffee house owl! The cashier is your muse! I know. Very well!"

This is extraordinarily gracious. Only officers can go to the coffee house when they wish. Officer cadets are only permitted there once a week, on Sunday afternoons.

I sit in the coffee house, contemplating revenge. A coincidence comes to my aid. Among my comrades is a young Jewish youth, a teacher, who at some inopportune hour has been declared fit to serve in the army. He is a scrawny fellow, almost a hunchback, neckless and with a sunken chest, a clumsy type who stumbles over his own feet. This pathetic specimen is overjoyed to be a soldier and, especially, an officer candidate. Whenever the first lieutenant approaches him standing in the ranks, and, in a gesture of contempt mingled with sympathy, slaps him on the shoulder, the poor fellow's eyes stream with tears of happiness.

This odd creature sticks in my mind as the subject for a story, and I share this with some of my friends. Now, sitting in the coffee house trying to think of a theme for the poem that I have been ordered to write, I see this same fellow pass by the window as if offering himself for the task.

Here is the subject for a romantic-patriotic-sentimental-military poem if ever there was one!

However, there is a fly in the ointment – not for me, but for the Honored Gentleman; the subject is Jewish.

Ay, what will this lead to?

Whatever happens, I've already been banished from the paradise of officer's rank. It's the end of the second month, and I am still a lowly rookie. What will be will be!

A moment later my friend with the dashing Christian officer's mien turns up. When I tell him my idea he jumps for joy, and then makes himself scarce.

I finish the poem by six o'clock. Entitled, "A Letter to the Colonel," its subject is the scrawny, misshapen Jewish corporal, lying mortally wounded in a military hospital, writing a letter to his *Herr* Colonel. In his letter be describes how he was born in the ghetto to sickly, impoverished parents. In his boyhood the children tormented him because of his pathetic, wretched physique, and when war broke out they yelled after him: "Emperor Franz Josef is waiting for you!" Then the God of the patriarchs took pity on him and made a miracle: he was found fit to serve in the army! Here at last success showed him her radiant face. He worked hard, studied, persevered in his training, and found favor with the sergeant. But the climax of his joy came when the colonel visited the cadets and went up to him, slapped him on his shoulder and said "You're a brave fellow!" Then he swore a sacred oath to die for the colonel, and this too was granted him by Divine Providence. When he went to the front and the battle was raging, he saw a Russian soldier aiming straight at the colonel. The poor corporal, faithful soldier that he was, interposed himself between the sniper and the colonel, and stopped the deadly bullet with his own body! Now that he was about to die he had but one last small request: Would the colonel please come and say to him once more, "You're a brave fellow?!"

And there you have it – a romantic, patriotic, sentimental and perfectly military poem!

"I'm a brave fellow."

When I present myself again to the first lieutenant and the expression on my face shows plainly that I have carried out the order, he greets me in the familiar person and tells me to stand at ease. Furthermore, he gives me a cigarette and asks me to sit down.

Then I read him the poem.

It makes such a powerful impression upon him that the fine gentleman keeps blowing his nose, moved by sacred military fervor. He quite forgets that the subject is Jewish. This bothers me quite a bit, but I hope he becomes aware of it and recognizes his own serious mistake.

When I finish, he again offers me a cigarette, and when I hasten to offer him a light he declines. Instead he offers me the burning match, saying:

"The colonel must hear this. He must. The colonel. Tomorrow night you will please read it to the colonel, too. He will be here, at my place."

The following evening, when I arrive at his quarters, the colonel is not there but his wife is. A simple Magyar woman of peasant stock, whom the colonel has fallen in love with and married many years before, she is well-liked by the men. She is a handsome, buxom specimen, and extremely kind-hearted.

She weeps bitterly when she hears the poem, keeps blowing her nose and saying:

"Poor thing! Poor thing! Poor Jewish corporal!" This brings on what I have been half-hoping and half-fearing: the first lieutenant finally becomes aware, falls into a sort of confusion, and says:

"Indeed, that's something of a great defect. A Jew. But surely he need not be a Jew. That is sort of, how shall I put it? We'll see what the colonel has to say about it."

"The colonel won't object," says his beautiful wife.

"Very good then. Tomorrow you'll read it to the colonel as well."

As I am leaving I hear the colonel's wife saying to the officer:

"How is it that he's still a lowly private? Not even a lance corporal?"

"Ah, that, well, that's nothing, madame. That doesn't mean a thing," says the first lieutenant apologetically. "It's a mere accident. Tomorrow he'll be promoted."

And to me:

"Tomorrow you'll come to me and report that you've been made a lance corporal. Understand? Well then, g'bye.

Next morning it is announced that I have been made a lance corporal; the men are delighted.

That evening I once again go to the first lieutenant's quarters. The beautiful woman is there again, with her younger son, a boy of thirteen. A charming and handsome lad. The colonel is still busy.

I read the poem once more. The boy jumps up with tears in his eyes and begins pleading with his mother, insisting that it's high time he is sent to the front. It's a disgrace to be at home, tied to Mommy's apron strings! He comes to me with childish affection and asks me for a copy of the poem. Then he turns to the officer:

"Oh, lieutenant! How come the *Herr* poet is only a lance corporal? Why is he not at least a corporal, like some of the others?"

"Ah, that... that... Well, it doesn't mean anything! Absolutely nothing!"

And to me:

"Tomorrow you'll come and report to me that you've been promoted corporal. Understood?!"

The following morning the order comes: I've been made corporal. Now the men are all astonished and envious – one day after the other?

That afternoon I am told to report again in the evening to read the poem, at long last, to the colonel himself.

The colonel is very pleased.

"Listen, you inkfish!" he says affectionately and in his own peculiar style, which cannot always be reported. "How is it you haven't even got three stripes? What are you, Napoleon, that you're content to remain a corporal? If I see you again with only two stripes, I'll send you back where you came from!"

The first lieutenant:

"Oh, well, that's nothing, nothing at all! Tomorrow he'll be made sergeant!"

He adds, stammering respectfully:

"What does your honor think? Wouldn't it be better, I mean, would it not be better if that corporal in the poem, I mean, if he were not a Jew, I think ..."

"Why?" exclaims the colonel, "On the contrary! Absolutely on the contrary! That's very good! That's something new. Excellent!"

And to me:

"Now then, out with you – go and sew on your third stripe this very evening. Understood?!"

He gives me his hand graciously and I take my leave. When I have sewed on the third stripe the men simply cannot believe their eyes – three promotions in three days? But I can't fall asleep. To this day I cannot say why – is it happiness, or the strangeness of the fact that I had written a poem, and a good one, to order?

An order, mind you, not from one of the great editors of the day such as Brandes, Ignotus or David Frishmann – but at the command of First Lieutenant Print.[5]

It would be interesting to see how the muse looks in uniform.

A week later I receive a letter from my friend the poet and editor Josef Patai:[6]

"Perhaps your best poem so far. Pity about the deplorable subject."

11 | The Great Reward

OUR BALL is attended by the entire higher aristocracy of Lucenec and its environs.[1] But when I stand on the stage to read the poem, all I can see before me are polished buttons and ivory stars. The audience appears to me like a awe-inspiring court-martial, headed by our commandant, the major, with his long drooping moustache, in his place of honor. I see him as soon as I step onto the stage, and am seized by terror. Fortunately, I also catch sight of the lovely lady, the colonel's wife, sitting beside her husband in the adjoining box. Then, when I stop in front of the prompter's pit, I am appalled to feel two hands grasp my ankles. I look down and see the face of the charming boy, the colonel's son. All my terrors immediately dissipate, and I read the poem most successfully. I see the beautiful woman wiping her eyes. Oh good. The audience is murmuring and I cannot tell if it means approval or distaste, acceptance or rejection. When I finish there is a burst of applause, which dies down at once, as if someone had stifled it. Only four hands do not succumb to the hesitation and continue to clap despite the silence – these are the hands of the beautiful woman and of the mischievous little fellow in the pit at my feet.

Then the *Herr Kommandant* rises and, in perfect military silence, amidst the total silence of the large audience, comes onto the stage. My poem is the concluding item of the ball. The Exalted Personage comes up to me, looks at me for a moment that seems like eternity, and then closes the evening with a short speech, directed more at me than at the audience:

"A fine Jewish poem, he says in a colorless voice. And the greatest reward you can get" – this more to the audience than to me – "is the gracious kindness of the Supreme Commander, His Imperial Majesty Franz Josef the First, who gives you the opportunity to die a hero's death for his sake."

Thunderous applause. Then the commandant adds, speaking to the rest of the participants who stand behind me on the stage:

"And that goes for all of you too!"

Again tremendous applause, and the Mighty One descends from the stage.

A few minutes later the first lieutenant's messenger comes backstage and says to me:

"To report!"[2]

To report? What for? Put that way it might mean a court martial.

But at once I reassure myself. I know that military jargon is none too precise, and it might simply mean an order to appear before the officer, and not stand trial before him.

But the *Herr* First Lieutenant Print informs me angrily that this time I really must appear before our commandant, presumably to be tried. Very graciously he adds, seeing my astonishment:

"You needn't always parade the fact that you are a Jew!"

In accordance with standing orders, he, as my superior officer, accompanies me to the Mighty One.

As we are walking silently I recall the final words: to die for Franz Josef. Is it Franz Josef's will that I should die for him. Who? Franz Josef? How odd. Ever since I can remember, Franz Josef has appeared to me as the image of the good-hearted, benign old patriarch, whose life has been full of inhuman pain, sorrow, family troubles and endless diligent paper work. When I was a child I thought of him as a "friend" of my grandfather, whom he used to receive in audience, and with whom he used to chat about horses and about the form of prayers at the synagogue. Whenever a new synagogue was built in any major city in Hungary, a special seat would be built for the Emperor in the eastern wing, and he, the nice old man, would come to the ceremonial opening and sit in his seat and listen the special prayers "He who gives salvation to kings"[3] and "A song. For the dedication of the temple,"[4] say Amen, then say a few words and leave, accompanied by the rabbi and the lay head of the community.

That was our Emperor Franz Josef.

Further: Every year the old emperor would spend a few days in Budapest, on the Buda side beyond the Danube, where he resided in the royal palace whose gates were open to all mortals.[5] We newspaper people, having finished our work at 3:00 a.m., would stroll into the royal palace gardens and there see the old monarch through the window, rising at exactly 4:15 a.m., bathing, dressing, drinking tea and sitting down at his desk to work. Every single morning.

That was Franz Josef, Our Supreme Commander, His Imperial Majesty Franz Josef the First!

We saw him continuously surrounded by tragedy: The tragic death of his beautiful wife Empress Elizabeth, glowing in the romantic light of Heine's poems and clasping his ivory cameo to her ample bosom. The tragic death of his young son Rudolph whose death remains unexplained to this day. Finally, the tragic death of his nephew and heir to the throne

Franz Ferdinand, whose murder by a black and bitter Serb lit the tinderbox of war. When the new crown prince, Charles the First, appeared before the old man to be anointed heir, Franz Josef lifted his eyes to heaven and said in a tearful voice:[6]

"Almighty God, this time do not show me the awful kindness of prolonging my days and seeing this young man die as well!"

That was our Kaiser Franz Josef!

Even later, when I became a fanatical socialist and loathed all royalty, even then I could not bring myself to hate the old emperor.

At most I could see him as a sort of charming operetta king whose crown is made of paper-maché and his sword of wood overlaid with silver and gold.

Now they tell me that Franz Josef wants me to die for him.

What a strange wish.

Perhaps his mind became a little scrambled in his old age?

If Mansie knew this, she would no doubt rush over to see him and ask him if it was true.

Meantime, we reach the quarters of the Exalted Gentleman.

To my great astonishment he sends the first lieutenant away, so as to speak to me in private. This is against regulations: in a court martial the commanding officer stays with the accused soldiers until a verdict is reached. But he sends him away.

When we are alone the commandant paces up and down the room for a few minutes and then turns on me suddenly and, as if bitten by a snake, snaps at me as if to frighten me:

"You're a Jew!"

"Beg to report: Yes, Excellency!"

He stares at me for a moment.

"Why are you so proud of it?"

"Beg to report: I'm not proud, Excellency, but when I am expected to be ashamed of it, I become proud."

"Hm. Hm."

Then suddenly:

"They say you're a good officer candidate."

"Beg to report: Yes, Excellency!"

"In that case, why are you provoking your comrades by showing off your Jewishness?" – He adds with a slight smile, "Wouldn't you like to be a general? Now General Kovacs was also a Jew, but he converted and became a general."[7]

He keeps looking straight at me. I make up my mind and answer:

"Beg to report: I do not wish to be a general, sir."

"Do you believe in your religion to such an extent?"

"Beg to report: I hardly believe at all, Excellency, which is why I don't believe in other religions either."

"Hm," he mutters again under his drooping moustache.

By now I am encouraged, and continue without waiting for his next question:

"It's exactly because I have no religion, that I cannot exchange it for another. A man cannot convert a coin he doesn't have."

His Excellency grows angry and shouts:

"I didn't ask you, *fratz*!" (*Fratz* meaning something like scum) he thunders at me.

I turn to stone. Then the Exalted Gentleman begins to reprimand me:

"You've been to the front already, you've tasted the worst. You should stay in the rear for a while longer, become an officer and then march out there. Understood?!"

"Beg to report: Yes, Excellency."

"Well, then?"

Suddenly his face became a monster mask of rage:

"You've got to throw that burdensome Jewish package to hell where it belongs, and not provoke people at such grave times! Understood?!"

The devil only knows how it happens, but at this point I draw myself up and presume to answer:

"Beg to report: No, Excellency!"

"What?! he roars at me, and without waiting for an answer shouts straight into my face "Quick march! Back to the replacement camp! To the front, you miserable dog!"

"Beg to report: Yes, Excellency! That's no punishment – that's my great reward! I want to die for the Supreme Commander, His Imperial Majesty Franz Josef the First!"

I leave him, saluting as I go.

The next day he sends me to the replacement camp, without officer's rank.

When we leave the city, on our way to the railway station, I march as an NCO at the head of my company. The entire population is out of doors. The cadets are known in the city, and everyone wants to see who has attained officer's rank and who has not.

Approaching the quarters of the Exalted Gentleman I see him standing there, ready to review the parade. Each NCO is supposed to give the order to his company to salute the commander who is standing on the sidewalk.

About a hundred paces beyond the commandant's quarters I see the lovely lady, the colonel's wife, standing there with her little boy, closely observing the rank and file. When I draw closer I see her put a handkerchief to her mouth, which is puckered as if she were about to burst into tears. With her other hand she strokes her little boy's head.

Suddenly the figure of the Great Gentleman arouses immense rage and repulsion in me. At that moment I feel as if I have to settle with him all my accounts and all the accounts of the Jewish people, from the Exodus to his venomous order to send me to the front ahead of time, because I insist on remaining a Jew. Let me provoke him a little. What do I have to lose? And so, as we march past him, I don't give my company the order to salute.

The men are puzzled, but march on without saluting. The fellows do not understand, but without an order nothing can be done. What do I have to lose?

It's a strange and terrifying moment. The Exalted Gentleman stands staring at my company with his green eyes, then pulls the ends of his moustache, looks this way and that, and raises his hand, as if to draw my attention so that I can correct my error. But I do not notice him. What do I have to lose?

But when we pass the lovely lady, I amaze my company by roaring at the top of my voice:

"Eyes right!"

The company straighten their backs and march past the lovely lady with a splendid salute.

Stormy applause rings up and down the crowded street. The public cheers us. And the lovely lady waves her handkerchief, bursts into tears, and smiles at us, all at the same time.

When we reach the railway station First Lieutenant Print comes to me and stares into my face for a long time, full of pity and fury:

"What have you done? he whispers. "Now even the Jewish colonel will not protect you. You're hopeless. You'll be sent to the front directly."

He, too, must have forgotten what the commandant had said at the ball. I remind him:

"Beg to report: The front is a great reward, not a punishment!"

We get into the train, and are off. On the way I find out that the colonel, the husband of the lovely lady and father of the charming little boy, is indeed a Jew as well.

12 | The Death Card

OUR REPLACEMENT CAMP is stationed in the town of Szatmar.[1] The first visit I pay there is to the chief rabbi of the local Progressive community, Rabbi Shmuel Jordan. He is a well-known Zionist, a rare phenomenon among Hungarian rabbis.[2]

The rabbi's family receives me with sad and tearful eyes – the war, the front… Especially the rabbi's younger daughter, Hannah, who is about fourteen. A dark and beautiful child, she is a perfect example of a young daughter of Israel, whose eyes wound and heal at the same time. She studies the Bible with her father and knows Hebrew well.

It's in this child's eyes that I first feel the terror of approaching death. I'll be gone and rot in a lime pit and she'll remain here, grow and flourish, become a beautiful woman, without me, forever. I become aware of the full horror of the war. The fact that I have already been in mortal danger once, and even wounded, doesn't enter my mind. It seemed like a mere incident at the time. Now, now it is really beginning. The war is beginning for me. Ah, little Hannah…

A new life begins for me in the replacement camp. Most of my comrades have been promoted officers, and I am the only failure, a good-for-nothing. I am given a few recruits to train in basic drill, marching, rifle-carrying and saluting. They, simple soldiers, mostly peasants, artisans and a few townsmen, look on me as a superior creature. They study diligently, listen to me with awe, and love me.

My new commanding officer, recently promoted colonel,[3] takes a dim view of the good relations between my soldiers and myself. He feels that I am too lenient with them. One day he comes up to me and says calmly:

"Did you use to go chicken-stealing with them? Spit in their faces right now!"

Spit in their faces? That isn't easy.

But the commanding officer won't let up:

"Spit in their faces, I said! Understood?!"

I look at their faces. Simple men, solid and guileless, learning the ways of war, getting ready to part from their families and die. How can I spit in their faces?

So I don't spit in their faces. What do I have to lose?

The result is that I am court-martialed and sentenced to a day in solitary confinement – in a narrow, dark cell, on bread and water, lying on the bare floor without cot or pillow.

It gives me time to think about patriotism. The enthusiasm of war burns with the flame of patriotism, love of the homeland. Orators preach it, women seduce their husbands and lovers to go and die for the homeland, poets compose verses to it, correspondents report – from the rear of course – about heroism on the battle-front in the name of love of homeland. And here I am ordered to spit in the faces of the would-be heroes and lovers of the homeland. Supposing I spat in a soldier's face, with his wife and children looking on?

When I am released from the cell I am approached by one of the recruits on his way to the day's training, a very young and strikingly handsome lad.

"Sergeant, sir, we beg you, all of us, if you're ordered to insult us please don't hesitate. Insult us! An order is an order. It doesn't matter. You shouldn't suffer on our account. Death is worse than insults."

"Go to your place, stupid!"

In the evening that same good-looking, eighteen year-old Magyar, who has volunteered freely, out of genuine and uncomplicated love of homeland, comes to see me. He says:

"Please, sir, I'd like to be your batman."

"Thank you, my friend. Only when I become an officer."

"It doesn't matter," he protests, "officer aspirants also sometimes have batmen, sort of unofficially. I'll serve you willingly. Please."

At once he begins to tidy up my things.

I look at him: beautiful as a virgin, large deep-blue eyes, glowing through long black lashes that shade their brightness like the sun rising from a deep forest. I fall in love with him. It's a pleasure to have him around.

From that day on he never leaves my side. He works for me, does all he can, makes every effort, always with respect, good manners, and extraordinary love.

He likes what I like and hates what I hate with the greatest intensity. Outwardly he is perfectly correct, but inside him I sense great force. He is like a faithful and handsome thoroughbred dog, with the heart of a lion.

His casual epithet for the colonel is "the horned pig" or "his piggishness" – on account of his extraordinary crudeness.

I find out on my second day with the troops that one of the basic rules of the army is vulgarity. Shamelessness and blunt directness. Everybody has to be able to curse and swear worse than any drunken whore. The foul curses hurled against all that is dear and sacred to man, from his own virtuous mother to the crucifix – or, among the Jews, the "phylactery strap" – are a kind of intoxication, like alcohol in the midst of the war atmosphere. Foul language assuages the pain and the sorrow and sense of helplessness. Some of the bitterness is dissipated and the mood lightens. Commanders understand this very well, and they praise and cherish those who best employ this style. The lieutenant explains it in different terms: according to him, this manner of speech is valued for its extreme brevity. Instead of searching for words and expressions to serve as euphemisms for matters that are not discussed in society, a single word is used, the simplest one, which requires no time for thought and leaves no room for misunderstanding. This kind of re-education often plays havoc with people. It happened that a well-born officer went home on leave, and while there, among cultivated people, suddenly spoke in a manner which shocked everybody. Eventually he hurried back to his troops to escape the disgrace.

There is one fellow among us who finds it especially difficult to get used to this style of speech. He is a former *yeshiva* scholar, by the name of Jacob Margolis, a skinny, swarthy fellow, short and hollow-chested, who speaks beautiful Hungarian. His inability to adjust to the accepted filthy speech causes him agonies. But he happens to be endowed with a natural sense of humor, almost a clown's talent, that saves him from the worst sufferings. Nobody ever sees him laugh – his face is unfailingly and almost provokingly serious, but his actions, his movements, voice and expressions can make the wildest beasts among the officers roar with laughter. This natural talent eventually helps him adapt, if not in speech, at least in actions. The fellow simply strips himself of all sense of shame, as our superior officer demands, and does everything possible to illustrate the required way of speaking and acting.

Before long Jacob Margolis has become a regimental favorite and his reputation extends throughout the division as well. As far as he is concerned, all he is doing is to carry things to the point of absurdity – "You want crudeness," he seems to say, "very well, here's crudeness for you!"

More than once he causes a breach of discipline in the midst of our work. It's a grave offence to make the men laugh while in training, and carries grave penalties.

"Just you wait!" the lieutenant says to him once, laughing in spite of himself. "You wait! The division commander will be visiting us soon, and then just you try some of your clowning. He'll knock your teeth out of your head, you bastard! (*Mamzer*, he says, which is Hebrew for bastard.)

"Why a bastard?" asks Margolis.

"All you *yeshiva* boys are bastards, ass-lickers, every one of you."

"Why ass-lickers, sir?"

"Stop asking questions, you piece of garbage! Because your officer says so!"

Four days later the division commander comes to inspect our regiment. We are out in the field, engaged in tactical exercises, keeping at it diligently and fearful of punishment. The commander appears, and watches us in silence for a while. When we stop for a rest he comes closer, looks attentively at Margolis and asks him:

"What were you in civilian life?"

Margolis, who has learned the lesson of brevity, answers:

"Beg to report: A *mamzer,* sir!"

"What's a *mamzer*?" asks the Great Gentleman.

"Beg to report: An ass-licker, sir!"

"What?!" the commander thunders. "Do you know what you're saying?"

"Beg to report, sir: I don't know. The lieutenant says a piece of garbage like myself isn't supposed to ask questions, sir!"

I stare at the lieutenant in horror, and he returns the same look. Then he faces the commander who pierces him with his eyes. After a moment's silence he gives the order:

"Continue!"

We go back to work. Later, when I line up my company for drill, and the lieutenant is standing beside me, Margolis' shrill voice suddenly pierces the air:

"*Herr* Commander, sir, beg permission to shit!"

This is in perfect compliance with the standing orders about military style of speech: don't waste time talking round and round when you have to do your business – speak briefly, use one word. This is plainly the one correct word. The lieutenant looks at Margolis and replies in a defeated voice:

"Go!"

Margolis runs off about one hundred paces and there does what he has to do.

A suppressed smile flickers on the commander's face.

We continue with the drill and Margolis still has not returned. We can hear him grunting and groaning, but he doesn't come back. Finally the commander grows tired of the joke and tells the lieutenant to order the soldier back.

"Margolis!" yells the officer, "run back!"

Margolis, good, disciplined soldier that he is, stops what he is doing and runs back to us, joining the ranks with his loosened trousers held in one hand and a husk of maize – which he had been using – in the other.

The spectacle shocks the commander into a stance of deadly seriousness. He adjusts his camera, photographs Margolis in this exemplary posture, and leaves.

Some days later the photograph appears in an army journal, under the caption: "An example of perfect discipline in the ordinary recruit." The entire regiment laughs over it, and Margolis is promoted lance corporal.

This military behavior spreads throughout the town where we are billeted, even the women are affected by it. But above all it is picked up by the children, and no amount of punishment, at school or at home, can cure them.

In time everybody becomes accustomed to it, as they do in other towns where the army is quartered, so that if an outsider comes for a visit, he might fancy himself in a different and strange environment.

And so, one fine day, I find that I too have become a typical soldier, a regular NCO, despite all my efforts to retain my civilian personality. I haven't even felt the transformation. I no longer suffer from the army experience: to share a coffee mug with scores of Gypsies, finish a cigarette begun by one of my comrades, or gobble up a hunk of bread that has fallen into the dirt, without so much as dusting it off first. All these have become second nature and no one gives them a second thought.

In the same way we grow accustomed to the idea of death, without regret, without nostalgia for our beautiful city and our beloved women far away.

Then a minor event hits us squarely in the face, and revives the sense of horror in all its magnitude. The sergeant distributes to each of us a small metal hinged locket made like two small book-covers, which can open and shut. Inside them are slips of paper with our names, ranks, date of birth and date of mobilization.[4]

They call it the death card. Every soldier has to hang it around his neck when he goes to the front. If his body is found in the battlefield, they will know who he is and be able to notify headquarters, who will in turn notify the family.

The death card makes our hearts stop beating for a few moments. The sergeant distributes them and explains their purpose. We take them in our hands, read their contents and hang them around our necks, under our shirts, everyone looking thoughtful and pale. Our young lives, with all their joys and events, flood our hearts.

Just then, I feel as if I have already died and been buried.

The officer notices our reaction.

"That's your diploma, fellows," he says mockingly. "All that you've learned and done from the day you were born until now, was done for this. So take care, boys, don't lose this little tin tag. Don't cause your families grief when you die. Why be lost without identification?"

We ponder about it.

He proceeds grimly:

"If they inspect you suddenly and you're found without the tin tags, you'll get three days in the slammer on bread and water. Understood?!

No, we don't. Is it so important to headquarters that we avoid bringing sorrow to the survivors?

When the officer leaves, Margolis comes up to me.

"I'm going to throw the damned thing away. What do I need it for?"

"Why?"

"I haven't any relatives."

"None at all?"

"No."

"Well then… what difference does it make if you do keep it?"

Margolis thinks a moment and then speaks, as if to himself:

"It's worse, if they report and there is no one to report to, they notify an empty grave. What for? Nobody will even say *kaddish* after me.[5]

"I'll say it for you," comes the voice of an elderly soldier who has recently been attached to my company. This is "Uncle Osterreicher," a Jew of about fifty, who had been a soldier before the war broke out and has been re-mobilized as a reservist.

The two soldiers, the young Margolis and old Osterreicher, shake hands and made a pact: whichever one of them survives the other will say *kaddish* after him.

"What about your sons?" I asked Uncle Osterreicher.

"I haven't any. I had two and both of them were killed last week. Almost on the same day. I have only daughters left, and a small grandson."

I regret having asked him.

The next morning my batman informs me with vindictive relish:

"The *Herr* Major has arrived. In full field uniform!"

I make inquiries and find out that the Exalted Gentleman has been sent here following a complaint. It seems that as a result of his "debate" with me on the subject of religion and Judaism, he was ordered to the front ahead of time.

So he too reaps the "great reward!" In the next dispatch, the one after us, he too will go to the front.

When he sees me, the major's face becomes contorted as if he was having a stroke. His drooping whiskers twitch like a grasshopper. He must have been "certain" that it was on account of me that this had happened to him.

Rabbi Jordan throws a little farewell party for me. Some resoundingly patriotic speeches are made. They speak of heroism, bravery, heroic death. One lady raises her glass and says in a voice full of pathos:

"What a glorious destiny for a poet – to die a hero's death. Your name will be cherished like that of Petőfi[6] (a classic Hungarian poet, who died in the war of liberation), with all the poets who have fallen on the field of honor!"

She drains her glass.

I sit there, listening and watching all those people who talk about death, about my own death, as if it were a beautiful game. Finally, I too raise my glass and say:

"If you find my death so delightful, I shall do my best to give you this pleasure."

The rabbi, who has been silent all this time, closes his eyes and turns to one side. Then little Hannah bursts into tears and runs out of the room. We can hear her crying:

"Enough! Enough!" She weeps bitterly.

They all rise, embarrassed and silent. They shake my hand in wordless farewell, shamefacedly. One, however, hopes that I obtain brilliant decorations. Finally the rabbi comes up to me, kisses me on the forehead and says with complete assurance:

"You won't die. You'll go to the Land of Israel, straight after the war. They are waiting for you there. Remember."

When I reach the door little Hannah comes to me and says:

"Come back without awards, without decorations and medals and bravery. Come back as an ordinary soldier, worn and ragged… even wounded… but come back! Come back alive!"

She kisses me and runs back to her room.

Once outside I can't recall any of the speeches, only little Hannah's moist eyes and her sweet voice: "Come back – worn and ragged – alive!" and the sweet touch of her mouth on my cheek. But I also recall the rabbi's words: "To the Land of Israel"… Odd. The old general, too, had said something of the sort: "Pray for me at the Western Wall."

In the replacement camp, he troops are ready to march. The band starts up, and we form ranks. Then my batman hands me a letter – from Mansie. I remember that I had sent her a letter: – "I release you, Mansie my darling. Live, love, drink, laugh and forget."

I read the answer. Two short lines:

"Don't you dare release me, you louse! Come back a simple private, but come back! Don't release me! I'm not your wife! – Mansie."

The parade begins, and I see my major approaching me. He comes up and whispers in my ear:

"So you informed on me, did you? We'll meet again, Jewish poet! You won't escape punishment this time!"

I start shouting at the top of my voice, astonishing the company (what do I have to lose?):

"That isn't punishment, sir! That's the great reward – to die for our Imperial Majesty Franz Josef the First!"

From behind me comes a voice shouting, in Hebrew:

"God damn you to hell!"

It's Corporal Margolis' voice, hurling defiance at the major.

13 | The Plague Village

WE ARE travelling to Galicia, loudly and excitedly. The commotion lasts a day or two, and then the contingent grow thoughtful and quiet. En route our officer joins us and shows us some photographs.

I look at them and see feet, feet… Nothing but soldiers' feet marching.

The officer explains angrily:

"What a gang of deformed cripples! The *Herr* Major photographed your feet when you marched. You walked like the lame and the infirm. It's a disgrace! You can't even march towards death in proper order!"

He turns to me:

"Aren't you ashamed? Is this how your company marches to the battlefront! Like ballet instructors, not soldiers! I'll teach you to march!"

Outrageous! Men marching to their death without knowing the first thing about marching!

Some days later – I have no idea how many – we get off the train, and proceed on foot. The order is to walk quietly and cautiously. We are approaching the front. In the distance the guns can be heard – dull, earthshaking sounds.

The Galician towns and villages through which we pass are all but abandoned. We see some pallid, exhausted, starving people who plead for a morsel of bread. In some of the villages and towns not a single house remains standing. Sometimes all that remains of a house is the stove, its desolate chimney rising against the gray sky like a funneled finger pointing to an ashen sky.

Often a starving cat sits on the stove, clinging to the remnant of the kitchen. Sometimes it's dying, mewing softly, sometimes it's already dead. Once my batman goes up to such a dying, wailing cat and tries to take it. But the cat hisses furiously at him, scratches him with its remaining strength, and remains where it is.

"Don't you know that cats never want to leave their homes?" says Uncle Osterreicher, who is going to the Galician front for the second time.

The mud come up to our ankles, the black, cloying mud of devastated Galicia.

The closer we approach to front, the more often we come across skeletons of horses, wrecked carts, and bicycles.

Near the village of Zlota-Lipa we encounter unexpected guests – cannon shells that have overshot their mark.[1]

Not far from the road, some two hundred paces away, we see a gaunt horse standing motionless. On the other side of the road a pitiful peasant is ploughing his field, with his wife and daughter pulling the plough. These four beings are the only living things between us and the horizon.

We stop for a rest. I walk up to the horse, try to talk to it, offer it a handful of oats from the fodder of our officer's horse. But the poor animal doesn't react at all. It stands there with its eyes half shut.

The peasant explains:

"It's the horse of a Hussar who was killed not far from here. He lay there for several days. The horse wouldn't leave his body. I took the Hussar and buried him and the horse followed me. I buried the Hussar right here, and since then the horse won't budge."

He adds: "It's a common sight. The horse of a Hungarian Hussar won't leave him. It will stand till it collapses, and then fall down and die from exhaustion and starvation. This one too will fall down and die beside its master's grave."

A few more shells fall nearby.

"Aren't you afraid?" I ask the peasant.

"Where would we go? No matter where you are, you can and you must die. This is my land. Perhaps peace will come soon."

He begs us for some bread. He kisses the hem of my overcoat and shares the bread with his wife and daughter. The daughter eats the bread and keeps ogling at me. She is willing to walk to the village with me, if I want her to. A typical Galician peasant woman, there are still some traces of beauty and robustness about her. But she is horribly thin, and her face looks dead.

The family eat the bread ravenously, but the peasant and his wife do not eat it all, and put some of it away. The man puts his in his pocket and the woman puts hers in her bosom. Only the girl eats all of her share, and asks for more, with a smile. A terrible smile. Like a death's head grinning, offering a kiss.

"Why didn't you go and fight?" I ask the peasant.

"Isn't it enough that the Jews took my only son to get killed?"

"The Jews?"

"Who made this war if not the Jews?"

"I'm a Jew, too, uncle" I say.

The woman stares at me open-eyed, then quickly crosses herself and mumbles a prayer. The daughter stops smiling at me and gives me a look of terrible disappointment. The peasant turns back to his field, saying:

"Go with God then, go."

I leave them and walked a little way with Margolis, who has acted as interpreter between the peasant and myself. He knows a little Ruthenian.[2]

"Well," says Margolis to himself. "Even at the very gate of hell itself they hate us."

We look at the Hussar's horse which is standing still, its head hanging low, beside its master's grave. It shakes us so much that we can't take our eyes off it. I notice that the eyes of the whole company are on it. Even after we have put a considerable distance between us and it, many keep turning their heads back to look at that horse.

Then the order comes to turn off the road and head for the town of Buczacz.[3] We turn right. We walk and walk, tired, sweaty, worn out, limbs hanging loose and powerless.

We pass villages which have recently known all kinds of hell. Finally we are billeted in a large village, in which almost every house has gaping holes smashed in them.

Within a couple of hours we notice a strange feature about that village. All the women, young and old, walk up and down, torn and ragged, scrawny bags of dried bones, pale, white-coated tongues endlessly flickering over their lips. Then we see that all of them have one great gaping tear in their rags – directly over their private parts.

At first it makes us laugh.

"It's impossible to walk down the street to fetch the food, damn them!" my young batman complains, blushing crimson with embarrassment.

Our officer expresses the opinion that Russian soldiers have done this when they raped them. But later we find out that they have done it themselves, to attract the men. When they pass a man they pretend to cover the torn spot, with their hands, smiling with feigned embarrassment.

A strict order is issued to confine the women to their homes, not to let them walk in the streets. But it's impossible to enforce. The women simply ignore all orders. They are not afraid of whipping or imprisonment. Not even of death.

One woman says to me, simply:

"What can be worse than hunger itself? Death? We'll all soon starve to death anyway."

There's nothing for it but to keep them in their houses by giving them bread. The next day's order states that they are all rotten with syphilis, and that whoever touches them will be sentenced to death by court martial.

One little girl, about ten years old, keeps walking up and down the street muttering repeatedly:

"I'm healthy. I have no syphilis. I'm healthy. You can examine me."

A group of soldiers and officers gather around her and listen to her mumbling with astonishment. Suddenly an NCO from the division headquarters arrives, listens to her for a few moments, takes out his revolver, and shoots her dead on the spot.

"Poor rotten wormwood blossom," he says, and goes to report to the headquarters. The colonel doesn't see any reason to punish him. On the contrary, he praises his action:

"The entire village should be burnt to the ground," he says. "I'm going to request permission to do so immediately. Why, they might poison the entire division, these plague-carriers!"

While we are still standing in the street, gazing at the child's body, a very old peasant comes up to us and mutters in Polish:

"It's the damned Jewesses who started it. They taught our women to become whores, damn their unclean souls!"

Margolis looks at the old peasant, nods, and says:

"Yes, old man. The filthy Jewesses. That's right."

Then he says to me:

"Ever since we got here I've been looking for a Jewish home, to spend Sabbath evening in. There isn't a single Jew in the whole village!"

Later that day we are ordered to vacate the village.

"Plague village!" growls the colonel disgustedly. "A real plague village!"

Margolis goes up to him, stands to attention and says:

"Colonel, sir! Beg to report: Not a 'plague village,' but 'the whorish city,' as mentioned in the Bible!"[4]

Lance Corporal Margolis is pleased – he has found his chapter and verse.

The colonel's command is carried out.

"You shall save alive nothing that breathes," quotes Margolis.[5]

14 | In Death's Vestibule

WE are heading for the town of Jazlowitz, a large village not far from the town of Buczacz. When we pass through Buczacz, I stop a Jew in the street and ask him, where does the writer I. S. Agnon live?[1]

The scrawny, famished Jew stares at me as if I have gone mad. Then he says:

"You've really found something to worry about... Agnon! I wish I knew where I live!" And off he goes, muttering to himself, "I. S. Agnon, I. S. Agnon..."

The synagogue is partially destroyed. I stand in the doorway and see — a few Jews are still sitting and studying sacred texts.

Then the cannonade begins – the front is not far. Before long shells begin to fall and explode in the town. There is no panic. People keep on walking in the street, weary and despairing. Only when they hear a shell whizzing overhead do they duck slightly out of habit, and continue on their way.

The fresh recruits among us begin to sense death's wings hovering overhead. We are drawing closer and closer to Jazlowitz, just behind the lines. This is the replacement camp where soldiers who have completed training are kept available, awaiting orders.

The town is shelled sporadically but with increasing regularity, without scoring a hit.

This is the first time that I see Uncle Osterreicher praying with his shawl and phylacteries on. I find out that he never misses any of the regular daily prayers. Even on the march he drapes himself in his shawl, winds on his phylacteries and prays – solemnly, intentfully, as usual.

"What will you do on the front, Uncle?"

"What do you mean, what will I do?" he asks simply, and adds slyly "That must be the reason our sages of blessed memory ordered us to put the phylacteries on the left hand. The right one is for shooting. There must have been an agreement between our sages and His Majesty Franz Josef!"

In Jazlowitz something new enters our lives. Or, to be strictly accurate, it begins en route, before we reach Jazlowitz. This had been our hardest march so far, but then comes the order, which must have been issued by headquarters to all the forces in the vicinity, to rush towards the village as fast as possible. Evidently, the war is going badly in that sector, and we might be needed there very soon. So we begin what is called "a forced march." A forced march is hell. No quarter is given. The regiment rushes down the roads, regardless of strength or conditions on the way. Faster! Faster! Until you are ready to drop dead. The officers are on horseback and we on foot, and they prod us on and shove us with the horses. If they could, they would yell at us and we, driven like cattle, would yell back. But we are too near the front, so their rage is bottled up, and finds other outlets – spurring and whipping the horses, whip and rifle-butt blows from the NCOs, who are also in a bad way, having to run forward when their legs can barely support them. Since nothing can be done without shouting, and that is forbidden, they whisper hoarsely, cursing viciously and helplessly under their breath.

Amid the low-voiced curses I hear Colonel Johann Figer's fierce growl:

"No mercy! Don't be sorry for the men. Men don't cost money! Only horses cost money! No pity for that rabble! Rapid march! Move!"

I noticed Colonel Johann Figer some days before. A handsome Austrian gentleman, tall, blond with dark eyes, extremely elegant, he has one special feature which catches my attention – his exquisite hands. They seem carved of ivory, their fingers long and delicate like figured Japanese art. I recall the fantastic hands of the medieval Magyar queen Elizabeth Bathory, who had maidens slaughtered so as to bathe her lovely hands in their supposedly beautifying blood.[2] *Herr* Figer's manicure would do justice to a first-rate Parisian beauty salon. His voice, too, is fine and soft, a most pleasant resonant baritone, as if he is about to burst into song. I keep thinking about Petronius, whose beauty, exquisiteness and sycophancy charmed the mad Nero.[3] I think about it especially when he stands at ease, or leans in a casual, aristocratic way, talking about science, art, philosophy and love – the epitome of the man of breeding and social standing, an example to all. The jaunty smile never leaves his lips.

It's still there when he is in the saddle, speaking and issuing orders in the language of a half-krone Kärnterstrasse[4] whore. Because, once mounted, *Herr* Figer changes almost beyond recognition. That is to say, he doesn't change, but his style does. That soft pleasant purring voice acquires a completely different and shocking meaning. He looks like a mask

– the mask of *Herr* Colonel Figer worn by a thief from the Prater.[5] Softly, with an affable smile and charming elegance, he points his swagger-stick at Corporal Margolis and says:

"Hey, Lance Corporal Margolis! What are you standing there staring at me for? You think you're looking at your beautiful mother wanting to fuck her, to sow her with your Jewish syphilitic seed, huh?"

Or, to the lanky Tyrolean:

"Listen, you limp dick! I'll stuff you into my horse's ass, maybe then you'll stiffen and stand straight like one of His Majesty's soldiers!"

Sometimes, directly after such remarks, he dismounts and comes to discuss Bergson's philosophical views about laughter with us.[6]

But one thing about him that arouses our soldierly suspicions. He is slightly lame in one leg. A lame officer is either a hero or the very opposite. He might have injured himself so as to go to hospital and get leave. The tall Tyrolean, who served with Figer at the front, whispers to us:

"He's more afraid of death than of vulgarity. He put the pistol in his pocket and shot himself in the foot through his trousers. We know him."

But the most infuriating thing about Figer is his supposed sincerity. Whereas the other officers are always at pains to disguise the sheer cruelty of military discipline, by justifying it as necessary to the army, *Herr* Colonel Figer does the exact opposite. He makes the viciousness a positive end in itself – cruelty for its own sake, torture for torture's sake.

"A soldier who isn't suffering isn't a soldier," he says with a saccharine smile. "I'll make you eat shit to make regular men of you, you charming rabble!"

This reminds me of something I have forgotten in the midst of my own suffering: that it was Figer who ordered me to spit in the faces of my soldiers, back at the barracks.

As the danger of death comes closer and closer, Figer becomes more and more vicious. I remember reading about the law of the jungle, how during a storm all animals gather together and don't harm each other – the boa constrictor with the deer, the fox and the birds and the leopard all together. *Herr* Figer reverses that natural law. At the whistle of a bullet or shell his eyes narrow, plump lips tighten, and he thinks up some extra cruelty, for which he always finds a good reason in the standing orders (which stress that officers must treat the men with kindness, so as to be on good terms with them).

His order "not to have compassion for the men, because they have no cash value," isn't original. He got it from His Royal Highness the Austro-Hungarian Crown Prince Franz Ferdinand, who had been assassinated in Bosnia just before the war broke out. The crown prince was known as the "Iron General," and that order really suited him. But the way it was carried out by his subordinate officer Colonel Figer would have given even Franz Ferdinand pause.[7]

Uncle Osterreicher is a special target of Figer's ire. The old soldier simply annoys him. He doesn't dare, or perhaps doesn't think, to order him to stop praying with shawl and phylacteries. At the front, in the army in general, praying is held to be a great virtue, almost as important as profanity.

Both must have a common psychological foundation – they intoxicate. Instead of drinking, one dispels the agonies and rage by swearing or by praying. But Uncle Osterreicher's constant praying attracts *Herr* Figer's special attention. During the forced march he suddenly orders the old soldier to run in front of his horse. Ostensibly this isn't so terrible, because the colonel's horse can hardly outrun the regiment, but trots alongside our column. But Figer keeps rushing backwards and forwards all the time, to check how the regiment is marching and make sure that nobody has surreptitiously ditched any part of his equipment, to lighten the immense load. Uncle Osterreicher has to run in front of the horse almost to the end of his strength, which never completely gives out. It's really a most amusing sight – a fifty-year-old soldier, a pot-bellied Jew with a little goatee beard and worry wrinkles in his parchment face, furrowed with worry about earning his daily bread, clumsily burdened with a back-pack, a folded overcoat strapped diagonally across his body, a rifle and cartridge belt, running before the horse, groaning and grunting, sweating profusely, legs ankle deep in the mud, kneading it with a sound like a dog lapping. He runs and runs, the horse snorting and blowing on his neck through its delicate, steaming nostrils: Run, Jew, Run!

None of us can understand how this exhausted elderly Jew doesn't stumble and fall flat on his face in that cloying, heavy mud which comes up to his ankles. What mysterious force is it that keeps his soul within his body and doesn't allow it to depart? *Herr* Figer gradually affects all the other officers, and they became more like him by the day. Another officer who has direct dealing with us is First Lieutenant

Stubniak, a Hungarian Slovak and commandant of the replacement camp. He is an obvious fool who doesn't allow any conversation except about women and dogs, but doesn't understand these either.

"A beautiful woman, eh? The beast! *Canaille*![8] The filthy piece of trash! Like a beautiful bitch!" he says with a grave smile whenever a woman is mentioned.

"Fine dog, eh? Goddamn! Sacrament![9] Like a pretty woman!" He says when speaking about a dog.

There is also Second Lieutenant Jony, an officer with a Jewish face that is truly repulsive when it expresses cruelty. Eventually we find out he is a converted Jew.

"Those converted Jews," says the tall Tyrolean naïvely, "they really make one wonder if there isn't some truth in the story that Jews slaughter Christian children for Passover."

Looking at Jony's arrogant, puffy, overweening face, I think about it and say to the Tyrolean:

"You're right, my friend. If there were such Jews who were paid by the priests to do those things, they must have been like this one."

The Tyrolean quite agrees.

Then there is Ensign Szegedy, a taciturn, intelligent Magyar, who has graduated from university and was a notary in a provincial city. He has the typical provincial's arrogance, from being used to peasants kowtowing to him, greasy hat in hand. Next is the dwarf-like Ensign Slezak, a young Czech with a round florid face spry as a Chinaman, always ready to obey an order or give one. The men call him "Jumping Jack." In fact, he is the nicest of the officers, but oddly enough this makes him an object of suspicion because at this time there are rumors about "Czechoslovakian perfidy" arising from the Czech liberation movement.[10]

This movement puzzles us greatly:

Czech regiments are traditionally devoted to Austria and to Franz Josef. Crown Prince Franz Ferdinand used to call them "my Czechs," and had greater faith in them than in the Austrian regiments themselves. The newspapers had a very human explanation for it – the crown prince's wife, the Crown Princess Countess Sophie Chotek, was Czech-born, and it was she who planted an affection for her people and its regiments in her husband's heart. Naturally, uniformed men had only contempt for such journalistic idle gossip without basis in fact. But now, suddenly, there are rumors of treason amongst "my Czechs." So we look with suspicion on the amiable little officer, who is no doubt trying to disguise his secret plans under the cloak of a sympathetic facade.

There are other officers and NCOs who learn from their superiors to behave arrogantly and scornfully to the common soldiers. We become used to seeing them swaggering about with their legs far apart, as if they all suffer from venereal disease, holding their heads back proudly, thwacking their boots with their crops and speaking through their noses:

"Rabble! Miserable rabble! Civilians!"

This epithet, *civilians,* is the greatest insult. Being a civilian means being a defective, a good-for-nothing, a coward, a fool, a worthless nonentity.

In addition to the officers, there are of course those pillars of His Majesty's armed forces – the sergeants themselves. Their bite is even worse than the officers, for it is they who have to carry out the orders. The soldiers call them "carcass skinners." One of these sergeants pays my insignificant self particular attention. Not that I am exceptional in this – a sergeant always detests those who may become officers, because he is all too aware that he may in the future have to stand at attention before them and obey their orders. So he uses what opportunity he can to show them that he is still in authority over them. He is not afraid that when the day comes he may pay for it – he has an infallible method of diverting the newly minted officer's wrath from himself to the soldiers. This is almost always successful. After all, there are many soldiers, and only one sergeant.

But my own sergeant excels the traditional enmity in his attitude towards me. Perhaps because I'm a Jew, and he feels certain that the colonel will never let me become an officer, because of my Jewishness. Or perhaps he knows in advance that even if I should be made an officer, I would never pour my wrath over the heads of the soldiers, or make them my scapegoats, and they would never have to suffer in my place.

It is here in Jazlowitz, in the rear of the front, that the officers' crops begin to thwack their boots with the greatest intensity and determination. They devise all kinds of methods "to accustom the men to the hardships of the front and strengthen their hearts in the face of war." First Lieutenant Erich Stubniak, a professional athlete, orders some of his men to run two hundred paces back and forth, and at each end of the track he stations a sergeant, whose business it is to see to it that every man, on arrival, pronounces correctly, without mistake, seven times in a row, the following words:

Allerhöchster Kriegsherr Seine Majestät Kaiser und König Franz Josef der Erste! (The Supreme Commander, His Majesty Emperor and King, Franz Josef the First!)

This treatment is applied with special care to the Magyars, to whom this German phrase is harder than swallowing a toad, and who loathe the German language even more than they loathe the sergeant.

Lieutenant Jony makes one of his soldiers eat five cigarettes, because he didn't throw away his cigarette when he, the officer, stopped him on the path.

The taciturn Ensign Szegedy makes his batman drink up the contents of his spittoon, as punishment for spitting on the floor in his quarters. The poor fellow retches up green vomit afterwards.

Mr. "Jumping Jack" catches a traitor trying to desert to the enemy camp during the night. Before handing him over to the court martial, he contrives his own punishment – he binds him and places him under a dripping tap, which drips on his head, drop by drop, all night long. The following morning, when the unfortunate man faces the court martial, he keeps gnawing the skin of hand, by reason of insanity.

This amiable Czech officer also changes, out of fear. He sees that his humane treatment of his soldiers is arousing suspicion. Everybody thinks that he is doing it out of cowardice, to cover his inner sympathies with the illegal Czech liberation movement. So he strives to be as brutal as the rest of the officers.

All this takes place under the direct command, and with full permission, of Colonel Figer, who is the Provisional Judge-Advocate General in that sector. (Later it transpires that the unfortunate soldier had not tried to desert at all, but that Ensign Slezak had done what he did – according to Figer's defense of him – "as a strict and conscientious officer, to prevent any possibility of such treasonous desertion.")

All this in death's vestibule, right next to the inferno, in a place where any one of us could at any moment be hit by a bullet and die. One of the soldiers says in a low voice that he cannot understand where all these wild beasts have suddenly come from. My young batman replies:

"Beasts? What beast does such things? Beasts don't hate at all, they simply want to eat."

My young batman generally keeps his mouth shut and performs his duties in exemplary fashion. But he guards me like the apple of his eye, and reports everything said by the officers to me. He picks up information in the officers' kitchen, where he meets the other batmen. He comes to cherish a deep-seated grudge and deadly hatred for anyone with officer's insignia on his collar. One day he reveals to me that First Lieutenant Stubniak has decided that I will never be made officer.

"That's none of your business, Pály," I say.

He burns with anger:

"All right. See if I care!" and walks off sullenly.

I call after him:

"What are you so afraid of? You'll find an officer to serve instead of me."

He stops in the doorway, rears up like a snake and bursts out in fury:

"Don't you dare pack me off to other people, sir! I'm not a whore!" He turns to go, but then stops and adds warmly:

"I wouldn't serve any of those rabbits pretending to be wolves! There isn't one among them who can boast the most insignificant medal on his cowardly chest! Why, even his piggishness hasn't so much as a lousy *signum laudis*! Instead he has a limp... A gun in his pocket!"

The *signum laudis* (badge of honor) is the lowest decoration for officers, a bronze medal.

That evening I'm summoned by First Lieutenant Stubniak, who forbids me to employ a batman. In vain do I try to explain to him that my batman has not been relieved of any of soldiers' regular duties, and that he has volunteered to serve me of his own accord and not at the cost of anything else he has to do. Stubniak thunders in his crackling voice:

"If he so much as polishes even one of your boots, you'll get solitary confinement! And you'll be bound!"

To be bound means being tied up against the wall, standing on tip-toe for hours.

A few moments later my batman comes in with my dinner, and on being told about the new order he stands to attention as if before an officer and shouts:

"Ensign, sir! Beg to report: I shall not leave you!"

"Go away, you fool!" I say. "You shouldn't address me by a title I don't have!"

"Ensign, sir! Beg to report: Tomorrow we go to the front, and there it will be us and not those rabbits who will decide!"

I scarcely have time to finish my supper when the order comes – tomorrow, at four in the morning, we are to go to the front.

We are ordered to lie down until four. My platoon is quartered in a large granary with its roof torn off, so that we can see the stars. Stars twinkle far away.

We lie down. Beside me lies my batman, who covers me carefully, like a tender mother. The approaching danger makes the young Magyar grow even more attached to me.

There is stony silence for a while. Suddenly we hear a distant cannonade, which keeps coming closer. I rise and go to my commanding officer, Lieutenant Jony, to see if there are any new orders.

Jony is in bed. He answers irritably:

"Go away! Go to sleep! What do you expect of me? It doesn't depend on me, but on the Russians!"

Strange. What a brilliant commander. It depends on the Russians. I cannot resist saying:

"Well, if it depends on the Russians, we're really in trouble!" and I turn to leave. When I reach the door I see that he has raised his head from the pillow and is glaring at me.

When I returned my batman is not there; As soon as I lie down – without undressing, of course – he returns.

"Where have you been prowling around at night?"

"I also wanted to study a little strategy, and see on whom it depends – us or the Russians."

He spits, disgustedly: "Pfui!"

I realize that he has followed me and overheard what the officer said to me. He lies down again and mutters fiercely:

"Why do you look for trouble, sir? Why go outside?"

"You're a fool, Pály. You think this barn is safer than any other place, inside or out?"

There is a lull. Then again, the low muffled sound of a Russian cannon. (Russian cannons have a different sound from our own) It's followed by a low shrieking sound which grows louder and louder, crescendoing over our heads, flying past like the angel of death and exploding nearby.

All sleepy heads are raised, looking at each other.

"Welcome!" says the tall Tyrolean. "*Dratuste*!" (Only a year later I discovered that he meant *Zdravstvuyte*, meaning "welcome" in Russian).

"God damn! says another. They don't even let a man gaze at the stars in peace!"

After that shell comes another, and yet another. I look at the men and see that they have all curled up tightly in their blankets, hedgehog-fashion, against the shells.

The lanky Tyrolean, who has rolled himself up so tight that he manages to look like a bear preparing to hibernate, grunts from inside his blanket:

"There's no better protection from Russian bombs than a blanket!"

15 | My Man Friday

AT THREE O'CLOCK they wake us up. "To the front!"

Strange – this is the second time that I'm at the front, and yet the sensation is new and so is the fear. Back then everything happened in a flash. Suddenly, hastily and shockingly, so that I didn't even have time to realize what was actually happening. This whole business, from the wild train journey and attack on the Cossacks in the Carpathians, to my brief passing out and finding myself in the hospital – was like a bad dream, a nightmare in a storm, continued noisily, ended by the hospital nurse with the gentle face and blue eyes, who smiled at me and stroked me, as if I were in paradise.

Here now are brand new faces. We enter a covered trench, with slits facing the enemy bunker. I calculate that the trench must be hundreds of kilometers long – from Czernowitz to Riga.[1] That's all.

We enter it at 4:00 p.m. exactly, walking down a steep path that leads from the outskirts of the village into our bunker, under a hailstorm of deadly bullets and explosions.

When we are all inside, we check each other. It's all right, we're all here. Faces look happy and pleased, as if we are safe inside the fortress of Przemysl.[2] Already we are accustomed to the roaring overhead, as if we have an agreement with the Russians to shoot *over* our trench, beyond our own lines.

We have absolutely nothing to do for the moment, having to wait for orders from above. Meantime they divide us into squads, and I am put in charge of a company of thirty men. I introduce myself to my new gang, and immediately recognize in it some splendid fellows, with whom one could die together lovingly. I don't know how it happened, but suddenly among them I discover Uncle Osterreicher and Lance Corporal Margolis. I am glad to see them. But there are other familiar faces there. The giant, ingenuous Tyrolean, standing smiling and announcing: "Sir! Johann Maria Braedl, infantryman, begs to report: there is no news!"

I shake his hand and hug him. My head reaches exactly to the middle of his flat chest.

The whistling overhead never stops. I check the rest of the men. There is the stunted Serbian, the half-Magyar, half-Serbian, "bastard," from the province of Banat.[3] His face is full of scars made by human beings – cuts and bites. One of his ears is partly bitten off. He has already won himself a reputation, even in the press, as one who, in a bayonet battle, would drop his weapon and attack the enemy, biting, scratching and choking.

"Sergeant sir! Laszlo Krechen, infantryman, begs to report: I'm an 'old fossil,' sir! Twice wounded!"

"Fine, my friend. I see."

Next I see the Croatian giant with the gold medal on his chest. He speaks broken Hungarian, but refuses to use any other language. He'll be a Magyar at all costs! Moreover, he is peeved because he did not get drafted into the "Homeland Defense Army," which is pure Magyar,[4] and instead has to serve in the joint Austro-Hungarian Army.[5] If one must die, one ought to die as a Magyar! He is the first person who impresses upon me the astonishing assimilatory capacity of the Magyar race, which is like no other in the world. He approaches me:

"Sergeant sir! Franz Rizic, infantryman, begs to report: Please could I be transferred to the 32nd Honvéd Regiment (for Defense of the Homeland)?"

"Don't you want to die with me, Rizic?"

"Beg to report: I would like to, but..."

"I know, my friends, I know. All right, we'll bury you with other Magyars."

He lowers his thick, trumpet-like nose.

Then there is fat Rosenberger, shaped like a barrel, very young, about nineteen, and as full of stories as a pomegranate is with seeds. He has a joke or proverb for every occasion, and it's impossible to shut him up. He volunteered, and has already risen to the rank of corporal.

"Sir! Corporal Bernat Rosenberger begs to report: at your orders, sir!"

"All right, just don't bother me with your stories just now."

Rosenberger grins broadly.

"Beg to report: It's hard to give up jokes at the front. Hangman Bali once asked one of the condemned men what was his last wish. The man said he'd like to hear a good joke. So the hangman told him this joke."

"Which joke?"

"Beg to report: The one I've just told!"

A few shells whine over the trench and freeze the mouths open in laughter.

Further:

"Lance Corporal Andras Madi begs to report: I'm an actor in the national theatre in Debrecen."[6]

"What sort of parts did you play?"

"Lackey parts."

Fat Rosenberger, speaking as a corporal without permission, interrupts:

"He turned the electricity on and off during 'Hamlet'!"

A deep, vulgar belly laugh arises at this and the actor reddens with suppressed, bitter anger. He quite literally gnashes his teeth.

"Who are you?" I ask the one who laughed. A big swarthy soldier, standing beside the actor.

"Beg to report: Benvenuto Gallieri, infantryman."

"Italian?"

"Yes, from Fiume."[7]

"Why did you laugh?"

"There are no lights in 'Hamlet.' The whole play takes place during the day."[8]

"Aha! During the day... And if it took place in the night?"

The Italian has no answer to this.

"What was your profession at home?"

"Cobbler, but also an expert leather worker."

I meet two more members of this Austro-Hungarian melting-pot. One is a student who, like me, has failed to become an officer, but hasn't even reached the rank of corporal. A coquettish fop who prinks and primps like a girl, he looks as if he uses lipstick. The other is a sculptor who has already exhibited his work with some success. His name is known to me, but we've hardly begun to talk when a commotion breaks out – the assault!

It's a ferocious, desperate battle. For two days it goes on at shelling distance, then we close in and fight with bayonets.

The Russians retreat, we occupy some of their trenches, and on the fourth day enter the town of Chestochowa.[9] We take it in blood, after a monstrous fight and many casualties.

We put up fortifications, and settle down for a little respite. I check my company: six killed and two seriously wounded. When the losses become known a deep, horrified silence falls over the company. I walk to and fro through the heavy silence, and suddenly hear my tall simple Tyrolean saying in a solemn voice: "They are lucky (*sie habens Gut*). They don't have a sergeant anymore."

I notice that our own sergeant is standing nearby and listening. He slinks up to me with soft predatory leopard steps and says:

"Watch out! You're spoiling the men!"

Then he goes up to the Tyrolean, pushes his bristly moustache into his face, and says, gritting his teeth:

"You'll eat a few more rats before you're rid of the sergeant!"

In the battle report which I have to submit to command, I mention the men who have shown outstanding courage and daring. Among these are Margolis, Uncle Osterreicher, and the Tyrolean. Margolis, the scrawny *yeshiva* student, bobbing through the tumult like a maddened bee whose hive has been invaded by wasps. Several times it was necessary to stop him from assaulting the Russian line single-handed with nothing but his gun, which he reloads with amazing speed.

Old Uncle Osterreicher, of course, did not fail to say his prayers with the phylacteries – though this time without the prayer shawl – and meantime fought on fearlessly. Together with the goyim[10] he yelled challenges and encouragement: "For our people and for God's cities!"[11] "In Your salvation I trust, O Lord!"[12]

I report all this in German.

The tall simple Tyrolean moves through the battle like a tank, his long legs stepping over all obstacles, trenches and broken fences, lighting cigarette after cigarette, and muttering furiously: "*Verfluchtes Biest!* (God-damn beast!)"

When I hand my report to my officer, Second Lieutenant Jony, he looks at it, reads it through, and tears it to pieces.

"Not so fast, my friend," he says, his eyes narrowing into slits. "You think the whole war is made just for medals?"

He thwacks his whip against his boots and turns to go. Then he looks back:

"Make out a simple report, without any heroics and smart alec statements. Drill in half an hour!"

Half an hour later we have a drill. At the front. This is something quite new to me. I have never heard of such a thing: in the trenches, in death's vestibule – drill, marches, standing to attention, calling on "The Supreme Commander, His Imperial Majesty Franz Josef the First!" and all the rest? And it's a proper drill, too, with all the vicious tricks and pranks known from base camp: running up and down, being made to eat cigarettes, and all the other inventions which here, in death's maw, are especially witty and imaginative. But the soldiers act very differently here. There is a kind of hilarity all along the line. At first I can't understand where those high spirits have come from. At any rate, the simple men take the torments that their officers inflict on them in their stride, with a jesting spirit that holds more contempt and mockery than pain. The tall naïve Tyrolean is ordered to run up and down the entrenchment twenty times. When he finishes the twentieth run he doesn't stop but keeps on running. The sergeant yells at him in vain, the man doesn't stop until the NCO grabs him by the arm. Standing, he goes on muttering automatically: "Fourteen, fourteen, fourteen."

"What fourteen, you idiot?"

"Fourteen!" the Tyrolean replies, with feigned naïveté. "The fourteenth run. I have to run six more times, sir!" He lies innocently and quite seriously.

At this point his comrades dare to chuckle quietly. Their laughter is poison to the "carcass skinner."

"You wait, you wait!" he says through gritted teeth. "I'll teach you military etiquette!"

He leaves, looking back at me with an ominous expression. We're relieved to see the back of him. The fellows sit down and began to talk, about the cursed battle, which has lasted for several days and in which three men – Margolis, the Tyrolean and Uncle Osterreicher – have distinguished themselves. Reports of their bravery have spread throughout the battalion. Everybody expects that the three will be commended and decorated, and their bravery makes the others smile. I begin to ask myself what made those men fight like lions, with such single-minded courage. I ask Margolis about it in private. He answers simply:

"How do I know? In such a panic you've got to do something. So what do you do? Stand by and look on? Or give other people orders, like *Herr* First Lieutenant Stubniak?"

Uncle Osterreicher explains it thus:

"I think that the main thing is Warsaw. If we take Warsaw we'll go home. My grandson will have his Bar Mitzvah a month from now, and I've got to be there. He's preparing a very fine speech. He's a lovely little prankster."

I ask the Tyrolean why he kept on shouting "*Verfluchtes Biest*" so furiously. Does he really hate the Russians so much?

"The Russians?" replied the Tyrolean. It's the sergeant. He's the goddamn beast! The accursed vermin! Blast him!"

"Aha."

Again I think about that word with which they ignite all the wars in the world – patriotism.

The actor Madi, who doesn't know I am a Jew, curses the Jews.

"Back there, in the theater, they gave me lackey parts," he says resentfully. "And here they're in line for medals! That rotten little yid," he means Margolis, "kept jumping up and showing off to get a medal. And you'll see, sir – he'll get it. He will. He won't rest until he's decorated. You hear, sir – the Jews everywhere are saying that our recent victory was due to the Jewish officers. Captain Schlesinger! I know him. He's a Jewish teacher who's afraid of his own shadow. Suddenly he's a hero! And that Margolis," he repeated enviously, "that rotten Margolis. That 'ay vay vay!'" He grimaces and spits.

"Why do you hate him so much?" I ask.

"Hate that choleric dog? Who hates him? You can't even hate that lot – they just make one sick!"

When I reveal to him that I am a Jew as well, he is not embarrassed. Speaking frankly, like a man who has nothing to lose, he says briefly: "My bad luck. Even here, I'm in the hands of a Jew!" From that day he attaches himself to the sergeant, who takes him under his benevolent wing and into his good graces. They scheme how to get at me.

The first is to take away my orderly, who has returned to me against orders. It's a tough nut to crack, because he is a regular soldier, and not, like officers' orderlies, exempt from general routine. So when the sergeant orders him to leave me, he answers:

"Sergeant, sir, beg to report: I volunteered freely to serve, and I also volunteered to serve the *Herr* sergeant of my own free will. I don't do it at the expense, but in addition to, military duties,"

But Second Lieutenant Jony finds a way – he commandeers him as his own orderly.

Then the Tyrolean turns up and announces: "Sir, today I'll bring you your dinner."

I feel rather strange being served by that giant soldier, who towers over me. But it doesn't last long. Pály comes in and states, quite openly and without lowering his voice:

"The first evening I shall dedicate one of His Majesty's bullets to him!"

"To whom, boy?"

"To that converted Jew! What do you need such disgusting Jews for? He makes me sick."

"Shh, don't shout, stupid! If you say such things again I'll knock your block off. Understand? Now march, make yourself scarce!"

The young soldier stands to attention and leaves me in correct, military style.

But precisely because of that, because he leaves me without another word, I grow very anxious. He will keep his word. That young Magyar, faithful as a dog and brave as a lion, doesn't beat about the bush. Lately, having tasted death, he has become totally fearless and resolute. He guards my honor like an intelligent Doberman Pinscher, who smells his master's enemy's every move from afar. The slightest injury to my honor, the merest hint against me, sinks into him like a poison, which ferments until it explodes. It has caused him to hate Second Lieutenant Jony and all antisemites with a ferocity that makes me wonder about his own origins.

"Tell me, Pály. Are there any Jews in your family?" The lad looks at me and answers simply:

"I'm a pure Christian, sir.[13] There are no Judas Iscariots in my family."

Wham!

"Well, then," I go on cautiously, "do you think all Jews should be despised as the betrayers of Christ?"

The youngster falls into confusion. He can't understand my question. What does he know? What am I getting at? This was what he was taught: "Judas Iscariot." What could possibly be the connection between his sergeant and that Iscariot? He loves his sergeant better than anyone in the whole battalion, and wouldn't permit anyone say a word against him.

I continue to question him.

"Do you hate Margolis?"

"Me, sir? Why should I hate him?"

"And Uncle Osterreicher?

"On the contrary, I love him. He prays for all of us."

"And Corporal Rosenberger?"

Finally he understands, "You think I'm an antisemite, sir? No! My father is a tenant on *Herr* Baron Freund-Tosegy's estate, and there is no Christian better than he. But, sir, if you think that I hate Jews," he adds in some confusion, "then...well, then, I'll leave you, if you want me to, sir."

I reassure him, saying that I should very much like him to be my friend and orderly. However, the second lieutenant wants him for himself.

The lad thinks a little and then said, as if speaking to himself: "That won't last long... But, sir, watch out for the 'carcass skinner.' He's a foul snake, and we have to be careful."

Then he returns to his new master, Second Lieutenant Jony.

That evening the first lieutenant appoints me quarter-master in charge of provisions and supplies for the entire platoon. I don't understand – why me? This is always the sergeant's responsibility. While I am thinking about it, my young orderly comes in and whispers:

"Don't take it on, sir. It's a dirty trick."

"You're a fool!"

"I'm a fool, sir. But it's a dirty trick. Please, sir, think up some way to avoid it. Believe me!"

I cannot think of any way to avoid carrying out the order, so I became the company quartermaster. Not an easy job, but not especially difficult at the front, and I do it competently. My men are very pleased. "Closer to the feedbags," they think. In a sense they are right. There are two self-evident truths in the army: one is that, while stealing at the front is a capital crime, it is quite legitimate to steal from the neighboring regiment. Secondly, while it's a punishable offence to appropriate special rations to favorites, it's only reasonable, in fact commendable, to give your own men generous portions.

Only my young orderly, who sneaks over to me whenever he can, is displeased about my new appointment, but can't explain why. He suspects something evil. He doesn't know what it is, but has a premonition of something evil that is sure to come to me (or, as he puts it, "to us") from this assignment.

Two days later the inferno begins again – a great offensive all along the front. As soon as the firing and the noise begin, my orderly turns, up and shouts respectfully:

"Sir – beg to report: I'm back!"

"You get back there at once, understand?

"Beg to report, sir: I won't!" he yells above the noise and commotion.

From behind me comes the voice of the tall Tyrolean:

"*Nicht lassen! Nicht lassen, Freitag!* (Don't leave him! Don't leave him, Man Friday!)"

We all rush out of the trench, towards death.

16 | I Am a Pilloried Thief

MY MEN'S affection for me isn't hard to understand. In addition to the spiritual community that I find under death's black wings, I also establish a material one, by distributing my allowance and the many gifts (mostly chocolate, delicacies, cigarettes, sent me from the city) amongst my comrades in danger. Some of them send the chocolates to their sweethearts and the small amounts of money to their mothers. For a few pennies sent to his mother, a humble Magyar can be a dog and a lion at the same time.

But gradually this affection becomes a source of hatred for me by the officers, a hatred stronger than death itself. If the mutual regard between me and my men began in the barracks, when I disobeyed the colonel's order to spit in their faces, here in the jaws of death, it has become genuine love. Money means nothing to me. I am so certain that I will soon die, that the only feeling left is the question, *When?*

One thing that puzzles me greatly is the elegant appearance of the officers whenever there is a break in the action. They spend their entire allowance, large or small, on clothes and fripperies. The most outstanding in this regard is the elegant *Herr* Figer, who lacks only earrings to complete the picture. His fingers are bedecked with gold rings set with precious stones, on his wrists are costly platinum bracelets, set with jewels. Those same decorations excoriated in women by the Prophet Isaiah.[1] By contrast, ordinary soldiers send the pittance they receive to their families – one to an aged mother, another to a wife, sister, or sweetheart, probably waiting for him back there with eyes swollen with hope and sorrow.

Thus our communal ways are anathema to officers, who retaliate by continuously transferring men in and out of my company. Second Lieutenant Jony, he of the Jewish physiognomy, keeps an especially sharp and hostile eye on me. He is my direct superior, and his loathing for me is reinforced by the fact that I am known to be a Jewish writer, and a Zionist. He is quite terrified that his comrades find out that he is a converted Jew himself.

His overriding fear is that I might be made an officer. There is only one sure method to forestall such a development – have me punished for some infringement of the regulations. The accusation alone, let alone the punishment for it, could keep me in my present rank.

The most recent battle, which raged for ten horrendous days around Czestochowa[2] and costs us many losses, brings about some changes in our regiment. It becomes known that almost all the Jewish officers have distinguished themselves by exceptional bravery. Most of the important achievements – taking of a strategically important hill, wood, village or seizure of a Russian battery, cannons, high-ranking captives – were done by Jewish officers, in fewer cases by Hungarian officers, never by Austrians. It may have been mere chance, but a fact is a fact, however maddening. It's the devil's work. And so the suppressed hatred begins to surface. The first to give it expression are Austrian officers. It comes to the point that a certain Jewish officer, Captain Neumann, is court martialed after an exceptionally victorious sally. Only he, his batman, and six soldiers survive the battle, and the eight of them not only drive a strong Russian battalion from its stronghold, but capture its heavy cannons, and a Russian colonel into the bargain. The charge is stupid, ridiculous and vicious: "Wasting ammunition!" (Meaning, presumably, that the victory was not worth the bullets). Further, it is charged that the officer "had used his batman as a shield to protect himself."

The rumor spreads through the camp like a shockwave. Captain Neumann was a teacher in his home town. He is a graduate of the only Jewish Teachers' College in Budapest, and has studied under Professors Bacher and Banozzi.[3] The charge against him is brought by Colonel Figer. But in the meantime, during the battle, an insignificant event occurs which only Pály notices – Figer has appointed the young convert Lieutenant Jony as his adjutant. This, to Pály, solves the mystery – the devilish cabal against Captain Neumann was Jony's perverted brain child.

The entire regiment impatiently awaits this disgraceful court-martial.

Some look forward to it with glee, others think about it with disgust and helplessness. Pály has an insane look about him, but is perfectly silent, like a person planning something terrible.

But before the trial can take place however, there is another assault and the trial is postponed indefinitely. Meantime I get a new commanding officer, a Magyar lieutenant, a devout Protestant,[4] bull-necked, taciturn and formidably honest. He has just been discharged from hospital, and when he hears about the court-martial he says to me:

"What sort of whorehouse have you made of this front?! What the hell is the charge?"

When I tell him that it is "wasting ammunition," his swarthy face grows even darker:

"What the hell? Is His Majesty suffering from a shortage of ammunition?"

He thinks a moment, then asks me:

"You're a Jew?"

"Yes, sir."

"Well then, tell me the truth, straight and without prejudice: how are the Jews in your company behaving?"

"Sir, you'll see with your own eyes and judge for yourself."

When the battle rages he sees for himself, and makes up his mind. He at once commends three men – the Tyrolean, Margolis and Uncle Osterreicher. The Tyrolean to be promoted to corporal, Margolis to sergeant and Uncle Osterreicher for a gold medal. This medal brings with it a financial reward, too, which means a great deal to the veteran Uncle Osterreicher, who has a dependent family.

He recommends that I be made an officer, an ensign.

I begin to stammer something about having little hopes of the recommendation being confirmed, since Colonel Figer…

He pierces me with his eyes and yells murderously:

"Shut up! I recommended you! I won't be a captain in a whorehouse! Dismiss!"

Among the battle casualties in our regiment – which comes to a total of 150 – is Lieutenant Jony.

The postmortem shows that the fatal shot came from behind. That is not unusual, since even in the course of battle people turn this way and that, and can easily get shot in the back. But the Tyrolean comments:

"A coward gets shot in the back, when running away from the enemy!"

Pály looks at him – he has not left my side throughout the assault:

"Don't curse him now he's dead. He was a bastard, but he didn't run away from this bullet."

Nobody understands, but these words pierce my heart like an arrow. I am astonished. I call him aside, make him stand to attention, and look at him for a long while. He looks right back at me for several moments, but finally cannot contain himself and says:

"I did it, sir!"

"You wretch!" I say. "What have you done? Don't you know what you'll get for doing this?"

"I know, sir. Don't worry, sir. I'll turn myself in to the court-martial. At your command, sir!"

I put my hand over his mouth:

"Keep your mouth shut, Infantryman Pály! Don't dare say a word without my permission! Understood?! Dismiss!"

He marches off, and half an hour later I am ordered to appear before the colonel. I am certain that I will return an officer. Instead, His Exquisiteness Herr Figer informs me with icy nonchalance:

"You wish to become an officer? You? Well then, you'll have to wait a little, until you've expiated your crime. I have been informed that you've embezzled your soldiers' money and rations."

"Sir…!"

"Shut up, *Herr* One Year Volunteer *Zugsführer*![5] Go tell your sergeant to bind you for two hours. Dismiss!"

I leave him more dead than alive, my head is spinning.

Me, a thief? A common thief?

I have stolen the soldiers' money!

Good Lord!

Me, of all people! My own soldiers' money!

Pály is white as a sheet. His virginal, dark-blue eyes look almost red, like the eyes of a wolf stalking its prey. He manages to say, in a tearful voice:

"That's Jony's legacy!"

Then he adds: "That actor, Madi. I saw him whispering to the sergeant."

The sergeant carries out the order. In the center of our trench is a kind of hut, which some officer or other must have had built for himself in an earlier round of fighting. It is on slightly raised ground, and a direct target not only for bullets but also for the heavy guns. In this damned hut, the sergeant makes me – the officer-candidate – stretch out on the makeshift cot. He ties my right hand to my left leg and says with sergeantly compassion:

"I'm sorry you slipped up this time. Out of respect for you I'm binding only one leg to one arm, and not both. You were given two hours. Stay here about half an hour, then untie yourself and get up."

As he is leaving, he repeats, quite seriously:

"Sorry you slipped up this time."

The blood rushes to my head:

"I shit on you, you red heifer!"[6] (He is red-headed.) I tell him in his own language: "My forefathers in ancient days used to throw this stuff which you accuse me of stealing to dogs like you. Get out of here, before I spit in your face!"

He is thunderstruck. It's the first time in my life that I see a sergeant startled by someone of lower rank. He makes no reply, but by the time he reaches the doorway he recovers and says to me, with an evil smile under his moustache:

"Look out!"

I lie on the wooden cot like a leper, and devote my time to thinking about my predicament. I come to the conclusion that my punishment is by way of "tit for tat." Because I have distributed my allowance among the soldiers, I am now accused of stealing their allowances for myself.

It's in keeping with the prevailing logic.

But before half an hour has passed my philosophizing comes to an abrupt halt. The Russians begin firing at us, at first in a broad sweep all along the sector and then, gradually, they begin to concentrate their fire around my little hut. The act of the devil himself. For a moment I think (a man is capable of fall sorts of foolishness in such a situation) that the colonel has arranged this attack with the Russians, to punish me. But things get more frightening by the minute. Shells fall all around my hut. It is not built parallel with the enemy line, but one corner is at a right angle to them. I am lying in a corner to the left of this central point, which faces north.

This is the Russian line:

This is our line:

This is the hut
with the cot on the
left:

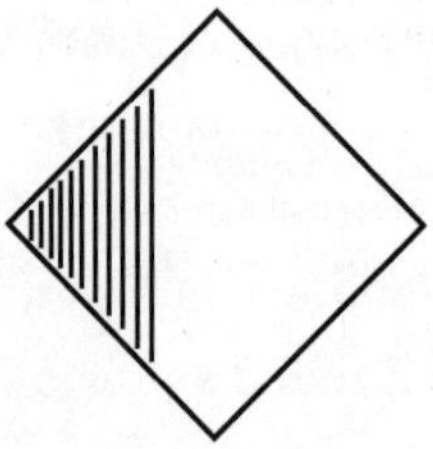

The shells keep falling.

Some fly over the hut, some explode before they reach me. I place my soul in the hands of the All-Merciful.

The sergeant has told me I need only lie there for half an hour, but a primitive stubbornness forces me to remain in my place for the full two hours. What? To live by the grace of the sergeant? Oh no! To die? What's the difference whether it is today or tomorrow? Suddenly a shell shrieks and almost concusses me, followed by an explosion.

I must be alive, because I feel pain.

The shell has sliced off the right-hand corner of the hut. Three corners are left, with the small addition of the two walls which still constitute the eastern and western corners,

Suddenly Pály appears, eyes bloodshot and tearful, and tries to drag me outside, against my will. I struggle with him, and explain that I don't want to profit from the sergeant's generosity. He lets go of me and says:

"You're right, sir."

Without another word he lies down beside me, muttering:

"I won't leave here either."

I don't try to drive him away. I know my man, and also – why deny it? – it's good to have someone beside me in the jaws of death. The devil knows what this means. Egoism? – I have no time to think about it, because shells are coming down fast and furious. We hug each other like two miserable insects, shriveled almost to the point of suffocation, and wait for the end to come. Hand-grenades fly all about the hut, whistling, stretching my already taut nerves to the point of snapping. I almost dare not breathe.

Two more corners of the hut are torn off, only one little corner remains standing, like a defective *Sukkoth* tabernacle with two incomplete walls and a roof. The shelling does not cease, but the Russians begin to aim their cannonade further away.

Suddenly I see the sergeant standing before us. He too is deathly pale, trying to speak and stuttering:

"What... what... wwwhat are you doing here?" he asks Pály.

The youngster looks back at him and answers calmly:

"I'm lying here dreaming about the sergeant's accidental death!"

The sergeant is stunned. He has probably never been spoken to so presumptuously by a soldier. Then he screams:

"Get out of here!"

"Stay, Pály!" I command.

Pály, unable to contain himself, adds:

"My place is beside my *Herr* ensign!"

A diabolical smile plays on the sergeant's lips. He stands over us leg stretched wide, swaying back and forth triumphantly:

"Perhaps you'll promote him ensign, eh, little boy?"

Then he screams at him again:

"Go and report!"

He leaves.

We do not get off the cot until the full two hours are over. Then we both present ourselves to my new superior officer, and I report to him as required by regulations:

"Sir, beg to report: I have received my punishment for stealing the men's allowances and embezzling their rations!"

The lieutenant doesn't understand. He thinks that I have gone out of my mind.

"What?!" he shrieks. "What did you say?"

I repeat my report. The officer grabs my shoulders and shakes me:

"Are you out of your mind?!" he roars.

"No, sir. At least, it is not I who is mad."

I explain the entire affair to him. He paces up and down like a caged lion, then suddenly stops in his tracks and says, quietly, as if speaking to himself:

"I'm going to put a stop to all this swinishness!"

He turns to my batman, standing to attention beside me:

"What about you?"

"Lieutenant, sir, beg to report: I could not leave my superior in that bitch of a situation!"

He explains the whole issue to him – about the hut, the shelling, everything.

The lieutenant listens, thinks, and then says:

"Come, show me the place!"

We show him the place, and he fumes with suppressed rage. He starts to walk away, then goes back to the hut, walks away, and returns again. Finally he makes up his mind:

"I shall put a stop to all this!" He looks me up and down. as if wondering how I survived it. Then he rebukes me for not leaving the hut when the shelling began. Not only was I permitted to do so – it was my duty! The punishment was not supposed to be death. When I explain to him why I stayed, I see in his face a terrible rage mingled with a kind of satisfaction. Finally he takes us to his quarters, gives us some cognac, and sends Pály back to his duties. He and I remain alone, drinking in silence, for about a quarter of an hour. Suddenly he stands up, raises his glass to me and says:

"A toast! To you, *Herr* Ensign – I drink to your health!"

We drink up, and he adds:

"Go and sew on your ensign's insignia. I guarantee it!"

When I return to my dugout and tell this to Pály, he does not jump up for joy. He makes me take off my tunic and, with a kind of joyous solemnity, sews the officer's insignia on the collar.

The following morning it is announced that I have been promoted ensign.

17| Hanina My Son[1]

War, madness, tempted fire and misery
And crowds drenched in prayer and blood—
Hanina my son, melody of all tempest,
Why has my joyful, divine spirit left
Your warm heart?
Beautiful is the cheer that your verse has killed—
Hanina my son, for all your life
You have hoped for these.

All your rhyme-stricken life,
You have thrust your two eyes through night's red glow,
They forever blaze, prisoner of mighty death,
With divine dying.
You have guided your heart
To receive the face of God;
And now, as thousands of suns yearn for you
Hanina my son, why do you fear
To gaze down the abyss?

Why have you set your eyes on the grave
Into which your tired image casts the past's harvest?
Hanina my son, will son of man perish
Where darkness spreads in the light of galaxies
And its song of mourning?
Did you not know that pain is welcome,
And sorrow is divine, divine seven-fold,
For my pure sons?

Sorrow is divine: I will reveal my secret to you:
My stormy worlds are sorrow's offspring:
Blessed is he who believes in my sorrow, which destroys
And designs all creatures: from bloody ant cells
To the horns of oryxes.
What else do affliction and despair come to teach you
Hanina my son, but that you are the groom of blood
And a Jew?

All my stormy world, holy to you,
Has been created for the family of song
For the Haninaites, elevating every sigh,
To a symphony for creating worlds beyond measure,
To a hymn of the abyss.
Hanina my son, look up on high:
The great brightness gradually blinds
With the light of the end of days.

The great brightness: this is the apple of my eye
At which all your living days you have gazed at with
  courage
The great brightness: where you may see me
While your tears enrapture you for a moment
And give life to verse.
All of life's joys are seen from this vantage:
In your mother's lullaby, your wife's kiss,
In idea and language.

This sorrow-filled crowd
Will amaze with its doom your tender heart:
Hanina, my son, rise up from the storm
Your hair burning in the sun,
And break out in song.
Happy is the hurrah and lovely is the reward,
Blessed is the lost, Hanina my son,
Who is not brought to the grave.

18 | Inferno

AT FIRST I hardly know myself how I feel when my batman dresses me in the tunic with its officer's collar insignia. Generally speaking, of course, I am glad, pleased and amazed. For the past four months I have been an NCO, giving orders, cursing and swearing like a sergeant, eating filth, drinking the undrinkable, crawling on my belly through muck and mud, preying zealously on mankind. I have even been declared a thief! In short, a proper soldier. Nevertheless, I experience a moment's shame at becoming an officer.

This atavistic shame, a leftover from the days before the deluge (namely, the war), is fully borne out by the present situation. To be a boon companion of Messrs. Stubniak or Figer is hardly an honor. And yet, I'm a soldier now, a totally different man. Then, when I recall that I may one day return to civilian life, I am deeply perplexed – what will I do among all those civilians? There is another strange thing – for all my loathing for *Herr* Figer, I have nevertheless – why deny it? – been doing everything possible to please him, and not only by his order. No, really… it's odd, but true.

I feel a momentary embarrassment of the new officer standing in my uniform. But only for a moment. The next moment I am perfectly contented. I look at myself in the mirror, which Pály holds up for me, and am pleased with what I see. I even find an excuse to justify my pleasure – from now on I will not have to carry the heavy burden of rucksack and heavy rifle. No more. Instead, I will carry a beautiful lightweight revolver. What a charming weapon. It's a pleasure to shoot it. You aim with one hand, as if it were a game, at that head over there – press, and Boom! – the head droops and the whole body sags and falls. Oh no, it's not just a shot, not a simple killing – it's something greater and deeper than that! Life and death held in one of my own hands. Just as my own life lies in the hands of some fellow over there.

And, of course, there are the creature comforts of an officer's existence. Not to mention the joy of my batman – now he's a regular, recognized batman. How he rejoices that I am finally, at long last, an officer! Now that is truly selfless joy. My own delight is really a reflection of his.

He, my young batman, has also been transformed, almost beyond recognition. His dog-like devotion has taken on a completely different quality. It resembles that of a faithful wife. Yes indeed, a loving yet capricious woman. These tantrums of love and devotion gradually became unbearable. He grows accustomed to ordering me about. Grumbling and complaining, he is constantly scolding me.

"Sir, again you haven't eaten the food that I brought you!" he says, and flings the dish of potatoes on the floor, roundly swearing by all that is holy. Or, if I happen to stand in a place of danger:

"Sir! What are you thinking of, sticking your rotten head up for the enemy?! Get out of here!" – followed by a resounding curse.

Or, if I put on my trousers before he has had time to mend and press them, he roundly abuses my ancestors and I, as far back as Moses.

He is devoted to me. He loves me. Very good, splendid. But it's too much! He's making my life impossible. He doesn't let me out of his grasp. A regular Xanthippe,[1] young and pretty, plaguing me incessantly. In vain do I try to shout him down, to scold him:

"Pály don't be vulgar. Don't curse at me, it's very bad manners."

Or:

"Pály, shut up or I'll beat the daylights out of you so badly that you'll forget your Creator!"

It's no use. He simply answers:

"What can I do, sir, if you haven't enough sense to take care of yourself?"

He gives me so much trouble that I feel quite worn out and more than once resolve to send him the hell away. Until one day his caprices irritate me beyond endurance, and then I remember the one unfailing military device that would stop him. This is after one of the officers has publicly humiliated Uncle Osterreicher, which so upsets me that I cannot swallow a morsel of food. I push the plate aside, light a cigarette and begin to write. My domineering batman looks at me for a moment, and pounces – he snatches the cigarette from my mouth, flings it down, and holds the plate under my nose.

"Sir, if you don't swallow your grub I'll smash it on your head! Understand?!" He holds the plate ready.

I stare at him, at my wits' end, wondering what to do, when suddenly I think of the answer:

– AttenTION! I roar at him at the top of my voice. The lad clicks his heels together and freezes, plate in hand.

"Now stay like that for half an hour!"

So I am rid of him for half an hour. He stands immobile, mute, petrified as a marble statue, and I can work on in peace.

After about fifteen minutes my kindly lieutenant comes in, sees my petrified batman plate in hand, and his serious face breaks out into a grin.

"Dismiss!" I order my batman as soon as I see the lieutenant, and rise to receive him. Pály leaves.

I explain the situation to the lieutenant. He laughs and says:

"Beware, my friend. You're becoming a disciple of *Herr* Figer!"

We have a pleasant, intimate chat, in the course of which I came to know more about this interesting personality. Scion of an old and noble Protestant family, he is an accomplished musician, plays the piano and organ, and has a large, choice library. His family, the Smerčany, is a traditionally democratic one.

While we are talking, Pály reappears with a plate of freshly made potato puree. He stands before me in the proper manner and says, almost in tears:

"Please, sir, don't stand me against the wall, sir. Eat, sir or… or… (his handsome face contorts) or I'll blow up this whole shitty world to pieces!"

I eat it, and he leaves. When he is gone, the officer says to me:

"Give me your batman, and I'll give you an original manuscript of Trismegistus."[2]

"What's the entire Trismegistus worth compared with the value of this young man, sir?"

"You're right," he answers thoughtfully. "There you have the terrible paradox of the war. This vile madness has one virtue – through it we discover qualities in people that we might never have known otherwise. Ye gods! what a little culture and civilization could make of such a young man! How handsome he is! By Allah's beard, if I were Jupiter, I'd have made him Ganymede![3]

During or conversation, he congratulates me on my promotion, but also has news for me. Now that I have been made an officer, I have to stand guard, with my company, on hill number sixteen. This hilltop is the most important site on our side of the front, and has cost us a great many lives during the recent engagements. Once, on a certain day, between 7:00 a.m. and 5:00 p.m., it changed hands eight times. The combat was terrible. Finally we have occupied it and protected it with a trench on the opposite side, facing the enemy.

And now I am to be given the terrible distinction of guarding this hilltop. Beyond, on the other side of the hill.

"From now on you'll be known as the 'fire officer,'" says the lieutenant, ironically and admiringly. "However, you're allowed to make a request, if you like, concerning the soldiers, the provisions, and so on. Think about it. You have till this evening."

He leaves.

"Think about it." What is there to think? I remember fat Rosenberger's joke. Perhaps I should ask Colonel Figer to tell me a joke before I go into that certain grave.

Suddenly the thought flashes through my mind. I go to my superior officer and tell him what I want. I should like to choose the men to take into that trench. I tell him that there is a precedent for it in the 66th Regiment. Could I be allowed to do the same?

It's agreed, that I can choose thirty men, half a platoon, from the entire regiment. When my lieutenant learns of my system of selection, he chuckles and is pleased. I select all the chicken-livered and nitwits, together with the wildest and rashest fellows. There are among them artists, Gypsies, *yeshiva* students, veteran horse thieves, notorious gamblers, professional card-sharks, and pickpockets. Since Margolis has in the meantime become a telephone operator (only God knows how; I discover later that before the war this Talmudic scholar had never so much as spoken a syllable on the telephone!), I recruit him as my telephonist. He is pleased, though for a moment he scratches his neck thoughtfully:

"I've an idea that I'll attain great heights over there on the hill. I'll be promoted heavenly telephonist." But he adds quickly: "Never mind, if I do, I shall respectfully send you all the reports from paradise!"

"You're so sure it will be paradise?"

"After the hell of our sergeant?! Why, the one virtue of our 'carcass skinner' is that he purifies and refines a person by ordeal so that he is fit to enter paradise."

Then I think that I should take that foolish actor Madi, who turned the lights on in "Hamlet" just to show him how the "cowardly Jew" Margolis conducts himself under fire. But while I am searching for him the awful report reaches me that Lance Corporal Madi has disappeared before the start of the battle. Next comes the appalling announcement that Madi didn't even wait for the start of the battle, but deserted and hid in the town of Jazlowitz,[4] where he has been caught, tried on the spot and sentenced to be shot.

Poor Madi! How that silly actor hated the cowardly Jews! With what deep-seated hatred, that he could not even disguise from me! And here he has been sentenced to die.

An execution at the front.

The reader who has never been at the front cannot imagine what a death sentence in the trenches means. Our civilization has no words to describe it. Here you are in a place where death lurks in ambush at every moment and at every step, a place where you're ninety-nine per cent certain to die, and you cling passionately to the one per cent chance of survival with every atom of your being. Then they come and take away that one flimsy per cent, and make death a certainty… It's revolting! I won't even try to describe this feeling to the reader.

I feel like fainting, like throwing up.

Half an hour later the order reaches me – I and my platoon are to execute the sentence.

I realize immediately that this is *Herr* Figer's brilliant idea, and am gripped with horror.

Shivers shoots through my veins. An idea occurs to me that I should somehow let Figer know that Madi is a rabid antisemite, and that it would give me pleasure to kill him. Perhaps then he would deny me the privilege.

But there is no time to do anything. The order is peremptory and has to be carried out at once. My world turns black.

The procedure in such cases is as follows: the condemned is taken to the rear, out of reach of enemy fire. There they stand him up and range the firing squad around him in a horseshoe-shaped formation. The condemned man doesn't stand within the open mouth of the horseshoe, but just beyond the center in such a manner that, if you joined the two ends of the horseshoe by straight lines to the point where the victim stands, you would get a pentagon with the victim at the intersecting point of the upper angle.

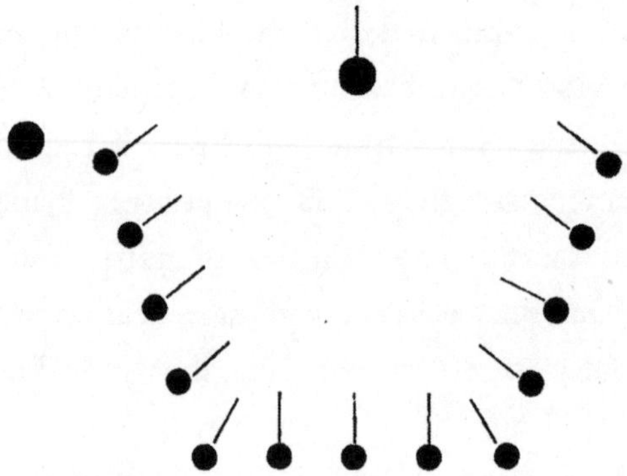

The condemned man stands with his back to the squad. The officer stands to one side of the last soldier on the left flank. He doesn't give the orders "ready" and "fire" by word of mouth, so that the condemned man would not become terror-stricken and move or try to run away. Not that he would do so deliberately – "a soldier does not try to escape military justice" – but he might do so in a fit of madness. Therefore the commanding officer gives the order by hand movement. The rule is that the condemned man's eyes must be blindfolded, but braver men insist on dying with their eyes open. There was even a case when a condemned officer insisted on standing open-eyed face to face with the firing squad, looking into the muzzles of the rifles trained on him. In such a case the officer in charge may give the order aloud.

I am to be the miserable wretch in charge of this horror.

And to do this to a soldier I knew personally! Moreover, to a man who is certain that I hated him, because he really hated me, and had done his best to give me a foretaste of the suffering in hell.

When Pály finds out, he began to shake all over.

"It's all the work of his piggishness!" he says. "God damn that lousy artist-comedian! He couldn't get killed in battle, he has to get killed by you, sir...! You of all people... Pfui!"

My head begins to ache. My temples pound like alarm bells. I think that I am going mad.

The only thing that keeps me going is the order – the peremptory order. That is what an order does to you. It steels the nerves like cold water on molten, white-hot iron.

When that wretched "lackey actor" Madi is handed over to me and he looks at me, I nearly pass out. It's plain that he is sure I have volunteered for the job, in revenge.

If only I could say something to him.

But that is strictly forbidden.

While walking to the place of execution I am filled with the wildest ideas. I think that it's a test devised by the Supreme Mysterious Mind, to test the Jew in me and the vindictiveness in my heart. For surely the Higher Mind knows that I have a very low opinion of revenge, that I think it is the lowest characteristic of man, because it reduces man to a level below that of a wild animal. The animal is not vengeful. It is the "unique gift" of *homo sapiens,* the thinking man. He knows, too, that I despise the dictum of the Talmud sage, Rabbi Shimon ben Yehuda, that "the pious scholar who is not vengeful and bears a grudge like a snake is not a pious scholar."[5] If that is a pious scholar, I want no part of it – let me rather follow our first great rabbi, Moses, who said: "You shall not avenge nor bear any grudge."[6]

Thinking all this, I am pleased to discover that not only do I not feel vengeful, but rather I feel deep compassion and pity for this poor unfortunate fool, who caused me to spend two hours in the pit of hell, two hours which have left me with an old man's palsy to this day.

We remain terribly silent until we reach the place of execution. There I arrange the men in the prescribed manner.

I realize that among them is fat Rosenberger. I take him out of the line and send him aside.

"You're a Jew," I whispered to him, and he understands.

Nobody hears what I said, only the condemned man catches the whisper. Or perhaps he doesn't hear, but only surmises what I have said. He salutes, stands to attention and says:

"Ensign, sir! I have one final request!"

"Speak, Lance Corporal Andras Madi!"

"You removed Corporal Rosenberger because he's a Jew, and you don't want him to commit any act of revenge."

"Yes, Lance Corporal Andras Madi."

"Well... I'm a Jew, too. I converted eight years ago."

My eyes darken. Lance Corporal Madi, the bitter anti-semite – a Jew? For a moment I can't believe him. Perhaps he is hoping for a reprieve. By representing himself as my racial brother, my "co-religionist," as they say in Hungary. But I realize that this is nonsense. I remain silent for a few moments that seem like an eternity, then swallow my bitter saliva and establish to my own satisfaction that I know what he is really after:

"Very well, Lance Corporal Andreas Madi. Uncle Osterreicher will say *kaddish* after you."

He, too, swallows his saliva, makes a strange, meaningless gesture and says:

"Thank you no, that isn't what I wanted to ask. I meant to ask, sir, that you leave me my lance corporal rank and shoot me without removing the insignia of my rank."

I stare at him speechless. My soldiers also stare at him, as well as at me. One of them even suppresses an awkward grin.

But, really, how did it happen? According to regulations, the condemned man is supposed to be degraded to the ranks before the execution. His stripes or insignia are to be torn off his tunic. It's a very strict rule where traitors are concerned. But neither the judge-advocate nor I have received such an order and I have not been ordered to do either, although the lieutenant gave me a long lecture on the procedure. I take advantage of this error and say:

"Very well. I have not received an order to degrade you, Lance Corporal Andreas Madi."

Then he says:

"Thank you. And one other thing: please give my trousers to Infantryman Laszlo Krechen and my boots to Infantryman Benvenuto Gallieri. They asked..."

"They asked for them? Very well, Lance Corporal Andreas Madi."

He salutes me respectfully, turns around and stands as ordered. I go up to him and take out my handkerchief to blindfold him, but he says:

"I have my own," and hands me his handkerchief.

That "I have my own" freezes the blood in my veins. "I have my own!" My hands shake badly and I can hardly manage to blindfold him. I see then that his cheeks are wet.

I finish everything in a hurry.

Thirteen shots hit his head. He stands a second, totters, and falls flat forward.

I begin to vomit. I collapse, and one of the soldiers gives me a little cognac from my own bag.

We return in silence. Only one man says quietly:

"He didn't even cross himself!"

It's the voice of the tall, simple Tyrolean. He knows no Hungarian and has not understood that the dead man was a converted Jew.

When I return to my dugout, I am almost grateful to *Herr* Figer for forcing me to do this hellish thing. After this, guarding the hill will seem like paradise.

It is very hard to die. It is a thousand times harder to kill, consciously, deliberately.

19| In the Name of the Holy Virgin

LANCE CORPORAL MADI'S last request becomes known throughout the camp and arouses respectful astonishment.

"Now there's a soldier!" says the officers. "There's a *proper* soldier!" they say enviously, and ask me:

"How did he ask you? How did it happen?

I explain it to all of them. He asked not to be degraded from his rank as lance corporal. He wanted to die a lance corporal.

This doesn't satisfy them. They want me to describe it in detail, to imitate his tone of voice – did he plead, did he speak brusquely, complainingly, did he demand it? How did it happen?

For a moment they forget about his treachery, his cowardice, everything.

Herr Figer is visibly stirred. He keeps studying his perfectly-manicured fingernails and walks up and down, deeply moved. "Now there's a soldier for you!"

Yet underneath his admiration there is a kind of envy, stronger than everything else. It has become widely known that Madi was a converted Jew, and that spoils everything. Firstly, a Jew, and a soldier! Secondly, the Jew died with his rank intact! *Herr* Figer cannot bear the thought that a Jew should have been so honored.

Moreover, the rascal had deceived them all this time. They had taken him for a genuine, born Christian! His entire conduct was that of a pure Christian throughout, without the slightest trace of suspicion. He always said his Credo aloud, with great devotion and piety. And whenever danger threatened, he was the only man in the whole battalion who would murmur repeatedly:

"By the Holy Virgin! By the Holy Virgin!"

Then he would fall to his knees and pray:

"Hail Mary, full of grace, the Lord is with You, blessed are You among women, and blessed is the fruit of Your womb, Jesus..."

In time the expression "By the Holy Virgin" becomes part of the camp vernacular in time of trouble or danger, great or small – "By the Holy Virgin!" And before long it is entered into the catalogue of brazen, vulgar cursing as well:

"May every vestige of you be blotted out, by the Holy Virgin!"

Or: "The Good Lord should have hacked your mother's belly to pieces before she shat you out, by the Holy Virgin!"

The one person who angrily objects to these profanities is Uncle Osterreicher. He just can't stand it. It makes him suffer. Uncle Osterreicher is the only person other than Madi who prays regularly. Madi to the Holy Virgin, and Osterreicher: "He that dwells in the secret place of the Most High shall abide under the shadow of the Almighty;[1] ... You shall not be afraid for the terror by night nor for the arrow that flies by day;[2] ... A thousand shall fall at you side and ten thousand at your right hand, but it shall not come near you[3]..."

The two devout worshippers are known even to headquarters. They are very pleased up there to have two worshippers in the camp. The officers are particularly satisfied with Lance Corporal Madi – there's a praying Christian for you! He not only curses and swears, he also prays!

And now it suddenly turns out that this Christian was a Jew.

I recall the lanky Tyrolean's comment and report to *Herr* Figer:

"Before dying, Madi did not cross himself."

Herr Figer opens his eyes wide, like one who has plumbed the depths of a matter – now he understands:

"But of course he didn't cross himself. He didn't dare cheat in the face of death!"

Then he adds:

"You realize, of course, that his last request was an act of cowardice, not courage, don't you?"

I don't realize that at all.

But what hurts *Herr* Figer the most is "the Jew's legacy" – the expression "By the Holy Virgin," which has become the by-word of our regiment, if not of the whole sector of the front. It introduces an entirely new element into the camp, the spirit of Christianity, not at all noticeable before. It begins to serve as a source of exceptional moral strength, as well as a ritually acceptable prayer shawl in which increasing antisemitism sanctimoniously cloaks itself.

Christianity has been on the ascent among us lately.

There is one person who finds another meaning in it, aside from anti-Jewish feeling, a curious and cynical one. It is difficult not to see some truth in it: the *erotic* significance.

The man who discovers this is Lieutenant Adolf Maising, a professor of psychology and pathology in Vienna, a disciple of Freud.[4] As far as he is concerned it is perfectly obvious:

"Healthy, vigorous men, strong as cedars, living for months, even years, without a woman, without so much as a whiff of woman! Their libidos seek various outlets. One of these is foul speech, in which you almost always find erotic-pornographic elements. Prayer, too, serves as an outlet – yes, prayer, which seeks to stifle this drive, struggles with it and usually succeeds in suppressing it. But what is more wonderful than a prayer which is itself erotic? – The prayer to Mary, Virgin of the Immaculate Conception!! You can see this for yourself," the professor continues wisely, "when you listen to our Croatian giant, Franz Rizic, pronouncing this phrase – with what fervor and emphasis! For him this short prayer is a literal catharsis!"

This is exactly what happens, The Croatian giant is the worst sufferer from the absence of women, sometimes, to the point of biting himself. For him, this is the absolute worst aspect of the war.

At any rate, the short prayer sweeps through the camp and the officers make it a slogan, a symbol, a hymn of hatred for the Jews, bringing it to the point of mania. They propound the theory that there can be no bravery without this prayer, no victory unless the men cross themselves and call on the Holy Virgin…

It is therefore self-evident that Jews can never be heroes.

"It is obvious."

The question of bravery is seen very differently here than back in the city. Under cannon and artillery, in the chaos and confusion of the battle, the concept "heroism" acquires a totally different meaning.

To start with, it sheds its patriotic cloak. What sort of patriotism could possibly be there? Nothing of the kind!

You're given the order to crawl stealthily behind Russian lines, well then you crawl – on your belly, in mortal terror, eyes half-shut and blinking. Often you duck your head, bury it in the mud, or behind a rock. Sometimes you quickly dig a little hollow and push your head into it, and lie on your belly, your body flattened, backside sticking up as a natural target for the Russians. Among the crawlers are usually one or two hot-tempered fellows, impetuous, thoughtless, and light-headed, who soon decide that this creeping on the ground makes them sick, and jump upright, resolving "The hell with it all!", shouting "Son of a bitch!" or "Hit him! He's not your father!", "Filthy bastards!", or even "Marusya!" (this female name is all we know of the Russian language), and rushing forward to assault the fearful enemy. They are usually followed by a few others, either from sheer inertia or sheer devilry, because they feel they have nothing to lose.

Recently they have added to their repertoire the war-cry "By the Holy Virgin!"

If one of these men survives the battle he is looked upon as a hero, wins a medal, gets a promotion or at least a pat on the shoulder.

Sometimes he wins all these on his grave, if he is unlucky and gets killed while screaming these curses.

This is what bravery has come to mean.

There are many similar manifestations of this. And it is mostly manifested by men who back in the city (and even here at the front) were terrified of cockroaches and mice.

Of late, most of these heroes are Jews!

But hatred finds an answer to this awkward fact – they can't be heroes if they don't shout "By the Holy Virgin!"

None of the Christians are sickened by it, or sense that it is blasphemous. They are not aware how they are degrading their Holy of Holies, the Mother of God, to the level of profanity – here, in the shadow of death.

Until one person succeeds in briefly opening their eyes. It's Lance Corporal Margolis, who among all the other curses adds:

"God damn you, in the name of Rahab the whore!"[5]

This makes them perceive their blasphemy, if only for a moment. By sheer coincidence we are then visited by a very important personage, the army chief chaplain. When he hears the name of the Mother of God bandied by the foul-mouthed soldiery he is horrified. But the officers find a remedy – they bring Margolis to him, for a sort of "court-martial." The priest happens to be a reasonable and warm fellow, intelligent and kindly, and Margolis explains to him that Rahab the whore serves as a symbol of victory in the Bible, as it was she who made it possible for Joshua to capture Jericho and then the rest of the Holy Land.

The reverend gentleman accepts this explanation with an understanding smile. After sending away the little Jewish lance corporal, he scolds the officers:

"Perhaps this lance corporal will help open your eyes and show you how low you have fallen, gentlemen! This little Jewish soldier is protecting the sanctity of your religion for you! Thank him that he has shown you the way to repentance."

But it can't be expected that this incident would change the regiment. Once a foul phrase has taken root, all the Jewish lance corporals in the world will not budge it. Rather, the priest's words serve to inflame hatred for us, especially for the dead Madi. *Herr* Figer walks around as if he were drugged, looking for some way to work out his rage. At last he hits on a terrible revenge – he orders that Madi's grave be opened and the lance corporal stripe be removed from his tunic!

It was the dead soldier's "good fortune" that he escaped this horrible punishment, because his tunic was not buried with him. The Serbian "bastard" is already strutting about in it, proud as a general – without the stripe of course.

But this whole Madi affair doesn't occupy us for long. At least, not those of us who have to go and defend that accursed hill. Only when Madi's two "heirs" come forward to claim his belongings – the Serbian "bastard" his good tunic and the Italian from Fiume[6] his fine boots – does the unfortunate wretch's image rise before my eyes.

"Why did he leave these things to you?" I ask.

"We asked him for them" they both answer.

"Excellent boots," says the Italian with relish.

"A tailored shirt," says the scarred Serbian, licking his lips. ("Tailor-made" means to have a tailor repair a garment obtained from the commissary).

"And you didn't hesitate to ask them of him, a man who was going to die, you scoundrels?!"

"Beg to report, sir: That's just it, he was going to die!" says the Serbian.

"It was all the same to him," adds the Italian. "Also, beg to report: I saw him offering them to the Jew."

"Which Jew?"

"Uncle Osterreicher."

"Yes, sir. He asked him to pray for him, after his death."

"And why didn't he give them to him?"

"Beg to report, sir: The Jew didn't want the things. He promised he would pray for him for nothing. What does a Jew know about boots?"

As I give them the "inheritance," I meanwhile recall that the Serbian had taken part in the firing squad which executed the man.

"Tell me, Infantryman Krechen, were you not one of his executioners?"

The "bastard," caught unawares, is startled and his face grows pale.

"Beg to report, sir: Yes, sir, I was."

"Hm. Don't you think you're a scoundrel?"

"Beg to report, sir: No."

"Did your heart not beat faster? Tell me the truth!"

"Beg to report, sir: No! I obeyed the order to fire."

"But meantime you could see the tunic before your eyes, couldn't you?"

The Serbian is quiet for a moment, then he says:

"Beg to report: Yes, sir. But I aimed at his head."

"So as not to spoil the tunic, eh?"

Again he is silent, then he replies:

"Beg to report: Yes, sir!"

I hesitate for a moment whether to give it to him, but decide to let him have it, after all. At least the fellow is truthful.

He takes the tunic like a child receiving a fine toy, tucks it under his arm, salutes me respectfully, and they both leave.

A few paces away they stop and examine their treasures with barely suppressed glee.

Suddenly I see them look at each other, at first with suspicion, then with anger. Finally they explode with violent curses:

"You son of a bitch, by the Holy Virgin! Just you wait!"

Later Pály explains to me what happened. It seems each of them had asked the condemned man for both items, and the poor fellow divided them between them. Which made them both mad. Each of them suspected the other of deliberately ruining his inheritance, but neither said a word about it to the other. Now, they discover that each has ruined the other's plans – both the tunic and one of the boots are riddled with bullet holes.

At the time of the disposal, I talk to the doctor about it, and he says:

"My friend, you can't boast that they are exceptional marksmen! I can understand a man aiming at the head and hitting the back – but to hit the foot instead of the head...!"

I don't tell him the story behind it. Why should I? How awful! Shooting a living man in the foot, so as to spoil his boot, to spite another man!

"Pfui, you swine, by the Holy Virgin!"

20 | The Madman

THE EVENING before we are to go to the trench in front of the hill I inspect my men in accordance with the Biblical injunction. Thus far in the war we have not been in such certain danger, and so I cite: "What man is there that is fearful and faint-hearted, let him go."[1]

To my amazement, nobody wants to remain behind. They all want to come and defend "the Hill of Venus."[2] This is the name the men gave to it, nobody knows why. It must have been nicknamed thus by someone and the name stuck. Whatever the reason,[3] the man was no ignoramus.[4] Once again Professor Maising explains it to us according to his theory: it's the erotic instinct that did it. The so-called Hill, or Mound of Venus, is the lower part of the woman's belly, and the trench we are to enter is below the hill. How pleasant for the libido to be able to say: I'm going into the trench below the Hill of Venus! Common soldiers, when they learn the mythological meaning of the nickname, give it a much blunter name of their own.

When I tell the professor, Lieutenant Maising, that all the men would willingly come to defend this dangerous hill, he literally dances with glee.

"Of course, my dear fellow! Of course! The name alone is enough to attract the fellows!"

Oh, well. It sounds like an exaggeration, but who really knows? The psyche of a soldier in battle is not easily explained by reason. Perhaps he is right.

He may be right that it's pleasant to go into the trench below the Hill of Venus. But when I remember how many deaths it has already caused us, the comrades who are gone, and to whose mothers I have had to write heartbreaking letters telling them the terrible news, my appetite for Professor Maising's theory deserts me completely.

Tonight we must enter the trap.

All the fellows sit down to write letters home. One writes to his mother, another to his sweetheart, a third to his best friend. All of them in utter silence.

The silence is truly terrible.

Whoever hasn't witnessed this ceremony of writing farewell letters before a decisive battle has never witnessed horror. The silence – which is so profound that one can hear pens scratching – is filled with the awesome mystery of death, till you feel your head pounding.

I watch one of my soldiers – large, deepset eyes, shaking hands, forehead creased like a philosopher thinking deep truths out. Who knows how many thinkers are lost among these simple folk?

I ask one of them to show me his letter, and he agrees before placing it in the envelope.

"Please, sir, my writing is not good – I am no scribe." The letter is only three lines long:

> My darling Ilonka,
>
> I'm about to enter the dugout of the "Hill of Venus" (you don't know what that is!) to defend the hill from the Mouska (Russians). It is your hill, and I am going to defend it. My darling Ilonka. If you want

me to live, then I won't die. You are my hill, my darling Ilonka.

Your Istvan, who will live only so long as you want him to.

I read a few other letters. The style varies, but the principle remains: the woman, for whom he lives and dies, sometimes the mother, sometimes both: the beloved and his mother. I relate this to our professor, and again he rejoices in the triumph of his Freudian scientific hypothesis.[5]

I go to say goodbye to my lieutenant.

When I arrive at his quarters I find a minor but important fuss going on. A group of officers, including our regimental doctor, surround First Lieutenant Stubniak. My own kindly Lieutenant Smerčany whispers to me:

"He is acting crazy, to try and fool us."

Then he adds:

"He's afraid of the hill. The order came for him to join you, so he's suddenly 'gone mad.' "

The silence in the room is punctuated by the doctor's voice talking to the "crazy" officer, and the latter talking to himself. He does it wonderfully well.

"Where did he learn how to do this?" I ask my lieutenant. in a low voice.

"Fear is a first-rate teacher!" he answers.

Officer Stubniak is a well-known coward: he is brave only against Jews. But, at the same time, he has a towering ambition to become a hero – without risking his life, of course. All this is so widely known, that even the minor medal that he wears on his chest is generally suspected as not genuine. There's a rumor that he has bought it for a goodly sum of money from one of his own NCOs, who succeeded in "capturing" a Russian enemy machine gun while he was out scouting in some forest with Stubniak's men. While Stubniak hid in a safe spot, his NCO captured the machine gun which Stubniak bought from him with money, thereby winning the bronze *signum laudis* for himself and boasting as a hero. The officers all know the story, but whenever they tell it they do not fail to add:

"Only a peddler-Jew could do such a thing – to sell his own triumph for money!"

Because, the NCO in question happens to be a Jew.

Once I put it to the NCO bluntly, and he answers:

"Why not? Such achievements are a dime a dozen, just like the *signum laudis* medals themselves. Big deal! A machine gun! Let him enjoy it,[6] be a hero, why not? I myself wouldn't have hung a bronze medal on my chest alongside my gold one!"

And now First Lieutenant Stubniak has "gone mad."

The doctor busies himself with him, straining hard to diagnose his condition. It's very difficult, because there is something very dubious about it. They have been in this quandary for the past two hours, and can't decide what to do. To decide, quite simply, that he is malingering would be unpleasant. He is, after all, a regular officer, product of the imperial military academy, a man who has trained all his life to be an officer, scion of an important family. It's very serious indeed.

Suddenly Lance Corporal Margolis comes in to report to my lieutenant, whose telephone operator he is. He has been ordered to install a secret telephone link between the trench and the Russian guard post, one of the most important and most dangerous tasks at the front. He's come to report about it.

Margolis, the little lance corporal, looks around and understands everything instantly. He glances at the "madman" and reports to Lieutenant Smerčany at the top of his proper soldier's voice:

"Lieutenant sir! Beg to report: I've set up the hidden line as far as the enemy's front! We'll be able to even hear him fart!

Everybody bursts out laughing – the so-called "madman" Stubniak almost bursts out laughing as well, but remembers in time and suddenly puts his hand over his mouth, trying to keep a serious face!

When the doctor, who is sitting beside him, sees this, he rises, puts his hand on the "madman's" shoulder and says very quietly and grimly:

"Scoundrel!"

He pushes him away contemptuously, and adds:

"March!"

"To report" (i.e., court-martial)!" roars Colonel Figer, purple with rage.[7]

The court-martial degrades the noble officer to second lieutenant, taking away one of his gold stars.

I ask not to be honored with his presence in the defense of the hill. My request is granted, so I'm going out there with my men, *sans* the heroic Second Lieutenant Stubniak.

The doctor, in the meanwhile, questions Margolis:

"How did you hit on the idea of making him laugh, Lance Corporal?"

"Beg to report: It's very simple, sir," says Margolis. "Only fools such as we laugh with us, not lunatics, who laugh when they feel like it. So now Lieutenant Stubniak is not mad, only a fool!"

21 | The Russian Christmas

On Night Guard[1]

Who goes there?
Attention! And speak.
(No weapons:
I am a brother).

No man shall pass here
And live!
What have you to say, speak!
(my Lord.)

Where have you come from?
Come forward. slowly.
(I have brought you a gift;
Eternal peace).

Who are you? What is your name?
Stand! Speak!
(I am the angel of death –)
Pass!

WE APPROACH the hill on a very "unpleasant," unsuitable night. The entire area is covered with pure, luminous snow, against which even a cat can be seen from two hundred paces away. The moon, too, sheds her light from behind the white clouds. We dig our path while walking through the snow, piling man-high walls on either side. A wretched Galician winter.

It takes us four hours and eight minutes to reach our trench on the other side of the hill.

The snow has prevented any active fighting in our sector for the past few days. This was why the enemy has not assaulted the hill, which had been captured by our side about a month ago. Only now is there a "report" that the Russians are planning a general offensive, and we have to prepare for it, standing watch.

But it seems that the snow is continuing to block the armies, so, for the time being, we live in the trench without having anything to do, and this leads to boredom.

Boredom at the front is nothing new. But if back home it's unpleasant to remain inactive for days on end, in a dugout it's infinitely worse, sometimes quite unbearable. It's sufficiently oppressive to sit and wait for something to happen without any distractions. It's a great deal worse to sit around waiting for the angel of death.

Nothing serves to dispel the awful boredom: neither the card games, nor the tall tales which soldiers spin. However, some of the simple stories that they tell are of greater interest than the finest literature – guileless folk tales, which could serve as great models for the art of story-telling. Here, for the first time in my life, I come into direct contact with the source of popular verse. The Hungarian people (like all other nations) abound in folk songs, which are more moving than all lyrical, classical, and modern poetry combined. Nobody knows who creates these gems.[2] Suddenly a song appears, words and music, which sweeps the country, towns and villages, and you will never know whose heart poured out its sadness and joy and shared it with the surrounding world.

I have often wondered about this, and here I am privileged to see the process of creation itself.

Story-telling is a favorite amusement of simple village Magyars. When four or five Magyars sit together in company, they at once begin to tell stories, or sing new songs, impromptu, on the spot, without any advance preparation. They compete with each other, try to produce something finer and fancier, and so it goes on and on throughout the night.

I think of the ancient Greek "symposium" (feast), in which the Attic sages competed with each other in presenting new ideas and logical arguments.[3] In the Hungarian "symposium" the subject of the contest is story and song, and the simplest peasant excels in it. A fresh, tender, and profound source feeds these tales, which sometimes remind me of ancient Egyptian, Greek or biblical stories. Biblical stories are uncommon, because every village Magyar knows them well. Instead, I am amazed to hear stories which seemed to have been taken from our own *Aggadah,*[4] imbued with characteristic Hungarian qualities, as well as the special contribution of the narrator himself. This is "Man" himself, the human being who is a child of his planet, unconfined by time and place, product of all generations and nations of the earth. All this can be found inside a tale which bears the specific features of Magyar culture that is to say, of the

Turano-Mongolian tribe which has been living in Europe for a thousand years, surrounded by the Latin, Germanic and Slavic civilizations.[5]

Here, I say to myself, are the sources for the inspiration of the romantic writer Maurus Jokai and the wild poet of freedom Petőfi![6]

This compensates me for all the trials and sufferings and the constant menace of death in this Great Madness.

It compensates me, but not the men. It may drive out boredom for a day or two, maybe as much as a week, but then it returns, stifling as ever. We decide to go for a "night stroll" – in the direction of the Russians.

When the battlefield is not several feet under snow, such a stroll means a sortie out of the dugout and through the no-man's-land between the lines: a scouting party. In the deep snow it also means digging through a straight ditch as far as the enemy line, to listen to what they are doing there.

What we listen to is unimportant. A simple villager says that we are hearing intrigues of the "cunning Mouskas" – what they are plotting against us over there.

One man with a thousand heads, or just the opposite: one head with a thousand bodies. When they plot against us they speak loudly, so that we can hear what they have to say.

I take Pály, Margolis and two other men, and we set out. Pály and one of the men shovel up the snow about one meter ahead of us, while the three of us toss it aside and broaden the path.

We make for the enemy line, which, as far as we know, is 500 meters away. We have, therefore, a good deal of work ahead of us before we get close enough to be in danger.

As we work, I wonder about this "stroll," which no one has ordered us to take, and is so fraught with mortal danger. Does it indicate that we are heroes? Of course not! We feel none of the sensations usually described as courageous. As for patriotism – what does that have to do with us?! Maybe we are just fools.

We walk on in a straight line, working and stopping for rests. A freezing but beautiful night. Peace and quiet. We work for about two consecutive hours. Again, a break – peace and quiet.

It's 2:15 a.m. A beautiful night.

Quiet! Suddenly we heard whispering behind us.

Yes, definitely behind us. Yet not exactly behind us – more to the left. Soft voices, whispering. In the beginning, sounds resembling our own shoveling sounds, after that low voices – even a slight cough.

I give the order to stop and turn back.

When we return "home" there is joy and gladness. Roasted potatoes, hot and floury. Marvelous.

But the other men are also bored. They also want to go for a "stroll." I choose three other men, but cannot do without Pály. Margolis also wants to come: he is needed to lay the telephone wire down the trench behind us, just as for a strategic advance. So I choose two other men by lot. Avram Marcus and Leib Adler, both Jews, as it happens. There is also one Magyar who asks to be added to the group, one Elek Fardi.

We hurry down the ditch and continue with our work.

Suddenly we hear soft voices, again a brief groan, a suppressed cough. Then someone saying Shh… and something that sounds like swearing and cursing.

We all say at once: Russians!

They are behind us, a little to the left.

We start back hastily.

Suddenly we heard a rough voice saying:

"*Stoi!*"[7] The man blocks our path. Bayonets ahead!

There is a brief commotion. Fardi falls down, pierced by a bayonet, yelling "By the Holy Virgin!" Margolis winds a telephone wire around the neck of one of the Russians, strangles him, and then runs away shouting, "By Rahab the Whore! I'm going to bring help!" He vanishes. I bring down one Russian with my revolver. More Russians showed up, shouting: "*Plen, plen pan!*"[8] They surround us. Someone grabs me from behind, and holds me tight. They stop shooting and thrusting.

We've been captured.

They take us a little way down our path, then turn aside and led us to the right.

I understand. We have been advancing towards each other, the Russians to our line, we to theirs. On the way, our paths cross. The distance between the two paths is not more than 7 or 8 meters!

God damn!

One of the Russian officers explains it all to me, but I don't understand a word he says. I understood this whole rotten matter all on my own.

At least Margolis got away. But he'll be too late to help. There's nothing for it. We've been taken prisoner.

Prisoner. It's a very strange feeling. Confused, unclear. Yet somehow like waking up from a dream to reality. All normal feelings one has ever known are involved in it – sorrow, shame, gladness, fear, freedom, hatred, love, laughter and tears, all mixed up together. It's hard to tell at first which is predominant.

Here is the fearsome enemy, face to face.

He's not terrible at all. Quite the opposite. They are smiling and talking as if with affection. One of them puts his hand on my shoulder (my revolver had been taken away), as if to pat me, and says:

"Officer."

I stare at him, astonished. Is this a dream?

He continues:

"*Nitchevo.*" This word I already know. It means "nothing." What does he mean, nothing?

Another one says:

"*Khorosho, Pan.*"[9]

We all know the second word. It means sir, or mister. What does *khorosho* mean? I haven't the faintest idea. A pity Margolis is not with us, he knows a little Russian. We walk and walk. Captives: very strange. Suddenly one of them takes out cigarettes and offers them to all of us.

But nobody wants to take them. The Russian is offended. I can see it on his face. He entreats us to take them. Avram Marcus looks at me: Shall I? I nod. He takes four cigarettes and gives them to us. He hesitates to be the only one. The Russian lights them for us. One lit match for two of us. But when the third presents his cigarette to be lit, the Russian shakes his head, puts out the match and lights another one.

Then he lights cigarettes for two of us. Strange. So this is the enemy! Suddenly I feel a strong desire to embrace him. I am ashamed to do so. I put out my hand and he shakes it, pressing it warmly and with his other arm he embraces me:

"*Khorosho, Pan!*"

I embrace him too, pressing his face to mine lovingly.

Everybody shakes hands all around.

My batman says:

"This isn't 'Mouska,' this is a man, just like us!"

Then, puffing on his cigarette, he looks at them and says:

"The enemy? They love us. Who knows? Perhaps they are all like these?"

I too look at them: they seemed like men from Mars.

Tall men, wearing ankle-length overcoats, big, brawny good men.

I am put in mind of Wells's Martians.[10]

We walk a bit further and reach their front line.

There are cries of joy. They are pleased to see us. Their dugout is a mess. Ours is a paradise, by comparison.

Suddenly my batman bursts into tears. He sobs and repeats:

"Mama! My sweet Mama!"

Like a little child. A pretty child crying for his mother.

"Don't cry, Pály! It isn't seemly!" I stroke him and try to quieten him down. But he keeps crying:

"Mama! My sweet Mama!"

One of the Russians grabs him by the shoulders quite affectionately, and says something to him. Then they give him a slice of black bread. I give him my flask, he sips a little cognac, and calms down.

"Aren't you ashamed, Pály? Crying? A soldier crying?"

"I'm not crying. But I am a prisoner."

One of the Russians grabs my flask, put it to his mouth and drinks avidly, like a thirsty camel. Another one grabs it from him and he too drinks and drinks. A third grabs it – but it's already empty. He swears, curses, and flings it down. The third man is the soldier who offered us cigarettes. Now he's sorry he did not take the flask from me on our way here.

This all makes a profound impression on me. A good impression – good men, simple and warm.

And this is the enemy? – It's complete madness.

The Russians consult among themselves, talking about us. They assign us to one of the men and part from us amiably. We are led behind the lines to a small farmhouse, a typical Galician farmhouse.

When we enter we are assailed by a stifling atmosphere full of liquor fumes and the odor of roasting pork. The little house is full of Russian officers, Cossacks, to judge by their uniforms.

In writing of these events I am again sickened. It's difficult to describe what we went through in that little farmhouse. Even now, the abomination makes me want to throw up.

In brief, what happened was the following: the drunken Cossacks informed us that it was their Christmas, the Russian Orthodox Christmas.[11] On the table, among the bottles of liquor, amid the spills, lay a human head, the head of a bearded man. He looked Jewish. The body was under the table. One of the officers, completely drunk, gave the order to force Avram Marcus to drink the blood of the dead Jew, mixed with strong liquor. Avram Marcus refused to drink it.

They forced his mouth open with the point of a bayonet and made him drink. He threw up blood and bile, and fell down dead. Then the officer gave the order to crucify Leib Adler on the wall. When they started to hammer nails into the palms of his hands, he went mad and began to beat and kick them with all his might. One of the officers shot him dead on the spot.

My Pály stood there the whole time, grinding his teeth ready to burst out and fall on them. I forced him to stand still. Then an officer gave the order to tie my hands, dig a grave for me and bury me alive. He could speak a few words of German, which was closer to Yiddish than proper German.

Pály fell on my neck and begged me to teach him a Hebrew prayer. He didn't want to be a Christian along with these evil beasts.

They took us out to be buried together. Dawn was breaking through the dark clouds. The Russian soldiers who were digging our grave in the yard spoke to us kindly whenever the officers weren't looking. One of them shook his fist angrily at the Cossacks carousing in the farmhouse.

We stood still and waited for our burial.

Suddenly we heard gunfire. Once, twice, three times. Shells began to explode all around. Some fell on the farm-house. There was a fearful panic. The soldiers drove us into the open grave, as the only place where "cover" was possible. The officers ran away as fast as their legs could carry them. The firing grew heavier, "accompanying" the retreating Cossacks with great precision, killing some of them. The little house was in flames. Soon the soldiers were all gone, except the two Russian soldiers who took cover in the open grave with us.

A few moments later my men arrived.

When we walked back under the arch of artillery fire, I noticed that my Pály had turned into an old man. His hair was completely white. Mine too had greyed considerably.

On the way back we found poor Fardi, dead from the bayonet wound, and the two Russian casualties, the one whom Margolis had strangled and the one whom I had shot. We carried them back with us and buried them with Marcus and Adler at the foot of the hill, near our dugout.

Private Margolis said *kaddish*.[12]

I returned to our headquarters and reported the whole thing to Colonel Figer. The fine gentleman listened, and then said, quite calmly:

"It's a very fine thing for a Jew to die on Christmas Day."

I left him, deeply shaken.

"God damn you, by the Holy Virgin!"

22 | Mockery

THESE EVENTS, together with the heavy snow, must surely have caused the postponement of the expected Russian offensive. We have plenty of time to think about what happened in that drunken farmhouse. We take no more "strolls," of course. Another stroll like that one and I would be 80 years old. Headquarters, however, views our sortie very favorably indeed. On my recommendation Margolis is promoted corporal.

When he comes to report it to me formally he says:

"Ensign sir! Corporal Jacob Margolis, telephonist to His Majesty, the Supreme Commander, Emperor Franz Josef the First, begs to report: Jacob Margolis Napoleon is now a 'petit caporal' – other than that, there is no news!" (I had told him that Napoleon's nickname among his troops was "le petit caporal," and now he is proud to be of the same rank). He likes the fact that, like Napoleon, he is short.

"Are you happy, Margolis?"

"Beg to report: Happy. But not completely."

"Why not?"

"If Madi were alive he'd have burst with envy!"

"Are you taking revenge on the dead, Margolis? Are you 'mocking the dead?'"[1]

"Beg to report: Quite the contrary. That's the whole point – I can't take revenge on him, because he's dead. If he were alive I'd do so, I'd talk to him all the time, so he'd have to keep calling me *Herr* Corporal... All the same, I want to thank you, sir. It's good to be promoted."

"What's so good about it?"

"I don't know. The devil knows… But you know the saying, 'where there are no men, try to be a beast like the rest of them.'"[2]

This saying, (which, incidentally, Margolis has stolen from Aharon Kaminka) reflects the entire psychology of the military species.[3] I find out that man's constant desire to appear extraordinary is not based on a noble impetus to rise above the common herd in the absolute cultural sense. Not a bit of it! Man wants only to rise above his immediate environment, whatever it may be. If he happens to be among professors, he too wants to be a professor, superior to others. If he is among officers, whose entire claim to fame lies in lack of logic and shiny buttons, he wants to be an officer, and shine more brightly than they do. That is all. Back in his *yeshiva*, the Talmud student Margolis aspired to become an *ilui*;[4] here, he is happy to be promoted corporal. By now, Jacob Margolis has forgotten how he used to view corporals in the old days.

I have plenty of time to reflect on all this, while waiting for the snow to melt.

We also have leisure to discuss the question of the "enemy," and the war as a whole. When we grow tired of the quiet songs and stories, Pály suddenly recalls the recent horror, our Russian captors, and especially the grave diggers. He reflects deeply about it, and then says:

"I've been at the front for a year and a half, but only now have I been able to see Russians with my own eyes. Previously, we kept shooting death at them from a distance, or else we fell upon them with bayonets in the night, in total darkness, where I could only see them by the flashes of gunfire."

"I'd so much like to see a Russian. At least one Russian," one of the least talkative soldiers says. "I think that they're a lot like us. Only their uniforms are different and peculiar."

"Well, I've seen them," says Pály rather smugly. "And I can't understand how we can kill them. The Cossacks, oh yes! Those are wild and evil beasts! I don't understand why the Russians let them rule over them. The Russians took us prisoners, but the Cossacks tortured us."

"Even the Cossacks aren't all wild and evil beasts" reflects Margolis. "There must be simple, good men amongst them. We also have drunken officers who are wild animals."

"They are the ones who make this war!" declares a third.

"Are there so many of them, that they can rule over all countries and force the world to make war?" asks a fourth.

"Why did you strangle that Russian?" A fifth scolds Margolis. "You could see he was a man just like you!"

"I… I strangled… of course I strangled him, because if I hadn't, he'd have killed me!"

"That's exactly my question!" Pály exclaims. "Why would he have killed you? And in general, why did they take us prisoner and why are we here making war against them? What is the war for, really? What do they want it for? I'm sure that they don't want war either. Who could be so stupid as to want to risk his life just to kill others? Where's the logic of it? The devil himself knows!… War!"

I listen, pretending to be asleep. I'm afraid that they would involve me in their discussion. If they ask me this question, what answer could I give?

No doubt the soldiers of Rameses, Hannibal,[5] King David and Julius Caesar and Napoleon must have had similar discussions in their camps.

But I fail to deceive them. I sneeze – which no man does in his sleep. The fellows realize that I am awake and at once rope me into the discussion.

"Ensign sir! Beg to ask: who's making this war?" demands the tall, naïve Tyrolean.

"Who's making this war? – Why, my dear fellow, everybody's asking the same question – the Russians, French, Germans, British – all of us are making it!"

There is a thoughtful silence.

The Tyrolean speaks again:

"But if everybody's asking, who knows the answer?"

"The answer is known to he who wants this war and makes it."

"And who is he, God damn his soul forever by the Holy Virgin?!" yells Pály. "If I could just get hold of him, I'd crush him like a spider!"

He presses on:

"Who is the person who is sending us to this war?"

I hesitate a moment, and finally answer him, very softly, without looking at him:

"Us? His Imperial Majesty, the Supreme Commander, Franz Josef." This makes some of them jump up, while others simply stare at me, as if a great secret has just been revealed to them.

General silence reigns, as if they have to digest a hard lump. Once they digest it, they react in different ways: some make odd, violent gestures, as if cursing wordlessly. One flings down the book he had been reading, another throws away a half-smoked cigarette. One spits on the ground with loathing, and another hits his own head and scratches it futilely.

Pály puts on his cap with a gesture of despairing rage:

"One man! By the Holy Virgin!" he says, and goes outside.

I want to say to them that in reality Emperor Franz Josef himself didn't want the war either, but I keep my opinion quiet.

It would have thrown me into worse confusion.

Poor old Franz Josef! Now he's the object of all the furious curses which his good soldiers are now hurling at him soundlessly, in their minds.

The problem would have continued to worry them, if it had not been for the thaw which sets in, and with it our great new Russian offensive.[6]

It's a mighty offensive along a front line winding for hundreds of kilometers in a zig zag line, from Czernowitz to Riga.[7] I stand for a moment in the midst of the battle, listening to the roar of gun-fire all along the line. Thousands of cannons and mortars on our side; thousands on their side. All pounding each other ceaselessly.

But none of us becomes deaf.

On either side of the line men with rifles, hand-grenades and bayonets all ready to kill, murder, expel, annihilate.

And not one of them hates the other.

Lunatics! Tens of thousands, hundreds of thousands of lunatics! All seized by a great madness, like a plague. But there is no doctor to examine them and diagnose their insanity.

What would happen if, instead, these tens of thousands are seized by another kind of madness, not to kill but on the contrary, to hug, to embrace, kiss one another, all along the hundreds of kilometers of the front?!

Even without love. There's no need for love to do this, just as there is no need for hatred in order to kill in a fit of madness. We don't hate at all.

Why is there no such madness as this? Seriously!

While thinking these thoughts I keep on giving the insane orders of battle:

"Right wing: don't advance! Sergeant Ritch: ammunition! Left: lie down, down! Target: two hundred and fifty paces! Right: advance ten paces! Rizic: on your knees! Braedl, damn you, what are you standing up for like a lamp post, as a target?! Fire! Fire! Fire! Not all together – in order! That's it, fellows! Margolis, don't get ahead of me with your wires! I don't need the telephone now! Greenbaum, Arbai. Djenga, Kaplanow! Get your heads down, down into the ground! Fire! Fire! Fire! Left: stop! Advance twenty paces – march! Right: stand still! That's it! Advance twenty paces – march! Right: stand still! That's it! Right: advance, catch up with left! March! Sergeant Ritch, ammunition, damn your mother! Margolis, lie down! That's it, fellows, that's it! Fine! Mouska's tucking in his tail now! That's right! Now – the whole line: advance, march! Fifty paces! Hurray! Shout, you pigs, or forever hold your peace!"

Meantime I'm thinking: what a loving assault.

"Hey! Orderly! Orderly! Maklin's been hit in the belly! Orderly! Mama! Orderly: to the right! Sergeant Ritch is wounded! Oh, Mama! Corporal Djelini to replace Sergeant Ritch!"

"Why can't there be a different type of madness?... What if all these men grew mad with love?"

"Ow!"

"March! Fire! Fire! Fire!"

"The bodies! Orderlies!"

"Go and eat now! Every fifth man, eat! The first, fifth, and tenth man, and so on. Go on, eat with appetite! Lance Corporal Gal, here's a cigarette for you!"

"Fire, fire, fire! Infantryman Kuhn, eat like a human being! Don't bolt down your food – you're not at a wedding party! Corporal Djelini, mortar fire! Fire! Advance! Follow me! Lie down! Fire! Hey! March!"

On the fourth day of the battle we take Chortkov. The Russians flee.[8]

My platoon distinguishes itself in the fighting. This band of hoodlums, artists, pickpockets and *yeshiva* students perform wonders, especially the four professional card-players.

Victory.

Six dead, fourteen lightly wounded, one seriously – Infantryman Maklin is wounded in the belly. He will die today.

Victory. The town is ours. Joy and rejoicing. Surely now it would be appropriate...

Yes, this would an interesting contest. Surely now we ought to meet with "the other side," shake hands, embrace and throw a party with speeches.

It's 7:00 a.m.

We sit down to eat, and, one after the other, fall asleep over our food.

I re-read the notes I made in my diary the day before, in which I described the battle, and see that they are worthless. Mere chatter. There is no trace in them of a single one of the myriad sights of the battle. Words, words, words… Nothing but words.

I don't think the genius has been born who can really do justice to this.

Perhaps if Beethoven and Dostoevsky were combined in a single soul![9]

When we get up, news begins to come in from all sides. Among the many items, one is especially "interesting." The entire 11th Regiment has been killed. But before dying, its men have won a tremendous victory – it was they who drove the enemy into the town, across the frontier, then fell into the range of the "Preobrazhensk guns" and perished to the last man.[10]

The eleventh company carries the day, winning eternal honor.

Was that victory?

Strange that this question should be asked, but it is.

There is a sight that is often seen at the front: a soldier lies on his belly, firing away, enthusiastically, exhaustedly, straining every nerve. For at least two days he hasn't slept, has hardly eaten anything, has done nothing but roll in the mud and keep firing away, jumping up, rushing forward to advance, yelling with might and main: "Forward! Forward!" – Then a bullet hits him in the head, he falls, his limbs convulse, he sprawls, sometimes continues to shout "Forward! Forward!" and he dies with the war cry on his foaming lips, and pride of victory in his heart. He remains lying in the mud and his platoon marches on to victory. He goes on to participate in the victory till the last minute, even after he has been lying dead for some time, and you seem to see the joy of victory on his pale face.

What does it mean? – Surely he knows he will never win now.

Not true. He is victorious. How? – Through his comrades.

Is this not a kind of mockery?

I don't know. Nor do I know how to solve this dilemma. There is something perplexing about this – a man dies – gladly, knowing that another man will take the crown and emerge triumphant.

Strange.

But there is something even stranger, a similar phenomenon, but on a larger scale. A regiment wins a battle, but all its men are dead. After the battle the victorious company is given an outstanding decoration, a flag, or something of that sort, and a formal announcement is made:

"Such-and-such a regiment has won a tremendous victory, having shown exceptional courage..."

And it is given the flag.

To whom is it given then?

To another company entirely! Because, after all, there are no survivors of the winning regiment. Some officer – who was nowhere near that monstrous battle, won by the poor creatures who are now rotting in a common grave – receives it on their behalf!

"The regiment has won a victory! Oh, the valiant company!"

The valiant regiment swells with pride.

The company sergeant swaggers with pride, as if he himself were a hero. He, the sergeant who during that terrible battle, where death ran rampant, happened to be away on leave smoking a cigarette.

At a time when his fellow sergeant. who won the battle, is moldering in his muddy grave.

The eleventh company received the flag. Poor regiment, poor fellows.

What a mockery!

Someone else has won a decoration, a large gold medal – Infantryman Andras Maklin. It wasn't pinned on his chest – It was placed on his grave, on the wooden cross they stuck on top of the mass grave in which Andras Maklin rots together with twenty of his comrades.

But he receives the medal, as well as a rifle salute. Over his grave. I can imagine Infantryman Maklin pulling himself up with pride, down in the earth;

"I'm a hero! They're firing the salute for me, and the medal on the cross is mine!"

What a great mockery.

23 | The Clenched Fist

FOLLOWING THE GREAT and bitter victory won through the agonies of hell in the Galician mud after the thaw, we are allowed a brief respite.

But we Jews are not to be allowed to enjoy the rest. Another roll call. It cannot be forgotten that some of the heroes are Jews. Once again those of us those who won medals are singled out for extraordinary hatred.

Now it's my turn to join the hated ones. Up till now the officers' hatred – by the Holy Virgin – has not been directed at me. Either I have been lucky, or perhaps I have staved off the hatred by the many discussions and exchanges of battle-front philosophy, which have been difficult for my fellow officers to digest. Whatever it is, I have so far been excluded from the openly displayed Jew-loathing. Even *Herr* Figer doesn't seem to feel any revulsion when we engage in our rather lengthy debates.

But now my turn has come. I am awarded a large gold medal, upon recommendation of my honest and noble Lieutenant Smerčany.

Colonel Figer himself pins the medal on my chest, saying:

"I've heard that you have Magyar blood in your veins, that one of your grandmothers was a pure Magyar, daughter of Bishop Kohani. That is not ordinary Magyar blood, but Calvinist blood, the bearer of the steadfast stubbornness and perseverance of John Calvin! This places a great obligation upon your shoulders. This blood demands that you overcome the Jewish blood in your veins."[1]

Here he stops a moment, as if regretting his frankness, and I take advantage of the moment to blurt out:

"Overcome the blood of the Maccabees, Herr Colonel?"[2]

His entire staff, which has been standing around us during this ceremony, is seized with horror at my presumption.

"Shut up, Ensign! I didn't ask your opinion, did I! I'm talking now!" shouts Colonel Figer. Then he controls himself, his face grows as pleasant and affable as before, and he goes on, thoughtfully:

"The blood of the Maccabees? Perhaps you do have the blood of the Maccabees in your veins. But it isn't too clear exactly how brave they really were. The people they defeated were not of pure Greek stock. Antiochus Epiphanes, Apollonius, Siron, Nicanor, Giorgias – they were not true Greeks.[3] Well, this is no time for debate. You have won a medal. His Majesty commends you and counts you among his heroes. You must now show yourself worthy of the honor!"

He shakes my hand.

Now there's a theory for you! What a shame that Judah the Maccabee didn't choose a pure Greek nation to defeat!

Henceforward I am marked as an object for open hatred. In a flash, my former friends become avowed enemies, without the slightest shame or compunction.

It's really astonishing how an officer can shed his personality in a twinkling of an eye and appear like a totally different person. For months past he has been your comrade, your bosom friend; he has played cards with you, gotten drunk with you, joked with you (Jewish jokes are popular even among the more antisemitic officers), asked your advice, and even read you letters to his mother and sweetheart. But all of a sudden he surprises you with a viciousness that makes your hair stand on end. Previously he has never made an issue of the formal salute due to him as your superior. On the contrary, he has always made a point of greeting you first, pleasantly and informally: "*Sevas*! *Sevas*!"[4] Now, all of a sudden, when you pass him, he yells out at you:

"Ensign! Don't you know you 're supposed to salute your superiors!!"

It throws you into a fearful agitation. You feel as if your world crumbling around you.

This is what happens to me after my unfortunate distinction. The officers make up their mind to prevent my further promotion at all costs. Nor, they resolved, should I ever win another decoration!

There is only one man among them whose friendly attitude hasn't changed: the good Lieutenant Smerčany.

"Spit on them, old fellow! What do you expect of those boneheads? Don't you know what an officer is? – An officer is a stupid mechanism walking on two gouty wooden pegs mumbling something that resembles human speech. Don't confuse them with real human beings!"

He is especially pained by what happens to kindly old Uncle Osterreicher. The old fellow finds amongst the Russian bodies a soldier whose features look Jewish. He examines him, and when he is convinced that he really was a Jew, he says *kaddish* for him.[5] That is enough to have him reported and sentenced to a day's fast.

The fast is no problem for him, since in any case he observes all the ritual fasts in the Jewish calendar. Corporal Margolis, when he hears about it, thinks up of a clever trick. He advises Uncle Osterreicher to report sick. This is easy enough, since he has been suffering from old man's bronchitis since the thaw, and the doctor has a soft spot for him because of his regular praying, complete with shawl and phylacteries, in accordance with Jewish law. Thus whenever Uncle Osterreicher tells him that he is feeling unwell, the doctor doesn't examine him at all, and promptly gives him sick leave for a day or two. Uncle Osterreicher takes Margolis's advice, and immediately gets a two day furlough. The penalty fast is therefore postponed until the third day, which is – as Margolis is well aware – a traditional Jewish fast, *Ta'anit Esther*.[6]

Typical Margolis cunning – if you must fast, at least do so when you should, and not at *Herr* Figer's express orders!

In this way our indignation at Uncle Osterreicher's punishment turns to a secret joke among the Jewish soldiers.

Lieutenant Smerčany appreciates the joke immensely!

From talking about it, we go on to discuss the various religions. The lieutenant seems to know a great deal about Judaism. He maintains that Jews are superior to Christians in one cardinal point – they aren't as superstitious as the average Christian. It's amazing, he states, how otherwise civilized Christians are given to senseless and meaningless superstitions, to the point of childish ingenuousness. Slavs especially, even the most intelligent amongst them who are atheists and believe in nothing, cannot shake off this nonsense.

I tell him how the Russian soldier lit our cigarettes, two to a match. The lieutenant has heard of this superstition, and says:

"There, you see! You can pound the Russian in a mortar but you can't get the superstition out of him!"[7]

This is a timely discussion. Among the many diseases which the army tends to catch at the front, that of obsessive superstitions is paramount. At every moment some completely irrelevant incident impresses itself on people and makes them to do the strangest and stupidest things. Amongst superstitions both in cities and village are: finding a horseshoe on the way, sneezing while eating, breaking a mirror, lending a pin or a needle without first pricking the borrower, and the like. At the front, hundreds of others are added. We all fervently adopt them: they adopt an almost religious significance. This is not surprising. Fear is a powerful psychological impetus to believe in every possible thing, both rational and irrational. The subconscious justification for it lies in the thought: why not do it, if people say it helps? If it doesn't help, at least it can do no harm.

So you do some stupid thing or avoid doing something, because of popular superstition.

I am convinced that this is what makes the very rich so religious. A man on whom Dame Fortune has smiled lives in constant fear that she will suddenly frown. That is why there are no atheistic millionaires.

Gamblers and performers are likewise superstitious. Before every performance Enrico Caruso used to kneel backstage and pray *Cara Mia Matera* with all his heart and soul.[8] Every prima donna carries some sort of "good luck" amulet in her bosom. People about to travel by airplane take some kind of stuffed animal with them "to save them from disaster," and so forth.

The soldier at the front, who is continually in the hands of a capricious fate, becomes full of such superstitions. He may laugh at himself for them, but won't give them up in the face of danger.

I experience this myself, and feel deeply ashamed.

I feel ashamed, but don't overcome my weakness. For the same reason – why not believe? It won't help, but it certainly won't hurt. So I succumb to the general foolishness.

The conversation about this becomes quite unpleasant for the cultured lieutenant and myself, because we both know that we are not immune to this accursed plague. He denies it emphatically when I point this out, and changes the subject.

A short time later, an ugly occurrence quite literally hits both of us between the eyes and forces us to confront it.

What happened was this:

I am sent out with ten men to scout the nearby wood in preparation for an attack. While we are there, the enemy spots us and opens fire with their heavy guns. Cannon are not adapted to firing on ten men, and the Russians must think that the entire regiment is advancing against them.

Then something extremely rare occurs – something that happens every thousand years. A shell lands right on top of my NCO – he simply disintegrates, as if he never existed. He had been lying beside me, on my left. There are only bits and pieces left of him to establish his identity and bury.

When the firing stops and I can get up I see that my left sleeve is blood-stained, one of my coat buttons is buttoned in the wrong hole, and the peak of my cap is turned to the right.

That I should have come out intact, when the man right beside me has been torn to shreds, is unbelievable luck. I almost say a prayer there and then.[9]

But I don't re-button my coat, neither do I turn my cap back from its absurd position which makes me look like a drunkard. It's plain to me that these things have saved my life.

But now I have to go and report the progress of my detail to my superior officer. To appear before him with my uniform awry is strictly against regulations. Men are punished for such things, officers especially, because they have to set an example for others.

But I'll be damned if I am about to tempt providence! I refuse to adjust my button and my cap, no matter what happens!

So, I appear before my superior officer looking drunk, my coat buttoned crooked, like a German professor's and my cap looking as if I have just been boxed on the ears.

I enter his quarters and stand at attention near the door. He responds in his usual amiable manner, but when he sees the state of my uniform he throws me a warning glance, as if hinting that I adjust my dress.

I ignore it.

He turns away, to give me time to straighten out my appearance. I ignore his generous intention.

Again he hints at my state, this time not so subtly.

Nothing doing.

When he realizes that this is no oversight but deliberate on my part, he changes his tune. Pretending not to notice, he says:

"Give me the report!"

I give him my written report and he signs it.

Then I notice something strange: he signs it with his left hand. It's a strain for him to write with his left hand but he does it nevertheless.

What is going on? When was he wounded in his right hand? We would have known about this.

Moreover, he comes up to me and shakes my hand – still using his left hand. He smiles knowingly, broadly, almost laughing out loud, when he says: "About face! Dismiss!"

That evening I find out the reason. Having narrowly escaped injury in the last battle, he discovers that his right hand was clenched tight. Now there is no power on earth that can make him unclench it for the next seven days.

My enlightened, cultured lieutenant, the doctor of philosophy!

24 | Woman! Woman!

SOMEWHERE, spring is making headway, though not around us, not in the ashen-gray Galician sky, nor in the forlorn, black, muddy earth. It is, however, to be discerned within us, in the souls of the miserable trench-dwellers.

We have grown accustomed to thinking of ourselves as a unique species, unrelated to the people who inhabit our towns and villages. Each one of us has people back there – father, mother, friends, relatives, acquaintances, but by now they seem unimaginably distant. What connection could there be between them and me, Infantryman Avigdor Feuerstein, who has been squatting in a trench for the past two years, sleeping quite soundly in deep mud, eating bread crusted with clods of earth, liable to die a violent death at any moment, sharing a cigarette with an infantryman who stripped dogs in civilian life? What connection could I have with any brother or friend back there, who is at that moment dozing in a cabaret, laughing at some joke or other about a fat mother-in-law?! Perhaps there is – if I could suddenly materialize before him, smack him soundly on his laughing face hard enough to stun him, grab him by the legs and swing him around like a broom, to bring all the other roisterers down, and then burn down the entire blasted cabaret together with all those accursed people performing on the stage! That's the connection I have with them!

It's insufferable! For the past two years, I've been living in constant peril of my life. Standing, sitting down, sleeping, eating, even smoking – at any moment a bullet may pierce my skull and put me in a mass grave, without so much as a burial ceremony, and no one would even know where my remains are buried.

Tens of thousands around me go insane
But my mind – it still remembers.
In a moment my time will come
And no one can foresee when.

Za-za-za: how beautiful is the death-hymn:
My heart chokes in my throat;
Za-za-za – oh mother, oh grandfather,
Oh my God, my Lord.

Drugged, my mind is sweaty, craven
Za-za-za, close your eyes quickly
In a moment – filthy ravens
Will crowd over you, cackling.

And your heart's blood will be clotted
And you will rot there under the bushes.
Za-za – please get rid of the body quickly
Without eulogy and shrouds.

Over there, in the city, men like myself are living their lives under peaceful, blue skies, without any airplanes shitting bombs on their heads, without shells and shrapnel, clowning around and laughing at a fat mother-in-law joke, enjoying the "fine art" of men screwing women. They are concerned only that their delightful whores should not rebuff them, but wear the most provocative crepe-de-chine dress and net panties. Why is *he* sitting there, and not I!! What makes him dearer to His Majesty than I am?!

Why should I be eating filthy eggs and have a constant rendezvous with death?

"This is the most painful feeling, and it consumes us here worse than anything else," writes my poor friend, Ensign Rubinsky, to one of his friends back in the city.

"Here we are, three or four of us, crouching under a wet shrub on a cold damp night. We lie in wait for death, which likewise lies in wait for us. Silence. Hours of silence. Then the enemy moves, right opposite us. He shoots, and a bullet whistles past my temple… And you, you back there in the city, are lying in a silken bed, kissing a warm woman.

"That's it!

"Woman!

"We have grown accustomed to everything, to every kind of misfortune. If the mud is too deep, and the quartermaster can't bring us provisions, we lie here like starved mangy dogs, scratching flea bites the size of olive pits, waiting for three days before we're allowed, by special dispensation, to open our tinned supplies. Poor Infantryman Guilani couldn't wait. He opened his can without permission – and paid for it with his life. Right there and then.

"Why? At that time you were sitting in a restaurant with your merry friends, guzzling beefsteak at a dinner party and washing it down with red wine. What happens if peace should suddenly come and we return home? I would first go to the restaurant and rip your gluttonous head off, then sit down and eat your dinner with gusto!

"Oh if the King would suddenly make peace!

"But we've gradually got used to that, too. Food? What do I care if my belly is full of toads, or roasted rats, so long as it's full? I have learned that one can be satisfied with anything.

"But there is one thing one can't get used to – the lack of a woman.

"How beautiful woman is! God, how beautiful she is!

"I sit down to eat, and facing me is a laughing woman with beautiful face and hands.

"I sit down to smoke, and facing me is a laughing women with white teeth and sexy voluptuous breasts.

"I lie down on the damp ground and try to sleep, and besides me lies a woman, warming me with her warm kittenish body, purring… Alas, It's my own body that I embrace, my own self that I press to my cold breast. It's my own hairy arm that I am licking, gritting my teeth, and my whole body convulses for a woman! A woman!

"Oh Bella!

"Bella, Margit, Emma, Mansie, Ilonka, Sara, Netta, Marie, Jophie, Clara, Anna, Rebecca, Cleopatra!

"Woman, Woman, Woman!

"The entire front groans with longing for absent women. The body has been hardened to withstand the worst trials, the heart has been petrified by so many bullets and shells, the muscles are knotted steel – but there is no woman into whom a man can sow his seed.

"Woman. Back there at home, in the city. She is playing with some scoundrel, who instead of waiting for death here beside me, is primping up his necktie and waxing his moustaches in order to kiss a woman there. A woman!"

Thus wrote my comrade Ensign Rubinsky to his friend, as his face turned all colors.

My men are sitting quietly, their silence overflowing with longing. A whiff of spring has touched their brown, trembling bodies, and they remain silent. Spring is torturing them. One of them gets up abruptly, sighs, and complains almost tearfully:

"Why can't we kiss a woman? Would it be so difficult for headquarters to bring a few women over here, at least once a month?!"

He sits down again and moans to himself:

"A fat lot His Majesty cares about it!"

But another soldier objects. He flings away an unfinished cigarette and shouts:

"By the Holy Virgin, if there were one he himself would kiss her!"

Most restless of all is the giant Croatian, Franz Rizic. He paces up and down like a mad bull, muscles bulging, blowing through his trumpet-like nose, snorting like a wild ox and swearing at the Holy Virgin:

"I'd tear a woman apart and eat her flesh without salt!" he says, eyes shining passionately. I feel deeply sorry for him. Suddenly he stops still and says with deathlike calm:

"Oh, how I would chase the Russians right back to Moscow, if only I could first sleep with my buxom Rosa!"

Then he says:

"I'm going crazy here. I'm losing my mind, it's going all dark. All I can see are women's tits and asses."

"And the head, you pig? What about Rosa's beautiful head?!"

"The head? I would swallow up it whole, first of all!"

His bulging eyes, turning my way, swell with tears,

Poor fellow.

Spring is making itself felt. The sun slowly disperses the clouds.

Above ground, on both sides of the trenches, grass sprouts everywhere. Here and there a little red or blue flower appears.

A bird trills high in the sky.

Look! There's a butterfly!

We're forbidden to stick our heads out and gaze a little at the land, which exudes spring everywhere.

Pály catches the butterfly on the wing, crushes and steps on it, exclaiming:

"Take that, you worm!"

"You vile beast!" I snap at him.

"*I'm* a vile beast?" says Pály, his beautiful eyes flashing. "*God* is a vile beast, by the Holy Virgin!"

He throws himself on his back on the damp earth and looks up at the blue sky, chest heaving.

A songbird warbles nearby.

The giant Croatian snatches up a clod of earth and flings it upwards with all his formidable strength:

"Get away, or I'll blow you into the nest of that sevenfold holy God Almighty up there in the heights of his hermitage!"

As for Lieutenant Stubniak, whose conversation has always been confined to women and dogs, he has descended to such vulgarity that even we are surprised.

One fine day he is court-martialed for sneaking into the village of Zlata-Lipa[1] and raping an old woman there.

He is sentenced to twenty-five lashes on his soles.

Before long another man is court-martialed for a similar offence. His punishment is more severe – he is degraded from corporal to a lowly private.

Then a third.

Headquarters issues an order that for rape, combined with unauthorized entry into a town, the punishment will from now on be death by hanging!

Imagine that! Hanging at the front! It involves more than just death!

But it doesn't help much.

Spring torments all of us, even those at headquarters.

I am especially concerned about my giant Croatian. I manage to keep him under restraint (or perhaps it isn't thanks to me). He bites his flesh, but remains where he is. The entire camp seems to be possessed: men sneak into town and disgrace the army. Above all, they undermine discipline! That is intolerable. Demoralization!

Finally, headquarters finds the answer – advance the line, assault the enemy!

That is real punishment. An offensive is considerably worse than defensive fighting. It's a soul-searing hell. You have to leave your trench, where you are concealed and can protect yourself from the enemy, and come out against him, while he is entrenched and able to hit back with all his strength.

But, strange to say, the fellows accept their punishment with satisfaction.

We have not yet taken part in such an offensive. All the suppressed energy, all the unrelieved sexual passion the soldiers have bottled up, is let loose upon the enemy. The Russian officers we capture ask us, what led to such a mad attack?

We attack like wild beasts, heedless and headlong, like wild animals that do not find their prey. The Russians retreat 70 kilometers to our rear!

Headquarters rub their hands with glee: Here is the reason for banning women from the front. Women consume the men's fighting energy!

And so it is. The giant Croatian, who has already won a number of respectable medals, does wonders this time. He plunges into the enemy camp like a maddened, deaf, dumb and blind beast, hardly firing his rifle, but using its butt to hit at the enemy left and right. He leads us into a bayonet fight without my order – and the fellows follow him like maniacs.

I feel the obsession of woman haunting my giant Croatian. Instead of growing wilder, he has grown increasingly subdued. But this is the calm before the storm, full of pain and sorrow. He has never been a big eater, this great bull of a man. (Margolis, the scrawny corporal, eats a great deal more than he does. Where does it all go?). He often shares his rations with one of his comrades. Of late he has been eating even less. Except for the mug of black coffee, which he drains with one gulp, he eats nothing till midday. Then he eats his soup and that's all. The rest he leaves for Margolis – only Margolis, under no circumstances anybody else. A mocking fate has brought these two men together, the towering seven foot giant Franz Rizic with the pigmy Jewish corporal, whose head scarcely reaches his friend's chest. Our one entertainment in the trenches is to watch those two walk arm in arm, the Croatian blowing Margolis back with one great sneeze, like chaff before the wind.

But lately the good Croatian has lost his sense of humor, together with his appetite. He wants a woman badly. Only a woman. He seems to be shrinking. I fear that this change is a bad omen. I feel he is coiling up so as to spring back suddenly at his cruel destiny.

During our rapid advance we enter the village of Zeshnenko, where we are ordered to stop and rest. We are dog-tired and fall asleep at once.

The next morning Pály brings me the latest news, as he always does at this hour. Among other things, he informs me that, in one of the village houses, a single Jewish girl has been found: she is insane.

"Why don't they detain her? They ought to tie her up and send her back to the rear," I said.

"She's perfectly quiet, says Pály. "She sits by the window looking at the forest, without moving. If you talk to her she doesn't answer. She just sits there, staring with open eyes, not saying a word. She's beautiful. Very beautiful, but thin, and her face looks dead. Do go and see her, sir. You should!"

I go.

The house stands at the end of the village not far from the edge of the thick forest, through which the Russians have fled. I enter. The house is in disorder. Broken furniture everywhere. On the table lies half a loaf of Russian army bread. There is a bed with bedding, which looks as though someone has just risen from it. It looks like a typical Jewish home.

There is no one in this room.

I enter the next room. It's a young girl's bedroom, reasonably clean and tidy. The white room of a Galician Jewish maiden. The white bed is ruffled. The mad girl is sitting by the window, looking out at the forest. She doesn't seem to notice us. I approach her, but she doesn't react. I try to speak to her, but it's as though I'm not there at all. She keeps staring ahead of her, with a frozen gaze. I take her hand and turn her face towards me. She looks at me for a moment with glassy eyes, which slowly close. When I let go of her head she turns it back mechanically towards the forest. I offer her something to drink, but she doesn't react. I offer her food, but she doesn't hear me.

She is beautiful. Although blonde, she is a typical Galician Jewish woman, like a Jewish Madonna. But terribly thin, wasted like a consumptive.

I try to move her from the window by force. At first she seems to yield, but when I set her on her feet and try to lead her, she pushes me away with such herculean strength that I almost fall.

I decide to report the matter to the army doctor.

While I am writing the report, Pály comes in and informs me that they had found another living soul in the village, an ancient crone. She is waiting outside. I go and bring her inside. I offer her a little brandy, which she drinks greedily and then asks for "something to go with it." I give her a wheaten rusk, from the officers' rations. She eats a little and stops, exhausted. She is very old.

"How old are you. grandmother?

"Last week I was 93."

"May you live to 120," I immediately say.

The old woman shakes her head:

"No need. Who needs such long life nowadays? The young ones are dying, and I drag myself around. I ask myself, who needs me? Why does The Almighty keep me here? As if to spite, no form of death overwhelms me. As if to spite me."

"Why did they leave you behind in the village?"

"They didn't leave me, dearie. I stayed. Where would I go? What for?"

I divert the conversation and ask her about the mad girl. The old woman tells me what happened to her. It's a fantastic story, difficult to believe. The Cossacks had come into the village and all but destroyed it. They murdered, slaughtered, abused, tortured. One Cossack killed the girl's parents before her eyes. He wanted to kill her too, but she fell at his feet and pleaded for her life, and he spared her. A couple of days later she was seen in the village, strolling arm in arm with the Cossack, clinging to him lovingly, like a young bride, laughing, gay and happy. Both the Jews and even the gentiles who remained in the village couldn't believe their eyes. If she had only looked mad – But no – she seemed quite lucid, even in love with her parents' murderer. She was their only daughter. When the Cossacks drove the surviving villagers out, she stayed with her lover. When our forces approached the village and the Cossacks beat a hasty retreat, she was left behind.

"The Cossack threw her away like a sack of rags," said the old woman. "I was at her house when it happened, because the poor girl loves me. He cast her off and ran away."

"Since then," the old woman concludes, "she has been

sitting by the window looking after him, towards the forest. She has been sitting like this for more than a week. She doesn't see, doesn't hear, doesn't eat or sleep. She just sits there, staring. Sometimes she dozes off, sitting there. She sits until she is exhausted and then falls asleep. Then she wakes up and goes on staring, without budging from her place. I've tried to give her something to eat or drink, but it's no use. It's a miracle her soul hasn't left her body yet. Who knows what it means – to fall in love with a murderer? Who can understand such a thing? God acts in mysterious ways."

The doctor examines her and thinks that there's no point in transferring her to a hospital. She would die in a day or two in any case.

I have no time to question him about the scientific explanation for this "sad marvel," as the soldiers have begun to call the poor girl, because the Russians have just opened up a fierce artillery offensive. We prepare for a stubborn defense. Then a strange and frightful thing occurs – a 28 caliber shell falls on the girl's house and, when the ruins are searched she is found torn to pieces, together with the giant Croatian.

Investigation discloses that the poor fellow ejaculated into the beautiful, half-dead girl.

There his destiny catches up with him. With the woman.

It takes a tremendous effort to spare him a disgraceful end. I succeed in having him buried honorably, together with the girl.

When we bury him, under a Russian barrage, little Margolis sheds tears. The old woman is there too, but she doesn't weep. Her tears dried up long ago.

Another strange thing happens. Lieutenant Stubniak, who had been degraded after his spell of "madness," is wounded in a peculiar way – a piece of shrapnel castrates him.

Little Margolis can't resist saying:

"From now on, no more women and dogs! That's the second degradation for playing mad – from man to eunuch!

"Such luck!" one of the men says enviously. "Such luck! Now he will be at peace, free of this cursed need for women!"

The poor fellow says this with tragic earnestness, from the depths of his heart, with genuine envy.

25 | Sublime!

A MAGNIFICENT AUGUST. Enough to drive one mad.

I receive a letter from Mansie. A very brief letter. It is the first I have received from her in months. She's working as a nurse in a hospital, and seems to excel at her work. As soon as I was sent to the front, she went to work in a hospital. She has abandoned the stage, the applause, wine and nightlife, and devoted herself to caring for the sick and the wounded.

> Avigdor,
> I've been having terrible dreams lately, insane nightmares. I see you dead already. I'm just about going out of my mind.
> Mansie.

A terrifying letter. Terrifying not because she is suffering, but because such letters bring death in their wake. Of late it seems that back in the city a spirit of prophecy has animated women who have sweethearts at the front. They seem to see their men's death as plainly as clairvoyants. One is ashamed to speak in such a way, but facts are facts. Lance Corporal Chizhik, a fine Slovak soldier who was a farmer and cobbler in his village, receives a letter from his fiancée in which she tells him that she dreamed that she saw him with a hole in his head. We laugh at the letter. A few days later the lance corporal is killed while eating – a bullet enters his left temple and exits through the right.

This is not an isolated case. The women's prophecies often come true. Of course, we only witness the cases when they do, not the cases when they do not. But only at first. After a few months these prophetic letters become a source of horror for the men. The great anguish and intense longings in the heart of a woman deeply attached to her man tauten and sharpen her nerves and senses to the point of prophetic epilepsy. If you haven't been at the front for at least a year, don't ridicule this. If it's at all ridiculous, then only we who have experienced these things have a right to ridicule it. We have seen what we have seen.

The commandant of our third battalion, Colonel Berger, is torn to pieces by a shell. In his pocket they find a letter from his mistress, telling him that she has made peace with his wife (what torture it must have been, that forced a mistress to make peace with her lover's wife! What torture must have led the wife to extend her hand of welcome to the mistress!), because she has dreamed that she saw him, the colonel, torn to pieces and pleading, in his final agony, that she should go to his wife and make peace with her!

General Gutthagen receives a very strange letter from his daughter. She writes: Dear father, Our maid keeps saying that there is a terribly bad smell about lately, and that it comes – please forgive me, my dear father! – from you, from your body. I can understand: I know you are all compelled to wallow in all sorts of filth over there. I do understand. I beg of you, dear father, to take good care of yourself. Bathe as often as you can, even there, for I know you like to wash yourself in cold water even in winter."

The general is puzzled by the letter, but also rather amused. His charming daughter, who is so exceptionally intelligent – did she imagine that generals too, have to wallow in filth? A general, after all, is housed in decent quarters even at the front. How could she pay attention to the silly servant's chatter?

But General Gutthagen's death bears out the servant's strange obsession. His batman goes mad (or perhaps he didn't go mad, only headquarters preferred to report that he had), murders his master, and buries his body in the outhouse in the courtyard of the Von Wilitzky mansion in Lazarovka.[1]

What is it? Telepathy? Prophecy?

Who knows? What are prophecy, telepathy, trances, insanity, clairvoyance, and the like?

The simplest souls have seen sights denied to the prophets.

But while in the rear grief and longings purify and sensitize the souls of women agonizing over their loved ones, the front-line soldier also experiences the presence of death. His soul is smelted by the crucible of war into a translucent substance, refined and sensitive to a miraculous degree. The nervous system, clarified in the fires of war, becomes a fine weblike net, which can both receive and radiate images, sounds, movements. Newspapers have recently been full of reports about a marvelous new invention capable of picking up sounds from all corners of the world and transmitting them to our ears. There is even talk about a "television" machine which will pick up pictures and project them across vast distances.

Who knows? – Perhaps such things will be possible. I myself believe implicitly that man can achieve greater wonders than these. And if such machines are possible, then I also believe in prophecy, which appears marvelous only so long as science has been unable to explain it rationally. Above all, I believe in the wonderful machine called *homo sapiens*, which may have the potential ability to radiate waves from itself over vast distances If the much-discussed hypothesis of Professor Einstein – to whom newspapers have recently devoted a great deal of space – is correct, and there is no separating space and time, and time is merely the fourth dimension of space,[2] why should it not be possible for our "soul machine" to receive not only that which is distant from it in space, but also in time from past and future? Why not? For, surely, according to this theory there is neither past nor future in time, as there is none is space?... Why not, indeed?

One thing is certain, our nerves here, in death's dugout, are no longer mere somatic threads of flesh. Observing us, my men and myself, I realize that neither our speech nor our conduct is in any way like what they used to be back home, before we had undergone all these experiences. We communicate in allusions, understand one another wordlessly. At times, words seem superfluous. Worse, they sometimes spoil communication. Who was it who said that speech is given to us to conceal our thoughts?[3] – It's true. I look at one of my men, Infantryman Gábor Balkani, and the love I feel for him is unlike anything I have previously felt for another man. The lad arouses a warm sympathy in me, but instead of revealing it, I say all sorts of other things. I chatter irrelevant phrases at him. But he feels my love for him *despite* those phrases! Another man is forever fearful for me, does all kinds of foolish things in the confusion of battle to protect me, to cover me, and when I survive intact, he stands or sits facing me, caressing me with his eyes, telling stupid stories. I see what he wants to say in his eyes, and the words he is uttering are totally unrelated. What he really wants to say is that he is so happy that I am alive, that he can see me with his own eyes and go on living beside me. As for my young batman Pály, who curses at me in the foulest language when I am careless, he always says the opposite of what is really on his mind.

But that is not the main thing. Far more important is the fact that almost every one of us can read the other's thoughts. We dream each other's longings, read each other's minds, even foresee each other's death as if in a dream. Together this all fuses into a great harmony, a love which no Greek philosopher or Hebrew prophet has ever dreamed of. This love is often revealed in an unexpected manner, without ever having been put in words.

A splendid, dazzling August day. A gentle hint of autumn has dressed nature in the cosmic cloak of its unsubstantiality. The setting sun glows, and we are lying on our backs, gazing at it. I seem to hear the roar of its colossal solar flares from a hundred and fifty million kilometers away. Oh yes, I can hear it. And while we lie here, a great, profound sadness spreads its black wings over us all, uniting us into one titanic soul, aching without wounds, tormented without knowing why, longing without knowing why.

Perfect quiet. Both here and over there, beyond our world, on the Russians' side.

They, too, are daydreaming, Together with us. We are merged together, separated only by the mighty longing to be with them physically, too, here, under the sun.

How we love them, those men over there, who are suffering with us, dreaming of the sun, of love, of women, of God!

Suddenly fat Rosenberger says:

"I'd give five years of my life to be the first to run across to them and give them a warm, fraternal greeting!"

"To do that and then die," says the lanky Tyrolean, as if continuing Rosenberger's thoughts without a break.

"I'm keeping a box of Memphis cigarettes that my Ada sent me for the first one of them that I meet," continues Barchi the professional hoodlum.

I realize that my own mind has been preoccupied with the idea of meeting the Russians. A few more exchanges, and I can determine beyond all doubt that all of us have been thinking the same thoughts. I perform an experiment:

"What were you thinking about just now?" I surprise Margolis, who has been lying there dreaming.

"I was thinking of a *minyan* with the Jews on that side" he answers without hesitation.[4] The first prayer we'll say will be *hagomel* (the prayer of thanks for deliverance from mortal danger)![5]

"How did you know what I was thinking, you little *yid*?!"[6] chides Uncle Osterreichcr, who seems to be asleep. He continues:

"I don't propose to get killed before I've prayed in one regular *minyan* with them – whether peace comes first or not! I swear!"

"*You* swear. Uncle Osterreicher?" I scold him.

"Yes. I swear."

"A righteous man proposes and the Holy One Blessed Be He fulfils," Margolis notes.

After a while he adds:

"How I should like just once to embrace a big Russian *goy*[7] and say to him, *khorosho, pan*![8] To embrace him and lift him up and throw him and wrestle with him."

"They are good fellows," says a stocky Magyar, who has served a long prison sentence for having murdered someone when drunk on his wedding day. "Simple fellows, who like a little drink, a good woman, fine horses. Just like us. It would be nice to meet them some time and drink with them a little."

"When peace comes, the first thing I'll do is to travel to Russia," says the scarred Serbian "bastard" half to himself. "I'll go there for a month or so and love them."

That's what he said – love them!

The sun is setting slowly. It fills our hearts with boundless joy and unimagined love. I think about the city and a unique joy sweeps over me, because I am here, suffering all sorts tortures in its defense, protecting the frontiers so that the enemy may not break through and disrupt its joys and pleasures. Just for a moment I feel a flash of resentment and envy against the city, whose inhabitants are lounging in theaters, laughing at some mother-in-law joke. But the next moment I am filled with pity, mingled with affection and compassion – let them rejoice, let them enjoy themselves, laugh, live the good life! I am happy to protect them, to shelter them from danger, to die a thousand violent deaths for them.

I'm happy.

What a wonderful destiny is mine – to die for others.

Only one thing hurts me – Mansie doesn't know that I'm thinking about her at this moment… Impossible! She must know.

The night is warm, soothing. Perfect quiet. The Russians aren't sending us any "gifts."

We lie here, thinking their thoughts. I light the lamp and write:

Blood and the Rose

It makes little difference to us wherever we may be,
Each kiss bears fruit and each color is blood,
Come to my grave, let us couple in a last embrace

Are you fearful? Please, don't be, for you shall find me
Over my clod of earth there you shall bend, with your glowing flesh,
And my fresh blood sap will bring you fragrant flowers.

In the land enriched with my sacred passion,
Come, kiss me for the last time with your trembling body
And let our Creator watch, and revel in His handiwork.

Let the maggots, boring through these crypts
Know how hallowed is the love of flesh for flesh,
Be fruitful and multiply and enjoy God's blessing.

And after we have, for eternity, been joined anew,
May you, O blood rose, blossom from my grave,
Stemmed from my marrow, glisten in the glorious sun.

A long, contented, agreeable silence.

Suddenly Infantrymen Djiga starts, as if from a nightmare and shouts:

"Tonight they'll attack! Tonight!"

"They won't. Not tonight," I say.

"They will sir! You'll see! I dreamed it. Some bastard has just entered their trench, a big bastard, and he himself has brought the order. You'll see, sir! Also, sir" – he added smiling "do be careful. Please! It was a bad dream. Be careful, sir!"

"You son of a bitch!" bellows my Pály. "*You'll* croak, not the ensign!"

The entire exchange seems half humorous, like all talk about dreams. But Djiga nevertheless gets up and dressed.

"I simply can't sleep, by the Holy Virgin!" he grumbles.

Less than an hour later the Russian offensive begins.

26 | The Whore City

DURING THIS BATTLE I receive an unpleasant visitor. The degraded Second Lieutenant Stubniak returns from sick leave, having spent some time in hospital recovering from his unique wound.

When he enters our trench somebody bursts out laughing. The rest of us, though we try our best to suppress it, are infected by the hilarity. There is no escaping the bad joke – the lieutenant has returned a eunuch.

At any other time the lieutenant would have angrily meted out stiff punishment to the entire platoon. But during an attack, with danger lurking everywhere, every private towers head and shoulders above him.

"Look at him, cowering like a dog," Corporal Margolis whispers audibly to Pály.

Lieutenant Stubniak doesn't bother me in the least. His notorious cowardice has only increased – or rather, whatever courage he had has only diminished several degrees since he left the front – or, possibly, since his castration. He sits quietly and drinks and drinks from his flask. Despite us being under a constant hail of shells (the Russians are shelling our rear trenches), we keep glancing at him, to see if we can spot the changes caused by his injury.

He doesn't curse or joke about women and dogs as he used to. He just sits there and boozes, pale and shivering. Whenever a shell flies overhead he seems to cringe and shrink into himself even more.

I feel tempted to bait him a little, to request orders. After all, he is there in his capacity as my superior officer.

He tries to get out of it by bravado, saying generously:

"No, no! He-He-He-You. That is, you're actually the commanding officer here – I'm, that is – I've been away, I haven't been back long" he stammers smilingly, slapping me on the shoulder. "I've become a rookie, my friend…Please – Please – Thank you very much – thank you…"

"Lieutenant sir! Beg to report: I won't do anything without an order!"

He stammers some more, cravenly, flatteringly, obsequiously, uttering compliments that nauseate the entire platoon.

The telephone shrills. We are ordered to send out an NCO with five men, to advance towards the enemy.

He passes on the order to me and adds generously:

"Do go on – Send that what's-his-name, the corporal, with five men, please."

"I need five men to come with me," I call out. Who will volunteer?

The lieutenant protests:

"Not you – Don't go, please! Only him, and them. You don't have to go!"

"*Herr Leutnant* sir! Beg to report: I never *send* men on such missions. I always *call* them to come with me."

"Why?" he stammers. "What for? There is no such order – I'm not ordering you – There's no need. Sit down, drink a little with me. There's plenty!"

Meantime five men and one NCO have lined up, and we all go over the top.

"You," I hear him mumbling behind me. "You are a valiant soldier, my friend. Good! Good! Go with God. I hope you succeed."

Hardly have we walked twenty paces when I hear a great gun roaring and then a whining noise A frightful blow knocks me down. Excruciating pain. –

When I come to, the army doctor is standing beside me, yelling orders to carry me away. He gives me a drink of brandy, shouting:

"Hurry and you'll be there in twenty minutes! Quick! Quick! If he dies on the way I'll wring your necks like – "

I don't hear the rest. Pain overwhelms me and I fall asleep. (Later I discover that I've fainted a second time).

I wake up in the headquarters field hospital.

The wound is massive and very dangerous, very near the heart. A ragged splinter of shrapnel, the top screw, about half the diameter of an egg, has entered my chest about three finger-breadths above my heart. The pain is overpowering. I can see and hear nothing. Only the nurse's voice comes through, again and again:

"You will recover, ensign, please God. It's all right. You'll recover. Only rest. The main thing is rest. Be at ease… The danger has passed. It really has, thank God. The operation was successful."

A few days later a young doctor comes to talk to me:

"Goddamn! That was a devilish injury – right beside the heart. Obviously, a poet should be wounded in his heart! How did you plan it so well? Directly beside the heart, yet not in the heart itself!"

He goes on to explain:

"You know that above the heart you have two great arteries which are actually one?"

I blink to show that I am following him. For the moment I don't have the strength for another reply.

"Well, then. The Russians, damn their souls, hit you with a piece of shrapnel right between both arteries! The fragment, the part of the screw, actually hit them both, but the arteries were gracious enough to allow it to pass between them, and they remained intact." If only one of them had been torn, why then – *kaputt*! You'd be lying there a dead hero."

I blink repeatedly, to indicate "No!"

"What no" he protests authoritatively. "I tell you, Yes!"

I blink again, and he becomes upset:

"You simply don't understand! What do you know about anatomy and medicine?! You only understand poetry."

But the nurse understands:

"The *Herr* ensign means, No, if the piece of shrapnel had hit the arteries, he wouldn't be lying here a dead hero. He'd be over there in a mass grave!"

I blink to show that I agree.

Then pain overwhelms me again.

I am transferred to the rear into Hungary itself. Here, at the hospital, I find out that my life is still in danger. Spells of fever come and pass, rising and falling sharply and suddenly.[1]

For two weeks my condition will not stabilize. The doctors do everything they can, try every possible means to reduce the pain and heal the wound, but nothing helps. They can't understand it. The wound was grave, deep and dangerous, but after the jagged piece of shrapnel was removed, the healing process should have proceeded smoothly and I should have begun to improve in a normal way.

Of course, they don't think of asking what I think. What army doctor would ever ask a patient for his opinion? At the front, the doctor prescribes one of two remedies for all ailments – aspirin or castor oil. For a headache or a stomach ache – aspirin or castor oil. For palpitations – aspirin or castor oil. For an attack of rheumatism following a week of lying in the wet – aspirin or castor oil. Two wonder remedies, which cure every disease under the sun. Manna from heaven!

This is the fate of all who fall ill at the front – until they are wounded.

Even cases of minor wounds are treated with aspirin and castor oil…Treated, that is, until the slightly injured men are carried off on stretchers to hospital with septicemia.

The reason for this is neither ignorance nor negligence. It's designed to deter the malingerers, the cowards and shirkers, who seek to avoid front line duty and hard work, and get some rest. Since a sick soldier who is not wounded and bleeding is quite obviously a malingerer, he is automatically sentenced to a regime of aspirin and castor oil. It happens more than once that such a malingerer breathes his last from the effects of the castor oil.

Little Margolis succeeds in reforming this wonderful regimen. He does it with the unwitting "help" of our divisional surgeon. The little corporal evinces a deep hatred for our own brigade doctor, who is an officious and untalented young man. He has hardly finished medical school when he is made a medical officer, and insists on "strict discipline" in dealing with soldiers.

Margolis has a slight wound in his elbow, which he is treating himself to avoid taking it to that unpleasant young man. But when he hears that His Excellency the surgeon major has condescended to visit our first aid station, he decides to go on the sick list. He enters the station at the right moment and is first in line. The surgeon major sits observing his junior at work

"What is it, Corporal Margolis?" asks the young doctor.

"Beg to request: Would you please give me some aspirin and castor oil, sir?"

Momentary amazed silence. Then the surgeon major himself steps up to Margolis and asks him, very cordially:

"What did you do back home?"

"Excellency, beg to report: I was a deputy rabbi!"

The younger doctor explains to his superior what a *yeshiva* student is.

"Aha, says the senior surgeon. "Well, how do you know what medicine you need? Did you study medicine as well? What's wrong with you?"

"Excellency, beg to report: I have a slight wound in the elbow."

He displays his wound. The surgeon major examines it carefully, then looks severely at the junior doctor, but says nothing. Then he turns back to Margolis, and the little corporal replies to his questions:

"Excellency, beg to report: I studied medicine at the front, not back home. I have learned here that there are two sovereign remedies: aspirin and castor oil!"

By this time the chief surgeon understands the situation completely. He examines the wound and doesn't like what he sees. It's already infected.

"Come here! he barks at his subordinate menacingly. What the hell is this?"

"It's just a minor wound," says the junior doctor, quaking with nervousness, and turns to Margolis: "How did you get it?"

The old doctor gnashes his teeth:

"What are you asking him for, you ignoramus? I'm asking *you*, what is the nature of this wound?"

It's apparent that the wound has been caused by a fall. A stone has torn skin and flesh right down to the bone. The minor wound has gradually become infected.

"Why didn't you come sooner? the senior doctor asks Margolis.

"Excellency, beg to report: Last year I had a terrible toothache. I was given some castor oil for it, and kept half of it. Three months ago I had a gnat in my eye: I was given two aspirin tablets, and kept one. Now that I have this wound I didn't wish to waste any time leaving the front, so I used those two medicines. But now I haven't anymore, so I came to ask for more."

The surgeon major listens, and a slight smile lights up his wrinkled face. He pats Margolis on the shoulder and turns to the young doctor, saying to him severely:

"The corporal is to have two weeks sick leave. Make a note! Meantime, his wound is to be treated with proper care, or he may lose his arm. Understood?! And keep the aspirin and castor oil for yourself!" (I hear this story in detail from Ensign Slezak, who is present). And so the cult of aspirin and castor oil is suspended for a very long time, and the young doctor is banished to the front line.

At the military hospital they don't treat patients with aspirin and castor oil, but the doctor-patient relationship differs entirely from that seen in peacetime. They don't bother to ask the patient how he feels, or what he thinks of his own condition. It is therefore a mystery to them why my wound refuses to heal normally. They don't understand it at all.

Had they asked my opinion, I would have told them the secret. It's the terrible revulsion and deep-seated nausea caused by my surroundings. I feel in the hospital that same indifference to, and mental detachment from, the men in the trenches as is the case for people in the city and coffee houses with their jovial civilian life. It's as if the thousands upon thousands of men condemned to die in their defense mean nothing to them.

Here my smoldering hatred of the city and its masses is increased to almost grotesque proportions. Just look at the conduct of these doctors, nurses, and orderlies, strutting about, among wounded men, who have been sent here from the heart of hell!

The young doctors are always exquisitely, almost foppishly dressed, as if on their way to a masquerade ball. To them the patient is an object, a subject of observation, a guinea pig to be experimented on.

The nurses are daughters of nobles and counts, or home girls with nothing to do, to whom work at the hospital is a type of amusement, an opportunity to preen themselves and show off their white hospital uniforms.

You observe them and realize that the whole world is nothing to them but a mirror in which to see their reflections and study their own actions.

A soldier lies dying in one of the cots, his groans are enough to break your heart. The oily-haired lieutenant-doctor looks right across him with a come-hither look at the young nurse, who responds with a promising smile and walks away from the patient humming a waltz, swinging her hips provocatively, shamelessly.

That's what stops my wound from healing – when I see this and think of my men over there, my blood boils.

Pity the heroes, pity their bravery!

There is one nurse in that hospital who walks about as if daydreaming, her eyes full of deep-seated Weltschmerz. Her name is Teresa. Her attitude to patients, the way she handles the wounded, her manner of speech, are themselves enough to ease their pain.

I ask the doctor to let Nurse Teresa look after me.

I find out later that the good Teresa had been a professional prostitute for a few years before the war.

Hers is the only soul in the place who feels the suffering of the war and sympathizes with its unfortunate heroes.

I find out many other things, which we never suspected. I hear that it is commonplace to see wives cheating on their husbands who are at the front. They lust especially after

Russian prisoners of war. Aristocratic ladies are drawn to common Russian soldiers, and women from the lower classes fall for captive Russian officers.

I discover too that there is one class of women who remain truly faithful to their lovers: the whores, nightclub entertainers, and frivolous dancing girls. These women volunteered for hospital work as soon as the war broke out, and have worked there with endless diligence and devotion, awaiting their lovers and the peace which must eventually come.

Those united in sacred wedlock have become strumpets, and the strumpets saints.

That good nurse heals my wound. I recover and leave the hospital. Only my left arm remains bandaged and in a sling, to prevent it from pressing too much against me.

I am given two months' leave. And so I go to "the city" – my beautiful, exciting and beloved Budapest.

It's then that I discover the staggering worthlessness of man in that stinking capital of corruption.

Budapest is second only to Vienna for gaiety. Its nightlife is notorious. The society of gay rounders which is a world unto itself, a government within a government. More than five thousand people live here entirely by night. Most of them are artists of all sorts, surrounded by a variety of frivolous people, playboys, spendthrifts and wastrels. Budapest doesn't need to apply to others for new forms of merrymaking.

But what they are doing now, during the war, is no longer carousing but killing. Killing every trace of human feeling and minimal respect for the millions who are suffering for the sake of these drones, enduring fiendish tortures, meeting all sorts of terrible, unnatural deaths, to preserve their safety and happiness, their drunken orgies.

I thought that I had been thoroughly familiar with this nightlife, but now I discover a new human species – human parasites. Nematodes and maggots who take special pleasure in considering everyone from the front as legitimate prey. It was the exact opposite at the beginning of the war. Then, on the contrary, the soldier was at an advantage, proud of the sacrifices he was laying on the altar of the city. And those worm-people, the dregs and scum of war, who had bribed their way out of service, walked humbly with tails between their legs, respecting those who went out into the filth and blood. But now it seems they have got used to war, and once they see that there is no danger in it for themselves, their cheerful lives continue on their course. They begin to hold their heads up, rebelling against their "slavish subjection" to righteousness, honor, and love for us.

But what I find most devastating is this most horrible fact – indifference of the wives to their husbands at the front. They seem perfectly contented with the state of affairs. The only feeling they still show for their husbands is to boast of "my husband's valor on the field of honor."

You see a civilian lady walking arm in arm with her prisoner of war, whom she has ransomed on her own surety "for housework," and with whom she lives a gay life, tasting the sweets of forbidden living. You hear her boasting, sighing like the true whore that she is: "Oh yes, my man is also bravely defending our homeland. Isn't it wonderful? He has already won three gold medals!"

And meanwhile she casts lecherous glances at her captive lover.

However, they are more generous than the men to us visitors from the inferno. On rare occasions, they actually prefer us to a Russian prisoner of war! This too they sanctimoniously garb in the cloak of purest patriotism.

"I detest those Russian prisoners," says an acquaintance of mine sitting in a coffee house late one night, her beautiful eyes ogling me amorously. "I also despise these trollops of theirs here, who lack all patriotic feeling, and instead of looking after" (that's what she said, "looking after") "our own wounded heroes, and giving them their love" (here she offers me her sweet mouth and swelling breasts) "they make love to the enemy! How disgusting! And you? How are you? How is your wound?"

I eat, suffering, saying nothing.

She helps me cut the cutlet on my plate.

I suffer in silence.

She tries to feed me a piece of it with the fork.

My patience snaps. I rise and yell:

"Waiter! Remove this whore from my table!"

General consternation. Even the dancing stops for a minute.

I pay and leave.

The city no longer understands such anger.

I stroll around the city, afraid to visit my friends. Even the nearest and dearest.

I go looking for Mansie, as a surprise. She is working at the hospital. When she sees me, she faints clean away.

The doctors speak very highly of her. They all admire her devotion to the wounded patients. She refuses to tend to any other class of patients. The hospital wants to transfer her to a civilian ward, but she threatens to resign.

She is working under an assumed name. Her real name is well-known as a cabaret dancer, and a temperamental one at that.

More than one doctor has tried to put the moves on her, but they soon find out that she is a dangerous woman. As soon as one tries to seduce her, she reports him to the head of the hospital.

The holy snake, that's what they call her.

My Mansie. My "whore" Mansie.

"Why didn't you write more often, Mansie?"

"What for? So you'll yearn for me more there in passionate helplessness? That's all you people need over there!"

"You people," she says. How well she understands the soul of an unfortunate soldier! Thanks to me she has obtained leave for as long as I am here. But she keeps weeping: her eyes are wet all the time.

"What should I give you? What do you want of me? Ask for something!"

"What should I ask for, silly girl?"

"Take whatever you want. Take my body, my soul, my life. I've been trying to remain beautiful and healthy for you. Not with paints and powders and creams. No. I've been eating a lot and doing exercises, though I have no appetite or desire for these things. But I have tried all the same to eat and look well and pretty. All for you. Now tell the truth – do you find me pretty?"

"Very pretty, Mansie."

"Seriously, tell me the truth! Because if I'm not, if you don't want me, I'll get you another woman, a very beautiful one. Tell me!"

"What a fool you are, Mansie. There isn't another woman as beautiful as you in the whole accursed city!"

She cries.

"Why don't you declare peace? I'm sick of it all. I'll go mad!"

"Mansie, if you love me, calm down, go on living a healthy and good life. Eat well and keep beautiful, Mansie, if you love me."

She thinks a moment and says:

"Love you? I don't know. I love not only you, but all the men out there. Why are you suffering? For whom? What for? Why, damn it?! It's horrible!"

"Come on, Mansie. Let's have a drink. We'll have your favorite – cherry brandy with Cointreau. Come on!"

"I shan't drink. Since you went out to that hell I haven't taken even a thimbleful. I don't need it!"

That is indeed the most sacred of all sacrifices.

And they called her a whore.

First – the soldier's wife, the honest and proper bourgeois lady. Today – the loose-moraled cabaret dancer.

The following day I pay a duty call – I visit the wife of my comrade, the painter and sculptor Ensign Diula Kerak. We have an agreement, that whoever gets to the city first would call on the other's family. I send her a note first, to say I have greetings from her husband.

She is waiting for me impatiently. But almost as soon as I come in I am struck by her less than warm interest in her husband. And yet I have known her, and her ardent passion for him – they had only been married a few months before the war tore him away. Now she seems more interested in me than in him.

I tell her about her husband, avoiding the worst, so as not to distress her unduly.

But she keeps returning to me.

As a last resort, I unfold the entire scroll of our sufferings over there, especially her husband's. I try to explain that underneath all the other hardships lies the greatest pain of all, that of longing for woman. And worst of all, a husband's jealousy of his wife, his terrible fear that she may be unfaithful in his absence. "Jealousy at the front," I say, "is unlike any other jealousy. It's a mental torture which combines three agonies in one: passionate longing, sexual deprivation and male honor."[2] Especially honor. The worst insult to it is the thought that she may be making love to some shirker, a useless good-for-nothing coward.

"That is especially true of your husband," I continue. "He is a great artist. The thought that his young wife might betray him with some worthless character with waxed, pointed moustaches drives him crazy."

She listens. Suddenly she rises, goes out and sends the maid out of the house on some excuse. I hear her shutting the front door. Then she returns, sits facing me, her knees accidentally touching mine, as though undesignedly.

"You too are a great artist."

I jump to my feet, my mind in a whirl, angry and offended at the same time with pain, anger, and shame. I close my eyes for a moment and then ask:

"What shall I say to Diula?"

"What should you say to him?" she stammers. "What should you say? Tell him that I'm waiting for him: that his creations are doing well. What else? – Nothing. I'm waiting for him."

"Very well," I say, and leave feeling thoroughly disgusted. I am really stunned. What should I tell the wretched husband?

I will have to lie to him as best I can.

I resolve to leave soon. It's all simply too much for me. This whorish city has stripped itself bare including its filthy chemise, and cavorts lewdly like a shameless harlot. I have to leave.

What will Mansie say, that pure soul of mine in the midst of the general vileness?

But I can't stay any longer. Staying here would be like the tortures of a captive in exile.

A few days later I am all set to return to the front. I am not going to use up the rest of my leave: there's no pleasure in it.

I go out and get drunk.

In this inebriated state I board an electric tram, and suddenly see a young woman smiling at me. She doesn't hesitate, comes up to me and introduces herself. She knows me, though I do not know her. Her husband is at the front. She has always wanted to make my acquaintance, even before the war, she says.

"Now you won't get away from me," she concludes amiably.

I get off and she comes with me.

A few moments later she invites me to her home. She is all alone.

I haven't meant to ask where her husband is, but now I decide to do so. On second thoughts, I change my mind. Why should I know? Better to know nothing.

"How long has your husband been at the front?"

"About two years."

"Does he know you're being unfaithful to him?" I ask her point-blank.

She is not at all embarrassed.

"Why should I care if he knows or he doesn't? What if he dies? Perhaps he's already dead."

I leave her without a word.

By some fiendish coincidence, I run into her the very next day. She greets me ironically.

"I didn't know you were such a coward."

She examines my collar for a moment, and says:

"Ah, you belong to the 65th Regiment! I have a friend who belongs to that regiment: Ensign Szegedy. He's here now. He was wounded and is recovered."

"Who? Ensign Szegedy? Where is he? When was he wounded?"

"Two weeks ago. A slight injury. If you'd like to see him, come and visit me this evening. He's staying with me."

She adds smiling:

"He isn't a romantic like you. He's a soldier, an officer!"

There is a nauseating bitterness in my mouth.

"Does he know that your husband is at the front?"

"Does he know? He's my husband's best friend. My husband belongs to the 66th Regiment, right next to yours."

I decide to go and see "my friend" Ensign Szegedy for myself. So I call on her that night. He is there. He really *is* living with her.

I don't say anything to him, but make up my mind that he will pay for it with his life.

The next day I ask headquarters to order me back to the front.

27 | The Trial

THE JOY of reunion at the front is unimaginable. You have to experience it to know what it means. There is a good deal of sadness in the rejoicing, but it's above all an outpouring of love, the sort of love you find only at the front.

My Pály is stunned to see me. He stands stock-still for a few moments, unable even to come to attention in the proper way. He is silent and his eyes overflow with tears.

"Well, Pály, how have you been?" He doesn't answer, just gulps and remains silent.

"Attention, Infantryman Gergo Pály!!"

He draws himself up and stammers, smiling through his tears:

"Ensign sir, beg to report: Welcome back!"

"At ease, Infantryman!"

I embrace him.

A moment later the entire gang surround me. Sixty-one men. There is no end to the questions; everyone wants to know if I have seen his mother, brother, father, sweetheart, wife, friend. How is life out there? How is everything going? What about peace? Especially, what about peace. Will there ever be peace?

I find a few changes. Some men have been promoted, some have received medals – because the war has not stopped in my absence. Two had been wounded – Ensign Szegedy and the lanky Tyrolean.

"The Tyrolean wounded? Where is he?"

"In hospital. A very serious belly wound. Fortunately it's in the side.[1] We've heard that he's recovering. He left you a note, sir."

"When did he write it? After he was wounded?"

"Yes. That is, no. After he was wounded he lay in the trench for a while and asked us to write down what he said. So we did."

They give me the letter. The dear Tyrolean asks me to receive his letters from home, especially from his sweetheart. I am to open them, and, if one of them is urgent, send it on to him at the hospital at once.

I have no idea what this means.

Ensign Kerak, the artist, comes to see me too. He is thrilled to hear that I have visited with his young wife…

Seeing him, my mouth dries up and I am afraid to speak.

I tell him everything he wants to hear. "She's going crazy without you." And so on.

He listens to me greedily, eyes shining. Then he sits down to write her a letter.

I gather three of my comrades, including Ensign Kerak, and tell them my impressions of the city. This, by way of introduction to the story about Ensign Szegedy's betrayal. Finally, I tell them all about it. None of us hesitates. We all sentence him to death.

We propose to draw lots, to pick the man who will carry out the sentence. But Ensign Kerak stands up:

"There's no need to draw lots. I'll do it. The first opportunity I get in the next battle, I'll shoot him like the dog that he is."

It's as if he senses that he is vindicating his own honor.

Is it really a coincidence?

Afterwards, I find out that the ensign from the 66th Regiment whose wife has betrayed him with the scoundrel Szegedy is also Kerak's good friend. He is thus vindicating his friend's honor, unawares.

Where is my little friend Margolis?

He, too, has won a medal. My lieutenant, who has in the meantime been promoted first lieutenant, has commended him for outstanding bravery. Margolis has succeeded in achieving something extraordinary – he managed to link our telephone line with that of the Russians, which runs through the forest. We are thus able to hear all their plans, even confuse them with some false orders. The outcome is impressive – our forces are able to capture the forest from the Russians. An important contribution to this achievement is made by a certain Russian prisoner of war, who had been batman to an officer who abused him cruelly. He deserted to our side and helped us.

When Margolis stands before me, proudly displaying his second medal, he snaps to attention and announces:

"Ensign sir! Beg to report, I've followed the biblical example:

"I will stir up Egyptian against Egyptian – brother will fight against brother, neighbor against neighbor, city against city, kingdom against kingdom."[2]

The pleasure of having found the right chapter and verse for the occasion is greater than the pleasure Margolis gets from the medal itself.

A terrible thing happens to Uncle Osterreicher: his head phylacteries have been pierced by a bullet, and he has to pray with defective phylacteries. Only someone as devout as he can imagine his distress. Poor Uncle Osterreicher is profoundly depressed. When I tell my first lieutenant about it, he decides to surprise the old soldier with a gift of new phylacteries. We call our resident Talmudist, Margolis, and he explains to the officer, at great length and in much detail, everything there is to know about phylacteries and their proper use. The Magyar officer listens attentively, and says:

"How very remarkable. This old Jew, who ought to be overjoyed that the bullet missed his skull by a tiny fraction, is in deep depression because his ritual prayer has become defective. I'm beginning to wonder, my friend, whether human life does really end with the phenomenon we call death... Perhaps Socrates was right![3]

"Beg to report, sir: Moses Mendelssohn was right, too!" interjects Margolis.[4]

I am amazed to hear that a devout *yeshiva* scholar is familiar with the free-thinking philosopher.

"Such extremist books sometimes did fall out of my pockets," says Margolis with a smug smile. He hastens to add: "But they didn't affect me!"[5]

The upshot of it is that an order is sent to Lwów,[6] the town nearest us, to obtain new phylacteries for Uncle Osterreicher, complete with a scribe's certificate of their absolute ritual purity.

A letter arrives for the Tyrolean. I open and read it. It is from his fiancée, Maria-Anna. Among other things, she writes: "I dreamed I saw you without arms and legs."

This is not a very urgent letter.

Ensign Szegedy returns to the front. I don't know how it happened, for I myself told no one but the three "judges," but by now everyone knows that he has done something loathsome while on leave in the city. But nobody knows exactly what it was, and there is intense curiosity when he returns to the trenches.

We receive him correctly, but with utmost coldness. At first he cannot understand the reason for this, and yet, as if sensing what is going on, he starts telling anecdotes about women and wounded soldiers, and the like. Nobody laughs; we remain cold as ice. Ensign Kerak avoids him. He is awaiting his opportunity…

He doesn't have to wait long.

Before the first great Galician snowfall predicted by the meteorologists, there is a fierce battle between the lines, and among the casualties of the 65th Regiment is Ensign Szegedy.

We are all relieved.

The evil has been purged from our midst.[7]

28 | Madame Pompadour

FOLLOWING THAT last battle, the subject of heroism in general, and of Jewish heroism in particular, again becomes the order of the day. This time it's presented in a new and improved light, though this had not been the original intention of the questioners who discussed it in the first place.

"What is it that makes the Jews so unconcerned about their lives, so heedless, like people to whom it makes no difference, and who have nothing to lose?"

Such is their form of question. By now there is no doubt whatsoever that the Jews excel in sheer bravery, even more than the purest Calvinist Magyars. Events keep confirming this fact, however unpalatable it may be. Since there is no way to doubt the facts, there has to be a way of disposing of their aura of glory. This is done by "analysis," that is, studying the facts as it were under a microscope. Needless to say, under that instrument, the face of the world's most beautiful woman looks like nothing more than perforated, hairy goose-flesh.

At first they say: "The Hungarian Jew has learned courage from his Magyar countrymen." This would make sense, except that of late despised Galician Jews have also shown outstanding bravery in combat.

Then they say: "It's not courage that makes the Jews do so well, but cunning. They trick the enemy on the battlefield, just as they trick the *goy*[1] in their business dealings back home."

This, too, might sound convincing, if it weren't for the many feats which simply cannot have been brought off by cunning. Not that unvarnished deceit is useless at the front. On the contrary, the task of commanders is based largely on this quality. It's called "the art of strategy." But the heroism of Captain Schlesinger, for example – who was a doctor in civilian life and volunteered for frontline service – cannot be ascribed to trickery by any interpretation of the word, when he saved the 15th Division from annihilation. In the battle for the village of Tolna[2] on the Dniester, when the entire division had been forced to retreat, he and his company remained behind in the village, and held out against the enemy, as though quartered in a fortress. Until the division sent him reinforcements after about a week, with his "fortress" as a base, he made constant sallies against the enemy who surrounded him like locusts in a small garden. For an entire week this action prevented capture of the village and the bridge, until the division commanders finally realized that he and his company had not been wiped out but were still very much alive, and sent him the necessary reinforcements.

We cross the Dniester – the largest and most important river on the entire front.[3]

In Schlesinger's company, most of the men who have distinguished themselves and won medals for bravery are Jews. Their Magyar comrades cannot say enough for their conduct in battle.

There are several other such achievements.

Take our little Jewish Corporal Margolis, that skinny telephone operator. There is no question that he is cunning as a snake, but no one can pretend that his latest feat is due to cunning alone. Every raw recruit knows that to link up with the enemy's telephone line is an ingenious idea. But to carry it out, to crawl four hundred. paces right under the enemy's nose and do what has to be done as unconcernedly as if he was amongst his own men – for that you need much more than cunning.

Then there is the report in the official army weekly that members of the Hungarian students' association "Maccabee" have enlisted. They didn't scatter to enlist with different regiments according to their birth. Instead they did a very fine thing. They organized themselves into one regiment, and went forth as one unit to fight the Cossacks in the Carpathians, where they performed great deeds. It was obvious that, massed as a single unit, they would lose incomparably more men than if they would have broken up and become one of hundreds in different regiments. But that didn't deter them.

There are also fellows known as Zionists, whose patriotism has been questioned, sometimes even by non-Zionist Jews.

And so the question comes up again, to the intense annoyance of the officers. It reaches such a stage that one of them thinks it quite all right to approach me with the following frank and foolish question:

"You've already got three important medals. But you're a philosopher. So tell me..."

He puts it in such a bumbling way, that I cannot repeat his words in any logical sequence. I reply abruptly:

"You want to know the secret? I'll tell you. It's your hatred for us. Nothing more. You have the power to hate us, and we have only one way to avenge ourselves upon you –

with our bravery. Engulfed with such bestial hatred we really have nothing to lose. Sometimes we feel that it's better to die than live in the midst of such senseless hatred."

This is the first time that I give vent unequivocally to this basic truth.

It is quite effective. The officer reports my words to his fellow officers, and, after prolonged discussions, a campaign is launched to stop their antisemitic speech.

Obviously, if the cause is removed, the effect – namely, the courage – would also cease to exist.

It is interesting to observe the struggle between hatred and envy. It is even more fascinating to see that envy and hatred have diametrically opposed interests.

No matter what, the excellence of Jewish soldiers disconcerts men of the "pure races" in this Austro-Hungarian-Serb-Ruthenian-Bosnian-Gypsy army – this marching Tower of Babel made up of about twenty different nations, which have been living side by side, their boundaries increasingly blurred, for generations.[4] In this polyglot army they keep on babbling about purity of race – a pure Magyar, a pure Italian, a pure Romanian, and above all, a pure Austrian! No wonder that there is even a Gypsy corporal, by name of Latzi Gentsche, who boasts of being a pure Gypsy!

Perhaps he's the only one who really has a right to such a boast.

After a while, Jewish boldness is labeled "Jewish impudence," and Jewish valor dubbed "Jewish panic!" Though, to tell the truth, even among gentile officers there are some objections to this term – how can you describe a reckless onslaught on the enemy as "panic"? Panic makes people run away, not storm headlong towards danger.

Only First Lieutenant Smerčany is silent and just smiles at these philosophic speculations. Until one day he loses his temper:

"You're walking round and round in circles beating about the bush. Sometimes I suspect that you're doing this deliberately, so as not to see the obvious: these Jews have for two thousand years been yearning for a national life, a heroic existence, epic achievement, to restore them to their ancient glory. They express their dreams in thousands of different ways – in prayers, in "the Holy Land," in crowning some mystic Hassidic rebbe like a king with his own court, and all sorts of similar things. Even the great Magyar patriotism of our own Hungarian Jews is no more than a desire to be absorbed in the glory of the Hungarian monarchy, to take part in its pomp and circumstance, by way of a substitute for their own country, in which they no longer believe. Who loves to dress up in our national costume, the mantle, the shako with the tail and the patriotic hip boots, more than Jews who have been successfully assimilated?!"

The other officers listen to him very attentively. Smerčany continues:

"Now, when they've had a whiff of the pomp of sovereignty in the shape of an army uniform with all the trappings, from the single stripe of a private first class to the red stripe, the lampases of the general's trouser leg, their natural heroic spirit breaks through liked a dammed up stream! Why all this sophistry? The Jew has turned out to be a hero, because his heroic spirit has been bottled up for two thousand years!"

General silence. Finally he adds, by way of conclusion:

"Let's try and give them their own country, and you'll soon see how Jewish cowardice will suddenly convert to Jewish bravery!"

This is the longest speech we have ever heard our laconic Calvinist first lieutenant make.[5]

No one has anything to say for a while. The officers drain their glasses and pull on their cigarettes in silence.

Without warning Ensign Slezak, the Czech "dwarf," speaks up cautiously:

"I've heard that there is such a plan at general headquarters!"

The men stare at him quizzically. He answers their unexpressed question:

"I heard that there is a plan to give Palestine to the Jews for them to establish their own homeland and government there."

"Who wants to give it away?" growls the Austrian Captain Walter angrily. "The English are planning to fool the Jews with some such plan! I've heard that myself."

"True," Slezak, says, "but our side means to do so as well. Perhaps it's in response to English treachery. I've heard that there is even such a proclamation, which is being distributed among the Jewish soldiers."

"Who signed that proclamation?" asks Lieutenant Smerčany, gravely and cautiously.

"I haven't seen it," Slezak replies. "But last night a friend of mine, who's been on the Western Front, visited me on the way to the 66th and told me about it. He said that the proclamation has been signed by Kaiser Wilhelm, His Imperial Majesty Franz Josef and the Turkish Sultan. At least, that's what he said."[6]

I listen to them and my mouth becomes parched. What does it all mean? Is it a cruel joke? – It must be. I see the dwarfish ensign's look at me as he speaks. They must have agreed beforehand to play a practical joke on me. Practical jokes are very popular at the front. I feel my face turning all colors, the blood rising from my heart to my head.

I control myself as best I can and say smilingly to the little ensign:

"Perhaps His Majesty The Ensign has also signed the proclamation?"

He is taken aback:

"Do you think I'm fooling you? I'm serious. This is what I was told by a friend from the Western Front. The proclamation has already been distributed there."

I finish my cigarette and return to my quarters. It isn't easy sitting with the others, flushing with embarrassment. I cannot understand it all. On the one hand, it sounds like a pure *canard,* on the other, it makes my heart beat faster. Who knows? So many peculiar things have been happening. That England has some such plan is not new. There have been rumors of it for some time. But of course, it's the well-known English perfidy.[7] But might it not be true that our side is responding with the same perfidy? Perhaps our "grand old man" has agreed with his two cronies to bring off not a trick, but a really historic act?

I cannot rest. I pace up and down, intoxicated like someone poisoned by a powerful sweet drug. Finally, I can't contain myself. I go to Ensign Slezak and ask him, cautiously and in private, whether there is any truth to the story. Now that we are alone, he speaks more excitedly.

He asks me:

"Would you pleased if it happened?"

"What? Palestine? You know that I'm a Zionist."

He hesitates a moment and then says, in the tone of one who really understands the issue:

"Be careful, my friend. In this place it's dangerous to display sympathy for such things."

"Why? If the three rulers have signed the proclamation?"

"Yes, yes... But just the same don't make a public display of it before you actually see and know the truth. You shouldn't dance before the wedding takes place, you know."

He says this with genuine and sympathetic understanding. It makes me suspect, just for a moment, that Ensign Slezak might himself be a Jew, even a Zionist. I have frequently been disabused of such misapprehensions at the front. Before long I find out the real reason: he is a Czech, and the Czechs – well, one mustn't even think about it. The thought alone dooms you to "hang on the nearest tree."[8]

The rumor sprouts wings and keeps fluttering amongst us more and more persistently. More men come over from the Western Front, and talk about it openly. I feel positively ill. My appetite vanishes, and I start to drink more than usual.

One day Margolis and Uncle Osterreicher come to see me. They have something to discuss with me privately. They want to "enjoy sweet fellowship" and take counsel about the situation.[9]

"I have news for the *Herr* Ensign!" Margolis announces secretively, trembling with excitement.

"Harbingers of the Messiah!" Uncle Osterreicher remarks.

"What news, Margolis?"

Margolis looks around carefully, then draws out of his tunic pocket a much folded sheet of paper, opens it up carefully, unrolling it like a precious scroll, and shows me the proclamation. It's a royal document addressed to the Jewish soldiers in the armies of Germany, Austria, Hungary, and Turkey and all their dependencies, stating in unequivocal words, without coloring, qualifications or provisos, the existence of a plan to establish a Jewish government in Palestine. The execution of the plan depends, of course, on our winning the war.

It is signed by Emperor Franz Josef the First, Kaiser Wilhelm the Second and the Turkish Sultan Abdul Hamid.[10]

I stand there with eyes bulging like a calf, staring at the proclamation, which is written in Hebrew and Yiddish and all the languages spoken by the Jews of Europe.

Then Margolis hands me a copy of the journal *Múlt és Jövő* ("Past and Present"), with the following editorial by Joseph Patai:[11]

> The international press has recently been greatly preoccupied with the subject of Palestine and Zionism. According to one English newspaper, England –

advised, supposedly, by no less a personage than Israel Zangwill – proposes to establish a neutral Palestine government.[12] A German newspaper states that Germany intends to set aside a billion marks to the Jewish commonwealth which is to be established there under its auspices. Meanwhile, there is a spate of articles about Palestine, its climate and inhabitants, its flora and fauna.

Now the Hungarian press has joined its full-throated tenor voice to the chorus. It devotes long articles and a rare gravity to the Holy Land, its past, present and future, the great work done over there by the Zionists in developing its trade and industry there with such outstanding success. In short, the war seems to have qualified Palestine and the Zionists for the best salons, since it has – in the words of the newspapers – crowned many ardent Zionists with the halo of heroic death!

But if, God willing, peace comes to suffering humanity, it will not be Germany or England, or even Turkey, which will make Palestine a Jewish state. This will be done by Jewish refugees fleeing from the lands of their exile to their ancestral homeland, there to continue its conquest and cultivation by the sweat of their brows. Then, will people again begin to speak of the resettlement of Palestine as building a "modern ghetto?" Or as being unpatriotic and disloyal to their country of adoption? Because what is permissible in war is not permissible in peace.[13]

I finish reading and rub my eyes. Again I peruse the proclamation, line by line, word by word, syllable by syllable. "Signed: Emperor Franz Josef the First; Kaiser Wilhelm the Second; Sultan Abdul Hamid"

Uncle Osterreichcr keeps repeating:

"Harbingers of the Messiah! Harbingers of the Messiah!"

Margolis, recalling our known "Jewish chutzpah," pronounces in the singsong voice of a Talmudic scholar:

"It is written: 'At the time of the harbingers of the Messiah's coming, there will be impudence and lawlessness!' Of which it is written: 'Blessed are those who wait and shall see the End of Days.'"[14]

"Let me have that proclamation, Margolis!"

This is the first time Margolis fails to obey my orders. He smiles awkwardly and doesn't know what to do.

"Corporal Jacob Margolis – *Attention*! By the Holy Virgin!"

Margolis stands to attention, hands at trouser seams, eyes glued to mine. He is frightened. I see in his face a fleeting suspicion that I am about to denounce him to a military court martial, as a traitor to the homeland.

A complete about-face of this kind is common among officers, and could be believed about any officer.

"All right, Margolis, at ease!" I pat him on the shoulder. "I'll give it back to you soon."

Margolis stands at ease and draws a deep breath.

"You really scared me there for a moment," he admits.

"You're a fool Margolis. Isn't the proclamation signed by the 'three kings of the east,' as predicted? – May your lot be amongst traitors like them!"[15]

"I... I..." poor Margolis stammers, "I thought perhaps it was only a trap... against us... to test us..."

Donner und Blitzen! He's right! It could be. At any rate, it's wise to be careful.

Be careful? It's easy enough with other people, but how can we be careful among ourselves? – After all, I think, isn't there an element of treachery in it? Even to think for a moment about another country? All right, I'm a Zionist. But not during the war! Good God! To be thinking of another country. another homeland, right here at the front, in the midst of the war?! Never!

"You're an idiot!" I say to myself. "Doesn't the king himself want it? Here he is, addressing us Jews... And if he himself says it, then surely we may think of it?

"What if it's a trap?"

"No! Joseph Patai himself writes..."

"And if Joseph Patai writes this," says Margolis, "you can believe the three kings, sir!"

I can't sleep a wink all night. I turn over from right to left, from left to my back, from my back to my belly. A thousand ideas rage in my mind. I begin to curse the whole situation.

"What joy! – How terrible! – Palestine! – Treason!..."

More and more rumors grow around this confounded subject. Now from "the other side" – Russia, England. Some really fantastic rumors.

How do the rumors reach us? Through Russian-Jewish prisoners of war, and they all center around the password "Madame Pompadour."[16]

Night falls.

It's so brilliantly moonlit that it inspires us with Circassian terror.[17] This is our own particular fear, the nemesis of the 15th Division, which has the special privilege of facing the Russian army's greatest snipers, the Circassians. We have a special name for them: "nose hunters." All along that section of our line opposite the Circassians, it's forbidden to stick even a finger above the trench. They shoot straight as an arrow, with hairbreadth accuracy, at a distance of three to four hundred meters, and hit their target without fail. If any man forgets himself and sticks his head out of the trench, he is sure to get a Circassian bullet right through the nape of his neck. The moonlight increases our "Circassian terror" considerably.

All along our front trench there is absolute silence. Or rather, the only sounds are those made by amateur musicians playing, pianissimo, many different tunes on all sorts of small instruments. Together the tunes combine into a wonderful but ill-starred symphony, which every one of us suspects of being his own swan song.

The reason for this suspicion is that the air is charged with anticipation of a major Russian offensive "which must end the war before winter." In this major assault it will be either them or us. We have been waiting for it for the past month with a mingling of terror, anticipation, hope, and a sense of doom.

Outside, perfect peace. The moon shines with that romantic light, under which sweethearts everywhere nestle against each other in bliss. Inside the trenches one sad all-embracing tune, a soft funeral march, the hushed symphony of death, to be climaxed by a tremendous roar of cannons along the length and breadth of the front. And then? – Who knows?

The music grows softer and quieter, becoming a secret serenade to departing life. A farewell to everything – one's dear mother, a capricious sweetheart back in the city, music, flowering fields and the bustling, carousing, whorish city, so far, far away.

Why does this mortal terror overwhelm us more than before?

Because the quiet is pregnant with an ominous feeling that had for some time been troubling us, and finally saturates us with a terrifying foreboding of certain death. It derives from the cloak of black secrecy with which the Russian Front has been shrouded for some time. For more than a year we have grown accustomed to knowing with a fair degree of accuracy what is happening on the other side of the lines. We've always known when the Russians will attack, and have been able to prepare accordingly. What the source of our information is, no one knows for sure. There are all kinds of conjectures and speculations. Some speak of high-ranking spies. Others, of a Polish princess living in Moscow, who is in love with one of Kaiser Wilhelm's sons. There are more absurd stories, that the queen, Her Majesty the Tsarina herself, informs our general headquarters of all decisions taken by the Russian supreme command in Moscow![18]

Recently the secret connection has been broken. There is no information, not a syllable, not a hint of a plan… What does it mean?

It fills us with panic such as we have never before experienced.

This fear resounds in muted tremolo through the entire accursed symphony that waits along the trench, quietly, painfully, as a last farewell.

Suddenly the telephone shrills.

"Hello! Colonel! My respects, Colonel."

"Listen, boy! There's no news. God damn those Cossacks! Not a murmur. Which is why we must attack, understood? – They mustn't attack us first, understood?!"

"My respects, *Herr* Colonel!"

"Everything is ready. How about you?"

"Yes, sir, Colonel! The entire Circassian artillery and their munitions dumps are as familiar to me as my own desk. I can even tell you where their general stores his cognac."

"You're a fine young fellow, my friend. Thank you! And what about Madame Pompadour and her companions?"

"Poppycock, *Herr* Colonel!"

"Well good… *Sevas*!"[19]

"My respects, Colonel!"

When I put the telephone down, I bite my lower lip and reflect. This is the first time that the colonel himself asks me about Madame Pompadour and her circle.

The subject of "Madame Pompadour" is not one we discuss aloud. It is something to whisper about, to smile and joke about in a low voice. But not to talk about openly. And here the colonel himself is asking me about it!

This has been the only piece of information which has filtered through the lines in recent days. Something about a certain "Madame Pompadour" and her circle. Although it's a plainly Jewish matter, it captures everybody's imagination, and becomes the subject of endless gossip. It certainly sounds curious, intriguing and enigmatic enough.

It seems that something is happening in Russia, something so devious and cunning, that only the cold, clever, calculating English machine could have devised it. An enigmatic woman named Madame Pompadour, evidently French, yet also Jewish, who actually took part in the fighting and lost one arm in an encounter has organized a Jewish legion, made up of Zionist men, for the purpose of conquering Palestine.[20] This Jewish Amazon is a one-armed Judith.[21] She has three comrades who help her, in three different countries of the alliance. One is a Russian, by name of Shabbatinsky – obviously a Jewish name, from the word Shabbat (sabbath). He is her commander-in-chief who has mobilized the Jewish troops for the conquest of Jerusalem. He has already recruited one hundred thousand men, all Zionists. The second is a certain Belfer – an obviously Jewish name, too. Originally a Russian, he has become a British subject, fabulously wealthy and a lord. He provides the money for the Jewish legion. The third is a truly terrifying man, who wishes to turn the Jewish Legion into the scourge of the world, destroying the entire German-Austrian-Turkish front in one day. His name is Wessman, and he is a professor of chemistry. He has invented a monstrous poison gas, which as soon as it comes in contact with the human body causes the flesh to instantly wither and drop, though the man remains alive.[22] Horrible! What a grisly individual!

But the moving spirit behind it all is the woman, Madame Pompadour.

This is the story that is whispered amongst us more and more frequently. Some discuss it jokingly, others in teeth-chattering terror. A monstrous war! A Jewish legion! That's funny! *Yeshiva* scholars, dreamy Talmudists on the march! And that Commander Shabbatinsky – he is a general who doesn't have to give orders. His power works like a spell – all he has to do is make a brief speech, and they all follow him like maniacs.

We whisper and gossip about it, trying to dismiss it as typical trench fantasy, product of nervous nightmares.

There are some Zionists among us – undeclared, of course, but lacking any evil intentions. Zionists are by no means suspected of harboring any evil thoughts in this war. The Zionists of Budapest have already achieved a great deal, and won the complete confidence of general headquarters, because they volunteered for the war without waiting for conscription. Moreover, they formed a Zionist brigade, headed by the leader of the Zionist sports association in Hungary, the redheaded Zsoldos, whom Max Nordau has nicknamed "the bullneck."[23] This regiment entered the front line 2,000 young Zionists strong, and in a single day lost almost all of them. They fought against the Cossacks and helped dislodge them from the Carpathians, and only a pitiful remnant survived. At least, that is what we are told. At any rate, it's the reason that we Zionists are not suspected of favoring the tales about Madame Pompadour and her circle. On the contrary, let her come with her legions – "the Zionists will soon make short shrift of them," is the reaction of those inclined to believe the story, who nevertheless believe a little of the legend about Madame Pompadour.

Nevertheless, the rumor affects us all. We, the few Zionists in the 15th Division, are consumed with curiosity, which gradually becomes a passionate obsession to know if there is any truth in those fantasies. Might there not…?

Under such circumstances, one's heart begins to beat a little faster. It is a Jewish heart which has been still for many generations. But the face suddenly blanches. One's features might reveal a titillating inner folly.

A Jewish legion! The idea casts a spell on us. Imagine, a Jewish legion conquering Jerusalem… Good God! How wonderful, how terrible! It is truly terrible – what if we encounter this legion and have to fight against it? In pitched battle?

No, no of course, there's nothing for it. If they come, we would know our duty to our homeland. Not one of us would hesitate even for a moment. God forbid we should dream of treason at the front. But a Jewish legion? Nonsense! There's no such thing.

We all laugh heartily.

"Harbingers of the coming of the Messiah," Uncle Osterreicher smilingly insists. "Harbingers of the Messiah!"

"What Messiah?! What are you talking about?! It's all nonsense!"

So we all say. But no sooner have we said it, when doubt begins to gnaw at us. A doubt combined with a shadowy hope, as well as fear – what if we do have to face them?… Oh God! What a dreadful confrontation! It's frightful to even contemplate.

We resolve, once and for all, that it's all a lot of nonsense.

Nonsense, had not something occurred in the meantime!

Nonsense or not, a new Jewish officer arrives at our regiment. He has been transferred from another regiment, and then we hear that he was from the "Zionist regiment," the one which reportedly had been all but wiped out.

When he comes to inform me that he has been attached to my company, and having stated it in formal terms, he adds in an informal whisper that this was done at his own request.

I am not surprised. Such incidents are not rare.

"Have you a friend in this company?" I ask him.

He grows a little pale and smiles embarrassedly. After looking around to see if anyone was listening to our conversation, he whispers in my ear:

"Madame Pompadour."

Without waiting to see the effect it has on me, he adds:

"Doctor."

The word "Doctor" instantly explains the whole thing. I know that the Zionists at the front, who are the only Jews to resist actively the insults of antisemitic officers, have adopted a sort of password that links them in this ethical-national battle whenever necessary. At first the password is "Doctor Herzl," but then, to make it quite unintelligible to the others, it is reduced to "Doctor" alone.[24]

This word, together with "Pompadour," is sufficient to flash a blinding, blazing lightning bolt in my mind and make my heart stop beating for a moment.

Within a few hours the entire fabulous riddle of "Madame Pompadour" is solved. Its origin is in another division, and it has spread to Budapest. My new fellow officer knows all about it.

"Madame Pompadour" is not a woman, but a Russian Jewish officer by name of Joseph Trumpeldor. "General Shabbatinsky" is none other than the Russian Jewish writer Ze'ev Jabotinsky, the one who has translated Bialik's poems into Russian. Lord Belfer is, of course, the English Lord Balfour, a British cabinet minister. And the grisly Wessman is Professor Chaim Weizmann, the noted chemist and Zionist leader, who lives in England.[25]

"So the stories about a Jewish legion are true?" I ask.

"Of course!" says the newcomer. He draws me aside and pulls out of his pocket another copy of the proclamation I have taken from Margolis and now keep in my pocket. This one is in Yiddish.

My comrade explains:

"God has made the one as well as the other."[26] This declaration is aimed at another one similar to it. The Entente – that is, the English – have issued a proclamation of this nature, and so... You understand? It's very simple."[27]

As to simplicity, I don't know about that.

But I feel my blood freeze in my veins.

My comrade continues: "Is it still a secret here? Among us it's talked about confidently and quite openly. And why not? If headquarters takes up the problem, why should it be taboo to speak of it?"

"What if it's a provocation?" I ask.

"Nonsense! In some regiments they have already formed groups around this proclamation, that is to say, around this idea. And the groups are recognized by headquarters. They're even speaking of a special flag."

"The orders will be given in Hebrew, I suppose?"

"You're pleased to joke, but it isn't a joking matter. The trouble is, not enough of the men know Hebrew."

I am beginning to feel rather warm.

As I stand there feeling like a dunce in the corner, the telephone rings. It's the colonel.

"My respects, *Herr* Colonel!"

"We won't attack. Not for the present. The devil knows."

"Perhaps there's some news, *Herr* Colonel?"

"News? From over there? The devil take them, no. Not even a murmur. It's enough to drive one mad. But just the same, for the present we wait. Something may happen yet. Understand?"

"Respects, Yes, *Herr* Colonel!"

He continues: "And what about the lovely 'Madame Pompadour?'"

The blood rushes to my head.

"Ha ha! The beautiful Madame Pompadour, *Herr* Colonel? Why, let her come, by all means! A beautiful woman can't hurt, can she, *Herr* Colonel? – Ha ha ha! I don't know about that, though. A beautiful woman does no harm, *Herr* Colonel. What do you think?"

"Well, not exactly – ha-ha-ha! Not exactly! Some turn the world upside down! There have been some beautiful women who caused revolutions, including the original Madame Pompadour! All France was in her hands! Ho ho ho!"

"In her hands, indeed, *Herr* Colonel. But they say that this Madame Pompadour has only one hand, ha ha ha!"

He laughs heartily and says goodbye.

"My respects, *Herr* Colonel!"

Whew! Cold sweat covers my feverish brow.

A cold sweat breaks out on my burning brow. "Beautiful women causing revolutions!" – "Madame Pompadour!" – That old drunkard doesn't know how prophetic he is.

My new comrade, who stands beside me and overhears this strange conversation, stares at me with astonishment.

"What? Is that all you people know about the Jewish Legion?"

"Yes."

"That isn't much. The harbingers of the Messiah sound muffled and remote at this end, my friend. But when those vapors reach us, we'll know more," he adds.

Hearing this my head begins to spin and I have to sit down.

Here we go again – the harbingers of the Messiah!

I am shaken and can hardly speak. I study that strange proclamation again. Yes, there it is plain to see. Kaiser Wilhelm is promising us Palestine.

So something really is happening, the fantasy is taking shape, evolving, developing, putting together many dreams, many visions. It's enough to make one feel drunk.

So we sit together, he and I, and think our thoughts in silence.

"What's going to happen?" I ask my friend at last.

"What's going to happen? he repeats. "Whatever happens!" He smiles, comes up to me, hugs and kisses me with memorable warmth. Then he seizes my shoulders and looks into my eyes, with exultant earnestness:

"Give me your hand!" he says.

He takes my hand, presses it with both of his and says:

"By this act, we hereby grant our dear wife. Hungary, a bill of divorcement.[28] By this same act, we take Madame Pompadour in holy wedlock. Say after me: 'Behold, Madame Pompadour, thou art hereby married to me according to the Law of Moses and Israel!'"[29]

I began to say: "Thou, Madame Pompadour…"

Again the telephone rings

It's the colonel again. After a few meaningless exchanges, he asks me again:

"Well, and how's Madame Pompadour, my friend?"

I shake myself and make an effort to control my voice. Then I laugh heartily and say:

"Ha Ha Ha! Madame Pompadour? I have just taken her for my wife, sir! You are cordially invited to the wedding party, Colonel! We'll drink a toast to it!"

The colonel laughs too, a warm intoxicated laugh:

"Ha ha ha! Congratulations! Congratulations! *Sevas*!"

When I put down the receiver my friend is already waiting with two filled glasses. He hands me one of them and says:

"*Mazal tov* (congratulations) Here's to Madame Pompadour!"

"*Mazal tov!*" I reply. "But wouldn't it be a good idea to invite our fellow officers of pure racial stock to rejoice with us? Even more in their joy in our betrothal, let them rejoice in our bill of divorcement."

The latent Jewish energy is beginning to pound in my veins.

Fortunately the attack begins soon, and provides an outlet for that energy.

29 | The Nest

Shuddering shivers quickly pass over me,
Cloudy, dim shades fall from my eyes –
My faithful batman Pály
This cold shadow standing opposite me
Is he satan or man?

Honored sir, I am on watch!

Last night he quietly appeared before me
And placed a crown on my decapitated skull –
My faithful batman Pály,
Why does his sunken eye blind so?
What does he look at with such scorn?

Honored sir, I am on watch!

Is he the angel of doom? – Yes, the good angel;
May his mission be holy, and his coming a blessing–
My faithful batman Pály,
Why is the torch in his hands upside down?
Draw your sword!

My father the son of Amram – unique in Israel[1]
My king sings sweet songs[2] on Mount Gilboa[3]
My faithful batman Pály,

Tell him: the Maccabee's son[4] shall neither fear nor
move
From doom and from death.

He shall raise his torch if his turn has come –
And you, if I go – raise your head high –
My faithful batman Pály,
Hand me my harp, let us go on together with eternal
song
Into the orchard of light!

Honored sir, I am on watch![5]

THIS POEM IS DEDICATED to my two comrades: Gergo Pály my lion-hearted batman, and my superior officer First Lieutenant Dr. Janos Smerčany. Both men have sung songs of my Maccabee ancestors to me, covering the hell of hate around me in a veil of past wonders.

From the first moment that First Lieutenant Smerčany reads the royal decree concerning a Jewish state in Palestine, he is so impressed that he begins to develop a theory about the government on so magnificent a scale that even the proudest of pure Magyars would not be ashamed to belong to it. He seems to concentrate his considerable general knowledge on planning the building of a Jewish country down to the last meticulous detail of national life. Remarkably, there is nothing in his theory of the well-known Mendelssohnian "mission" of the Jewish people "to bring light to the gentiles."[6] In his imagination, he constructs a simple country, a normal state like any other, except for one element which his straightforward gentile mind associates with it. The source and center of peace between the three rival religions would be in Palestine and constitute what he calls "the third covenant."

"The first covenant," he reflects, "is the Old Testament, the covenant of the unity of God, or the covenant of the human God. The second, the New Testament, that of Jesus of Nazareth, is the covenant of the divine man, and the Koran of Muhammad corresponds to it. Now we must create the third testament, the covenant of peace. And the only way we can achieve this is through Mother Earth to whom we must return, from whose bosom Providence has torn us away."

When my Pály hears these things he becomes excited and gives me no peace until I explain to him what the first lieutenant – "who isn't at all like an officer, judging from how he speaks" – has said. I explain it to him again and again, whenever I have the opportunity. The young Magyar listens intently, absorbs and digests the words, until they become part of him. Then his imagination begins to sprout the most amazing blooms, astounding in their simplicity. This Magyar is not a typical devout Christian. He is not especially fond of the prayers and symbols of his faith. The cross does not appear on the outside of his church, but only within. On top of his steeple he places a weathercock, the symbol of the dawn. The Magyar talks to God the way he talks to his father, or rather, to his best friend. He argues with him and sometimes curses him in the manner of a loving friend. The truth is that, although for centuries past the Magyar god has been clothed in Christian form, he remains essentially the

Hunnish-Turanian-Mongolian divinity "Eleveh," who is more of a human hero than a mysterious heavenly Providence.[7] The Hebrew "My Lord is a man of war" is much closer to the Magyar concept than any other.[8] No other people can more intimately understand this human concept than the Magyars.

Through this prism, Pály views the Kingdom of Israel "which the good old patriarch Franz Josef, by virtue of his long life, has been privileged, as destined instrument of prophetic divination, to establish at the close of this horrible war." In Pály's opinion, this is a war between Gog and Magog.[9]

Between them, these two men, the educated, commissioned officer and the common soldier, spin an astonishing future here, in the pit of death.

Now it has become much harder to reconcile oneself to dying. To die now? After this proclamation?!

Sometimes I indulge in forbidden thoughts – what great plan is being set in motion, over there, by Trumpeldor, Jabotinsky, Balfour, and Weizmann? How can I die while it is going on?[10]

Ah well!! Whatever happens, all roads lead to Jerusalem – Uncle Osterreicher is right: The signs of the coming of the Messiah are plain to see!

I no longer feel the bitter, mordant animosity around me. What do I care about this foolish hatred, when this proclamation has been published?!

I lose several of my men in the last attack. The Serbian

"bastard" Krechen is torn apart by a grenade, while wearing the "tailored tunic" he inherited from the unfortunate Lance Corporal Madi. Why did he wear it in battle? Did he sense that he was going to die, and wanted to appear before his Maker in dress parade, in a tailored coat?

The next one to leave us, artist-sculptor Kerak, is killed immediately after Krechen. How fortunate for him that he never lived to discover how his faithless wife has betrayed him. Sometimes death is a consummation devoutly to be wished.

After them Corporal Bernat Rosenberger, the fat joker who was all of twenty-one years old, falls. Who will now tell us the good old banal jokes for the thousandth time? How terrible it is to recall the jokes of a dead comrade. I see his jokes fluttering over our orphaned heads.

And so they go, one after another.

I personally feel that I have paid too high a price for the insignificant victory won in that last battle.

The simple, lanky Tyrolean comes back from leave. A pleasant surprise awaits him – he has been promoted from private to corporal at one stroke. But his happiness is mingled with deep grief. He is overwhelmed by the deaths of Krechen, Rosenberger and Kerak.

It is terrible to watch him weeping silently for his comrades. I try to console him, but he pays no attention. After a long silence he gets up and says in a fatalistic tone:

"Now it's my turn."

How can I give him his fiancée's letter after this? But he asks me for it.

"I know there is a letter from Maria-Anna. I met her on leave. I even know what's in it, because she told me."

I give it to him. He reads it and broods for a while.

"Of course it's my turn now. But what difference does it make? I told her that I free her of her love for me. I gave her a divorce without a priest. Our wedding was without priest or clergy as well. She cried. Silly, what is there to cry about if a man dies?"

He says this with eyes still wet and red from his own tears for his dead comrades.

How much love there is among us, the common soldiers.

How much hate there is "up above" among the officers.

After the last attack we expect to have a long rest. The bitter winter arrives, bringing an exceptionally heavy snowfall. Snow buries everything as far as the eye can see.

We all begin to repair and improve, even beautify our individual dugouts.

A nest, that word most aptly describes a dugout in which each soldier in the front line settles himself. The entire company lives and sleeps in one large "hall," a sort of wide, dark cavern which has to be illuminated by lanterns even during the day. But the officers and even NCOs "build" themselves small individual quarters in the sides of the cavern. That is the dugout: Twentieth century man's nest, regression to our primordial cave-dwelling ancestors, seventeen million years ago.

Pály decides to build me a "regal palace." My poem has moved him profoundly.

"The *Herr* Ensign is a descendant of biblical kings," he explains.

"We are all descendants of kings, Pály."

"No, sir. Our kings were once slaves to your eastern kings. Jerusalem was the first city in the world. Before Jerusalem there were only small robber villages, big and small.

"What about Rome?"

"The Romans were robbers. I know. I've read about it. How could they be decent folk, if their gods were drunkards, lechers and murderers? It's the same with the Greeks. Marauders all. Now Jerusalem – I know King Solomon's prayer by heart."

He begins to recite Solomon's prayer upon the completion of the Temple:

"I have surely built a magnificent temple for You, a place for You to dwell forever."[11]

In Hungarian, of course.

Almost all the Magyars in my company carry small Bibles in their rucksacks.

The nest construction grows apace. We improve the walls, dig out special niches to keep all sorts of things in. We make a table and suspend two bunks, one above the other – the upper one for me, the lower one for Pály.

This quiet time in the midst of a white, snow-covered world has a unique atmosphere about it. Living in our cave, warming ourselves beside the makeshift stove, we feel completely removed from society and the clamorous civilization of the city.

Work on the nest is never finished. There is always something to improve and repair. You find a stick of wood, or a piece of sheet metal, a shard of glass, a nail or a broken pot, and at once you have some use for it. Everything can be utilized; everything is beneficial.

The nest becomes more and more improved, cozier and cozier. You become deeply attached to it, with a deep atavistic attachment, sad and sweet at the same time.

The colonel invites me over for a drink. He lives in a splendid dugout. The army craftsmen and locksmiths have built him a princely dwelling, complete with tapestries, paintings, books – everything.

But when I return to my own nest I despise his opulence. After all, I have built my stove and my bed with my own two hands.

It's my own nest. I live in it. I sit and think in it, I await death in it.

We've been living like this for two months. The snow keeps falling, and we sit in our dugouts. Our only duty is to check the gun embrasures, the "windows of death," Pály calls them. They have to be kept clean, free of snow, so that we can always have an unobstructed view of the sector between us and the Russian lines.

After such an inspection we creep back to our nest, warm ourselves at the stove, and dream under the blanket of snow.

Once in a while one of the officers makes a tour of all the dugouts, for the purpose of requisitioning. "The NCO's nest is a very fine one," they report to the commissioned officer, and the latter, now envious, becomes anxious to move in and take over.

He enters and the NCO jumps up in bewilderment, stands to attention and announces:

"Lieutenant sir?! Beg to report: There is nothing to report, sir!"

The officer braces himself, legs wide apart chews his cigar between his gold-capped teeth, thwacks his whip against his boots and says:

"Very nice, corporal. Very nice… It's a regular officer's quarters. You will evacuate at once, and change your address for mine!"

"Yes, sir!"

The officer departs, and the poor corporal remains stunned, his eyes bulging out of his head with anguish and humiliation. He flings away his half-smoked pipe and curses God for a pig. Then he begins to evacuate his nest.

Ah, the nest that he has put so much into, that he has dug out of the ground with his fingernails, improved with his heart's blood, to which he is so desperately attached!

Given enough time you can get used to anything – to the endless mud, to continual sleeplessness, to hunger, a snatched meal, eating roasted rats, running for hours without stopping to catch a breath, to the officers' contempt, to their sadistic punishment.

But there is one thing you simply cannot compromise and resign yourself to, and that is to be robbed of your own nest.

A deed like this quenches even the feeling for singing.

As an NCO, it has been my lot to suffer from this more than once. My nest seems particularly attractive to the officers.

Yesterday it happened to the tall, awkward Tyrolean. Being a corporal, he has built himself a separate little room, fixed it up, and decorated it to suit his simple, innocent taste.

His ingenuity has improved it even further. Then Ensign Slezak, the little "Jumping Jack" Czech officer, comes and robs him of it.

I hurry to tell Lieutenant Smerčany about it. He doesn't have to think twice. As soon as the marauding ensign has ensconced himself in his new finely appointed abode, the first lieutenant informs him that he wants it for himself. He needs it, that's all.

There is nothing for it. Ensign Slezak has to go to the trouble of looking around for new quarters. He finds that his former dugout suits him best after all.

The modicum of respect that I felt for Slezak, following our talk about the proclamation has entirely disappeared. I feel prejudice, even hatred, for him now.

Needless to say, the first lieutenant restores his nest to the Tyrolean.

Only Lance Corporal Margolis (excuse me: *Herr* Corporal Margolis) knows how to preserve his nest from robbers.

He keeps two or three dead rats hidden just outside, and whenever he suspects that a marauding officer might be on the prowl, throws them under his bunk. When the officer comes in and announces that he likes the place well enough to take it for himself, Margolis informs him:

"Oh sir! Beg to report: This is really a splendid place! You'll feel most comfortable here. The only trouble is, devil take them, it's full of this vermin" (and he points to the dead rats under the bunk) "which have been eating me up alive. I have no peace at night. They insist on coming right into bed with me. Last night I caught three of them. They took a walk on my belly, if you please, sir! God damn them! But it's not too bad. You can poison them. Here, I'll give you some of this very good poison I've got."

While speaking, he produces some yellow powder (actually just plain brick dust) and shows it to the officer.

By which time the worthy gentleman is usually outside.

Gentlemen robbers do not like to fight against rats.

There are no medals to be won in such a battle.

30 | The Dog

PÁLY BRINGS ME a dog. A wretched creature: scrawny, mangy and mute. Yes, a dog that is mute.

But he's got a pair of eyes that throw you into confusion. They're terrible to look at. All the sorrow of the war looks through them.

The dog cringes before me. I feed it, but it eats very little.

"He has forgotten how to eat," says Pály. "Who knows when he last had a meal?"

We clean him very thoroughly, with paraffin oil, benzine, snow, soap and water. The paraffin oil also cures his skin, which is covered with a vile mange.

If only he would bark! His muteness breaks my heart. He looks at me and whimpers, but doesn't bark.

Pály talks to him, pleads with him, threatens him, tempts him – nothing works.

He remains silent.

Pály tries to rouse him by making all sorts of animal noises: a cat, a frog, a calf, horse, donkey, pig, even a dog. Nothing doing. The dog stays silent.

At last there is some good news. Pály takes the dog with him when he goes to the officers' kitchen to get my food. On his return he announces joyfully:

"Bende barked!" (Pály has named him Bende after a much detested sergeant who was killed last year.)

"What happened?"

"Lieutenant Stubniak tried to pet him, and he barked at him."

"You're lying, Pály!"

"I swear it, sir."

He adds:

"He won't allow any officer to pet him. They drove him away with beatings before. But he really barked angrily at that pig Stubniak! Corporal Margolis suggested that I show him one of those officer types. I thought he was joking, But it turned out he was right."

The dog recovers and becomes quite handsome.

In a short time he becomes a great favorite with the entire platoon. In time, he becomes a regimental mascot. A very precious mascot indeed, since he has come to us on his own. The angel Gabriel must have sent him to us.[1]

The dog becomes a good friend to both of us. Back home I had always liked dogs. But here, it becomes a true companion.

One day Pály catches me in a piece of foolishness. I am having a long conversation with the dog, as if it were a good friend who understands me well. The young man is alarmed. He has been worried about my recent bouts of depression. Now, when he comes in and hears me talking to dog for a whole hour, he thinks that I am really losing my mind. He says that I have wept as well.

Who knows? Perhaps I am going out of my mind. I feel as if I am. The snow keeps coming down. My men are sitting around all day, yearning for the living and the dead. The officers are vicious brutes. I am slowly going crazy.

> Your eyes and mine are set on the filthy ground,
> On the body of our harlot earth slaked with heroes
>   blood –

You are sad, so sad, my canine comrade,
Why has your black face fallen so?
Why are you so silent?

You walk around me in an orphan's trembling stillness
And hide your tail in the depths of your heart –
Do not fear, do not dread, my canine comrade,
Approach my living grave and sit here at my side,
Let us warm each other together.

Let us warm ourselves in the light of despised dog grief,
I have not spoken for a while with somebody to my liking.
Do not glorify me, My canine comrade,
For I, like yourself, am a barker, a prophet,
A dog, the son of prophets, for generations.

For I, much like yourself, spent my life licking
And with canine joy have adored every shadow;
We share one fate, my canine comrade,
Like you I howled at the darkness of night
At the cold moon.

Ah! At the cold moon, silent and dead:
The corpse dragged at the height of secrets,
Where both of us decided, my canine comrade,
To please our God, and thank Him for His grace,
For the remnants of the set table.

For the table remnants of mighty absent owners,
Object of their cheerful song forever
We will devoutly turn, my canine comrade,
And deceive ourselves: like a bird on a branch
We will sing a psalm of freedom.

A psalm of freedom – woe to all of us, dogs of song,
Who bark so fiercely yet bite with fear –
Sit beside me, my canine comrade
Perhaps we can both, together
Hurl a curse to the sky.

To vomit forth our terrible grief, stifled and putrefying:
This foul pus-infected beauty which we share.
Teach me, my canine comrade,
To howl out such a curse
Damned, clear, and liberating.

Why do you look straight at me with such wondering
eyes? –
O, how I have thirsted for such eyes,
For tearless eyes, my canine comrade,
That conceal miracles in holy howling,
With love, with ancient truth.

I, my comrade, have not howled as I pleased
And my singing maw is drenched with blood;
Only my eyes wander, my canine comrade,
East, south, north and west,
Towards this cursed life.

Towards a life, where I shall walk on all fours,
A free dog, peeing on the horns of the altar –
I shall try no more, my canine comrade,
To justify any impurity and instill falsehoods
Into the garbled language of man.

No more shall I attempt to rattle my doleful depths,
To share a kind word for my coming successors –
I shall lie no more, my canine comrade
With eternal questions: why? what for? –
At a time fixed by God's mercy, I will be silent.

In another moment or two – a molten spark will
explode
My dreaming brain into ten thousand pieces.
And you – you, my canine comrade
Sit and wait a few moments
Sighing for my inarticulate life.

Howl over my life lost in the noise of lies,
With a silent moan mourn me forever –
Afterwards - slowly tear my body to shreds
And lick up my reddening blood.

Lick up my delirious blood[2] – wallow,
And vomit out a bark full of forlorn poison -
Perhaps, oh perhaps, my canine comrade,
You will bark out what was prevented from my song:
To poison the world with my grief.[3]

After a while Pály grows jealous of the dog.

When I comment on it, he says brusquely:

"He's your best friend sir. Perhaps you'd like him to be your batman?"

He falls silent for a moment, then adds:

"I'm going to chase him out of here to hell and gone!"

Of course, he doesn't. Right now, before a battle, to chase away our sole "guardian angel", that the whole regiment believes will protect our lives?! Never!

31 | Mene, Mene

THE IDLENESS and boredom of these long wintry days and nights inevitably produces strange behaviors and living conditions which we have been witnessing lately. Officers have shed the last vestiges of their civilian decencies, and appear before us in their most loathsome repulsiveness. These superior beings spend all their time eating and drinking, smoking, cursing, and playing practical jokes.

In addition, they boil over with hatred. Simple, senseless hatred. At first they hate Jews, then they come to hate everybody, that is, anyone who is helpless or humble, above all the common soldiers. This hatred was born early, two years ago, and has increased and spread instead of being obliterated by the sense of common danger. It has extended and flourished, until now it takes on the form of real bacchanalia.

The temper amongst the officers can best be defined as a combination of physical and spiritual orgies. The orgy of the body manifests itself in the usual way: extreme drunkenness with all sorts of mixed drinks. In the absence of women, sexual desire finds another outlet: inquisitorial persecution of human beings. If the hypothesis that there is a sadistic element in the erotic impulse is true, here, at the front, that single factor completely displaces the sexual experience itself.

Orderlies are the very first victims of these perverted officers. Punishment has ceased to be a matter of observing the rules and become an essential ingredient of daily life – something that comes within the bounds of the routine experience of these irrational, deluded men. They take special pleasure in devising unique punishments for each minor infraction – an improper word, an unauthorized gesture.

The Grand Inquisitor is *Herr* Colonel Figer. His Exquisiteness Figer, he of the perfect manicure and aesthetic theories, is the most punctilious in punishments which combine both physical and mental torture. For example, if one of the officers forces his batman to swallow the contents of the spittoon, he considers it inadequate punishment. His improvement on it is to force the victim to raise the vessel and say "To your health!" and then drain it. Afterwards he must express pleasure in it by saying: "Ah, that was good! May I have another?"

The officers compete with each other in devising new punishments. Soon they appear to have completely lost their reason. They hit on a brilliant notion – to punish men according to their civilian occupations. Thus the carpenter is made to eat wood shavings, the locksmith to swallow nails, the shoemaker to eat his glue, if perchance he makes a pair of shoes that don't please the officer. And so on.

The execution of every punishment is an occasion for a hilarious drunken celebration.

There is one unfortunate soldier who addresses a new lieutenant as *Herr* Ensign. He has been accustomed to addressing him thus for two years, the officer having only that day been promoted to lieutenant.

"What did you do back home?" the officer asks.

The man replies that he had been a gardener. So he is punished by being made to stand outside the trench like a scarecrow for a whole hour, a perfect target for Russian bullets. We watch horrified as he stands there for an entire hour, turning his head this way and that, trying to dodge the bullets that whistle around him, swaying like a lone tree in a storm.

It seems the gods protect this wretched creature, who is only hit in the arm and not in the head. Because of this he is "released" from standing there any longer.

One of the drunken officers sees fit to bandage the poor man's wound with wine, before handing him over to the medical orderly.

This abusive treatment, this bacchanalia of cruelty, has become second nature to them: wine, profanities, torturing the common soldiers, and drunkenness to the point of unconsciousness.

In the meantime, however, they continued to hold philosophical discussions about God, art, religion, and psychology.

An uninterrupted, continuous orgy along the front lines, "on the field of bravery and honor!"

Only two of the officers take no part in it – my First Lieutenant Smerčany, engrossed in his books, who has recently gone on leave, and Second Lieutenant Stubniak, for the obvious reason that he no longer has the sexual desire to stimulate in that way.

Headquarters knows absolutely nothing of any this. How could they? Who would report it to them?

The fact is that hundreds of men witness this moral leprosy. They suffer the mental and physical torments of hell enough to drive them insane, but not one of them dares to burst his bonds and raise a hue and cry of protest that would reach the ears of headquarters, which does, after all occasionally send high-ranking officers to inspect the regiment.

Is the theory which says that the people, the masses, make a revolution the correct one? I doubt it.

There are millions of men in distress here from all walks of life – workers, scholars, merchants, illiterate peasants – all suffering together like sick dogs for the past two and a half years. And one small cabal amongst the "higher ups" holds them tethered to an iron chain, bending them to their slightest whim!

Only a select few can initiate a revolution from among these higher-ups. If a general were to give the order for demobilization or a march against the royal palace, we would all either disband or march on the palace!

If a revolution comes, it can only be from above, with help of some of the generals. After that, it would continue without them, Only the first order is important, the order that liberates. The other processes continue on their own momentum without, even against, the wishes of those who gave the initial order in the first place.

Ah, yes, generals. A few of those could affect the great change, the cataclysm, the great redemption. But they, of course are not the ones who are suffering!

If only one general were made to drink the contents of a spittoon!

But no – the war has made that species into great prima donnas. Who, before the war, was even aware that such persons as Ludendorff or Mackensen existed?[1]

Who ever paid attention to these creatures except prostitutes, or they themselves?

Now their names are one everyone's lips, and newspapers are full of their fame and glory!

Why should they of all people make any changes – are they crazy?

Ensign Slezak has become completely demented lately. His mania is catching traitors who want to cross the lines and desert to the enemy. He keeps catching them and providing them as "spiritual nourishment" for the officers.

Margolis explains it to me in a way that seems reasonable and logical:

"The only one who really wants to cross over to the Russians is Herr Slezak himself. How that fellow hates all Magyars! And I know something else," Margolis continues, "Almost everyone knows that the leader of the Czechs, some professor whose name I don't know,[2] is now in Russia, preparing the revolution that is to liberate Czechoslovakia from our 'grand old man.' So! 'If one habitually claims that others are flawed, he disqualifies himself with his own flaw.'[3] Herr Slezak goes out of his way to unearth traitors so that no one would suspect him of wanting to take a stroll across the lines!"[4]

Of late there have been rumors of Jewish soldiers "who deserted to the Russians and betrayed all our secrets."

They have to be Jews, of course.

Not the Czechoslovaks, nor the Ruthenians, who state almost openly that the Russians are their kinsmen. Only the Jews are to blame. It's known that Ruthenian peasants in the Carpathians tell their children stories and sing songs about the "Matzkali" (Russian), who will come at the end of days and liberate "the world." They have been awaiting the "Matzkali" as Jews await the Messiah.[5]

But rumors always mention "Jewish traitors."

Meantime, we become genuinely good soldiers.

The snow is beginning to melt, and we can see the Russians mending the "roofs" of their frontline trench. It has always been understood that, when both sides are engaged in the same activity – such as removing dead bodies – neither side fires on the other. Therefore, while we repair our positions after the thaw, the Russians are not afraid to come out and work on theirs.

However, a new art form has recently become popular among us – "hunting." Men stand at the "windows of death" and shoot at the "target" over on the other side. Great rejoicing whenever somebody hit a bull's eye.

Pik! One.

Pik! Two.

Pik! Three.

That each "pik" is a family man, a living, suffering human being, doing his duty and wanting to go on living as much as any of us – that thought doesn't even occur to us.

A man's living soul is reduced to a mere "pik!"

If, to cap it all, you can hear the man's death rattle, so much the better.

I observe with what calm satisfaction the boys take pot shots at human "foxes" and "hares."

In the end we pay for it with the life of a fellow who is very dear to us. The lanky Tyrolean has gone up on the roof of our dugout to make some repairs. He is certain that the

Russians won't fire at him, since I had stopped the "hunting game" four days ago. But the Russians obviously haven't forgotten our violation of the unwritten agreement, and the Tyrolean suddenly falls head forward – dead.

So now he is also gone.

How awful it is to lower him down, to bury our tall, simple Tyrolean in the rotting hole that is his grave!

I remember his words – "Now it's my turn."

We stand speechless around his body, now rigid in death. Margolis sobs softly.

Uncle Osterreicher keeps moving around in circles as if hesitating about something. He exchanges a few whispered words with Margolis, and then stands over the body and says *kaddish*, the prayer for the dead.

And so our simple. Christian Tyrolean gets what thousands of Jewish soldiers die without.

The final words of the prayer are choked with sobs and a hoarse cough of advancing age.

The old soldier is crying.

Amongst the "higher-ups," in the meantime, the orgy grows ever wilder, and now boldly emerges from behind closed doors, breaking out of the officers' mess. Of late, the officers have been dressing as though for a wedding. They preen in gorgeous clothes, bedecked with gold and precious stones, shimmering inside the trenches like Satan's treasure-hoard in hell. They strut about like puffed-up turkey cocks that some drunken maharajah has decorated with gems, and, for greater debauchery, has them drink from his own wine. They stagger about in circles and gobble strangely, incomprehensibly. The officers have also changed their manner of speech. They now speak through their noses, which they believe is a sign of lofty nonchalance and superior indifference which prides itself, so to speak, on lassitude and aristocratic laissez-faire. They have given up pronouncing certain consonants, especially the francophone "r." Instead they pronounce something like the German "ch." This is believed to be more aristocratic, as ordinarily heard amongst the sons of counts in their clubs.

Margolis has a different explanation. He says that they are imitating the Galician Jews, who always pronounce their "r"s that way.

Having made this scientific discovery, the little corporal becomes angry with one of the Jewish officers who is strutting about with the affectation of nobility, puffing himself up and imitating the accent of the nobility to perfection. While discussing guard duty near the telephone, Margolis suddenly asks him:

"Excuse me, *Herr* Ensign, sir, do you pronounce the 'r' like this naturally, or did you learn how to do it?"

The stupid Jewish ensign stares even more dumbly at the little corporal. Then he gathers his few wits together and replies, restraining his temper:

"Yes, Corporal Margolis, it's natural."

"Oh," says Margolis matter-of-factly. "Then you are a Galician Jew, sir."

The ensign instantly becomes as angry as a raging bull. He cannot find the words to express his fury. He goes right up to Margolis, until their noses almost touch, grits his teeth and roars threateningly:

"Just you wait, you stinking *bokher!* I'll teach you to be respectful! (*bokher* is the Hungarian Jews' word for *yeshiva* student.)

To call an assimilated Hungarian Jew a Galician is probably the deadliest insult he can receive. How much more so, when he's preening himself and straining every nerve to speak through his nose and puff himself up, to nasalize and strut like a noble Magyar.

"What have you done, you wretch?" I ask Margolis when he tells me about the incident. "Now he'll eat you alive!"

"When?" says Margolis. When can he eat me alive? Not just now. The general offensive is about to begin, now that spring is coming. This offensive will bring with it the coming of the Messiah!"

This is the general opinion in the camp. The war simply cannot go on much longer, can it? It's already more than two-and-a-half years! Where are the additional men and material going to come from?

We are out of strength, out of patience, out of the will to go on living like this, out of everything. Only one thing must happen, and then peace will follow. There has to be a "day of reckoning and revenge"[6] first – a mighty offensive, both on our part and the enemy's, in the course of which "all accounts will be settled."

This settling of accounts means the great revenge upon the officers.

There is only one man who doesn't believe in the final "Day of Judgement," and he is Infantryman Johann Kretschery. None of us have managed to find out his ethnic origin. He is a very thin man, red-eyed and red-headed.

Under "nationality" his papers bear the description "Austrian." But what does that mean? Can the word "Austrian" exactly define a man's nationality? There are any number of different kinds of "Austrians." A deputy from the upper house of the Hungarian parliament once exclaimed: "Austria, thy people are as numerous as thy peoples!"

In fact, Kretschery displays the characteristics of many different nationalities. To begin with, he understands all the principal languages of the Empire. He even speaks Hungarian, the most difficult language in Europe, like a pure Magyar.[7] In addition, he speaks German, Czech, and several other languages.

We ask him, unable to contain our curiosity:

"Tell the truth, Kretschery, are you a Jew?"

He answers drily:

"When I die, Uncle Osterreicher will no doubt say *kaddish* after me."

This seems to suggest that he is Jewish. But then once he happens to mention, in the course of a story spiced with sharp and sarcastic jests, that he was born circumcised.

At which point we give up trying to figure out his racial origin.

One day Margolis springs a question on him:

"Do you like *cholent* (a traditional Jewish Sabbath dish)"?[8]

"Who doesn't like *cholent*?" replies the redhead. "Anyone who doesn't like that dish is no friend of mine!"

It's useless trying to figure him out. And what a name – Kretschery!

Kretschery doesn't believe in anything, neither in God nor in the devil, neither in Jupiter nor in Jehovah. That is to say, he has only one belief which he must have evolved during the course of the war at the front. He delights in demonstrating that belief with all sorts kinds of proofs and logical theorems.

What it amounts to, in brief, is this:

"God is neither a pure spirit nor the most refined matter. Nor even dynamic energy, as you seem to think. Energy too, requires someone to apply it. No, God is a creature, mightiest in the mightiest. A creature with an intelligence superior to ours, but a creature nonetheless. God is a cruel and most wicked creature, crueler than any we know. This creature has dominion over all that exists, both within and beyond the grasp of our finite brain. Its reign is absolutely cruel and unlimited. Once you understand this, you understand everything. You'll understand why 99.9% of life in this world is one great mass of monstrous cruelty, a mighty program of abuse and torment against mankind in general, but also against all species of living creatures. Suffering, misfortune, affliction, and pain. You don't have to be a mathematician or philosopher to figure out the preponderance of suffering and minimum of happiness that there is in life. The man who first came up with that piece of nonsense that "My Lord is a compassionate merciful God"[9] was trying to deceive both himself and the wicked creature to whom he prayed. Being at a loss, he thought to cajole and flatter it, as you flatter a murderer who's holding an axe over your head. For what is our entire, life, if not a continued sadistic torture devised by someone or other?

"And let me tell you," Kretschery concludes, "if you want to approach God, you have to be like him – cruel, murderous, sadistic and contemptuous of his victims. You have to bait your victim and laugh at him. You have to make every effort to be like God himself."

This is the catechism of Infantryman Johann Kretschery.

The doctrine is well received by our officers. They burst out in laughter at his words, but it's plain that they have great appeal for their drunken souls. At any rate, they receive firm support for their conduct, in which they have indulged without the need for philosophic backing.

They decide to throw a party – a "philosophical ball," as they put it – in honor of Infantryman Johann Kretschery.

When told about it, Kretschery initially says nothing. Later he says:

"Let 'em hang themselves without me! What do they need me for? They're wild enough brutes without my help. I won't go."

He doesn't want to appear, even though many of the soldiers envy him – an ordinary soldier whom the officers honor by arranging a party in his honor! It's a remarkable breach of military etiquette.

In the end he is forced to attend the party.

He doesn't abstain from his share of drinking once he is there, but he utters not a single word. They simply can't get a sound out of him.

When the officers notice this, they decide to bait him. "Let the reader of the letter be its messenger."[10]

Their orgy rages all that night.

The soldiers in the trenches sit waiting for the great Day of Judgement, for the war of Gog and Magog, which will bring about the final cataclysm prophesied by Isaiah and in the New Testament.[11]

That is the apocalypse awaited by the common soldiers through the long wintry days and nights that exhaust their nerves. Everything is leading to "the end of days."[12] Everything is proceeding in good order. Everything.

Then one night, while the officers are carousing in their mess, there is suddenly a great uproar. The next morning Pály hears about it from the other officers' batmen in the kitchen. Something terrible has happened there, an astounding miracle, the like of which has not been heard of since biblical times.

Pály described it all to me, genuinely awe-stricken.

"At 3:00 a.m., at the height of the drinking and singing and carousing, an inscription appeared on the wall, the exact duplicate of what was written in the times of the Bible, Sir! They said it was terrifying! Colonel Figer almost went out of his mind, sir!"

"Who saw it?"

"Lieutenant Stubniak's batman was in the room, sir, and he saw it with his own eyes. It was exactly like in the Bible, sir!" he adds with awe but also an inner joy.

I am intrigued into the affair. Indeed, it seems that the inscription appeared on the wall, in luminous letters: MENE, MENE, TEKEL UPHARSIN.[13]

I do not doubt it for long. It occurs to me that Margolis had something to do with it.

It proves to be so. Margolis, who has become an expert in telephone technology, has recently also made a study of electricity. It is he who produces the terrifying miracle in the officers' mess, by means of electrography. The drunken officers who see it go out of their minds and flee for their lives. The officers' mess is very quiet for a long time thereafter.

Amazingly, even after they find out that it was Margolis' doing, they do not punish the little corporal. On the contrary: The writing on the wall makes such an impression on them that they grow afraid of the stratagem's cunning!

Such is the power of belief, especially in the heart of a drunken officer who goes beserk in the courtyard of death.

The common soldiers feel that Margolis's trick matters not in itself but rather as proof that the "end of days" has really arrived. Thereafter each one of us, asleep or awake, sees before his eyes the inscription:

MENE, MENE.

32 | Diomedes and Glaucus

ANOTHER SPRING HAS ARRIVED

We clean, repair, and improve our trench "city." Everything is neat, orderly, and pleasant.

Outside, above us, the Galician sun, as though by a supreme effort, seems for once to be rivalling that of Italy. We can hear birds singing here and there. A lark in full flight passes over our heads, trilling exultantly. There are a few butterflies as well.

This time we respond to the spring differently from last year. Hearts are calm, the quiet before the storm, before the end, at least so we all feel and believe. The yearning for life, for liberty, for the city, for women and for a simple trade, no longer makes us rage and gnash our teeth. All those longings have blended into a single deep-seated pain, which imposes a sort of calm. We wait quietly, without fretting, in a pleasant state of enervation, within which lies a new seed of hope – a prospect for peace.

It seems that there is a similar feeling. "over there."

Nevertheless, within this calm a single assured and terrible expectation is implicit. We all know that before long a great new spring offensive will come. The worst part of it is that all through the winter we have received no information from the other side. The secret thread which has always kept us in constant contact with them, and through which we have obtained important news, plans and sketches of positions in the past, has snapped. It is generally believed that the other end of that thread has been in the hands of the Tsarina – though the reason for this belief could never be found. The devil knows why.[1]

At any rate, the thread has been broken, which means that we have to make our preparations without knowing anything of the other side's intentions.

Despite this, we believe that the offensive will not begin until early June, and it's now only April.[2]

"We'll be able to arrange our Passover Seder here at the front," Uncle Osterreicher says to me with perfect confidence. "Then, the Day of Judgment will come!"

We all feel this way. The "great wedding" will be held in June.

We strengthen our positions, devoting special attention to the concrete bunker behind our frontline trench, about thirty paces to the rear. There we will wait for the assault. When the Russian artillery begins its work of destruction we will withdraw to our fortified concrete bunker and there await the infantry attack.

And meantime, we are filled with quiet and yearning, even yearning towards the enemy.

There are some among us who have never in their lives seen a Russian in person, not even at a distance. The Russian man becomes a fantastic figure, provocative, mysteriously appealing in the eyes of a plain soldier. There is something about this appeal that lures him, as though by some hidden, inner force.

There is in this fascination a feeling which one could undeniably call love.

Our most intense yearning concentrates on a single strip of land no more than three hundred paces wide – no man's land.

For several months now there have been no encounters between the lines. We sit here, daydreaming, singing, playing and yearning. On the other side they must be doing the same thing.

Now that the snow is gone and the ground reappears, everything becomes covered with marvelous green grass. Here and there flowers of different colors dot the grass, and butterflies hover over them. Above everything the lark warbles in the sky.

We peep at all these marvels from the trenches, gripped by a mighty, agonizing longing – Oh, just once to come out of the trench and stroll in that "Garden of Eden" (our name for no man's land), to walk, run, skip and roll like a colt on the fragrant soft grass, in company with the shadowy, distant Russians!

Oh, to roll and wrestle with the Russians, like mischievous children in the open!

This is the most beautiful of our dreams so far.

I vow that if I survive this war, the first thing I will do is return to this very spot with Mansie and my sister, and sit down on the grass with them. Then I will bury my face in it and just cry, cry, cry my heart out.

Uncle Osterreicher receives his new phylacteries from Lwów.[3] How he rejoices in them!

"I will not depart this world," he announces wrapped in his prayer shawl and bound with his phylacteries, "until I have prayed in a *minyan*[4] with them over there!"

"Uncle Osterreicher, you're making a vow in your shawl and phylacteries!"

"Yes, I am! I want to obligate The Almighty to grant me this privilege. That's the one thing I want to do in my life, to pray with them. They pray over there just as we do, and with the same ritual, don't they? Our prayers are the same all over the world" he continues meditatively. Finally he repeats:

"A *minyan* – with them – in peace!"

"The Lord grant it!" the Italian Benvenuto Gallieri responds. "I too would like just once to have a drink with them! To share one glass of wine with them, by the Holy Virgin!"

We are ordered to go and reconnoiter the thick woods which stretch between the lines to our left. The Russians had been there last fall, but then they left.

Now, in preparation for the spring offensive, we must reconnoiter it. Who knows, we might be able to bring back some information.

I have the privilege not to go myself, but send my men instead. But now, not only my customary habit impels me to go along with them as always, but more especially the powerful, unconquerable longing to leave the trench and stroll through the "Garden of Eden."

I take seven men – all volunteer.

Among them is Uncle Osterreicher. I don't want to take him, but he actually pleads with me. I have never seen him plead like this before.

What can I do? I take the old man along for the "stroll."

Of course Margolis as well. He understands Russian.

We climb out of the trench at exactly 3:00 a.m.

It's a moonlit night, except that the moon is mostly concealed behind dark clouds.

As we crawl through the damp grass we roll around on it, over and over, like young colts, freshly released from the stable after an idle, sluggish winter.

"Too bad we can't neigh, whispers the old horse-thief Adam Ballah. "I have an unconquerable desire to give a loud, Exultant neigh… Iyy!"

"Shut up, you horse's ass!"

We crawl on, towards the wood. By the time we reach it we are drenched from head to foot.

Once inside the wood we stand up and advance cautiously.

After some fifty paces I am startled to suddenly see a human shape ahead of us.

Normally one would shout "Halt" – but here, now, under these circumstances?

We all stop in a broad line, each man about five paces apart.

We all see the man, standing behind a thick tree.

We too stand each one behind a tree.

Suddenly, as if the devil is spiting us, the moon emerges from behind the dark clouds, and bathes us in a lustrous stream of light!

Now I can see plainly: Russians. Not one – eleven of them.

We stand behind the trees, frozen, immobile. We hold our rifles ready, trained at them. Not aimed precisely, but at the ready with butts resting against our waists.

They do the same.

Two rows of riflemen, facing each other, standing as if petrified.

Who will move first?

As soon as one of them moves, I'll shoot.

They must be thinking the same thing: as soon as one of us move, they would fire at us.

And so we all stand, not daring to stir.

A few minutes pass, then a few more. Our hearts pound furiously. The moon shines brightly.

Then one of our men coughs accidentally.

After that one of them coughs as well.

What does this mean? An answer?

I try coughing as well.

Again, a cough from the other side.

Now we are certain that it's a reply. I decide to try again, but Uncle Osterreicher anticipates me.

Again an answering cough.

We take it for granted that this is a reply.

Well, then, we are the initiators, and as such are in command of the situation. This is most important in such an encounter. It's a basic law in war – the side that makes the opening move always has a better chance of victory, even though he is much weaker than the other.

I stand there for a few moments longer, and a forbidden thought flashes through my mind: a truce.

I know what a grave crime it is, yet I cannot suppress it. I struggle with myself, but the idea wins.

I make up my mind!

I slacken my grip on the rifle, pointing it at the ground.

The Russian facing me does the same.

By way of an experiment. I raise my rifle to its previous position. So does he, so do my men. That being so, I slacken my grip again. He does the same thing.

Very good.

After me, my men do the same thing. So do the Russians.

Now both rows of soldiers stand with their rifles pointing downwards. *Iacta alea est!* For better or worse, I thrust my bayonetted rifle into the ground. Whatever happens, happens!

My answer seems to be the correct one. They do the same.

Then I say: "*Pan!* (Sir)" – and am startled by my own voice.

At once the answer comes: "*Pan!*"

At that point, I come out from behind the tree and stand facing the Russian, but I order my men, in the meantime, to keep under cover where they are.

The Russian comes forward, too, I stand still for a moment, but he keeps walking towards me.

That's good! That's very good! It bodes well.

The Russian comes right up to me and again says: "*Pan!*"

I offer him my hand, and in the meanwhile order my Italian to walk towards the enemy lines and beyond them, to see if reinforcements have been planted there. Perhaps it's a trap?

Gallieri takes his rifle along, for protection, and walks confidently ahead. Margolis, at my order, comes over to us and engages in conversation with the Russian. He asks him if there are any more men back there. A Russian NCO replies.

"What did he say?" I ask.

"He said, God forbid!"

"Good. So tell him there isn't any force behind us either."

Gallieri returns and reports: not a soul back there.

We all breathe a sigh of relief. Margolis jokes with the Russians. Then we all sit down on the ground.

I keep in mind that we could all be sentenced to death for this.

Who cares?! The devil take it!

We chat a little, of course barely audibly.

They give us some peculiar tobacco. It looked like chips of cut stalks mixed with crumbled green and yellow leaves. The Russian explains that this is "makhorka." He makes a tiny funnel of a small piece of tough paper, pours a pinch of these scraps into it, seals the top of the funnel – and there you have a cigarette!

Very strange.

I take the gift and wait. He wants to roll another such cigarette for himself, but I don't let him. I offer him one of my own. He thanks me, "*Spasibo, pan!*"[5]

I hand out cigarettes to all of them.

We light them with utmost caution, inside our caps, which screen the light on all sides, and smoke.

Then we share our liquor with them.

They enjoy it immensely.

Unexpectedly, the Russian in command of the patrol speaks up. Margolis interprets:

"He proposes that we exchange a few prisoners."

"What does he mean?"

"He'll give us a few of his men as prisoners, and we'll give him a few of ours in exchange."

I think about it. It's a peculiar idea, but a striking one.

"Well, boys," I turn to my men, as a sort of experiment, "which of you would like to make peace with the Tsar, a pox on him?"

"With the Tsar, a pox on him, no. But with these fellows. yes," says the Italian.

The Russian explains some more, and Margolis interprets:

"They have an abundance of food. White bread and meat. too. They have everything, he says, not like us!"

Pály flares up furiously, but contains himself for the moment:

"You tell him, *Herr* Corporal: In a pig's eye! You have no more than we do! They can stuff themselves till they burst, on our side as well! Tell him, Corporal!"

"Shut up, Pály!"

"Madjar. Madjar!" says the Russian.

He recognizes a Magyar when he sees one.

"Mouska!" says Pály. "Mouska!" (Muscovite).

The Russian offers his hand to Pály who hesitates a minute then, despite what he has said, decides to shake it.

I decide to send Uncle Osterreicher with them, to take a much needed rest. Let this veteran, with his large, dependent family, live out his life, waiting for peace in captivity, and there await the Messiah. Why should he get killed in the spring offensive?

At first Uncle Osterreicher protests. Why him, of all the men? Later, however, when the Italian agrees to go too, he hesitates a little.

"Why not, Uncle? You've got your phylacteries. There you'll have your *minyan*. Why should you die a few days before the armistice? Think about it!"

Uncle Osterreicher turns to Margolis to have him ask the Russian if they wouldn't kill him over there.

The Russian makes a broad gesture in emphatic protest.

"He says 'God forbid,'" explains Margolis.

Eventually we come to an agreement: I will give him four men, and he will give me five. A profitable deal.

I tremble all over. It could mean a sentence of death.

Oh, devil take it, why not! The Italian does so much want to go on living. Uncle Osterreicher is an elderly Jew with a family – Why should "the Old Man" back in Vienna mind if I exchange these men for some Russians? I am confident that "the Old Man" would agree, and if he did, the hell with all those drunken swine over there!

"We're not going to give them our rifles, though, devil take them!" say our four "captives" almost in unison. "Please take our rifles with you!"

We part with kisses and embraces. Uncle Osterreicher weeps. So does one of the Magyars. Before we part, I suggest that we all fire a few shots in the air, to signal an encounter between us.

(Note: As I write these lines I am myself a prisoner of war.[6] When I get here I find out that both the Italian and Uncle Osterreicher died on the way, in Chortkov, even before they entered Russia proper.[7] The other two survived, so I cannot mention them by name. They could be executed for this. And I? – If ever I publish this journal, I'll erase this entire chapter).

When we return to camp, my conscience makes me positively ill.

Then I remember the Trojan war, and the two enemies, the heroes Diomedes and Glaucus.[8] They became friends on the field of battle and made a truce between them, before the eyes of the warring armies. If the Greeks could allow such a thing, how much more so should we!

33| The End of Days[1]

AT THE BEGINNING of June our tense anticipation of the spring offensive reaches hysterical proportions. The concrete bunker is complete and ready.

Just to spite us, spring is superb, moving our hearts and souls to tears.

One evening, while my batman is preparing my bunk, he suddenly says:

"The fun will begin tomorrow morning, or I'm a mad dog!"

"Why tomorrow morning?"

"Why? Why? Just like that, that's how. You'll see if I'm wrong, sir."

"You surely must have heard some rumor."

"Must have heard. Of course I have heard! But who listens to these rumors? I know for sure – tomorrow morning. At dawn."

Because of this he has everything prepared, packed and ready.

We go to sleep.

Never before have I slept so soundly and well, when a massive shell – a "thirty-two," probably – violently shakes our entire encampment, with its shriek and then explodes about fifty paces to our right. It has been aimed directly at our front lines.

The noise instantly arouses me from sleep. After the explosion we enter our concrete bunker and abandon our front line trench to the withering barrage, which all but bursts our eardrums.

My nest is the target of this annihilating fire.

I remember every tiny detail of my nest. The window with its pentagonal pane, (we did not have the necessary tools to cut it into rectangular shape), the bench, the bunk bed, the coat-hanger, the hollowed-out "cupboard" that had been chiseled shaftwise into the wall, and the pictures – among them "the forty great rabbis," from Maimonides to the *ketav sofer*.[2]

The noise inside the bunker is hellish. It's about 5 meters deep, and the roof, level with the ground, is 3 meters thick. It is constructed as follows: a layer of boards, each more than a half-meter thick; upon this a layer of concrete; and on top of everything – earth.

Beneath this roof we sit pressed tightly together and listen to the roaring of the shells, which rend the heavens and shatter our entire front line.

When one of these shell hits our roof and bursts, we feel as if we are going to suffocate. We sit for a few seconds with mouths gaping and, with a choking breath that resembles a protracted, stifled sneeze, wait for air to come up of our smothering lungs. The sneezing lasts for several minutes.

We sit in two long lines, facing one another, closely crowded, waiting for the order to abandon the position.

To abandon it – after the enemy has finished destroying our front line, begins to shell our rear lines and our artillery, and then starts sending his infantry to attack us.[3]

To go forth – while on the outside a shell explodes on every square meter, at least one shell in each meter! A shell powerful enough to demolish a three-story building without leaving a single brick in place.

To go forth under a rain of death. How fortunate that the science of war has laid down that one must emerge only after the enemy has ceased to rain down death and when his troops begin to advance.

Then suddenly the order comes: "Send out patrols!"

Sending out patrols means leaving trenches, stationing men in a long line, twenty paces apart. The men must lie down in the midst of this terrible hail of bullets and watch for the upcoming infantry attack.

The order is received by *Herr* Colonel Figer in person. He has been sent to our position by headquarters and condescended to join us in the concrete dugout because it's a little safer than his cozy nest. He transmits the order to me:

"Send out twenty men as lookouts, and tell them that whoever volunteers will receive a decoration. If he already has one, he'll get an even higher one. Those who distinguish themselves will be promoted."

I call out:

"Anyone who wants to come out with me..."

The colonel interrupts:

"You needn't go outside, Ensign. Why should you?"

Colonel Figer has suddenly become the milk of human kindness. He's concerned about somebody else's life beside his own. Alas, this is not an exceptional case. Oh no! In times of danger these gentlemen officers suddenly become charming and kind, courteous and affectionate, positively sisterly.

Sisterly, though, not brotherly. Brothers are men. These gentlemen turn into soft, effeminate women.

"Sit down a little. You must be tired."

Or: "Don't trouble yourself, let me do this."

Or: "Don't risk your life. The army needs men like you." Now *Herr* Figer is concerned about my life. I shouldn't go outside myself. I should send an NCO out there, into that certain death up above us.

"Colonel, sir! Beg to report: I never *send* my men. I always *call* them to face danger."

I go on with the announcement of the terrible order.

Sixteen men volunteer.

"Any more? Who else? Well, what do you say, boys?"

Another man volunteers.

The air in the bunker is almost unbreathable, it's so tightly compressed by the explosions overhead.

Hik! We gulp, mouths gaping, lungs bursting, eyes bursting out of their sockets.

"Well any more? Who else?!"

Nobody. I need three more men.

This is the worst part: to point to three men and force them to go outside with the rest.

The only thing comparable to this volcanic upheaval of one's moral life is to take a fellow soldier and shoot him, by order of a court-martial.

Those who volunteer enjoy a moral advantage, a satisfaction that eliminates a large part of the terror of death. It's a form of autosuggestion that is immensely valuable at such times. A man who willingly risks his life pulls himself together and goes out courageously.

But the man whom I must order to go outside is a truly unfortunate wretch. Especially after he has not volunteered like his comrades. And I must compel this miserable fellow, who after all did not volunteer because he was afraid, to go outside and meet certain death.

I must single him out amongst all his fellows.

For him I represent cruel, inexorable fate. Fate itself.

That is pure hell.

I actually implore them to volunteer. I plead with them in every way I know.

To no avail.

So I play "Babel" with them. I order all those who have not volunteered to get together in a group. Then I pass down the line with my eyes shut and walk the entire length of that row of men. When I return in the other direction I pick them out at random:

"You – You – You!"

Then I open my eyes and see whom I have chosen for the "burnt offering."

The three chosen men stand before me – wretched, pathetic, miserable. They don't even have the satisfaction that the courageous act of volunteering gives.

I whisper to each one of separately:

"It doesn't make any difference to me, my friend, that you didn't volunteer. You'll get a medal just like the others."

Now we have to go outside.

The concussions of roaring bombshells shake everything around us, but we emerge from the bunker in full view of the enemy. Seeing us, he adds the "little devil" – the machine gun – to his cannons, and aims directly at us.

I crawl forward at the head of my men.

We are all outside, on top of the concrete roof.

All hell breaks loose around us. The machine guns rattle away, right in our faces.

We crawl on, but before I can place four of the men in position, two are already gone. They have simply disappeared.

I wonder if I myself am still alive. Who can tell in such roaring turmoil?

I post the rest of the men in a line, ten paces apart. At first I keep ducking, throwing myself flat on the ground, seeking hollows to bury my head in, terrified and gasping for breath. After a few minutes I remain still, waiting doggedly for the bullet or shell that would blow me to hell.

But after some time passes and death, spitefully, fails to come, I throw precaution to the winds and stand up. I really stand upright. What could happen to me on my feet that couldn't happen otherwise?

So I stand up and encourage my men.

In that moment I wonder about it. What is this? Heroism?!

Heroism, hell! It's the ultimate despair. It's the only way to preserve my taut nerves from snapping in the terrible tension.

Suddenly I see Pály crawling out of the concrete dugout and advancing towards me. He wasn't there when I formed the patrol, and when he returns and sees that I have gone outside, he follows me.

I point my revolver at him: "Get back! At once!"

He ignores both my gesture and my revolver, and crawls towards me gingerly, eyes blinking, closing and opening with a wide stare. When he reaches me he tackles me about my feet and drags me down to the ground.

I pass cigarettes to the men, and lie down as well.

The only way to get that damned batman back inside is to go with him.

So I start to crawl back "home." No sooner do I start, but two or three of the men began to follow me.

"Get back, you pigs!" I yell, aiming my revolver at them.

There is nothing for it. It's a basic law of nature – in the absence of his officer, the bravest soldier may lose his courage. So I remain, and Pály, of course, remains with me.

Finally the order comes for me to bring them back. They aren't needed outside yet. The enemy isn't ready to advance.

Bring them back? By then there are only fourteen men left. The rest have been torn to pieces, died of wounds, or simply disappeared without a trace.

When I get back inside and see Colonel Figer, I boil with fury and hatred. It's as if an acute attack of nausea rises in me at the sight of this loathsome, drunken coward. The sight of his polished fingernails makes me want to shoot him on the spot with my revolver.

From that moment on, this feeling of revulsion and detestation grows stronger and stronger inside me, as he goes out of his way to be kind and pleasant to me.

Pály goes mad and laughs in the colonel's face. He openly mocks him.

"Pály," I whisper in his ear, "you'll go mad with the punishment he has waiting on you for this!"

"When? When, sir? Tomorrow? The day after? There is no more tomorrow or the day after! There is only today, sir! And he's not going to survive it, by the Holy Virgin, sir!"

The Great Gentleman stares at him in silence.

The Russians shell our positions continuously all this day and night, the next day during the day and night as well, without letting up for a second. Only on the third day is there a sudden silence, at midday.

I go outside at once to see what is happening.

The enemy has still not tried to advance.

The quietness after two and a half days of continuing bedlam is like heavenly nectar spreading through the body.

At last after this hellish shelling we can telephone the other dugouts and ask for news.

Only, there is no telephone – the shells have ripped up the lines.

Where in the world is Margolis?

Margolis is nowhere to be found.

Within the hour, the cannons began to roar again.

If that were remotely possible, even worse than before!

It's impossible to establish telephone communications with even the nearest field headquarters.

Suddenly the telephone rings!

Extraordinary joy.

"Hello! Yes? Respects, Excellency!" says Colonel Figer into the telephone. "What? Who? Who repaired the telephone wires? I've no idea, Excellency! What? No, I didn't send anyone out to repair them. How could I send anyone out, at such a time? What? Yes, Excellency! As soon as I find out, I'll let you know.

"Yes, Excellency! My respects, Excellency!"

He passes the message to me: it's the commandant in person who has sent me, as the "fire officer," his personal congratulations as well as that of the entire division. He trusts me completely and thanks me very much. He also wants to know who has repaired the telephone lines here and all along the front line of our regiment, in this inferno.

I am convinced that it's Margolis. That devil is capable of doing anything! And the proof? He is absent, and no one knows where he is.

Deathly panic suddenly hits me. What has happened to him?

Only let the little fellow remain alive with me, dear God! Don't take that young boy away from me now!

I would gladly give my life for his, for his safety.

But I don't have to worry long. He turns up.

"Good lord! What a face! You look terrible, Margolis!"

He is covered with mud from head to foot, his hair wildly disheveled and his clothes torn to shreds and bloody.

I hurriedly examine him all over.

"Where are you wounded, my poor fellow? What have you done?!"

He draws himself up and announces:

"Ensign, sir! Beg to report: All the telephone wires have been repaired, sir! Mouska can shoot even the Tsar himself, but he can't disconnect our telephone lines anymore. A plague on his head!"

"Where are you wounded, Margolis?!"

"Right here," he says, and shows me his ankle. A minor scratch, a tear in the skin that wouldn't scare even a child. That's his injury.

"This isn't mine sir," he says, pointing at the blood on his clothes. It's my comrade's, the telephonist from the adjoining regiment. He got killed and belched his blood onto me."

I embrace him give him some brandy.

Only then do I realize that instead of reporting to the *Herr* Colonel, he has reported to me, in the colonel's presence.

I pinch his side and whisper:

"Go and report to him now. Do you hear?"

"To whom?" he asks, almost audibly. To that female over there with the whore's manicure? Let the devil report to him! I won't! I want nothing to do with him! Have I ever stolen chickens with him?!"

The telephone rings again. It's the commandant asking to speak to the "rescuer repair man" himself. To his surprise, Margolis answers:

"Excellency, beg to report: All my life I've talked with God over the telephone!"

That night, at 2:00 a.m., the Russians emerge from their holes and begin to advance towards us in hordes.

The battle is very bitter. My men fight like maddened lions.

Pály sings the entire time, chanting some tune or other in the midst of the raging tumult.

A kind of jesting spirit breaks out amongst the men in the very midst of this hell. Everyone is shouting, joking, singing. The Russians must think that we have all gone mad.

At 3:30 p.m. after an hour-and-a-half's firing, the sergeant comes to report:

"There is no more ammunition, sir!"

"I'll put a bullet through your head! Why didn't you prepare enough for such an emergency?"

"Sir, for the past half hour I've been asking the *Herr* Colonel to give the order, but he's sitting in the bunker, completely confused. He's terrified and can't say a word! He just keeps drinking."

"I'll get the ammunition for you!"

I descend into the bunker myself.

The colonel is seated there, drinking. He can hardly sit upright. Seeing him thus, all the devils in the universe enter my mind and rekindle all my loathing and hatred for him. In a flash I recall at that moment the entire record of this creature's filth, impurity and cruelty, and feel that I have nothing to lose. It's the end of days!

He senses it and began to stammer:

"Why – You – You know that – that I trust you – I've always trusted in – in – your courage —! You are – He rises and tries to slap me on the shoulder.

I push his hand away and scream at him:

"What am I? What am I?" I scream with all my might, feeling released from all bonds of regulations and discipline. "What am I, *Herr* Colonel?! I demand ammunition, sir! Ammunition! You hear me, you son of a bitch, you! Ammunition! Why are you standing here like an idiot? – Out! Get outside! To the war! *Get out!*"

I threaten him with my revolver.

"You'll die here, you filthy dog!"

Behind me Pály yells:

"Put a bullet in his belly, sir! A bullet in his pig's belly!"

I will never forget that miserable scene: a pathetic trembling creature, half drunk and half dead with fright. When I scream at him, he stammers:

"Please don't! – Don't –! You're a hero!"

I spit in his face and go outside to get the ammunition.

I return to find an astonishing change. On both flanks of my company – absolute silence. No one in sight. My company is spread along a hundred and fifty yards of the trench, and that is all that was left of our front line. All the others have been taken captive.

How did it happen?

I don't know.

The Russians keep pouring on by the thousands. When one of their waves falls, a second follows, and then a third and a fourth, a fifth and a sixth, there is no end to their forces. We have only three lines, that's all. And they are twenty, thirty lines thick.

"Who in the world has produced them in such crazy numbers?!" yells Pály, firing ceaselessly.

"That's one thing they know how to do!" Margolis yells back. "They know how to multiply, God damn and blast them!"

"I think that today they also know how to win," I reply, trying to keep up the spirits of my shrinking platoon, which is losing about a man a minute.

Our artillery isn't doing us any good either.

What has happened?

Has the artillery been captured as well?

I send up rockets of all colors, pleading for support. There is no answer.

We are alone.

Suddenly my sergeant says:

"Look, sir! Behind us! Mouska is there as well!"

"What? Behind us?"

I snap the order: "*Gendarmerie*!"

That means that the platoon must divide into two sections, one facing the front and the other back to back with their comrades, facing forward and firing from that position.

Suddenly I hear someone yelling behind us:

"Avigdor! Avidgor! Don't shoot! We're all lost!"

It's the voice of my dear friend First Lieutenant Smerčany.

He has been taken captive and the Russians were leading him away behind our lines – leading him straight towards us. With him is a whole crowd of our men.

I immediately understand that the Russians have broken through our front lines to the left or to the right of us, penetrating our rear and defeating one of our adjoining regiments. Now they surround us and have captured the entire division.

It could not have been otherwise.

Meanwhile, however, the Russians are also advancing towards us from their own front. I rally my platoon and we continued to defend ourselves on that side.

There are only twenty of us left.

Then four men fell, one after the other.

Then another three.

And another one.

Then two more.

From behind us somebody yells:

"Don't fight! It's useless! All is lost!"

But are we firing? It's the rifle that fires, not the man!

A Russian officer walks towards me, flanked by soldiers on both sides.

I fire at him with my revolver. I fire and fire, but fail to hit him.

What's the matter with me? Am I drunk? Or blind?

But he doesn't shoot. He keeps on coming towards me without saying a word. He seems to be smiling.

A tall man, strikingly handsome with open, kindly features. Smiling, he approaches and raises his hand:

"*Nie nada, pan! Nie nada!*"[4]

He points at something behind me. I look – there they are, our men, all captive.

I see them and give the order to lay down our rifles.

My men – only six are left – thrust the bayonets of their rifles into the ground. We stand and wait.

The handsome Russian officer comes up to me. I hand him my revolver.

He fires the remaining bullets into the air and puts it in his pocket.

Again he smiles at me, slaps me on the shoulder and says something.

Margolis translates:

"He's saying you're quite a man, sir!"

The Russian produces a cigarette case and offers me one.

I take out my own cigarette case and offer him one of mine.

We both light up.

The Russian proposes that we exchange cigarette cases. I agree.

Margolis is sorry to see me exchange my gold case for the Russian's silver one.

The Russian shakes my hand warmly. He notices my belt and admires it. He takes off his own belt and we exchange them, buckling them on each other's waist.

Again he shakes my hand, almost embracing me, and repeats the words he had said before, adding several which I don't understand:

"*Iei bogu! Molodetz!*"[5]

He hands me over to his sergeant, to accompany me to their headquarters. He warns him to take good care, so that no harm befalls me on the way.

We walk away. We are captives.

On the way we stumble upon Russian corpses, also some of our own.

Margolis looked at them intently, and after a long silence says to me:

"Well, then, tell me, sir: what was all this game about? Couldn't I have simply bought a ticket to tour Russia by train?

Was it necessary to make all this tararam for this? Was it, sir?"....

(Haydn)

Notes

Introduction

[1]Anatoly Steimatzky, The Gnazim Institute of the Hebrew Writers Association in Israel, 119/א-38992 א/119.

[2]Uri Kesari, Feuilleton, "Hashigaon Hagadol." *Doar Hayom* 5 January, 3, 1930.

[3] Yediot Gnazim, 74:D, 9th year, Nisan, Tashla, 1970, 790.

[4]Ruthenians and Ruthenes are Latin exonyms formerly used in Western Europe for the ancestors of modern East Slavic peoples, especially the Rus' people with an Eastern Orthodox or Ruthenian Uniate Church religious background.; A "shabbes goy" was a non-Jew who performed tasks not permitted to an Orthodox Jew on sabbaths and festivals.

[5]Avigdor Hameiri, *Arsi Eretz Hakarpatim, Betoch Hakarpaturos. Encyclopedia of Diaspora Communities, Memorial Books of Diaspora Countries and Towns,* volume 7. Jerusalem-Tel Aviv: Encyclopedia of Diaspora Communities, 1959, 587.

[6]Emil Feuerstein, Avigdor Hameiri: Personal communication. *Ma'ariv* 26 July 1974.

[7]Bratislava (Slovak Republic).

[8]David Tadhar, *(Menahem) Avigdor Hamieiri,* Encyclopedia for the Pioneers and Builders of the Yishuv, volume 3 (Tel Aviv: Rishonim, 1958), 1260.

[9]Alon Rachamimov. "Collective identifications and Austro-Hungarian Jews (1914–1918). The contradictions and travails of Avigdor Hameiri," In Laurence Cole and Daniel Unowsky (editors), *The Limits of Loyalty: Imperial Symbolism, Popular Allegiances, and State Patriotism in The Late Habsburg Monarchy.* (New York and Oxford: Berghahn Books, 2007), 185; Eliezer Ben Yehudah (Eliezer Yizhak Perlman, 1858–1922), Hebrew lexicographer and newspaper editor, and the driving force behind the revival of the Hebrew language in the modern era.

[10]Yosef Sa'aroni, *Avigdor Hameiri, Moznaim* 6, 1 (31) – 6 (36), 1937–1938, 522.

[11]Ernest Roth, *A Tale of Three Cities [Vienna, Budapest, and Prague]* (New York: Charles Scribner's Sons, 1971), 90.

[12]Avigdor Hameiri, "Halomo shel Lilian: mitoch bli Tina al yedidai veson'ai," *Tesha Ba'Erev,* 128, 3rd year, 11 August 1939, 4.

[13]Idem., "Halomo shel Lilian: mitoch bli Tina al yedidai veson'ai," *Tesha Ba'Erev,* 116, 3rd year, 23 May 1939, 5.

[14]Ibid.

[15]Avigdor Hameiri, Letter to Nahman Sirkin, 21 Kislev, Tarpa (22 December 1921). The Gnazim Institute of the Hebrew Writers Association in Israel, 119/A-45327.

[16]Avigdor Feuerstein, *Shlihei Hasatan, Ha'aretz,* 29 December 1921, 2.

[17]Joseph Roth (1894–1939), Austrian journalist and novelist, best known for his family saga *Radetzky March* (1932), about the decline and fall of the Austro-Hungarian Empire. Died of chronic alcoholism; Stefan Zweig (1881–1942), Austrian novelist, playwright, journalist and biographer. Zweig's memoir, *Die Welt von Gestern (The World of Yesterday)* (London: Hamisch Hamilton and Stockholm: Bermann-Fischer Verlag AB, 1942), is noted for its description of life during the waning years of the Austro-Hungarian Empire under Franz Josef I and has been called the most famous book on the Habsburg Empire. He committed suicide with his wife.

[18]Words possibly borrowed from an essay by Ahad Ha'am (Asher Zvi Ginsberg) (1856–1927) "Imitation and Assimilation."

[19]Avigdor Hameiri, *Reah Moledet. Hadoar,* 7 November 1924, 4–7.

[20]Ibid.

[21]Mukachevo (Western Ukraine).

[22]Avigdor Hameiri, *Tiyuta Lane'um,* The Gnazim Institute of the Hebrew Writers Association in Israel, 119/כ-2542, Ramat Gan 1955. *Epikores* means non-believer, denier, heretic; Theodor Herzl (1860–1904), father of modern Zionism; the Tetragrammaton (*hashem hameforash*) was only known to the High Priest who used it only on Yom Kippur during the ritual sacrifices, After destruction of the Second Temple in 70 CE, the name became forgotten, and we do not know it today.

[23]Moshe Kleinman, Book Review, *Haolam* 54, 27.12.1929, 18.

[24]Avigdor Hameiri, *Masa Be'eropa Haperait, Rishmei Agav Anakroniyim* (Tel Aviv: Va'ad Hayovel, 1938), 14; *Sikarikin, Doar Hayom,* 01.01.1932, 5; Idem, *Voyage into Savage Europe. A Declining Civilization,* (Brookline, MA: Academic Studies Press, 2020), 55.

[25]*Népszava,* Socialist-Democratic Hungarian language newspaper.

[26]Chapter 2.

[27]Endre Ady (1877–1919), Hungarian poet and journalist regarded by many as the greatest Hungarian poet of the twentieth century.

[28]Chapter 10.

[29]Lee Congdon, "Endre Ady's Summons to National Regeneration in Hungary, 1900–1919." *Slavic Review* vol. 33 no. 2. Association for Slavic, East European and Eurasian Studies, June 1974, 321.

[30]Lev Nikolayevich Tolstoy (1828–1910), Russian writer regarded as one of the greatest authors of all time; Alexander Sergeyevich Pushkin (1799–1837), Russian poet, playwright, and novelist of the Romantic era, considered by many to be the greatest Russian poet; Alexei Maximovich Peshkov (Maxim Gorky, 1868–1936), Russian and Soviet writer, a founder of the socialist realism literary method; Leonid Nikolaievich Andreyev (1871–1919), Russian playwright, novelist and short-story writer, who is considered to be a father of Expressionism in Russian literature; Romain Rolland (1866–1944), French dramatist, novelist, essayist, art historian and mystic; William Shakespeare (1564–1616), English poet, playwright, and actor, widely regarded as the greatest writer in the English language; Henri Barbusse (1873–1935), French novelist and a member of the French Communist Party; George Bernard Shaw (1856–1950), Irish playwright, critic, polemicist and political activist; Oscar Wilde (1854–1900), Irish poet and playwright; H. G. Wells (1866–1946), English writer; Upton Sinclair (1878–1968), American writer; Walt Whitman (1819–1892), American poet, essayist, and journalist; Anatole France, born François-Anatole Thibault (1844–1924), French poet, journalist, and novelist

[31]Count István Tisza de Borosjenő et Szeged (1861–1918), Hungarian politician, prime minister, political scientist, international lawyer, macroeconomist. The prominent event in his life was Austria-Hungary's entry into World War I, when he was prime minister for the second time. Tisza was initially against declaring war.

[32]Chapter 5.

[33]Chapter 3.

[34]Herzl, born in Budapest, was the feuilletonist of the *Neue Freie Presse* in Vienna.

[35]Chapter 1.

[36]Chapter 2.

[37]Herzl was the representative of the *Neue Freie Presse* at the 1894 trial of Alfred Dreyfus (1859–1935). The resultant antisemitic rallies, with calls of "Death to Jews," were pivotal in his Zionist awakening, and in turning him into the father of the future State of Israel.

[38] *Fabula* and *syuzhet* are terms originating in Russian formalism and employed in narratology that describe narrative construction. *Fabula* is the chronological order of the events contained in the story, *syuzhet* is employment of the narrative.

[39] Yosef Nadav, Conversation with Avigdor Hameiri In *Bitzaron, Yarhon Lemada, Lesifrut uleba'ayot Hazman*, 23rd year, (volume 45), Tishrei Heshvan, Tashkav (1961), booklet 1 (226), 62. The goal by the German historian Leopold von Ranke (1795–1886) of presenting history *wie es eigentlich gewesen ist* is an impossible one.

[40] Avigdor Hameiri. *Hashigaon Hagadol. Reshimot Katzin Ivri Bemilhama Hagedola,* edited by Avner Holzman (Tel Aviv: Dvir Publishing House, 1989), 285.

[41] Chapter 28.

[42] Ibid.

[43] Chapter 9.

[44] Louis Barthas, *Poilu: The World War I Notebooks of Corporal Louis Barthas, Barrelmaker, 1914–1918,* translated by Edward M. Strauss (New Haven, CT and London: Yale University Press, 2014), 144.

[45] Chapter 25.

[46] Avigdor Hameiri, *Al HaFashizm VeSio: Milhama*. Speech at the Official Opening of the Second National Conference "Antifa". Tel Aviv: Association for the Assistance of Victims of Fascism and Antisemitism "Antifa" May, 1935, 4.

[47] Chapter 4.

[48] Chapter 9.

[49] Ibid.

[50] When Hameiri is taken captive, he asks a Russian general to be housed with Pály and Margolis, not with other officers: Avigdor Hameiri, *Hell on Earth,* translated by Peter C. Appelbaum (Detroit, MI: Wayne State University Press, 2017), 35.

[51] Chapter 29.

[52] Chapter 28.

[53] Chapter 9.

[54]Albert Einstein (1879–1955), one of the most famous theoretical physicists of all time who developed the theory of relativity; Arnold Zweig (1887–1968), German writer, pacifist and Socialist; Karl Kraus (1874–1936), Austrian writer and journalist, known as a satirist, essayist, aphorist, playwright and poet.

[55]Holtzman, *Avigdor Hameiri and War Literature,* (Tel Aviv: Merkaz Koved, Maarkhot Stage for Military Research, 1986), 76.

[56]Chapter 3.

[57]Avigdor Hameiri, *Voyage into Savage Europe. A Declining Civilization,* translated and edited by Peter C. Appelbaum (Brookline, MA: Academic Studies Press, 2020); Idem., *Of Human Carnage—Odessa 1918–1920* (Middletown, RI: Stone Tower Press and Boston, MA: Black Widow Press, 2020).

[58]Holtzman, *Avigdor Hameiri and War Literature* (Tel Aviv: Merkaz Koved, Maarkhot Stage for Military Research, 1986), 32.

[59]Ibid., 145.

[60]Chapter 4.

[61]Chapter 24.

[62]Chapter 30.

[63]Letter from the Committee for Culture of the Jerusalem Worker's Union, 24.02.1938, The Gnazim Institute of the Hebrew Writers Association in Israel, 4207/11.

[64]Letter from "Antifa" to Hameiri, The Gnazim Institute of the Hebrew Writers Association in Israel 24.02.1938, archives 4206/11.

[65]Avigdor Hameiri, *Al HaFashizm veSi'o,* Speech at the Second National Conference of "Antifa" in Support of the Victims of Fascism and Antisemitism. Tel Aviv, May 1935, 6-7.

[66]Chapter 6.

[67]In his doctrine of transcendental idealism, Immanuel Kant (1724–1804) argued the sum of all objects, the empirical world, is a complex of appearances whose existence and connection occur only in our representations. Kant introduces the thing-in-itself as follows: "And we indeed, rightly considering objects of sense as mere appearances, confess thereby that they are based upon a thing in itself, though we know not this thing as it is in itself, but only know its appearances."

[68]Deuteronomy 8:3.

[69]Chapter 6.

Editor's Preface

[1]Avigdor Hameiri, *Hashigaon Hagadol. Reshimot Katzin Ivri Bemilhama Hagedola* (Tel Aviv, Mitzpeh, 1930).

[2]Idem., *The Great Madness,* translated by Jacob Freedman (New York: Vantage Press, Inc., 1952).

[3]Idem., *The Great Madness,* translated by Yael Lotan (Haifa: Or Ron, 1984).

[4]Idem., *Hell on Earth,* translated and edited by Peter C. Appelbaum (Detroit, MI: Wayne State University Press, 2017).

[5]Idem., *Of Human Carnage. Odessa 1918–1920,* translated and edited by Peter C. Appelbaum (Middletown, RI: Stone Tower Press and Boston, MA: Black Widow Press, 2020).

[6]Idem, *Voyage into Savage Europe. A Declining Civilization,* translated and edited by Peter C. Appelbaum (Brookline, MA: Academic Studies Press, 2020).

[7]See introduction by Avner Holtzman, Appelbaum, *Hell on Earth,* 7.

[8]Avigdor Hameiri, *Hashigaon Hagadol,* edited and with an introduction by Avner Holtzman (Tel Aviv: Dvir Publishing House, 1989).

[9]Heinrich Heine (1979–1856), German poet and literary critic. Heinrich Heine, *Ne'imot Ivriot,* translated by Avigdor Hameiri (Tel Aviv: Sinai, 1948).

[10]Hanns Heinz Ewers (1871–1943). See Wilfried Kugel, *Das Unverantwortliche: des Leben des Hanns Heinz Ewers* (Düsseldorf: Grupello Verlag, 1992).

Author's Introduction

[1]An obvious impossibility.

[2]Maurice Maeterlinck (1862–1949), Belgian playwright, poet, and essayist; Albert Einstein (1979–1955), one of the greatest theoretical physicists of all time, who developed the theory of relativity.

[3]Chortkiv (Ukraine).

Chapter 1

[1]Constantin Brunner (1862–1937), pen-name of German Jewish philosopher Arjeh Yehuda Wertheimer. He lived in Germany until 1933, when, with the rise to power of the Nazi party, he moved to The Hague (site of the Peace Palace, opened 28 August 1913) where he died on 27 August 1937. Esperanto is the most widely spoken constructed international auxiliary language It was created by Polish ophthalmologist L. L. Zamenhof (1859–1917) in 1887.

[2]Albert Einstein (1879–1955), German-born theoretical physicist who developed the theory of relativity, one of the two pillars of modern physics (alongside quantum mechanics).

[3]Thomas Alva Edison (1847–1931), American inventor.

[4]Wilhelm II (1859–1941), Kaiser of Germany.

[5]Hameiri is referring to *Ich und Du* by Martin Buber (1878–1965), published in German in 1923 (Leipzig: Insel Verlag), which deals with his philosophy of dialogue, a form of existentialism centered on the distinction between the I–Thou relationship and the I–It relationship.

[6]Alfred Redl (1864–1913), Austro-Hungarian counter-intelligence officer and one of the leading figures of pre-World War I espionage, who was also a highly paid spy, working for the intelligence service of the Imperial Russian Army. The original has the incorrect name of Bulman; Przemyśl (Poland), Austrian fortress city west of Lviv (Ukraine), site of fierce fighting during the war.

[7]Budapest night club named after Orpheus, legendary musician, poet and prophet in Greek mythology. Apollo taught Orpheus to play the lute when he was an adolescent.

[8]*Privatdozent:* academic title conferred by some European universities, especially in German-speaking countries, to someone who holds certain formal qualifications that denote an ability to teach independently at university level.

[9]Baruch (Benedict de) Spinoza (1632–1677), Dutch philosopher of Portuguese Sephardi origin. One of the early thinkers of the Enlightenment and modern Biblical criticism, including modern conceptions of the self and the universe, and one of the great rationalists of seventeenth-century philosophy. Logos: principle of order and knowledge.

[10]Johann Sebastian Bach (1685-1750), one of the greatest of all classical composers.

[11]According to Immanuel Kant (1724–1804), the categorical imperative is an objective, rationally necessary and unconditional principle that we must always follow despite any natural desires or inclinations we may have to the contrary. All specific moral requirements, according to Kant, are justified by this principle, which means that all immoral actions are irrational because they violate it.

[12]After Leviticus 19:18.

[13]The closest star system and closest planetary system to Earth's Solar System at 4.37 light-years from the Sun.

[14]Oral lesions of secondary syphilis are infectious.

[15]Thomas Hobbes (1588–1679). The state of nature is a "war of all against all," in which human beings constantly seek to destroy each other in an incessant pursuit for power.

[16]The appendix, an embryonic remnant, is a small, pouch-like sac of tissue that is located in the first part of the colon (cecum) in the lower-right abdomen.

[17]"Australian primate." (original).

[18]Rabbi Shlomo ben Yizhak (Yizhaki) (1040–1105), medieval French rabbi and author of a comprehensive commentary on the Talmud and commentary on the *Tanakh.* Rashi studied in the Worms yeshiva.

[19]Camille Flammarion (1842–1925), French astronomer and author.

Chapter 2

[1]*Népszava,* Social-democratic Hungarian language newspaper.

[2]Franz Josef I (1830–1916) was Emperor of Austria from 1848, and King of Hungary from the *Ausgleich* (agreement) of 1867, until his death.

[3]Victor Emmanuel III (1869–1947), King of Italy.

[4]Original: "Australian primate."

[5]Hameiri is referring to Max Nordau (1849–1923), *Paradox* (Leipzig: Elischer, 1885)—*Paradoxes: From the German of Max Nordau,* translated by J. R. McIlraith (London: Forgotten Books, 2012).

[6]Michelangelo Buonarroti (1475–1564), Florentine sculptor, painter, architect and poet of the High Renaissance, who exerted an unparalleled influence on the development of Western art; Niccolò Machiavelli (1469–1527), Italian Renaissance diplomat, philosopher and writer, often called the father of modern political philosophy; Giuseppe Garibaldi (1807–1882), Italian general, patriot, and republican who contributed to Italian unification and creation of the Kingdom of Italy.

[7]Italy began the war neutral, but as a nominal supporter of the Central Powers.

[8]See chapter 1.

Chapter 3

[1]The Hussars were an Austro-Hungarian army regiment who invaded Serbia after Austria declared war on Serbia on 28 July 1914; The Karađorđević was a Serb dynasty, founded by Karađorđe Petrović, the *veliki vožd* ("grand leader") of Serbia in the early 1800s during the First Serbian Uprising. Peter Karađorđević (1844–1921) was King of Serbia when the war started; Count Mihaly Karolyi von Nagykaroly (1875–1955), Hungarian politician who served as Hungary's last Prime Minister before its independence from the Habsburg Empire in November 1918.

[2]In 1914 the Russian Army attacked the Austro-Hungarians in the Carpathians. Through fall 1914, the Habsburgs suffered numerous defeats against numerically superior Russian forces pushing into Galicia and the Carpathian foothills in the northeast corner of Austria-Hungary and capturing the fortress city of Przemyśl.

[3]Szabolcs-Szatmár-Bereg is an administrative county in north-eastern Hungary bordering Slovakia, Ukraine, and Romania.

[4]*Sunt lacrimae rerum* (see Chapter 6, notes 1 and 7,).

[5]*Du* instead of *Sie.*

[6]Eduard von Schweitzer (1844–1920), Jewish lieutenant field marshal in the Austro-Hungarian Army.

Chapter 4

[1]John of Giscala (birth date unknown; death date after 70 CE), was a leader of the Jewish revolt against the Romans in the First Jewish-Roman War.

[2]This poem is included in the Freedman, but not the Lotan translation.

[3]Jewish study hall separate from a synagogue. Hameiri uses it in the sense of a school.

[4]Endre Ady (1877–1919), turn-of-the-century Hungarian poet and journalist. Regarded by many as the greatest Hungarian poet of the twentieth century. Hameiri's translation of his poetry was published in 1954.

[5]Judah Aryeh Blau (1861–1936), teacher at the Budapest rabbinical *Beth Midrash,* and its director from 1914 and author of many papers on Jewish subjects.

[6]Szeged: city in Hungary; Austro-Hungary invaded Serbia on 28 July 1914.

[7]Paul von Hindenburg (1847–1934), German field marshal and statesman who led the Imperial German Army during World War I and later became President of Germany from 1925 until his death during the last days of the Weimar Republic.

[8]During August through the fall of 1914, the Austro-Hungarians suffered numerous defeats against numerically superior Russian forces pushing into Galicia and the Carpathian foothills in the northeast corner of Austria-Hungary.

Chapter 5

[1]The original states Journey to the Land of Hottentots. Hameiri was fond of invoking Africa as a metaphor for the savagery that he saw around him. Hottentots is a term historically used to refer to the Khoikhoi, the non-Bantu indigenous nomadic pastoralists of South Africa.

[2]Sigmund Freud (1856–1939), Austrian neurologist and the founder of psychoanalysis, Freud pioneered interpretation of dreams.

[3]Familiar salutation used in many parts of Central and Eastern Europe.

[4]Budapest night club.

[5]A group of pacifist newspapers.

[6]Lev Nikolayevich Tolstoy (1828–1910), Russian writer regarded as one of the greatest authors of all time; Alexander Sergeyevich Pushkin (1799–1837), Russian poet, playwright, and novelist of the Romantic era, considered by many to be the greatest Russian poet; Alexei Maximovich Peshkov (Maxim Gorky) (1868–1936), Russian and Soviet writer, a founder of the socialist realism literary method; Leonid Nikolaievich Andreyev (1871–1919), Russian playwright, novelist and short-story writer, who is considered to be a father of Expressionism in Russian literature; Romain Rolland (1866–1944), French dramatist, novelist, essayist, art historian and mystic; William Shakespeare (1564–1616), English poet, playwright, and actor, widely regarded as the greatest writer in the English language; Henri Barbusse (1873–1935), French novelist and a member of the French Communist Party; George Bernard Shaw (1856–1950), Irish playwright, critic, polemicist and political activist; Oscar Wilde (1854–1900), Irish poet and playwright; H. G. Wells (1866–1946), English writer; Upton Sinclair (1878–1968), American writer; Walt Whitman (1819–1892), American poet, essayist, and journalist; Anatole France, born François-Anatole Thibault (1844–1924), French poet, journalist, and novelist

[7]Count István Tisza de Borosjenő et Szeged (1861–1918), Hungarian politician, prime minister, political scientist, international lawyer, macroeconomist. The prominent event in his life was Austria-Hungary's entry into World War I, when he was prime minister for the second time. Tisza was initially against declaring war.

[8]lya Ilyich Mechnikov (1845–1916), Russian Imperial zoologist of Moldovan-Jewish origin best known for his pioneering research in immunology for which he was awarded the Nobel Prize in 1908, together with Paul Ehrlich (1854–1915). His book *Research in Human Nature — An Optimistic World View* was published in 1903. Another essay on the same subject was published in 1907. Mechnikov pioneered the study of gerontology.

Chapter 6

---

[1]The tears and laughter of things.

[2]Imaginary land in South America, rich in treasure and sought by Spanish explorers in the sixteenth century.

[3]Chapter 5 note 8.

[4]Exodus 5:10-15.

[5]Hebrew: *lehitpager* (also to be dead tired, exhausted). *Peger* is a corpse.

[6]The *Shahnameh* (Book of Kings) is an epic poem by the Persian poet Ferdowsi (c. 940–1020) between 977 and 1010. It is the national epic of Greater Iran and, consisting of 50,000 couplets is one of the world's longest epic poems.

[7]In this passage (book 1, line 462) from the *Aeneid* (c. 29–19 BCE) by Publius Vergilius Maro (70-19 BCE), Aeneas gazes at a mural found in a Carthaginian temple dedicated to Juno that depicts battles of the Trojan War and the deaths of his friends and countrymen. Aeneas is moved to tears and says *sunt lacrimae rerum et mentem mortalia tangunt* (There are tears of things and mortal things touch the mind). The title of chapter 6 is a modified quote.

[8]Camille Flammarion (1842–1925), French astronomer and author.

[9]The 1812 Overture by Piotr Ilyich Tchaikovsky (1840–1893) was composed to commemorate the Battle of Borodino (7 September 1812) between Imperial Russia and French troops under Napoleon. The work ends a combination of The Marseillaise and the Tsarist Imperial anthem "God Save the Tsar."

[10]Gravediggers scene (*Hamlet* Act V Scene 1).

[11]Gaius Julius Caesar (100–44 BCE), Roman general and statesman who played a critical role in the events that led to the demise of the Roman Republic and the rise of the Roman Empire.

[12]Auguste Rodin (1840–1917), French sculptor; Isadora Duncan (1877/1878–1927), American dancer; Lev Nikolayevich Tolstoy (1828–1910), Russian writer who is regarded as one of the greatest authors of all time; Endre Ady (1877–1919), turn-of-the-century Hungarian poet and journalist regarded by many as the greatest Hungarian poet of the twentieth century; Shneur Zalman of Liadi (1874–1812), Orthodox rabbi, founder and first Rebbe of Chabad, and author of many works, including the *Tanya* — a work on Hasidic mystical psychology and theology which serves as a handbook for daily spiritual life in Jewish observance.

[13]Shabbat 114a.

[14]William Shakespeare (1564–1616), English playwright, poet, and actor, widely regarded as the greatest writer in the English language and the world's greatest dramatist; Gabriel-Maximilien Leuvielle (1883–1925), known professionally as Max Linder, French actor, director, screenwriter, producer and comedian of the silent film era.

[15]In his doctrine of transcendental idealism, Immanuel Kant (1724–1804) argued that the sum of all objects, the empirical world, is a complex of appearances whose existence and connection occur only in our representations. Kant introduces the thing-in-itself as follows: "And we indeed, rightly considering objects of sense as mere appearances, confess thereby that they are based upon a thing in itself, though we know not this thing as it is in itself, but only know its appearances."

[16]Deuteronomy 8:3.

[17]Kant was not a hunchback, but his fellow-philosopher Moses Mendelssohn (1729–1786), with whom he corresponded but whom he never met, did have such a condition.

Chapter 7

[1]Ernst Theodor Amadeus (E.T.A.)Hoffmann (1776–1822), German romantic author of fantasy and Gothic horror, jurist, composer, music critic and artist.

[2]*Tefilat HaDerech.* "May it be Your will, Lord, our God and the God of our ancestors, that You lead us toward peace, guide our footsteps toward peace, and make us reach our desired destination for life, gladness, and peace. May You rescue us from the hand of every foe and ambush, from robbers and wild beasts on the trip, and from all manner of punishments that assemble to come to earth. May You send blessing in our handiwork, and grant us grace, kindness, and mercy in Your eyes and in the eyes of all who see us. May You hear the sound of our humble request because You are God Who hears prayer requests. Blessed are You, Lord, Who hears prayer."

[3]This did in fact happen. Russian arms supplies at the start of the war were woefully inadequate, but improved with time.

[4]Jacob's elder brother and progenitor of the Edomites.

[5]The Maccabees were a group of Jewish rebel warriors who took control of Judea, which at the time was part of the Seleucid Empire. They founded the Hasmonean dynasty, which ruled from 167 to 37 BCE, being a fully independent kingdom from about 110 to 63 BCE.

[6]Zalman Schneur (1887–1959), prolific Yiddish and Hebrew poet and writer. Schneur spent the war years in Berlin, working in a hospital and studying at the University of Berlin.

[7]Sarcasm: tefilin are worn on the left arm.

Chapter 8

[1]Hameiri sarcastically uses the word "intelligentsia" to denote a status class of educated people engaged in the complex mental labors that critique, guide, and lead in shaping the culture and politics of their society. The intelligentsia includes artists, teachers and academics, writers, and literary *hommes de lettres*. Individual members of the intelligentsia are known as intellectuals.

[2]Non-commissioned officer (NCO).

[3]Platoon leader.

[4]Zadar (Croatia).

[5]"The Hope," Israeli, not Hungarian, national anthem.

[6]Judges 7:4-6.

[7]Wilhelm (Benjamin Ze'ev) Bacher (1850–1913) Jewish Hungarian scholar, rabbi, orientalist and linguist. Teacher at the Budapest Rabbinical Seminary from 1877, and its head from 1907 until his death.

Chapter 9

[1]Wilhelm Bölsche (1861–1939), German author, editor and publicist. Bölsche was not a trained naturalist but a popularizer of natural science as a layman to the general public.

[2]Count Otto von Bismarck (1815–1898), conservative German statesman who masterminded the unification of Germany in 1871 and served as its first chancellor until 1890, in which capacity he dominated European affairs for two decades. Grunewald is a forest located in the western side of Berlin on the east side of the Havel, mainly in the Grunewald locality. At 3,000 hectares (7,400 acres) it is the largest green area in the city of Berlin. In Germanic mythology the linden tree is associated with Freya, the motherly goddess of truth and love. According to German folklore, it was not possible to lie while standing under the linden tree.

[3]Werner Sombart (1863–1941), German economist and sociologist and one of the leading Continental European social scientists during the first quarter of the twentieth century. His book *Die Juden und das Wirtschaftsleben (The Jews and Modern Capitalism)* (Leipzig: Duncker und Humblot, 1911) was much used by the Nazis.

[4]Michelangelo Buonarroti, Florentine (1475–1564), sculptor, painter, architect and poet of the High Renaissance who exerted an unparalleled influence on the development of Western art.

[5]Karl Marx (1818–1883), German philosopher, economist, historian, sociologist, political theorist, journalist and socialist revolutionary.

[6]Franz Joseph Haydn (1732–1809), Austrian composer who composed the melody for the Austro-Hungarian national anthem "Gott Erhalte Franz den Kaiser." The theme comes from his *Kaiserquartett* (Hob. III:77), second movement (theme and variations). Haydn was Austrian, not German; German opera composer Richard Wagner (1813–1883) had to flee from Saxony in 1849, after having played a minor role in the unsuccessful May Uprising in Dresden.

[7]Count Lev Nikolayevich Tolstoy (1828–1910), Russian writer regarded as one of the greatest authors of all time. Tolstoy served as a young artillery officer during the Crimean War and was present at the eleven-month-long siege of Sevastopol. Appalled by the number of deaths involved in warfare, he left the army after the end of the Crimean War.

[8]This is very true. The Old Testament is full of war and bloodshed. Contrary to popular belief, Jews are not pacifists.

[9]Matthew 10: 34.

[10]Friederich Nietzsche (1844–1900), German philosopher whose work has exerted a profound influence on modern intellectual history. *Thus Spoke Zarathustra,* chapter 6, "The Pale Criminal": "Thus speaks the red judge: "Why did this criminal commit murder? He meant to rob. I tell you, however, that his soul wanted blood, not booty: he thirsted for the happiness of the knife!"

[11]Rabbi Pinchas of Koretz (1726–1791), a Galician Hasidic rabbi and disciple of the Baal Shem Tov (c. 1698–1760), founder of Hasidism.

[12]Camille Flammarion (1842–1925), French astronomer and author.

[13]The Rabbi Akiva mentioned here could be his hometown teacher (see chapter 4), or Akiva ben Yosef (c. 50–135 CE), leading Jewish scholar and sage; Wilhelm (Benjami Ze'ev) Bacher (1850–1913), Jewish Hungarian scholar, rabbi, Orientalist and linguist; Elijah ben Solomon Zalman (the Vilna Gaon) (1720–1797), Talmudist, halakhist, kabbalist, and the foremost leader of non-Hasidic Jewry of the past few centuries.

Chapter 10

[1]Hameiri's journalistic pen name before the war. Kova is Hungarian for stone. "Feuerstein" was Hameiri's original name.

[2]Endre Ady (1877–1919), Hungarian poet and journalist regarded by many as the greatest Hungarian poet of the twentieth century.

[3]Hameiri is talking about himself. His first poetry collection (*Mishirei Avigdor Feuerstein*) was published in 1912.

[4]*Sie* instead of *du.*

[5]Georg Brandes (1842–1927), Danish critic and scholar who greatly influenced Scandinavian and European literature from the 1870s through the turn of the twentieth century; Hugó Veigelsberg (1869–1949), noted Hungarian editor and writer who usually published under the pen name "Ignotus" (Latin for "unknown"); David Frishmann (1859–1922), Hebrew and Yiddish writer and editor, literary critic, translator, and poet.

[6]József Patai (1882–1952), Hungarian Jewish scholar, author, and journalist, founder of the Jewish cultural journal *Múlt és Jövő* (Past and Future), which he established in 1911, first as an almanac, and then, a year later, as a monthly. Patai was Hameiri's friend and literary patron.

Chapter 11

[1]Lučenec (Slovak Republic).

[2]*Zum Rapport.*

[3]Psalm 144:10.

[4]Psalm 30.

[5]After the *Ausgleich* (Agreement) of 1867, Franz Josef became Emperor of Austria and King of Hungary,

[6]Empress Elizabeth of Austria (1837–1898), Bavarian-born wife of Kaiser Franz Josef, mortally wounded in Geneva by an Italian anarchist; Heinrich Heine (1797–1856), German poet, writer and literary critic best known outside Germany for his early lyric poetry; Crown Prince Rudolph (1858–1889), only son of Kaiser Franz Josef and Empress Elizabeth, died in a suicide pact with his mistress, Mary Vetsera, at the Mayerling hunting lodge; Archduke Franz Ferdinand (1863–1914), heir to the throne and Franz Josef's nephew, assassinated with his wife Sophie Chotek in Sarajevo

on 28 June, 1914; Charles I of Austria/Charles IV of Hungary (1887–1922), last monarch belonging to the House of Habsburg-Lorraine before the dissolution of Austria-Hungary in 1918. Hameiri does not mention Franz Josef's brother Maximilian I of Mexico (1832–1867), executed by the Mexican government.

[7]Unlike Germany, an unconverted Jew could rise to high rank in the Habsburg Army. Generally (but not always) conversion was necessary to attain the rank of brigadier or higher.

Chapter 12

[1]Satu Mare (Romania), near the Hungarian border. At the end of the nineteenth century, site of frequent arguments between different sects of Orthodox Judaism. After a large number of traditional Ashkenazic Jews had settled in the town, the Jewish community split in 1898, when a supporter of the Hasidic movement was elected chief rabbi, into an Orthodox and a Status Quo community. The Status Quo Zionist community erected a separate synagogue in 1904.

[2]Rabbi Shmuel (Sandor) Jordan, head of the Status Quo Szatmar community from 1902. An active Zionist, in 1911 he founded the first Jewish kindergarten in Hungary and taught in the elementary school between 1922 and 1929.

[3]The original: *Sar Haelef.* This is a biblical term taken from 1 Samuel and 1 Chronicles which means roughly "captain of one thousand," but has no exact English equivalent. Lotan translates this as colonel, and Freedman as lieutenant colonel.

[4]The precursor to dog tags.

[5]Jewish prayer for the dead.

[6]Sándor Petőfi (1823–1849), Hungarian poet and liberal revolutionary, considered Hungary's national poet, and one of the key figures of the Hungarian Revolution of 1848. He is the author of the *Nemzeti dal* (National Song), which is said to have inspired the revolution in the Kingdom of Hungary that grew into the Kossuth war for independence from the Austrian Empire. It is most likely that he died in the Battle of Segesvár, one of the last battles of the war. A collection of his poems, translated into Hebrew by Hameiri, was published in 1952: *Sándor Petőfi, Mishirei Sándor Petőfi,* translated by Avigdor Hameiri (Tel Aviv: Sinai, 1952).

Chapter 13

[1]Zavaliv on the banks of the Zolota Lypa River (Western Ukraine).

[2]Ruthenians and Ruthenes are Latin exonyms formerly used in Western Europe for the ancestors of modern East Slavic peoples, especially the Rus' people with an Eastern Orthodox or Ruthenian Greek Catholic religious background. In its broadest usage, Ruthenians or Ruthenes refers to peoples who were ancestors of the modern Belarusians, Rusyns and Ukrainians. In the Austro-Hungarian context, Ruthenians means Ukrainians.

[3]Buchach (Western Ukraine).

[4]After Isaiah 23:16.

[5]Deuteronomy 20:16.

Chapter 14

[1]Yazlovets', Buchach (Western Ukraine). Shmuel Yosef Agnon (1888–1970), author and future Nobel Prize winner, was born in Buczacz.

[2]Elizabeth Bathory (1560–1614), Hungarian noblewoman from the noble family of Báthory, and niece of Stefan Bathory King of Poland (1533–1586) who owned land in the Kingdom of Hungary (now Hungary, Slovakia and Romania), known for her supposed cruelty.

[3]Gaius Petronius Arbiter (c. 27–66 CE) was Roman courtier during the reign of Nero. He is generally believed to be the author of the *Satyricon*, a satirical novel believed to have been written during the Neronian era (54–68 CE); Nero Claudius Caesar (37–68 CE), Roman emperor known for his cruelty.

[4]Vienna's main shopping street between the opera and St. Stephen's Cathedral.

[5]Amusement park on the outskirts of Vienna.

[6]Henri-Louis Bergson (1859–1941), French philosopher influential in the tradition of continental philosophy, especially during the first half of the twentieth century until the Second World War. Proponent of the concept of *élan vital.*

[7]Archduke Franz Ferdinand (1863–1914), heir to the throne until his assassination in Sarajevo on 28 June, 1914. His Czech wife Sophie, Duchess of Hohenberg (1868–1814) was murdered with him.

[8]Vulgar rabble.

[9]Here used in the form of an oath.

[10]This is a very contentious issue. Hameiri comments on it repeatedly in his books, and it is mentioned in the writing of many other Austro-Hungarian soldiers. The reader is referred to Manfried Rauchensteiner for a dispassionate discussion on the subject. *The First World War and the End of the Habsburg Monarchy 1914–1918* (Vienna, Cologne and Weimar: Böhlau Verlag, 2014), 335–40.

Chapter 15

[1]Czernowitz was capital of the Habsburg province of Bukovina. Modern day Chernivtsi (Western Ukraine); Riga (Latvia).

[2]The fortress city of Przemyśl (Poland) was occupied by the Russians in March 1915 after a long siege, and reoccupied by Austro-Hungary during the Gorlice-Tarnów Offensive in May 1915.

[3]Geographical and historical region straddling between Central and Eastern Europe that, before 1919, was part of Hungary. It is currently divided up between Romania, Serbia, and (a small part thereof), Hungary.

[4]*Kaiserlich-Ungarische (k.u) Landwehr Armee* (Royal Hungarian Honvéd Army).

[5]*Kaiserliche und Königliche Armee* (Imperial and Royal Austro-Hungarian Army).

[6]Hungary's second largest city.

[7]Harbor city near Trieste, part of Austro-Hungarian Croatia before 1919. Modern day Rijeka (Croatia).

[8]Manifestly untrue.

[9]Częstochowa (Poland) site of the monastery of Jasna Góra, home if the Black Madonna painting.

[10]Perjorative term for non-Jews.

[11] 2 Samuel 10:12.

[12]Genesis 49:18.

[13]The original Magyars were Calvinists.

Chapter 16

[1]Isaiah 3:21.

[2]Częstochowa (Poland), site of the monastery of Jasna Góra whicb houses the Black Madonna painting.

[3]Benjamin Ze'ev Bacher (1850–1913), prolific writer on Jewish subjects, teacher at the Budapest Rabbinical Seminary from 1877, and its director from 1907 until his death; József Bánóczi (1849–1926), Hungarian Jewish scholar, served from 1892 until his death as director of the Budapest normal school for the education of teachers.

[4]The original Magyars were Calvinists.

[5]Platoon leader.

[6]Hameiri is referring to the red heifer (Numbers 19), whose ashes were used for purification of an Israelite who had come in contact with a corpse, but which rendered the priest performing the ritual impure until that evening. No clear rabbinical explanation for this commandment is available and it is expounded as a *sod* (secret).

Chapter 17

[1]Hanina my son: Name synonymous with a completely righteous man (tzadik), according to what is said about Rabbi Hanina Ben Dosa (Berakhot 17b): As Rav Yehuda said that Rav said: Every day a Divine Voice emerges from Mount Horeb and says: The entire world is sustained by the merit of Hanina ben Dosa, my son, and for Hanina, my son, a *kav* of carobs is sufficient to sustain him for an entire week, from one Shabbat eve to the next Shabbat eve. For the significance of this symbolist poem, the reader is referred to Andrew Sanders, *Hanina my Son. A Novel of The First Century* (Jerusalem: Gefen Books, 2000). Hanina lived during a time of the terrible shock that came with destruction of the Second Temple in 70 CE, and subsequent renewal of the Jewish spirit.

Chapter 18

[1]Wife of Socrates, synonymous for an ill-tempered woman who nags her husband.

[2]Hermes Trismegistos may be associated with the Greek god Hermes and the Egyptian god Thoth. Greeks in the Ptolemaic Kingdom of Egypt recognized equivalence of Hermes and Thoth, and the two gods were worshiped as one. The *Hermetica* are Egyptian-Greek wisdom texts from the second century or earlier, mostly presented as dialogues in which a teacher, generally identified as Hermes Trismegistus, enlightens a disciple. The texts form the basis of Hermeticism.

[3]In Greek mythology, Ganymede is a divine hero whose homeland was Troy. Homer describes Ganymede as the most beautiful of mortals. Zeus fell in love with his beauty and abducted him, to make him cup-bearer on Mount Olympus.

[4]Yazlovets' (Western Ukraine).

[5]Yoma 22b–23a. The quote is by Rabbi Yohanan in the name of Rabbi Shimon ben Yehotzadak.

[6]Leviticus 19:18.

[7]Jewish prayer for the dead.

Chapter 19

[1]Psalm 91:1.

[2]Psalm 91:5

[3]Psalm 91:7

[4]Sigmund Freud (1856–1939), Austrian neurologist and founder of psychoanalysis.

[5]Rahab the whore let Israelite spies into Jericho. Joshua 2:1-24, thereby helping them to capture the city.

[6]Modern-day Rijeka (Croatia).

Chapter 20

[1]Deuteronomy 20:8.

[2]*Mons veneris:* The technical term for the external female genitalia.

[3]Hameiri uses both Hebrew words for why: *madua* (past), *lamah* (future).

[4]Ethics of the Fathers 2:5. Rabban Gamliel said: "A boor cannot fear sin."

[5]Sigmund Freud (1856–1939), Austrian neurologist and founder of psychoanalysis.

[6]Hameiri is being sarcastic. The expression comes from the prayer *Yedid Nefesh*: "For to him your love is sweeter/Than the dripping honeycomb, and any taste at all."

[7]*Zum Rapport.*

Chapter 21

[1]Not included in the Lotan translation The entire chapter is not included in the Freedman translation.

[2]Original: "Words of the Living God" (Gittin 6b, Eruvin 13b).

[3]In ancient Greece, the symposium was a part of a banquet after the meal, when drinking for pleasure was accompanied by music, dancing, recitals, or conversation.

[4]Non-legalistic exegetical texts in classical rabbinic literature, particularly in the *Talmud* and *Midrash.* In general, *Aggadah* is a compendium of texts incorporating folklore, historical anecdotes, moral exhortations, and practical advice in various spheres, from business to medicine.

[5]Hameiri is incorrect. Contrary to popular belief, the Magyars originated from the Ural Mountains region, between the Urals and the Volga.

[6]Móric (Mór) Jókay de Ásva (1825–1904), writer of romantic Hungarian novels; Sándor Petőfi (1823–1849), Hungarian poet and liberal revolutionary.

[7]Stop, or freeze (Russian).

[8]You're captured, sir.

[9]Good, sir.

[10]Invaders from Mars, according to *The War of The Worlds* (1898) by H. G. Wells (1866–1946).

[11]The Eastern Orthodox Church, in accordance with the Julian Calendar, celebrates Christmas on 7 January.

[12]Jewish prayer for the dead.

Chapter 22

[1]"He who mocks the dead blasphemes his Creator" (After Proverbs 17:5; Berakhot 18a).

[2]A sarcastic play on Hillel's saying "Where there are no men strive to be a man" (Ethics of the Fathers 2:5).

[3]Aharon (Armand) Kaminka (1866–1950), rabbi and author. One of the first to translate classic Greek and German literature into Hebrew. He served as rabbi in Frankfurt an der Oder and Prague and lectured at the Vienna Theological Seminary from 1900.

[4]Young Torah and Talmudic prodigy or genius.

[5]Ramesses II (c. 1303–1213 BCE), aka Rameses the Great, Third Pharaoh of Nineteenth Egyptian dynasty; Hannibal (247–181/183 BCE), Carthaginian general and statesman who commanded Carthage's main forces against the Roman Republic during the Second Punic War.

[6]Hameiri is referring to the The Gorlice–Tarnów Offensive (2 May–22 June, 1915) in which the Central Powers pushed east reoccupying Lemberg and Przemyśl and occupying Warsaw, to a line roughly between Riga and Czernowitz.

[7]Chernivtsi (Western Ukraine); Riga (Latvia).

[8]Chortkiv (Western Ukraine). The same town where Hameiri would be captured in June 1916, during the Brusilov Offensive.

[9]Ludwig van Beethoven (1770–1927), one of the greatest of all Classical composers; Fyodor Mikhailovich Dostoevsky (1821–1881), Russian novelist, short story writer, essayist and journalist.

[10]The Preobrazhensky Life-Guard Regiment was one of the oldest and most elite guard regiments of the Imperial Russian Army.

Chapter 23

[1]John Calvin (1509–1564), French reformer, pastor, and theologian active in Geneva during the Protestant Reformation, and principal figure in the development of the system of Christian theology later called Calvinism. The original Magyars were Calvinists.

[2]A group of Jewish rebel warriors who took control of Judea, which at the time was part of the Seleucid Empire.

[3]Antiochus IV Epiphanes (c. 215–164 BCE), Hellenistic king of the Seleucid Empire from 175 BCE until his death. Notable events during the reign of Antiochus IV include his near-conquest of Egypt, his persecution of the Jews of Judea and Samaria, and the rebellion of the Jewish Maccabees; Apollonius, man of the Seleucid Empire who lived in the second century BCE; Nicanor (d. 161 BCE), Syrian-Seleucid General under Antiochus Epiphanes and Demetrius Soter; Giorgias: Syrian-Seleucid general of the second century in service of Antiochus Epiphanes.

[4]A corruption of *Servus*, the familiar Austrian greeting.

[5]Jewish prayer for the dead.

[6]Fast in memory of Queen Esther the day before Purim.

[7]A riff on Proverbs 27:22. "Though you grind a fool in a mortar, grinding them like grain with a pestle, you will not remove their folly from him."

[8]Enrico Caruso (1873–1921), perhaps the greatest Italian operatic tenor in recorded history. *Cara Mia Materna,* Roman Catholic prayer to the Virgin Mary.

[9]*Birkat hagomel*: A prayer said after recovering from a serious illness or surviving a dangerous journey.

Chapter 24

[1]Zavaliv on the banks of the Zolota Lypa River (Western Ukraine).

Chapter 25

[1]Lazarovka (Ukraine).

[2]Albert Einstein (1879–1955), one of the greatest theoretical physicists of all time, who developed the theory of relativity.

[3]Charles Maurice de Talleyrand-Périgord (1754–1838), French diplomat: "Speech was given to man to disguise his thoughts."

[4]*Minyan*: Quorum of ten adult men necessary for an Orthodox service.

[5]Blessed are You, Lord our God, ruler of the world, who rewards the undeserving with goodness, and who has rewarded me with goodness.

[6]*Yid*: Opprobrious epithet for a Jew. Uncle Osterreicher uses the word against another Jew.

[7]*Goy*: Opprobrious epithet for a non-Jew.

[8]Good, Sir.

Chapter 26

[1]Post-operative infection. No antibiotics were available during World War I.

[2]*Gavrut, gever.* Modern Hebrew didn't at the time (and to an extent still doesn't have) words for male and female genitalia and intercourse.

Chapter 27

[1]In the pre-antibiotic era, penetrating abdominal wounds were almost uniformly fatal because of peritonitis.

[2]Isaiah 19:2.

[3]Socrates of Athens (c. 470–399 BCE), one of the founders of Western philosophy.

[4]Moses Mendelssohn (1729–1786), creative thinker whose writings on metaphysics and aesthetics, political theory and theology, together with his Jewish heritage, placed him at the focal point of the German Enlightenment (*haskala*) for over three decades.

[5]The *haskala* was anathema to most strictly Orthodox Jews.

[6]Lemberg (Lviv, Ukraine).

[7]Deuteronomy 17:7

Chapter 28

[1]Opprobrious epithet for non-Jew.

[2]Talne (Ukraine).

[3]Westernmost of the three great rivers (Dniester, Dnieper, Don) that flow through Ukraine to the Black Sea.

[4]This is not exactly true. The only German that many Slavs in the Habsburg Army could understand was the eighty basic commands, and nationalist feelings – especially Slavic ones – remained very much alive.

[5]The original Magyars were Calvinists.

[6]The British authorities made a series of promises to both Arabs and Jews regarding the fate of the post-World-War I Ottoman Middle East, including Palestine. Approximately 30,000 Jews from Eastern Europe had immigrated to Ottoman Palestine between 1881 and 1903, to establish farms and agriculture, and more came through 1914 in response to Theodor Herzl's call for establishment of a Jewish State. The British wanted their support to fight the Turks. In late 1916, Sharif Hussein bin Ali of Mecca had (with the aid of the British and T. E. Lawrence) begun an Arab revolt against the Turks. However the British and French had, behind the scenes, already negotiated a treaty dividing the postwar Middle East into French and British spheres of influence, as set out by the Sykes-Picot Agreement. The British issued the Balfour Declaration "viewing with favor the establishment of a post-war Jewish State" on 2 November 1917, after the treaty had been promulgated. No reports of a similar declaration by the Central Powers could be found and the purported proclamation is almost certainly a rumor. I thank Michael Simonson and his colleagues at the Leo Baeck Institute, New York City for their help researching this issue.

[7]Hameiri is exactly right on this point.

[8]See Chapter 14, note 10. Hameiri is talking about supposed Czech treachery.

[9]Psalm 55:14.

[10]Sultan Abdul Hamid II Thirty-fourth Sultan of the Ottoman Empire and the last Sultan to exert at least partial control over the fracturing state. Turkey was in effect governed by the triumvirate of Enver, Talaat, and Djemal Pasha. It is highly unlikely that they would have agreed to such an arrangement.

[11] *Mult és Jövő* (Past and Future), a Hungarian Jewish periodical established in 1911 by the poet, scholar, and Zionist leader József Patai (1882–1953), still in existence today. I was unable to obtain the article in question.

[12] Israel Zangwill (1864–1926), British author at the forefront of cultural Zionism during the nineteenth century, and close associate of Theodor Herzl (1860–1904). He later rejected the search for a Jewish homeland in Palestine and became the prime thinker behind the territorial movement.

[13] *Quod licet Jovi non licet bovi* (Latin): literally "What is permissible for Jupiter is not permissible for a cow." The origin for the phrase is the novella *Aus dem Leben eines Taugenichts* (1826) by Joseph Freiherr von Eichendorff (1788–1857), although it is not clear that he coined the phrase himself. In his play *Heauton Timorumenos* Terence (c.195/185–c.159? BCE) coined a similar phrase, *Aliis si licet, tibi non licet* ("to others it is permitted; to you it is not permitted"). The phrase is often translated as "Gods may do what cattle may not." It indicates the existence of a double standard (justifiable or otherwise), and means "what is permitted to one important person or group, is not permitted to everyone."

[14] Mishna Sota 9: 15; Daniel 12: 12.

[15] Hameiri is sarcastically comparing the three monarchs of the Central Powers to the three kings of the east, who came with gifts for the infant Jesus.

[16] Marquise de Pompadour (1721–1764) mistress of Louis XV of France.

[17] Region and ex-country in the North Caucasus and along the northeast shore of the Black Sea, and ancestral homeland of the mostly Muslim Circassian people.

[18] The wife of Tsar Nicholas II, Empress Alexandra Feodorovna, was a German princess (Alix of Hesse), granddaughter of Queen Victoria. Despite rumors to the contrary, her loyalty to Russia was absolute.

[19] *Servus,* colloquial "goodbye."

[20] Vladimir Jabotinsky proposed that a Jewish legion be formed to join the British in liberating Palestine from the Turks during World War I, but the British resisted the idea of Jewish volunteers fighting on the Palestinian front. Instead, they suggested the Jews serve as a detachment for mule transport at another location along the Turkish front. Joseph Trumpeldor subsequently formed the 650-strong Zion Mule Corps, of whom 562 were sent to the Gallipoli front. Both men were instrumental in formation of the Jewish Legion in the World War I British Army.

[21]The Book of Judith is a deuterocanonical book, included in the Septuagint and the Catholic and Eastern Orthodox Christian Old Testament, but excluded from the Hebrew canon. It tells of a Jewish widow, Judith, who uses her beauty and charm to destroy the Assyrian general Holofernes and save Israel from oppression.

[22]German Jewish chemist and Nobel laureate Fritz Haber (1868–1934) played a major role in the development of the non-ballistic use of chemical warfare in World War I.

[23]Jenö Zsoldos (formerly Stern) (1896–1972), Hungarian literary scholar and philologist. Born in Budapest, Zsoldos fought as an officer in the Austro-Hungarian army during World War I; Max Nordau (1849–1923), Zionist leader, physician, author, and social critic.

[24]Theodor Herzl (1860–1904), founder of modern Zionism.

[25]Joseph Trumpeldor (1880–1920), early Zionist activist who helped to organize the Zion Mule Corps and bring Jewish immigrants to Palestine. Trumpeldor lost his left arm fighting for Russia during the Russo-Japanese War (1905); Vladimir (Ze'ev) Jabotinsky (1880–1940), revisionist Zionist leader, author, poet, orator, soldier and founder of the Jewish Self-Defense Organization in Odessa. With Joseph Trumpeldor, he co-founded the Jewish Legion of the British army in World War I; Hayim Nahman Bialik (1873–1934), modern Hebrew national poet; Lord Arthur Balfour (1848–1930), British Conservative statesman who served as Prime Minister of the United Kingdom from 1902 to 1905. As Foreign Secretary in the Lloyd George ministry, he issued the Balfour Declaration in 1917 on behalf of the cabinet; Chaim Weizmann (1874–1952), Zionist leader and Israeli statesman who served as president of the Zionist Organization and later as the first president of Israel. Weizmann was also a noted biochemist, considered to be the father of industrial fermentation. He developed the acetone–butanol–ethanol fermentation process, which was of great importance in the manufacture of cordite explosive propellants for the British war industry during World War I, which facilitated issuance of the Balfour Declaration.

[26]Ecclesiastes 7:14.

[27]The 1917 Balfour Declaration was real.

[28]A *get*, a Jewish bill of divorce.

[29]More sarcasm. Hameiri uses the vow made by a Jewish man when he puts the ring on his betrothed's finger "Behold you are sanctified to me with this ring according to the laws of Moses and Israel."

Chapter 29

[1]Moses. Deuteronomy 34:10.

[2]*An'im zemorot* (I will sing sweet songs). *Shir hakavod* (song of praise) recited in some synagogues prior to the additional service of Sabbaths and festivals.

[3]Site of Saul's defeat by the Philistines and Saul and Jonathan's deaths.

[4]Judah Maccabee was a Jewish priest and son of the priest Mattathias who led the Maccabean Revolt against the Seleucid Empire (167–160 BCE).

[5]This poem does not appear in either English translation.

[6]Isaiah 49:6; Moses Mendelssohn (1729–1786), philosopher whose writings on metaphysics and aesthetics, political theory and theology, together with his Jewish heritage, placed him at the focal point of the German Emancipation for over three decades. The *haskala* of the German Jewish emancipation (and that in other countries) saw the scattering of the Jewish diaspora as God's will, making the Jews bringers of the message of monotheism to the nations of the world.

[7]The Magyars actually originated from an area between the Ural Mountains and the Upper Volga River, not from Central Asia.

[8]Exodus 15:3.

[9]The war between Gog and Magog appears in Ezekiel 38, Revelation 20: 7–8, Quran 21:96, and legends of many other civilizations.

[10]See chapter 28.

[11]I Kings 8:13.

Chapter 30

[1]Dogs are important companions for lonely soldiers. The only living creature to whom Adolf Hitler became attached in the trenches was a fox terrier.

[2]1 Kings 21: 23; 1 Kings 22: 38.

[3]This poem does not appear in either translation.

Chapter 31

[1]Erich Ludendorff (1865–1937), German general, politician and military theorist. After August 1916, he emerged as the chief policymaker in a military dictatorship with Paul von Hindenburg (1847–1934) that dominated Germany for the remainder of the war; August von Mackensen (1849–1945), German field marshal on the Eastern Front and Romania.

[2]Hameiri is referring to Tomáš Garrigue Masaryk (1850–1937), Czechoslovak politician, statesman, sociologist and philosopher, and first leader of an independent Czechoslovak state after World War I.

[3]Kiddushin 70a.

[4]See chapter 14, note 10.

[5]See chapter 13, note 2. "Moskali" is a derogatory Ukrainian word for Russians. Hameiri is being sarcastic. I thank Yohanan Petrovsky Shtern for language assistance.

[6]After Deuteronomy 32:35.

[7]Hungarian is a Finno-Ugric language similar to Finnish, Estonian, Lappic, and Khanty and Mansi spoken in Russia.

[8]A traditional Jewish stew of meat, potatoes, beans, and barley simmered overnight and eaten for lunch on the Sabbath. Cholent was developed over the centuries to conform with Jewish laws that prohibit cooking on the Sabbath. The pot is brought to a boil on Friday before the Sabbath begins, and kept on a hotplate or left in a slow oven or electric slow cooker until the following day.

[9]Psalm 86:15.

[10]Bava Metzia 83b.

[11]See chapter 29, note 9. In Isaiah 41:22 and 66 the end of days is prophesied without mention of Gog and Magog.

[12]*Aharit* or *ketz hayamim* (Hebrew).

[13]The writing on the wall during Belshazzar's feast (Daniel 5:26–28). "God has numbered the days of your reign and brought it to an end. You have been weighed on the scales and found wanting. Your kingdom is divided and given to the Medes and Persians."

Chapter 32

[1]See Chapter 28, note 18.

[2]This proves to be correct (see chapter 33).

[3]Lviv (Ukraine).

[4]Quorum of ten adult Jewish men.

[5]Thank you, Sir.

[6]Hameiri's experiences as a Russian prisoner of war are described in his second World War I novel, *Hell on Earth*: Avigdor Hameiri, translated and edited by Peter C. Appelbaum (Detroit, MI: Wayne State University Press, 2017).

[7]The death of Uncle Osterreicher is mentioned in: Hameiri, *Hell on Earth*, 43–44; Chortkiv (Ukraine).

[8]Homer's *Iliad* 6:232–236. In the *Iliad,* Glaucus – a Lycian and ally of Troy – met Diomedes of Athens in the field of battle in face to face combat. In response to Diomedes' challenge to him, Glaucus said that as a grandson of Bellerophon, he would fight anybody. Upon learning of Glaucus's ancestry, Diomedes planted his spear in the ground and told of how his grandfather Oeneus was a close friend of Bellerophon, and declared that the two of them despite being on opposing sides should continue the friendship. As a sign of friendship, Diomedes took off his bronze armor worth nine oxen and gave it to Glaucus. Glaucus gave Diomedes his golden armor, said to be worth 100 oxen.

Chapter 33

[1]The Brusilov Offensive was the greatest Russian feat of arms of the First World War. It began on 4 June 1916 and initially made great inroads. However it petered out in late September due to lack of supplies. It broke the back of the Austro-Hungarian Army which lost approximately 750,000 men killed, captured, or missing, but also exhausted the Russian Army and contributed to the 1917 Russian Revolution. For a frontline witness to this offensive, see: Bernhard Bardach, *Carnage and Care on the Eastern Front. The War Diaries of Bernhard Bardach 1914–1918*, translated and edited by Peter C. Appelbaum (New York and Oxford: Berghahn Books, 2018), 127–157.

[2]Moshe bem Maimon (Maimonides) (1135/1138–1204), medieval Sephardic Jewish philosopher who became one of the most prolific and influential Torah scholars of all time. He was also a preeminent astronomer and physician; Avraham Shmuel Binyamin Sofer (*ketav sofer*, writ of the scribe) (1815–1871), one of the leading rabbis of Hungarian Jewry in the second half of the nineteenth century and head of the famed Pressburg Yeshiva.

[3]The Brusilov Offensive saw the first use of storm troops.

[4]No need, sir.

[5]Good for you! What a man!

About the Author

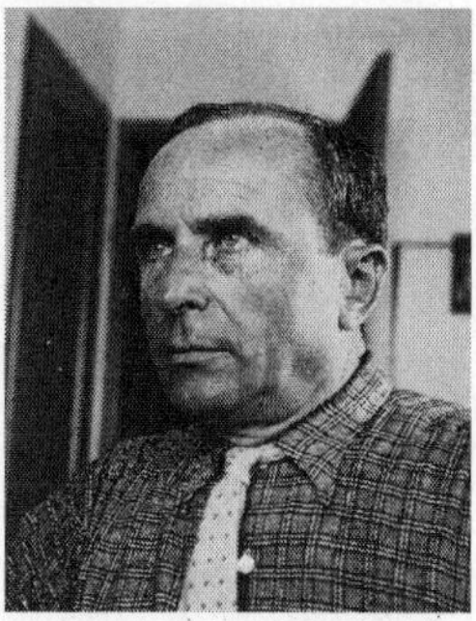

Avigdor Hameiri (Feuerstein, 1890–1970) was a Hebrew poet (the first Poet Laureate of Israel), novelist, editor, and translator. Hameiri was born in Ó-Dávidháza, Carpatho-Ruthenia (then Hungary but present-day Ukraine). His first Hebrew poem "Ben he-Atid," appeared in the weekly *Ha-Mizpeh* (1907). His first volume of verse, entitled *Mishirei Avigdor Feuerstein*, was published in 1912. In 1916 he was captured by the Russians while serving as an Austrian officer on the Russian front, imprisoned in Siberia, and released in 1917 after the October Revolution. In 1921 he immigrated to Palestine, joined the staff of the daily *Haaretz*, and edited several journals. In Tel Aviv, he founded the first Hebrew social satirical theater, *Hakumkum* (1932). Hameiri published a number of novels, short stories, and poetry collections that gave literary expression to his war experiences, the Third Aliyah, and later, the Holocaust. In his work he attacked the stagnation of Jewish life, described the carnage and hatred that engulfed all of humanity during World War I and particularly the vulnerability of Jews of this time to its consequences. Hameiri's power as a storyteller is most revealed in his war stories; observational, often cinematic in the vividness of the moment and place capturing the peculiarly tragic fate of the Jewish soldier fighting wars which are not his, and of the Jewish residents' fate in wars' aftermath. He won the Bialik Prize in 1936 and the Israel Prize in 1968. His other works of fiction include the important novel *Ha-Shiga'on ha-Gadol* (*The Great Madness*—a new translation forthcoming 2021). His books have been published in 12 languages. He died in Israel on April 3, 1970.

About the Editor

Peter C. Appelbaum, M.D., Ph.D., is Emeritus Professor of Pathology, Pennsylvania State University College of Medicine. After more than four decades in infectious disease research, Dr. Appelbaum is spending his retirement years writing and translating books on modern-day Jewish military history. He is the author of *Loyalty Betrayed* and *Loyal Sons* (Vallentine-Mitchell, 2014) and, together with James Scott, has translated an anthology of war essays and poems by Kurt Tucholsky (*Prayer after the Slaughter*, Berlinica, 2015) and *Broken Carousel: German Jewish Soldier-Poets of the Great War* (Stone Tower Books, 2017). He is also the translator/editor of *Jewish Tales of the Great War* (Stone Tower Books, 2017). Dr. Appelbaum has also translated *Of Human Carnage—Odessa 1918–1920* (Black Widow Press and Stone Tower Press, 2020), *Voyage into Savage Europe* (Academic Studies Press, 2020), and *Hell on Earth* by Avigdor Hameiri into English from the original Hebrew for the first time (Wayne State University Press, fall, 2017). For that work, he was the recipient of the TLS-Risa Domb/Porjes Prize for Hebrew-English Translation for 2019. He also has translated Theodor Lessing's *Jewish Self-Hate* (Berghahn, 2021) and *Enemies in Our Country: Satires and Novellas* (Black Widow Press and Stone Tower Press, 2021).

BLACK WIDOW PRESS POETRY IN TRANSLATION

Approximate Man and Other Writings by Tristan Tzara. Translated and edited by Mary Ann Caws.

Art Poétique by Guillevic. Translated by Maureen Smith.

Beginnings of the Prose Poem. Edited by Mary Ann Caws, Michel Delville.

The Big Game by Benjamin Péret. Translated with an introduction by Marilyn Kallet.

Boris Vian Invents Boris Vian: A Boris Vian Reader. Edited and translated by Julia Older.

Capital of Pain by Paul Eluard. Translated by Mary Ann Caws, Patricia Terry, and Nancy Kline.

Chanson Dada: Selected Poems by Tristan Tzara. Translated with an introduction and essay by Lee Harwood.

Earthlight (Clair de Terre) by André Breton. Translated by Bill Zavatsky and Zack Rogow. (New and revised edition.)

Essential Poems and Prose of Jules Laforgue. Translated and edited by Patricia Terry.

Essential Poems and Writings of Joyce Mansour: A Bilingual Anthology. Translated with an introduction by Serge Gavronsky.

Essential Poems and Writings of Robert Desnos: A Bilingual Anthology. Edited with an introduction and essay by Mary Ann Caws.

EyeSeas (Les Ziaux) by Raymond Queneau. Translated with an introduction by Daniela Hurezanu and Stephen Kessler.

Fables in a Modern Key by Pierre Coran. Translated by Norman R. Shapiro. Full-color illustrations by Olga Pastuchiv.

Fables of Town & Country by Pierre Coran. Translated by Norman R. Shapiro. Full-color illustrations by Olga Pastuchiv.

A Flea the Size of Paris: The Old French Fatrasies & Fatras. Edited and translated by Ted Byrne and Donato Mancini.

Forbidden Pleasures: New Selected Poems 1924–1949 by Luis Cernuda. Translated by Stephen Kessler.

Furor and Mystery & Other Writings by René Char. Translated by Mary Ann Caws and Nancy Kline.

The Gentle Genius of Cécile Périn: Selected Poems (1906–1956). Edited and translated by Norman R. Shapiro.

The Great Madness by Avigdor Hameiri. Translated and edited by Peter C. Appelbaum with an introduction by Dan Hecht.

Guarding the Air: Selected Poems of Gunnar Harding. Translated and edited by Roger Greenwald.

Howls & Growls: French Poems to Bark By. Translated by Norman R. Shapiro; illustrated by Olga K. Pastuchiv.

I Have Invented Nothing: Selected Poems by Jean-Pierre Rosnay. Translated by J. Kates.

In Praise of Sleep: Selected Poems of Lucian Blaga. Translated with an introduction by Andrei Codrescu.

The Inventor of Love & Other Writings by Gherasim Luca. Translated by Julian & Laura Semilian. Introduction by Andrei Codrescu. Essay by Petre Răileanu.

Jules Supervielle: Selected Prose and Poetry. Translated by Nancy Kline & Patricia Terry.

La Fontaine's Bawdy by Jean de La Fontaine. Translated with an introduction by Norman R. Shapiro.

Last Love Poems of Paul Eluard. Translated with an introduction by Marilyn Kallet.

A Life of Poems, Poems of a Life by Anna de Noailles. Edited and translated by Norman R. Shapiro. Introduction by Catherine Perry.

Love, Poetry (L'amour la poésie) by Paul Eluard. Translated with an essay by Stuart Kendall.

Of Human Carnage—Odessa 1918–1920 by Avigdor Hameiri. Translated and edited by Peter C. Appelbaum with an introduction by Dan Hecht.

Pierre Reverdy: Poems, Early to Late. Translated by Mary Ann Caws and Patricia Terry.

Poems of André Breton: A Bilingual Anthology. Translated with essays by Jean-Pierre Cauvin and Mary Ann Caws.

Poems of A.O. Barnabooth by Valery Larbaud. Translated by Ron Padgett and Bill Zavatsky.

Poems of Consummation by Vicente Aleixandre. Translated by Stephen Kessler.

Préversities: A Jacques Prévert Sampler. Translated and edited by Norman R. Shapiro.

RhymAmusings (AmuseRimes) by Pierre Coran. Translated by Norman R. Shapiro.

The Sea and Other Poems by Guillevic. Translated by Patricia Terry. Introduction by Monique Chefdor.

Sixty Years: Selected Poems 1957–2017 by Mikhail Yeryomin. Translated by J. Kates. *(forthcoming)*

Through Naked Branches by Tarjei Vesaas. Translated, edited, and introduced by Roger Greenwald.

To Speak, to Tell You? Poems by Sabine Sicaud. Translated by Norman R. Shapiro. Introduction and notes by Odile Ayral-Clause.

BLACK WIDOW PRESS MODERN POETRY SERIES

WILLIS BARNSTONE
ABC of Translation
African Bestiary (forthcoming)

DAVE BRINKS
The Caveat Onus
The Secret Brain: Selected Poems 1995–2012

RUXANDRA CESEREANU
Crusader-Woman. Translated by Adam J. Sorkin. Introduction by Andrei Codrescu.
Forgiven Submarine by Ruxandra Cesereanu and Andrei Codrescu.

CLAYTON ESHLEMAN
An Alchemist with One Eye on Fire
Anticline
Archaic Design
Clayton Eshleman/The Essential Poetry: 1960–2015
Grindstone of Rapport: A Clayton Eshleman Reader
Penetralia
Pollen Aria
The Price of Experience
Endure: Poems by Bei Dao. Translated by Clayton Eshleman and Lucas Klein.
Curdled Skulls: Poems of Bernard Bador. Translated by Bernard Bador with Clayton Eshleman.

PIERRE JORIS
Barzakh (Poems 2000–2012)
Exile Is My Trade: A Habib Tengour Reader

MARILYN KALLET
How Our Bodies Learned
The Love That Moves Me
Packing Light: New and Selected Poems
Disenchanted City (La ville désenchantée) by Chantal Bizzini. Translated by J. Bradford Anderson, Darren Jackson, and Marilyn Kallet.

ROBERT KELLY
Fire Exit
The Hexagon

STEPHEN KESSLER
Garage Elegies
Last Call (forthcoming)

BILL LAVENDER
Memory Wing

HELLER LEVINSON
from stone this running
LinguaQuake
Lurk
Seep
Tenebraed
Un-
Wrack Lariat

JOHN OLSON
Backscatter: New and Selected Poems
Dada Budapest
Larynx Galaxy
Weave of the Dream King

NIYI OSUNDARE
City Without People: The Katrina Poems

MEBANE ROBERTSON
An American Unconscious
Signal from Draco: New and Selected Poems

JEROME ROTHENBERG
Concealments and Caprichos
Eye of Witness: A Jerome Rothenberg Reader. Edited with commentaries by Heriberto Yepez & Jerome Rothenberg.
The President of Desolation & Other Poems

AMINA SAÏD.
The Present Tense of the World: Poems 2000–2009. Translated with an introduction by Marilyn Hacker.

ANIS SHIVANI
Soraya (Sonnets)

JERRY W. WARD, JR.
Fractal Song

BLACK WIDOW PRESS ANTHOLOGIES / BIOGRAPHIES

Barbaric Vast & Wild: A Gathering of Outside and Subterranean Poetry (*Poems for the Millennium,* vol. 5). Editors: Jerome Rothenberg and John Bloomberg-Rissman

Clayton Eshleman: The Whole Art by Stuart Kendall

Revolution of the Mind: The Life of André Breton by Mark Polizzotti